THE LOST ONES

THE LOST ONES

ACE ATKINS

G. P. PUTNAM'S SONS

NEW YORK

PUTNAM

G. P. PUTNAM'S SONS
Publishers Since 1838
Published by the Penguin Group
Penguin Group (USA) Inc., 375 Hudson Street, New York, New York 10014, USA •
Penguin Group (Canada), 90 Eglinton Avenue East, Suite 700, Toronto, Ontario M4P 2Y3,
Canada (a division of Pearson Penguin Canada Inc.) • Penguin Books Ltd, 80 Strand,
London WC2R 0RL, England • Penguin Ireland, 25 St Stephen's Green, Dublin 2, Ireland
(a division of Penguin Books Ltd) • Penguin Group (Australia), 250 Camberwell Road,
Camberwell, Victoria 3124, Australia (a division of Pearson Australia Group Pty Ltd) •
Penguin Books India Pvt Ltd, 11 Community Centre, Panchsheel Park, New Delhi–110 017,
India • Penguin Group (NZ), 67 Apollo Drive, Rosedale, North Shore 0632, New Zealand
(a division of Pearson New Zealand Ltd) • Penguin Books (South Africa) (Pty) Ltd,
24 Sturdee Avenue, Rosebank, Johannesburg 2196, South Africa

Penguin Books Ltd, Registered Offices:
80 Strand, London WC2R 0RL, England

Library of Congress Cataloging-in-Publication Data

Atkins, Ace.
The lost ones / Ace Atkins.
p.   cm.—(A Quinn Colson novel)
ISBN 978-0-399-15876-6
1. Mississippi—Fiction.   I. Title.
PS3551.T49L67   2012   2012010936
813'.54—dc23

Printed in the United States of America
1   3   5   7   9   10   8   6   4   2

BOOK DESIGN BY AMANDA DEWEY

This is a work of fiction. Names, characters, places, and incidents either are the product
of the author's imagination or are used fictitiously, and any resemblance to actual persons,
living or dead, businesses, companies, events, or locales is entirely coincidental.

While the author has made every effort to provide accurate telephone numbers and
Internet addresses at the time of publication, neither the publisher nor the author assumes
any responsibility for errors, or for changes that occur after publication. Further, the
publisher does not have any control over and does not assume any responsibility
for author or third-party websites or their content.

For Jess

A man is sent to war and taught how to kill;
but after, the unlearning of it is left up to him.

—Elmore Leonard, *Last Stand at Saber River*

When you're on the march, act the way you would if
sneaking up on a deer. See the enemy first.

—Rogers' Rangers Standing Order No. 5

A COUPLE ROUSTABOUTS HAD BEEN ASKING ABOUT GUNS AT THE TIBBEHAH County Fair, but by the time the word had gotten back to Donnie Varner, they'd long since packed up their Ferris wheel, corn dog stands and shit, and boogied on down the highway. He'd tried for them at a rodeo up in Eupora and the fall festival over in Hernando, but it wasn't until he pulled off the highway into a roadside carnival in Byhalia, Mississippi, that he knew he had the right spot. It was late, past nine o'clock, and the edge of Highway 78 was lit up in red, blue, and yellow neon, the fairway spreading out past the gas station and into an open cow field, bursting with folks carrying popcorn and balloons, little black kids and white kids, Mexicans working the stands. The air smelled like burnt sugar and cigarettes.

"*¿Dónde está Alejandro Ramírez Umana?*"

A fat brown woman running a stick around a cotton candy dryer nodded to the flashing lights of a Tilt-A-Whirl called the Cool Breeze. As Donnie walked closer, he could see the little cars spinning and zipping up into a fake ice tunnel where folks would scream when getting blasted with cold air and mist. Donnie's white T-shirt was already soaked through from his ride up from Jericho with no air conditioner in a busted-up Dodge van he'd borrowed from his church.

How the hell else could he have brought a sampling of the fifteen AK-47s, two Mossberg 12-gauge shotguns, three MAK-90 assault rifles, a Ruger Mini-14, and a .223 caliber AR variant rifle? There was a mixed bag of ammunition, scopes, magazines, and gun cases to show that he meant business and could deliver more.

A dark girl with long legs was taking tickets, black hair pulled back from her face with a pink scarf, wearing a white tank top and shorts, a fat pink belt around her small waist. She was tall and thin, with muscular brown thighs. She wore a pair of old cowboy boots.

Donnie smiled at her and repeated: *"¿Dónde está Alejandro Ramírez Umana?"*

"I speak English."

"Where's he at?"

"Who are you?"

"A friend."

"I don't know you."

A couple kids muscled by Donnie and handed the girl tickets. Both boys looked at the Mexican woman in the damp white tank top and smiled at each other. Their heads swiveled as they made their way up the ramp, nearly tripping over themselves into the Cool Breeze tunnel.

"I heard he needed some guns," Donnie said.

"That's not true."

"Fine by me."

"Don't talk so loud."

"I'll be getting a hot dog over at that stand."

"What is your name?"

"Donnie Varner."

"Alejandro knows you?"

"Just tell him about the guns."

Donnie pulled out a pack of Natural American Spirit cigarettes and thumped them forward, ripping open the box. He fired one up and strolled over to a clump of vendors selling Polish sausages, pizza, barbecue, and Coney Island dogs. He paid two dollars for a footlong and dressed it with mustard and relish, wishing he had a cold Busch beer to wash it down.

The best thing about going to Trashcanistan and coming back was enjoying every goddamn moment you got. In the good hours, the pleasures seemed more intense. He could smoke cigarettes on his dad's porch all night long, watch the sun rise off the hay his father had rolled and baled. During the bad hours—maybe why he didn't like to sleep—he'd think he was still over there, hearing that market bomb explode near three of his buddies, with parts of forty civilians getting shredded with them. How do you make sense of that?

He'd had three surgeries to remove all the shrapnel that had decorated his back. But the first words out of his father's mouth on a cell phone call from back home was: "Y'all get the bastard?" He had to tell his dad, No. This wasn't Vietnam. These people really didn't have no objective besides blowing themselves to heaven and screwing seventy-two black-eyed virgins.

You could smell the turn of the season mixed in the corn dogs and funnel cakes. Mississippi still had hot days, but there was a gentleness to those hot breezes, signaling fall was coming on, chillier weather. Cotton gins were running. People were turning over their crops and planting collards and harvesting pumpkins.

Donnie wiped the mustard off his chin and stood and stretched, scratching his chest and lighting up another Spirit. Down the midway in all that neon glow, he spotted that fine Mexican woman, hands in tight pockets of those white shorts, wiggling down the worn path. Cowboy boots kicking up a bit of dust till she got near him and didn't smile but just pointed.

"And?"

"Go to the motel."

"Where?"

She pointed again to a little, squat two-level facing a cow pasture and Highway 78.

"Oh, there."

"Room 211."

"Do I look that goddamn stupid?"

"I'll wait with you."

"I don't know you."

"Or you, us," she said. "If you have a wire—"

"I ain't wearin' no wire."

"But if you are—"

"Alejandro will chimichanga my ass."

She raised her thick eyebrows and nodded, walking ahead of him, making Donnie sweat by the way she walked. He was enjoying the white shorts and cowboy boots, but he wasn't altogether stupid, reaching up under his T-shirt and making sure the .38 Special was tucked in his branded belt.

She had a key and opened the door on the second floor. Donnie hung back, waiting to hear something, blowing out a thin trail of smoke and staring down at the neon carnival facing the cotton fields, cars headed north to Memphis.

"Come on."

"I'm good."

"Come on," the girl said.

Donnie shrugged and wandered in, keeping cool, looking to other doors and then back the way he came. He walked back to the bathroom, heart jackhammering in his chest, checking behind the shower curtain and then strolling out nice and easy. He found the girl facing him, arms across her nice chest, but frowning. "Take off your shirt."

"Come on now, sweet thing."

"Luz." She had a slight bead of perspiration on her upper lip and rings of sweat under her arms.

"What kind of Mex name is that?"

"An old one."

He peeled off his T-shirt, fronting the girl so she couldn't get a glimpse of his pistol.

"And your blue jeans."

"Hell."

Donnie shook his head, took the lit cigarette out of his mouth, and placed it in an ashtray by the bedside. He reached behind him slow, grinning, and showed her the gun loose in his right hand. "OK?"

She nodded.

"Be a lot easier if you'd show me, too."

"You came to us."

"A fella can at least try."

She waited till he'd taken his jeans down to his cowboy boots and made a slow turn in his boxer shorts. Her face dropped when he looked at her, and he knew she'd seen the thick, rubbery scars on his back. He pulled his pants up and reached back for his .38, sliding it into his belt, and then slipped into his T-shirt.

She dialed a number on her cell and sat down on the sagging bed, the cheap bedspread stained and sun-faded. She didn't say anything. She lolled her head in a shrug and crossed her legs, swinging her booted foot back and forth.

Donnie walked back to the front door and waited on the balcony, leaning over the railing while he smoked two more cigarettes. He'd heard about these bad dudes down in Biloxi from this fella in Jericho named Ramón, gangbangers from Mexico and out west that blew in after Katrina and decided to stick around and do business, run whatever they could back and forth to Old Mexico. He didn't know nothing about their politics or business, only that they paid in cash.

A Mexican man turned the corner from the stairwell and nodded at him.

Alejandro Ramírez Umana's entire face had been scrawled in jailhouse tattoos. He was short and muscular, with a shaved head and small mustache. The black scrollwork on his face showed numbers and letters and drawings of demon horns.

Alejandro said something fast and harsh in Spanish. Donnie caught about none of it, watching while he pointed out to the wide parking lot, already starting to empty out for the night. She nodded. "He wants you to bring them here. To the motel."

"Two miles down the road is a Walmart," Donnie said. "Y'all can meet me in the parking lot for a little look-see. I got a brown Dodge van. Just you and him."

She told him. He answered her, seeming like he was pissed off, keeping an eye on Donnie. Donnie Varner smiled and winked. Alejandro stared at Donnie, seeming kind of like he was an insect, before turning and bounding down the metal steps.

"He will want to shoot the guns."

"That can be arranged."

"First we see the guns. How many can you get?"

"How many y'all need?" Donnie grinned at Luz. The smile seemed to make her nervous.

"Many."

"Baby, you're too pretty to be at this freak show."

She finally smiled. He handed her a business card.

"See y'all in Tibbehah County."

2

QUINN COLSON DID NOT WANT OR NEED TO ATTEND THE ANNUAL GOOD OLE Boy party out at Johnny Stagg's property. But Chief Deputy Lillie Virgil had pointed out it was an unwritten requirement of being sheriff in Tibbehah County, even if Quinn had only been sheriff since a special election in the spring and that election had been against Stagg. And now it was fall. Stagg's behemoth metal barn where he kept tractors and earthmovers had been cleaned out and filled with long tables covered in red-and-white-checked oilcloth and folding chairs borrowed from the three Baptist churches in Jericho. A well-known master of barbecue had brought in his crew from Sugar Ditch, and dozens of steel washtubs had been filled with ice and cans of cheap beer and Coca-Cola. A bonfire blazed at the edge of Stagg's land, where politicians from all over north Mississippi gathered despite the lack of chill in the air.

"Johnny Stagg may be this county's biggest asshole," Lillie Virgil said, slamming the door to Quinn's old Ford truck, "but he sure knows how to throw a party."

"How long do I have to stay?"

"Do I need to remind you that sheriff is an elected position?"

"Do you recall Stagg telling everyone that I suffered from post-traumatic stress and was a loose cannon?"

"He would've said worse about me."

Quinn shut the driver's door and followed Lillie down a gravel road where conversion trucks were parked alongside Cadillacs and Mercedeses. Men had driven north from Jackson or south from Memphis to check out this year's political climate, whether it was for U.S. Senate or the coroner of Choctaw County. There would be stump speeches and political alliances made. After the speeches came the long prayer, and then the meal where hundreds, maybe a thousand, would listen to a country band down from Tupelo fronted by Kay Bain, a spitfire in her seventies who didn't stand much taller than five feet and who could wail as good as Tammy Wynette.

"I used to come out here with my uncle," Quinn said.

"See," Lillie said. "He hated Stagg back then, too. But he knew it was part of the job."

"I'd like to punch Johnny Stagg in the throat."

"Are all you Rangers so damn charming?" Lillie asked.

Quinn stood tall and rangy, hair buzzed high and tight, wearing a pressed khaki shirt with two front pockets, pressed blue jeans, and shined boots. He kept a Beretta 9mm on his hip, the same one that had served him on numerous missions in Iraq and Afghanistan as a Ranger in the 3rd Batt, 75th Regiment. A patch of the sheriff's office star was sewn on his left pocket.

His face was all sharp angles, a hint of Cherokee from some time back. He looked to be a hard man even though he'd yet to turn thirty.

"If I were you," Lillie said, "I'd walk right up to Johnny Stagg and shake his hand."

"Smile as you walk through the cannon smoke and give 'em hell?"

"Stagg would hate it if you showed you were a bigger man."

Quinn regarded Lillie as they met the edge of Stagg's land. He looked at her brown curly hair pulled into a ponytail and freckled face without a trace of makeup. She was nearly his height and a hell of a looker when not wearing an oversized sheriff's office jacket and laced clunky boots.

But if he ever complimented her, she took it as an insult.

Quinn said hello to several folks who'd supported him in the election against Stagg, the boldest supporter being old Betty Jo Mize who ran the *Tibbehah Monitor*. With wry humor, she'd described Johnny Stagg's entire sordid history in her columns—his strip club truck stop and association with criminals. Quinn was pretty sure that's what won him the election.

He hugged the old woman and she winked at him, whispering into his ear. "Glad you're here. That prick will hate it."

"Where's the beer?"

Betty Jo smiled and pointed the way.

Quinn found a cold Budweiser and met up with Mr. Jim, a veteran of Patton's 3rd Army who ran the town barbershop, and Luther Varner, a Marine sniper who'd served in Vietnam. Mr. Jim was talking about shutting down the barbershop again, a rumor he'd been spreading since Quinn was a kid. Luther Varner just smiled as Mr. Jim talked, smoking down a long Marlboro red. He had a faded *Semper Fi* tattoo on his wrinkled forearm and a face fashioned from granite.

"God damn," Varner said. "How long are these folks gonna talk? I'm getting hungry."

"They hold the meal just so we have to listen," Mr. Jim said.

"Are you listening to this horseshit?" Varner asked.

A nervous young guy in a tieless suit stood on the small stage filled with guitars and a drum set. He spoke about his love of country and his personal relationship with Jesus Christ. "I am a family man and an avid hunter. No one will take that away from me."

Quinn drank his beer.

"This is more than an election to me," the candidate said. "It's a crusade. We will restore morals to our country and put God in charge."

The speeches were limited to two minutes, sometimes Stagg having to get on stage and point to his golden watch. The Good Ole Boy was good-natured, the candidates black and white, male and female. A black woman was running for circuit judge and offered the only speech that contained facts about her office. There were coroners and county clerks, two U.S. Congress candidates trading veiled barbs about mean-spirited television ads Quinn had not seen.

The smell of the chicken smoke blew in from a cold breeze inside Johnny's shed. A prayer was said and everyone finally lined up with paper plates and plastic forks. Quinn grabbed some chicken with baked beans and coleslaw and found a place to sit outside on a hay bale. Kay Bain and her band started into "Fist City" by Loretta Lynn, and the smell of the hickory smoke and the sparking bonfire under a full harvest moon wasn't altogether unpleasant.

"Glad you came, Sheriff."

Quinn looked up from his plate to see the craggy, comical mask of Johnny Stagg. Stagg wore high-waisted jeans and a white snap-button shirt. His brown dye job was slicked back into a ducktail, and his ruddy Scotch-Irish face shone from a recent shave.

Quinn nodded.

Stagg offered his bony hand.

Quinn stood. He saw groupings of people turn, watch, and whisper. Lillie stood by the mouth of the barn, nodding to Quinn as she held a drumstick of chicken.

Quinn shook Stagg's hand.

Stagg showed off his huge veneers and laughed, holding the smile for a while and nodding with some surprise. "You ain't gonna give me a talkin'-to?" Stagg asked.

"About what?"

"I guess you know all that mess was just politics."

"Sure, Johnny."

"And I figure you know that I intend to keep my position over the Board of Supervisors."

"It's a small county," Quinn said. "I may have heard something about that at the Fillin' Station."

"Long as we're OK on that."

Quinn nodded. He wanted to sit back down and eat some chicken. He waited a beat, and said: "I've been hearing about some action out at your truck stop. Gambling, girls, and such. You wouldn't know anything about that?"

Stagg grinned and laughed.

He turned and quickly took the arm of the U.S. senator and led him to the front of the line to get a plate of chicken.

"That was a good start," Lillie said. She handed him a fresh beer.

"Can I go wash my hand?"

"You're maybe the best outdoorsman I ever met," Lillie said. "You respect the woods, and that includes the animals that could kill you."

"If I see a rattlesnake, I blast it with my shotgun."

"No you don't," Lillie said. "You kick them out of the way, knowing they're just a part of the forest."

"Thanks for the beer," Quinn said. "You can keep the advice."

Lillie smiled at him. The firelight caught the little blond hairs at the nape of her long neck and freckles across her nose and cheeks.

"What?"

Quinn grinned and looked toward the bonfire.

Anna Lee Amsden—Quinn still thinking of her by her maiden name—and her husband, Luke Stevens, stood at the edge of smoke and sparking light. Luke was a good man, having been in Quinn's graduating class, and had come back to Jericho to serve as one of the town's few doctors and now county coroner. Quinn never thought he'd see Anna Lee with someone else long term, but there she stood with her arm hooked in Luke's, nearly eight months pregnant.

Quinn finished the beer and crushed the can.

The country music stopped, and Johnny Stagg again assumed the role as master of ceremonies, ring leader, and preacher, launching into a big-grinned thank-you to all the donors and politicians and cooks who made this possible. He also said he was thankful to Sheriff Colson for showing up.

Quinn stood and craned his neck over the crowd.

"The supervisors wanted to present the new sheriff with something to show a new beginning in Tibbehah County," Stagg said from the stage. "And how much we appreciate a young man and decorated soldier coming back home."

Headlights shot on from up the gravel road, and a truck rolled slow down the path, past the barbecue pit, bonfire, and stage. The horn honked, scattering the onlookers, and blue lights flashed from the dashboard. A brand-new Dodge Ram 2500 painted a golden brown idled at the mouth of the barn. The gold star of the Tibbehah County Sheriff's Office had been painted on the door. The truck boasted a two-ton winch, dual exhaust, four-wheel drive, and roll bar decked out in a set of massive KC lights.

"Jesus Christ," Quinn said.

"I had no idea," Lillie said.

One of Quinn's new deputies—he'd fired all the old ones except Lillie for years of laziness and corruption—got out of the truck and walked to Quinn, smiling and holding the set of keys. The onlookers gathered around the truck and admired the golden paint and leather seats, a big-haired woman with fake breasts tooting the horn and hitting the siren.

"Kenny," Quinn said to his deputy. "Hand the keys back to Mr. Stagg."

"Come again?"

"I don't want it," Quinn said. "Tell him I've always been a Ford man."

"Come on, Quinn," Kenny said. "Board of Supervisors approved the funding last month. It's all legal."

Kenny was a thick guy with a short goatee and shaved head. He was a trusted friend and a good man, but the whole idea of it made Quinn sick to his stomach.

"Tell Mr. Stagg and the board I appreciate it," Quinn said. "But taxpayers' money can be better spent."

Stagg stood over by the massive truck and offered a wave, the moonlight shining off his pompadour and big teeth. Quinn just stared at him and nodded as he turned to the gravel road.

"You coming?" he asked Lillie.

Lillie put down her half-eaten plate of chicken and followed.

"Don't I always?"

3

THE NEXT MORNING, LUKE STEVENS CALLED THE OLD FARMHOUSE. QUINN had inherited the place from his dead uncle along with a stockpile of hunting rifles, rusted farm equipment, and a cattle dog named Hondo. He'd just finished eating some fried eggs with country ham and placed a black skillet on the floor to let Hondo finish off what was left. The dog's coat was a patchwork of gray and black. He had two different colored eyes.

"Good to see you last night," Luke said.

"Sure thing."

"Wish you'd come over and said hello," Luke said. "With Anna Lee pregnant, we haven't been going down to the Southern Star much. Too damn smoky. You should stop by the house sometime for a beer."

"What's up, Luke?"

"Strange thing this morning," he said.

Quinn looked at his watch, noting it was nearly 0700.

"Woman named Janet Torres. You know Janet? Used to be Janet

Sanders. Clerk at the Dollar General, tips the scales at more than three hundred. She has a face that would stop a Mack truck cold."

"Maybe."

"Anyway, Janet brought in this little girl," Luke said. "Child was three. She'd suffered massive head trauma, tons of bruises, and a broken leg. Janet says the girl fell out of a shopping cart at the Piggly Wiggly."

"I bet."

"You think you can pay a visit before I get child services involved?"

"Sounds like you better start that process."

"Quinn?"

"Yep."

Hondo polished off the skillet and looked up at Quinn. He scratched the dog's ears for a job well done. He reached for his 9mm and wallet with sheriff's star.

"I think she's got some other kids out there," Luke said. "Some kind of foster deal out of South America."

QUINN MET UP WITH KENNY at Dixie Gas on the edge of the Jericho Square, and they rode out in Kenny's patrol car, finding the Torres property in the south part of the county near some bottomland that adjoined the Choctaw Indian rez. A cattle gate fronted the highway, shut with some old chain and a padlock. Kenny searched in the pocket of his deputy's uniform and pulled out some chewing tobacco. He offered Quinn some Red Man, and Quinn declined.

"You try their phone?" Kenny asked.

"Couple times," Quinn said. "You know this woman?"

"I know who she is," Kenny said. "She used to have a place called Little Angels Daycare in the city. I hadn't seen her in a while. I know she married some Mex fella, and had an ass the size of Texas. Mean disposition."

"Sounds like a winner. Can't wait to meet her."

They got out of the sheriff's cruiser, hearing a pack of dogs begin to bark deep down through the second-growth pines and up a slight hill. Quinn looked to Kenny and hopped the cattle gate. Kenny, who was double Quinn's size, hefted himself up onto the gate and nearly toppled over before finding his feet, some of his chew spilling on the lapel of his shirt.

"Son of a bitch."

"If the woman says anything," Quinn said, "we had some urgent information from Dr. Stevens."

"Is that baby still with her?"

"Luke got the child airlifted to Memphis. St. Jude's."

Quinn could see the house as they got about a quarter of a mile from the highway, a ramshackle place perched on top of a small hill. A gauntlet of small cages and pens surrounded the property, the sound of the dogs barking and yipping and howling just about deafening as he and Kenny walked closer.

"Damn, Quinn," Kenny said. "You smell that?"

"Hard to miss."

Dozens and dozens of chain-link pens and rabbit hutches were crowded with puppies and full-grown dogs with matted fur. The ground was a sticky mud clumped with dog hair and crap. The damp dogs smelled of urine and rot. One cage held two hound puppies, both dead.

"Holy hell," Kenny said.

Quinn walked ahead through the maze of cages and pens and yipping dogs that scratched and cried for him, looking at him with their sad yellow eyes. A crude set of steps had been fashioned with some old two-by-sixes, the façade of the house looking to have been cobbled from parts off a trailer. The house was old and crooked, with a rusted tin roof and a patchwork of blue tarps stapled on top that fluttered and bubbled in the cold morning.

Quinn knocked on the door.

"I guess Janet ain't the homemaker type," Kenny said.

Quinn knocked again. He tried the knob. The shitty, thin little door had been dead-bolted. He looked to Kenny and shrugged. Kenny stepped back to the path.

Quinn stepped back and leveled the heel of his boot at the lock, busting open the door.

The smell inside knocked them backward.

Kenny walked inside behind him, covering his face with the edge of his jacket. The big deputy didn't make it halfway inside the house before he turned and ran back outside, throwing up his breakfast and tobacco over the railing.

Quinn kept his breathing slow and easy, reaching for a bandanna in his pocket, the stench at least better than bloated bodies and backed-up latrines. The house was dark. He tried the light switches, but there was no electricity. He turned on his Maglite and spotlighted the room. Piles of dishes filled the kitchen sink. Mounds of dirty clothes and diapers sat in heaps on the vinyl floors. A massive easy chair with large holes and tears faced a brand-new flat-screen television. Stacks of *Us Weekly* and *People* magazine littered the ground next to wrappers for Jenny Craig weight-loss bars.

Kenny ventured down the hallway. Quinn heard doors opening and closing.

The house looked to be stuck in time, with appliances nearly thirty years old. The gas oven contained half of a pizza. The pizza waited, stale but not covered in mold. It looked like some squatters had entered a time warp, not bothering to change anything, only trash what was there. An old hi-fi system sat in the corner loaded down with a Peggy Lee 33.

Quinn followed Kenny into the back rooms.

"Quinn?"

Quinn stopped at a closed door, opening it wide with his knuckles.

The room had been painted pink several decades ago and splattered with wallpaper murals of bunnies, chickens, and baby frogs. There were rainbows and big shining suns. Most of the murals hung halfway off the wall, the glue weakening from years of summer heat. The room stank of fermented urine and the open jugs of spoiled milk on the filthy blue carpet.

Kenny moved ahead, tripping on the toy trucks and stuffed animals worn down to the thread. He turned to Quinn. The big man's eyes filling, unable to speak.

Thirteen rickety cribs patched from lumber scraps filled the room.

All thirteen were empty.

4

"Not much to do," Quinn said. "They'd shagged ass out of the county, probably the state. We've got bulletins out on their vehicles."

"And the children?" she asked, out of earshot of her grandson Jason, who'd wandered over to an old shed where Quinn kept the cane poles and fishing tackle.

Quinn shook his head, watching Hondo following the boy, nudging him at the butt to hurry up. Both boy and dog impatient to get to the pond.

"Memphis police are keeping watch," Quinn said. "Girl's in rough shape, Momma."

Jason returned and tugged at Quinn in the fading golden light, a stretch of pecans behind him. He wore a snap-button rodeo shirt and Wranglers with knee-high rubber boots. Sometimes when he was with Quinn or his grandmother, people would stare. He was a light-skinned black child with the eyes of Quinn's father, an over-the-hill Hollywood stuntman who no one had seen in years.

Jason had been with Quinn's mom now for the last three weeks, left for the fifth time by Quinn's sister, Caddy. There were excuses, legitimate reasons, and promises to return at Christmas. A cell phone number she'd left turned out to be disconnected.

"He doesn't have to stay," Jean said. "I know y'all are busy."

"I'll call if we get word on the Torres folks."

"Is Lillie coming over?" she asked.

"Why do you ask?"

"No reason."

"You asked."

"She's not as tough as you think."

"Lillie was the top shooter on the Ole Miss rifle team," Quinn said. "I've seen her knock a three-hundred-pound man to his knees. You want to me to buy her roses?"

Quinn's mother grinned and walked back to her Chevy, wearing a new sweatshirt she'd bought on a recent trip to Graceland for Elvis's seventy-fifth birthday. After a few glasses of cheap wine, she'd recount that time in '76 when The King touched her hand at a show at the Mid-South arena, sighing his signature finale of "Can't Help Falling in Love," draping a yellow scarf—that she still owned—around her neck. Romantic to a fault.

Jean waved and drove off, Quinn waving back and reaching into his old Ford to the gun rack for his Remington 870 pump. He pocketed a few 12-gauge shells, and then snatched the cane poles from the shed.

"Ready?" Quinn said, pulling Jason's ball cap over his eyes.

Jason nodded, taking the poles from Quinn, serious on the walk down the well-worn path, through the rows of cedar and oak, scrub pines, and gum trees that had grown tall in the neglect of the old property. They stopped at the edge of the levee, sun setting over the water.

"Stay here."

Jason stood still. Hondo stayed, panting, at the boy's side.

Quinn crested the levee and spotted a pair of fat water moccasins sunning themselves on the banks. He moved slow and careful through the grass and blasted a fat one in half and reracked a load, sending the other one dropping in pieces into the water.

"They dead?" Jason asked in a soft country accent.

"Just scared 'em a little," Quinn said, toeing his boot at a piece he missed, Jason not seeing the bloody parts as they rolled into the pond with a plop.

DONNIE VARNER EXPECTED the Mexicans at four, but they didn't get to his gun range till nearly six, Donnie having to turn on the lights fashioned into his tall pines to give them a decent enough view to shoot. There were four more of them and Alejandro and the girl, the fine-looking one named Luz. She wore jeans and pointy-toed boots and a bright red leather jacket, black hair spilling over her shoulders and down her back, reminding him of a horse's mane.

He smiled at her when she climbed out of the back of the black Cadillac Escalade and surveyed the bare hills and ruined land around the range, the trailer where he kept his shop, another he rented to Tiny, and up the hill to the small Airstream he called home. The sign out on Highway 9 read SOUTHERN COMFORT.

He was glad to see her. But, man, Alejandro sure was a freak show.

The tattoos of the horns and numbers and shit looked even stranger in the harsh artificial light. He burned off a cigarette and reached for another. Three of the other men were big hard-looking Mexes in T-shirts and jeans. The other was just a boy, Donnie figuring him not to be much more than fourteen, holstering a goddamn Glock 9 on his belt.

No introductions asked for or given.

"Thought we agreed on just you and Alejandro?" Donnie asked.

Luz shrugged. "They wanted to shoot."

"What's to stop them from shooting my ass and taking the goddamn guns?"

She looked to the tree line where Donnie had spread out his boys Tiny and Shane with deer rifles just in case the party got a little ugly. She turned to him and smiled and said, "The guns?"

He walked the Mexicans over to some tables built with scraps of lumber, a rusted tin roof nailed overhead on four-by-four posts. Donnie snatched a blue tarp from a big table and showed off the weapons along with some ammo. Right then, it started to rain.

Alejandro, who hadn't said a goddamn word, muscled by him and picked up the Mossberg 930 and snicked open the breech, knowing how to ghost-load extra rounds. The other two men and the boy joined him, studying the fresh weapons in the light and smiling.

"Who's Junior?" Donnie asked.

Luz stood back, arms folded over her chest. She didn't answer him.

"Damn, he doesn't look old enough to wipe his ass."

"Watch him shoot."

"That Mossberg he's got was voted 2009 shotgun of the year," he said. "A five-hundred-member academy made it so. Just don't want him knocked on his ass."

"You can bring your friends out if you wish," she said.

"What friends?"

"The ones in the woods."

"That's all right, darlin'," he said. "Excuse me if I don't trust y'all just yet."

She walked back to the Escalade and leaned against the grille, watching the Mexicans shoot shotguns and automatics in the light rain and bright artificial light. She had a graceful way about her as she stood with her hips forward, completely at peace in the middle of a gun deal. Donnie followed and offered her a smoke.

"How 'bout you and me get a cheeseburger at the Sonic after this deal is made?"

"Do you know who I am?"

"Does it make a difference?"

Alejandro let out six fast, thumping shots from the Mossberg, blowing thick holes in the cardboard target of the black robber Donnie had set up. He looked up the hill to nod his approval of the gun, but his smile faded when he saw Donnie close to Luz.

"You and Tattoo Boy?" he asked, lighting a cigarette with a Zippo.

"Alejandro works for my boyfriend."

"And your boyfriend ain't no preacher?"

Luz didn't answer. Man, it sure was raining.

QUINN STOOD WITH JASON on the weathered dock as the rain came in. The little boy took his fishing seriously. Quinn smoked a La Gloria Cubana, Hondo sleeping at their feet.

"What do you want for dinner?"

Jason looked up at him and smiled. "Waffles?"

"I can make some waffles," he said. "How about I fry some chicken, too?"

Jason nodded. "Chicken and waffles?"

"Sure," Quinn said. "Why not."

He'd inherited the property and the family farm late last year after the death of his Uncle Hamp, the former sheriff who'd died in disgrace and turmoil. Most of the acreage had been overgrown with scrub pine and privet bush, but in the summer, he and his friend Boom had reclaimed a lot of the land, putting in a new well, rebuilding a barn that had been burned by some thugs, and cutting trails into his woods. The old house had been repainted, floorboards mended, and a new stove bought from Sears. He'd planted corn, tomatoes, and hot peppers.

Quinn's deep freezer was ready for the deer he'd kill after Thanksgiving. It wouldn't take much to supplement what he'd shot and grown. He bought his whiskey and cigars in Memphis.

"How 'bout we head on in?" Small drops of water flecked the shoulders of his khaki shirt.

"Watch TV?"

"You know I don't have a TV."

"*Scooby-Doo?*"

"We can read books."

Jason checked his line. A crappie had taken the cricket. He didn't seem too worried when he turned to Quinn and handed him the cane pole and empty hook. "Call Momma?"

"Soon," Quinn said. "She's been askin' about you."

God damn, he hated to lie.

"SO WE GOT A DEAL?" Donnie asked, looking into Alejandro's screwed-up face. The wiry little guy just stared back and nodded before walking back to the Escalade.

He returned thirty seconds later and tossed Donnie a manila envelope crammed full of cash. Donnie opened her up and poured out the money. He started to flip through the bundles of twenties and hundreds, and in a few minutes he knew it was all there. The rain hit hard on the tin roof of the range.

Donnie offered his hand to Alejandro. The little man shook it.

"Y'all want a drink?" Donnie asked. "I got a bottle of Jack in my truck."

Luz shook her head. "They don't drink."

"Not even tequila?"

"No."

"Signs and wonders."

The boys and the kid gathered the guns and ammo and packed the car.

"A true pleasure," Donnie said to Luz.

"He wants more," she said.

"OK."

"You said you could get M4s."

"It'll cost you."

"That's not an issue."

"How many?"

"A hundred."

Donnie laughed, feeling a smile creeping up. "Really?"

"Can it be done?"

"Maybe."

"You will find out?"

"You have the most beautiful hair I've ever seen."

"You will see about the guns? Military grade. Not Chinese rip-offs."

"Yes, ma'am," he said. "Sure about that burger?"

Luz's eyes wandered over his sorry ass. "You can call later if you wish."

She walked off in the tall cowboy boots and got inside the Escalade, the wipers working overtime. A broad swath of headlights turned and passed over his face before disappearing in the rain.

Shane and Tiny emerged from the woods. Shane was country skinny, with a goatee, and wore a Toby Keith T-shirt. Tiny wore Carhartt overalls, and was as big and fat as a guy named Tiny should be. Both of them had served with him in the 223rd on his first visit to the Shitbox.

"Crack open the beers, boys," Donnie said. "Tiny, go get that bottle of Jack in my truck."

Donnie fired up a Spirit and tossed them both a wad of money. "And y'all thought I was a liar when we were back in God's Armpit."

Them boys sure could grin.

5

QUINN GOT THE CALL AT TEN AND DRESSED, PULLING ON HIS TIBBEHAH
Sheriff's jacket and official ball cap as the farmhouse door slammed behind him. His mother had picked up Jason earlier, and he was glad of it,
hearing the urgency in Lillie's voice when she called. Ten minutes later,
he was nearing the black section of Tibbehah County called Sugar Ditch
and the infamous Club Disco 9000 juke. He braked in the gravel lot,
beaten jalopies and battered trucks parked at crazy angles around him.
The juke wasn't much more than rusted tin and scrap wood.

Lillie waited for him as he climbed out of his truck, already walking
toward the front door and the sound of driving blues guitar.

"How bad is it?"

"Spam's pissed."

"Spam's always pissed," Quinn said. "Property damage?"

"Yep."

"Anyone hurt?"

"You know it."

"This makes for how many?"

Lillie held up three fingers and kept walking. The inside of the juke house was lit with Christmas lights and a few red bulbs swinging from the ceiling. An old black man sat down while playing a guitar on stage. His drummer, also black, looked about eighty. A gaunt white man in a trucker hat took a guitar solo as Quinn made his way to the bar through the overturned tables, busted chairs, and broken beer bottles. Behind the bar was a poster of a black woman in a bikini holding a Mickeys Big Mouth.

Boom Kimbrough wobbled on a stool, nursing a forty and dog-cussing a man hiding behind the bar. The man was bleeding, holding a bloody towel filled with ice to his cheek. Spam, the bartender, stood in front of the man, making a real show to Quinn and Lillie about point-ing out Boom on the stool down the way. At six-foot-five and two hun-dred sixty pounds, Boom wasn't too hard to spot.

"You better get his ass outta here," Spam said, slamming shut the register. "His crazy shit ran my crowd out of here. Damn if he didn't beat up four of my best customers. Got damn."

Boom rambled on with some more nonsensical words. He laughed a bit at what he'd said and tipped back the forty-ounce with his good arm. His other had been lost in a roadside explosion while he'd been delivering water out of Fallujah.

"Next time he come in and act a fool, I'm gonna shoot him. I swear to it, Quinn."

"No you won't," Quinn said. "Boom?"

Boom wobbled and looked at him with glassy eyes. He smiled back at him in a wavering and unknowing way. Lillie stepped up and put her arm around him. She whispered in his ear. He nodded. Boom kept drinking.

"How'd it start?" Lillie asked.

Spam twisted up his mouth. He shrugged. "Shit, I don't know. I think one of them dumbasses said something to Boom about how at least he got one hand to jack his monkey. And that shit just kinda set him off. I don't think they meant nothin' by it. They was just sayin' it was a good thing he got one arm left."

"For monkey jackin'," Quinn said.

"We was jes playin', man," said the bleeding man.

"Shut up," Lillie said.

Quinn nodded. "Boom gets testy when he drinks."

"No shit," said the bleeding man.

Quinn just stared at him.

"Would you please get his ass outta here?" Spam said. "Maybe I can at least pay the light bill. Ain't good for business to have this crazy-ass nigger charging like a bull."

Quinn nodded. Lillie gripped Boom's arm and whispered again into his ear.

He shook his head.

"Come on, Boom," Quinn said.

"Naw."

"It's Quinn."

"No it ain't," Boom said. "You the law. Quinn Colson ain't no law. Quinn Colson a crazy-ass motherfucker."

"Now he's both," Lillie said.

Quinn looked to Lillie and Lillie grinned. She hooked her arm within Boom's and tried to lift him from the stool. He shook his head and kept drinking. A thick scar shone at the base of his skull, hair growing unnaturally around it.

Spam raised his eyebrows to Quinn. "If it was up to me, I'd say tase his ass."

Quinn reached out and gripped Boom's belt and pulled him upward. Boom shook his head and swung at Quinn's head. Quinn stepped back, feeling his face fill with heat, but also seeing that day when they'd chased rabbits down by Tom Cat McCain's place, Boom helping him waist-deep out of a frozen creek. Boom built a fire and dried out Quinn's boots while Quinn sat there chattering and shaking in Boom's dry jacket.

Quinn put down his hands and took a step back. Boom lunged for him, toppling over a chair and spinning in a half whirl before landing flat on his ass and passing out.

Lillie walked up to Quinn's side. They both stared down at their pal.

"I guess that works, too," Lillie said.

Boom snored.

"You want to carry him?"

"I'll pull around the cruiser," Lillie said. "Get some help."

"I got it," Quinn said, studying the thick scars on Boom's face. "You get a statement from Spam and whoever else you can find."

"Just how I wanted to spend my night."

"Why are you all dressed up?"

Lillie wore a tight black V-neck under her sheriff's jacket, nice jeans, gold earrings, and her good boots. Quinn smiled, taking her in for the first time.

"Hard to believe," she said, "but I have a life."

"You have a date?"

"I'll get the statement," she said. "You take your buddy to jail."

"Just how I wanted to spend my night."

6

"QUINN?"

"Yep?"

"What are we doing?" Boom asked, raising up in the passenger seat and looking out at the acres of newly planted pine trees.

"Riding around."

"Why?"

"Waiting till you sober up."

"What happened?"

"You beat the crap out of four men at Club Disco," Quinn said. "Spam wanted me to use a taser on you."

"Why?" Boom asked. He rubbed the back of his head and let out a long breath.

"One of 'em told you that it was a good thing you could still jack your monkey."

"What's wrong with that?" Boom asked.

"Don't know," Quinn said. "But for some reason, you seemed to take some offense."

"You gonna take me to jail?"

"Nobody seems to remember shit," Quinn said, watching the long gentle stretch of gravel road open up in the hills. He could only see as far as the headlights. "Lillie took statements from two guys who were bleeding pretty bad. Both of them said they'd tripped."

Boom nodded. "Folks don't care too much for the law in the Ditch."

"Hearts and minds," Quinn said. "That's where we'll find ultimate victory."

"Shit."

"You been to see your counselor at the VA?" Quinn asked, taking a cut-through road down to 9W and south to Jericho.

Boom stayed silent, his head lolling with every pothole and crack on the back highway. "Stop it, man."

"I'm not busting your balls," Quinn said, "but we had an agreement you'd go up to Memphis twice a month."

"Naw, man," Boom said. "I mean, stop the motherfucking truck."

Quinn hit the brakes, and Boom had the passenger door open even before they stopped rolling. He vomited out most of the night's beer and then hopped to the ground to relieve himself on an old oak tree.

After a bit, Boom hopped back in the truck. "I could eat."

Quinn shook his head and popped the truck into gear.

THE SONIC LIT UP the south end of Main Street, a couple blocks down from the Town Square, in red-and-yellow neon. Teenagers took nearly every parking slot around the drive-in, wandering from car to car as an old Tanya Tucker song played on the loudspeakers. Girls in tight jeans and cowboy boots mixed with the FFA boys in their camo ball caps and football players sporting their letterman jackets. Six girls sat together at a table in front of the kitchen, huddled against the wind and smoking cigarettes.

"Man, this shit takes me back," Boom said.

Quinn ordered a couple hamburgers, fries, and black coffee.

"I don't drink coffee," Boom said.

"Maybe it's time to start."

Boom nodded. The waitress rolled by on skates and passed along their burgers and coffees. They sat there for a while, watching the high school kids and listening to the sheriff's radio.

"What set it off?"

Boom drank some coffee and made a face. "I can't drive."

"You don't have a car."

"I tried to drive my daddy's truck to the co-op for some feed and something happened."

Quinn nodded. He unwrapped a cheeseburger and started to eat.

"Hard to explain."

"Try me."

"I seen something on the side of the road."

"So you pulled off?"

Boom nodded. He hadn't touched his food.

"What was it?"

"Goddamn trash bag."

"But you thought it was an IED," Quinn said.

Boom nodded again. He reached into the bag for the fries and burger. Quinn kept eating. One of the girls at the smoking table opened a small flask for whiskey from her purse and poured into a couple other girls' cups. Quinn remembered being the one who'd go to Tupelo with his Uncle Van and buy quarts of Jack Daniel's for field parties. He hardly seemed the right man to try and stop it now.

"You remember how my Uncle Van used to get us beer and whiskey?"

"Got me weed, too," Boom said.

"You think that's wrong?"

"He got paid."

"You're right," Quinn said. "Had to give him twenty bucks a run."

"Good to get the beer," Boom said. "Makes this town more interesting."

"Try not to make it too interesting," Quinn said. "I can't keep doin' this shit. People will talk."

"That's all we got in Jericho, Miss-ippi."

A silver Toyota Tundra with a roll bar and Edelbrock dual pipes circled into a slot across the way. The glare of the lights and the neon across the windshield made it tough to see. But Boom didn't seem to have a problem, swallowing half the cheeseburger and pointing. "You know Donnie was back?"

"Heard something about it."

"Last time I seen his country ass was at Camp Anaconda," Boom said. "We played cards and drank some rotgut shit some of his Guard boys had made. Rough, rough shit."

Boom was out of the truck first, with Quinn following. The teen-age girls went quiet as Quinn passed, heads bowed, cups under table. Quinn hung back and watched Boom lean into the driver's side of Donnie Varner's Toyota and shake hands. There was a woman with him, and Boom nodded at the woman. They laughed.

Quinn walked over to the window.

"God damn, Sheriff Colson," Donnie said. "The world's been turned upside down."

"What's up, Donnie?"

"My daddy sent me newspaper clippings about what happened," Donnie said. "Holy shit. Meth dealers, crooked-ass preachers, and here comes you, bigger 'an shit. Can't say I was surprised about Wesley. But hey, man. Sorry to hear about your uncle. He was a good man."

"If you say so."

"Got to forgive, brother," Donnie said, grinning wide. "That's what the preacher man says."

Quinn walked closer and noted the woman seated beside Donnie. She was very dark, eyes and hair both almost black. She had done little to acknowledge Donnie's friends besides stealing a momentary glance. Her delicate bone structure and wide eyes reminded Quinn of something you'd see in a very old painting with women wearing black and lace and holding fans. Something almost regal about her.

"Who's your friend?" Boom asked.

Donnie's face colored a bit. He took a sip of his milk shake. "This is my friend, Luz. Luz, these are my boys Boom and Quinn. See that star? This son of a bitch is the goddamn sheriff. Used to be people in this town locked up their trucks and their daughters when he was around."

Quinn shrugged.

"Army made an honest man outta him," Donnie said. "Wish I could say the same."

"Good to see you, Donnie."

Donnie nodded and shook his hand. Quinn smiled at the woman. She looked away and covered her left cheek with her hand.

"How's your momma?" Donnie asked.

"Loving Elvis."

"Caddy?"

"Don't know."

"Your dad?"

"Still gone."

"He was my hero," Donnie said, big Edelbrocks growling behind him. He smiled. "I had all them movies he was in on VHS and used to study the shit out of his stunts. If you paused the frame just right, you could see it wasn't Burt Reynolds at all. Shit, it was Jason Colson."

Quinn nodded.

"I wanted to be a stuntman more than anything," Donnie grinned and gave a two-finger wave and backed out slowly.

Quinn followed Boom back to the truck. They sat there and finished their coffees until the kids all drove away and bit by bit all the neon and light was gone. Jericho was getting ready for Sunday morning. You could hear the wind and the fall blowing into town.

"Donnie's into some shit," Boom said.

"Yep," Quinn said, and cranked the truck.

"What you gonna do?"

"I got bigger shit to deal with," Quinn said. "Did you read about the fucking mess Janet Torres left at her house?"

"I heard."

"Know anything about it?"

"Nope."

"Nobody else seems to, either."

7

THEY CAME FOR THE TORRES'S DOGS AT DAYBREAK MONDAY, FIVE DIFFER-
ent humane societies from around state, packing the matted, flea-
infested animals in crates and into vans, chugging exhaust into the cold
air. Some of the dogs held their ground and had to be snared with long
poles and wire loops. They'd starved and shit and pissed on themselves
so long that human contact seemed strange. Kenny and Quinn had
been looking after them since the first of it, making sure they had food
and water. Kenny wandered over to one cage and looked in on an old,
tired black Lab and asked if it would be trouble if he put her in his
truck.

"Don't see why not," Quinn said.

Kenny waddled into the cage and scooped the filthy animal up into
his arms, talking to her, the dog licking his fat chin and goatee. The
animal moved weak and slow.

"These are some class folks, Sheriff," said a woman who'd come up
from Jackson.

"You ever seen anything like this?" Quinn asked.

"Only every week or so," the woman said. "Mississippi isn't too big on animal welfare. Most we can cite them with is neglect. Legislators can't tell the difference between family pets and animals to hunt. They think we're all nuts with PETA, trying to tell people what they can do with their property."

"What's this amount to?"

"Hundred-dollar fine."

Quinn stayed until all the dogs had been taken, the smell of them still lingering. He lit up a cigar just to clear his head out, knowing most of the dogs would have to be put down for their own good. Many would have severe heartworms, congenital problems from the inbreeding, and other behavior problems like nipping the hands trying to save them. Lillie told him yesterday that Janet Torres had made a bundle by selling Chihuahuas crossbred with miniature poodles on the Internet, some at five hundred dollars a piece. She called them Chi-doodles and had bragged she'd coined the name.

Lillie walked around the mud in tall rubber boots, taking pictures of the empty cages, horrible conditions, for when they'd go to trial.

"You want to kick around the house some more?" she asked.

"Can't hurt."

Quinn followed her up into the Torres place, unlocking the padlock on the front door and heading through the little kitchen. He and Kenny had left the windows open, and that had helped with the putrid smell a bit. But not much. The trash, rotten food, and busted toys remained. Children and Families had taken pictures, but Lillie shot off a few more digital images, twisting open the blinds, letting a little light inside the property.

"I called every single number off three months of her cell phone bill," she said. "Called a lot in Mexico, and had Javier from the El Dorado stop by and help."

"That's pretty stand-up."

"He called Torres an embarrassment to the Mexican people," Lillie said. "He and some other Mexican business folks have offered a reward for them."

"On my tenth birthday, I ate so many tacos I puked in one of his sombreros."

"He get mad?"

"Thought it was funny," Quinn said. "My dad threw the party, and slipped out the back door after charging up a dozen margaritas for him and his girlfriend."

"The movie star?"

"The other one," Quinn said. "The cocktail waitress from Tampa."

"He really double for Burt Reynolds?"

"Six movies," Quinn said, opening up cabinets and shining his Maglite inside. "Got fired for showing up drunk on the set of *Stroker Ace*. That's when my folks were still together."

"You check the Torres bedroom?"

"They kept separate bedrooms," Quinn said. "You got to walk knee-deep through garbage to get to her poor bed. Torres had a small bed in a guest room. Kept a lot of pornography, stuff it looked like he was selling. Multiple Mex bootlegs."

"Anything good?" Lillie asked.

"It's all there," Quinn said. "Check it out for yourself. I think Kenny took a couple home."

"Dog and pony stuff?"

"Hell, I don't know," Quinn said.

"Bullshit."

"You check out her bedroom again, and I'll check around the room with the cribs," Quinn said. "You get far with those bills?"

"She'd run up fifteen credit cards to the max, eight of them more than ten thousand dollars."

"What'd she buy?"

"She collected shit off QVC," Lillie said. "Crazy shit that she stored in that shed out back. Collector dolls signed by Marie Osmond. You walk into that shed, and they are all arranged in rows staring out at you. It creeped my shit out."

"That's crazy."

"Do I lie?"

Quinn worked through the kitchen and the children's room, feeling his stomach kick up a little, a stark emptiness in his gut, as he shined the light under the thirteen empty cribs and through the long wall closet littered with busted toys, sun-faded and cracked. Two cases of expired milk formula, diapers from Walmart, and quart jars of Vaseline.

He found a small taser gun in with the stuffed animals, electric tape wrapped tight for a better grip.

Quinn smoked the cigar down to a nub, crushing it out on the front steps, looking down the hill at all those empty cages and rivers of shit and piss heading down into a gulley. He hoped he could convince the county to take the property and burn it all. He'd go back to the office, take a hot shower, and change into some fresh clothes, use some saddle soap on his boots. You got warned about catching all kinds of diseases before heading into missions, but no one thought about this kind of shit in America.

Lillie joined him on the old crooked porch. "Ever know a woman who could wear a size twelve double E?"

"Yeah," Quinn said. "But she had a hell of a personality."

"Janet liked shoes, mostly house slippers. Sexy shit, with feathers that matched her negligee."

"You want me to get sick?"

"Think she'll come back for these?"

Lillie cracked open a shoe box, showing off thick rolls of cash bound with rubber bands.

"How much?"

"First few rolls are hundreds," Lillie said. "If they're all the same, I'd say about twenty grand."

"Seems like the first thing she would've grabbed."

"I don't think they ever came home after taking that baby to see Luke," Lillie said. She fanned away the cigar smoke as if it was worse than her cigarettes. "The Torres family hauled ass the moment they knew he wasn't buying that horseshit story."

"Be an incentive to come back."

"Especially if the place was locked up tight, everyone gone," Lillie said. "How do you want to rotate?"

"We can work in four-hour shifts," Quinn said. "I'll take one just like everyone else. I wouldn't want anyone out here for longer. This smell, it gets into your clothes and in your skin."

AT TWILIGHT, the sky lit up orange, pink, and black over the shape of the Rebel Truck Stop and the red neon sign of the sexy mud-flap girl kicking her legs back and forth along Highway 45. Donnie Varner drove around the complex with its twenty pumps, mostly diesel, and a big diner that served the best chicken-fried steak in north Mississippi. Around back was a big metal barn called The Booby Trap, where truckers would work out a little loneliness over cold cans of Coors or Bud. Women worked the poles and a back room filled with ragged vinyl chairs facing mirrored walls. Before he shipped off to the Sandbox the first time, Donnie got eight lap dances from a pregnant girl from Eupora named Britney who promised she'd be using his money to fund her college education. She said she wanted to study dolphins. She also said for two hundred bucks, she could go and make Donnie's willie sneeze, Donnie saying, "For two hundred bucks, I can make my own willie sneeze, darlin'."

Now, after doing business in Atlanta, Las Vegas, and OK City, this place seemed kind of quaint and homey to him, not that den of iniquity like his preacher had called it. This place was pretty minor league talent; any girl with a decent ass and boobs could find work in Memphis or New Orleans, maybe Sammy's Go-Go in Birmingham.

"Mr. Stagg in?" Donnie asked a fat guy named Leonard who'd been a deputy sheriff for fifteen years before Quinn Colson had run him off. Leonard looked up from the sports page of the *Daily Journal* and nodded, leaning forward and stubbing out the cigarette between his fingers.

"He call you?"

"He knows I'm here," Donnie said.

"I'll ask."

"Just open the fucking door, Leonard," Donnie said. "Shit. Don't be such a goddamn hard-on."

Stagg had two offices, one in downtown Jericho, for meetings on his development company and county business, and the real office behind the pole dancers, right next to the back room where high-stakes poker was played. Stagg was even so goddamn ole-time corny that he ran a Faro game on Sunday nights. The only person Donnie'd ever heard of who played Faro was Wyatt Earp.

Leonard opened the door and waved him inside.

Stagg was on a phone call, giving him that Johnny Stagg wink and pointing out an open chair. Donnie took in the office with heads of dead animals and mounted fish, framed pictures of folks who'd sent glamour shots to him; people who were only famous in northeast Mississippi but somehow meant shit to Johnny Stagg. Maybe Stagg thought if he collected enough of them he wouldn't be the son of some dirt farmer out by Carthage who had to peddle his soul and rape thousands of acres of land to make that first million.

"Donnie," Stagg said. "You got something to discuss?"

"Oh, I don't know, Johnny. Maybe I just came on out for a beer and a pecker tug. Did I walk in the right room?"

Stagg grinned.

"Yeah, I got business."

Stagg propped up a pair of oxblood loafers on his desk. Stagg dressing like an old frat boy, with his button-down shirt, red sweater-vest, and Ole Miss team belt, wanting so damn much to be accepted by the folks in Oxford that he gave a decent amount of income to the athletic program there, Donnie hearing he was about to get a full seat on the board despite having barely graduated high school in Tibbehah County. He'd come a long way from cleaning out bedpans for the old people he conned out of land for nearly a decade.

"Guns."

"What you got?" Stagg said, his weathered face a road map to hell. "I could use a good deer rifle."

"Not to sell," Donnie said. "I'm buying."

"I don't sell guns, Donnie."

"Johnny, you'd sell your own mother if there was money in it."

"I don't appreciate that kind of talk," Stagg said, scratching his cheek. "My momma's been dead for twenty years."

"Would that make a difference?"

"Your daddy is a fine man," Stagg said. "War hero, at that. He know you're out here?"

"My daddy hadn't wiped my ass for some time."

"And the proposition?"

Donnie reached into his blue jeans jacket for a torn piece of notebook paper, reading it off like a grocery list: "Eighty Mossberg shotguns, fifty

AKs, seventy-two Glock 19s, and fifty or so M4s. Oh, and a couple grenade launchers. I wasn't so sure about those last two."

Stagg just smiled, showing off his tombstone teeth, and laughed like Donnie had said something funny. Donnie just waited, deadpan.

"Took all I could from a shitty situation in the Guard, Mr. Stagg," Donnie said. "Got out with a few toys. I got forty-six M4s left, but they're wanting a hundred. I can get most of what they want. M4s, being military grade and all, are a little trickier."

"Can't help you, son."

"Is that really a picture of you and Tim McGraw or one of those phonies you get made up at Six Flags?"

"Tim came to one of my parties at Ole Miss last year," Stagg said. "His wife sang me 'Happy Birthday.' "

"Is she just as pretty in person?"

Stagg smiled and walked past Donnie, Donnie thinking the son of a bitch was throwing him out, but instead he called in Leonard. Leonard stood, splayfooted and nearly cross-eyed, the long-running joke being that he'd been the only deputy who could keep his eyes on two suspects at once. "You get Dara for me?" Stagg asked.

"I don't need to pay for no girl," Donnie said.

"Call it a welcome-home gift," Stagg said. "Thanks for all you done for America."

"Hell," Donnie said. "If you put it like that."

The girl was too good for The Booby Trap, Donnie halfway impressed Johnny could recognize the talent or maybe had at least gotten lucky. She was not hard-looking or wrinkled or drugged-out. She seemed almost shy at first, with a thick head of curly blond hair and wide-set brown eyes. She smelled like cherry perfume, a nineteen-year-old, barely legal wet dream who sat him down in a ragged chair in that empty mirrored room—a goddamn thousand Donnie Varners—shitty dance music playing so loud he couldn't hear himself think as she straddled his waist and pulled her tank top over her head. The girl kept on a pair of cotton panties, and Donnie got a good bit of ass in his hands.

She pulled down her bra strap by strap, showing off a natural pair, soft and drooping, not like those rock-hard things girls got in *Playboy*. She leaned into him with hot cinnamon breath, letting him smell the cherries in her hair and neck, and then pulled back, helping him out of his jacket, rubbing his chest, pulling off his boots.

"What the hell?"

But then she rubbed his feet and ran her hands up each of his legs, spreading his knees wide apart and then moving the flat of her hand around the old bulldog. Donnie closed his eyes, wishing he had a cold Coors in one hand and a smoke in the other. And, damn, if she didn't pull up his shirt, kissing his stomach and then peeling down her panties, bending over to give him the whole show.

Johnny Stagg was a good man, Donnie thought, as she fell back into him and twisted up his shirt and ran her hands over her chest before she stopped cold as the houselights flicked on and the music stopped, Leonard's ugly face looking down on him.

He was sucking his teeth.

"God damn, Leonard," Donnie said. "You sure made it shrink up."

"He's clean," Dara said, reaching for her little panties and thin tank top, fanning out a match after she lit a smoke and disappearing behind the bar to pour herself a Jack on ice.

"And I thought you loved me," Donnie said, heaving himself into his Levi's jacket, walking to her, and stealing the smoke from her mouth. "I am truly hurt."

The girl toasted him from behind the bar.

Leonard opened up the back door, motioning Donnie with two

fingers. The red light from the neon mud-flap girl, kicking high and low, high and low, outside.

"Mr. Stagg will be in touch," Leonard said.

"You ever get deputy of the month?" Donnie asked.

Leonard scowled at him.

"Guess not."

8

QUINN RELIEVED KENNY AT TWO A.M. A COUPLE DAYS LATER, BRINGING IN
a thermos of black coffee and a cold sausage biscuit, a Maglite, and a
ragged Louis L'Amour paperback he'd found at the farmhouse. Kenny
had been standing in the kitchen when he opened the back door, chain-
smoking cigarettes and staring into the darkness, dog tired and deep in
thought. Quinn moved past him, patting him on the shoulder, but
Kenny didn't move, a big fat shadow with the glowing red tip of his
cigarette in his mouth.

"I had to shower three times to get this smell out," Kenny said.
"Washed my hair with lemon juice."

Quinn sat down on the Torres's old sofa and screwed off the cap
from the end of his thermos and poured a cup. "You hear anything?"

"Walked in from the north end of the property, just like you said.
Been quiet."

"I brought a book."

"What is it?"

"Quick and the Dead," Quinn said.

"Didn't they make a movie out of that?" Kenny said.

"Yep. Sam Elliott."

"He was real good in that *Lebowski* picture," Kenny said in the darkness. "Funny as hell."

"You don't have to stay, Kenny."

"I'm good," he said. "Drank a couple Red Bulls. Been just kind of thinking a lot. Took that Lab to see Jess Colley. Jess says she's got mange and heartworms. Gonna cost five hundred dollars to get her healthy."

"What are you gonna do?"

"I don't know," Kenny said. "Get her fixed up, I guess."

Quinn drank some more hot coffee and felt for the flashlight and paperback at his side. He leaned back into the sofa, knowing that four hours wasn't a damn thing. On training and in missions, waiting could be days or weeks, sometimes while wearing face paint and blanketed in a ghillie suit. Being a Ranger was full-tilt shitstorm or nothing. When you weren't shooting, you were running, and when you weren't running, you were jumping out of airplanes. He knew keeping still was an art.

"Quinn," Kenny said. "You mind if I ask you something?"

"Shoot."

"Me and you kinda lost track of each other after graduation," he said. "I didn't write you or nothin'. Hadn't seen you in almost ten years. How come you gave me this job?"

"Not many folks I could trust."

Quinn could only still see the outline of Kenny, watching the end of the cigarette glow red-hot, and then heard the hiss as he tossed the butt in the kitchen sink.

"I can't really imagine what y'all went through."

"What's that?" Quinn asked.

"Do you wake up in night sweats like you see veterans do in movies? Or just driving around and get a flashback, thinking about your best friend getting killed in the line of duty? I imagine that can mindfuck you good even if you don't lose a limb like ole Boom."

"You try and keep your head clear."

"How do you do that?"

"Some of my buddies find God," Quinn said. "Most of them still like to fight, in bars or in the ring."

"You see folks die?"

"Yep."

"You kill some?"

"I did."

"Buddies get killed?"

"Kenny, it's pretty late."

"I'm sorry," Kenny said. "Didn't mean to push. I mean, we just hadn't talked at all since I come onto the department. And I guess I'm just sayin' I appreciate you for coming back. I know things been different."

Quinn drank some coffee. Kenny's Bic flicked back on, and he lit another cigarette. The room filling with tobacco smoke over the kitchen counter and into the family room, cold night air breathing through the cracked windows.

"You think I should save that dog?" Kenny asked.

"Good to have a dog," Quinn said.

"Better 'an my ex-wife," Kenny said. "Found out she gave our youth pastor a blow job. And the kicker was, I figured the son of a bitch was gay. He had his hair frosted like you see on old women and wore leather bracelets and shit."

"You want some coffee?"

"I got to git," Kenny said. "Sorry about askin' about war and all that. I know you got to keep them things secret."

"I don't mind the talk."

They both heard the wood creak on the old porch at the same time. Kenny's fresh cigarette hissed into the sink as Quinn stood and unholstered his gun. He saw the large shape of Kenny step back from the kitchen and into the living room, raising his weapon as the door jimmied open and a hand fumbled for the lights. The voice of a girl saying "Shit" when she realized there wasn't electricity.

Keys dropped onto a countertop.

Quinn got a good sense of a short girl, low and fat, arms down by her sides and hands empty. He clicked the Maglite up into her wide face. She squinted and covered her eyes. Kenny giving a hell of an unnecessary "Hold it."

"Mara?" Quinn asked.

The girl didn't say anything. Her face was white and doughy, with bug eyes, under a pink John Deere ski hat, expressionless in the flashlight beam. Kenny moved behind her and gripped her by the thick arm, reaching for his handcuffs. Mara Torres just stood there, chunky and short, a not-quite-miniature version of her mother.

"Where are they?" Quinn asked.

"I'm alone," her voice soft and thick country. "Hell."

"Kenny, go check the road," Quinn said. "I'll take Miss Torres to the jail."

"My name ain't Torres," she said. "That Mex bastard ain't my father."

9

DONNIE ATE SUPPER WITH HIS FATHER EVERY THURSDAY NIGHT AT THE
Jericho VFW Hall right after Bible study. This had pretty much been
the deal since his momma died when he was twelve, and Luther Varner
looked forward to taking his son to that big meal at the old cinder-block
building at the edge of town. Donnie wasn't complaining. No, sir. They
had row after row of fried catfish (with the tail on), French fries, coleslaw, baked beans, and sometimes a little barbecue if the cook—usually
a large black man—decided to get a little creative. All the old soldiers
in town—and there seemed to be more and more of them, a helluva lot
more of them than when Donnie had been a kid—just ate that shit up.
The Jericho VFW spanned World War II to what people called the
Global War on Terror but what Donnie just called a big fucking mess.

He and his daddy had a lot in common, he figured. His daddy had
been a Marine sniper in Vietnam. But like all old soldiers, his daddy
never said a word about it. About as close as he'd ever come to knowing
what old Luther went through was watching him bawl during the

annual showing of *Sergeant York* on TBS. Something sure got to him there.

"What'd you think about the talk tonight?"

"I think Joseph's brothers were a bunch of assholes," Donnie said.

"Pretty tough on that kid for a damn coat."

"Must've been some coat."

Luther Varner stood about six-foot-four, with a silver crew cut, leathery skin, and a *Semper Fi* tattoo with a smiling skull on his right forearm. He lifted that forearm to burn off another smoke, squashing it into his coffee cup, and reached for another piece of fried catfish.

The VFW was clogged with so much cigarette smoke that the goddamn air purifier had turned yellow.

"You ever have crazy dreams like that?" Luther asked. "Like that ole pharaoh?"

"Sometimes."

"Skinny cows devouring fat cows. Grain eating other grain. Hell."

"Crazy."

"I hate to dream," Luther said, taking a bite of catfish.

Donnie looked up on the wall and spotted a photograph of old Judge Blanton, a Korean War vet who'd been a good friend to his dad. His father caught him staring.

"You make it through the Chosin Reservoir and get offed at the Dixie Gas station in Tibbehah County."

"He made a stand," Luther said, working the white meat from the fish's bones. "He was a good man."

"I heard he done got himself killed 'cause he felt shame for throwing in with Johnny Stagg."

Luther shot Donnie a look, the kind of look that used to mean Donnie'd be left with a sore ass from the flat of his daddy's hand. He didn't talk for a long while, reaching for some Tabasco. "Heard you were over at the truck stop the other day," Luther said.

"Damn, you can't take a shit in this town without someone smellin' it."

"You got business with Stagg?" Luther asked.

"Just getting my piston greased."

Luther nodded, but, god damn, that old coot knew. What'd he want, for Donnie to keep working a shift at the convenience store?

Luther said: "You can work for me some more. Pick up an extra shift."

"I'm making money."

Luther nodded again, scraping up some more on his plate, washing it down with some sweet tea. Donnie got up to buy a dollar beer and sat back down, his daddy's eyes with that rheumy, faraway look that he always thought of as being on Da Nang time.

"I'm sorry for what happened to you, Donnie."

"I'm here, ain't I?"

"Sometimes I can't sleep," Luther said, "me being the one pushed you into the Guard."

"Can't drive a truck forever," Donnie said. "Ain't shit to do around here since the plant closed."

Luther nodded, thinking the best thing about the VFW might've been the cold beer. They damn sure know how to ice a son of a bitch.

"You seen Quinn Colson since you been back?"

Donnie nodded.

"I know he's been trying to round up a couple more deputies."

Donnie snorted so hard, some Budweiser flushed out his nose. "Shit."

"How's that?" Luther said, stubbing out his millionth cigarette, starting up a new one.

"I got everything in hand," Donnie said.

"What's wrong with being on the right side?"

"You believe Quinn Colson won't find a way to get himself paid?"

"He grew up."

"Well, good for him, Dad."

"SO WHO IS YOUR FATHER?" Lillie asked Mara in the Tibbehah County Sheriff's Office conference room less than an hour later.

"Fred Black."

"The welder?" Lillie asked.

Mara nodded.

"I know Fred," Lillie said. "He built a nice wrought-iron fence for my mother. Is he still in Jericho?"

"Yes, ma'am."

Quinn hung back against the glass door. He'd been sheriff for six months, and this was the first serious interrogation he'd ever watched. Lillie took the lead since she had more law enforcement experience than anyone in the department, with her five years as a cop in Memphis.

"Can I get you something to eat?" Lillie asked.

"No, ma'am."

"Listen, Mara," Lillie said. "I'll put it this way: I don't think you're a part of all this. How 'bout a Coke?"

"I'm not talking."

"I just want to get you a Coke, Mara. That doesn't mean anything."

"I only came back to get some clothes," she said. "What's wrong with that? I didn't do nothin'."

"We got warrants out for your mother," Lillie said. "You're eighteen and can be prosecuted as an adult. But I don't think that's right. I don't think you got much choice in all this."

"I just needed clean underwear."

"How about a shoe box full of money?" Quinn asked from the wall.

"I'll take that Coke," Mara said.

Quinn walked to the back of the department to a Coca-Cola machine that had probably been there since the 1960s and got a bottle, cracking off the cap. He headed back into Lillie's office and handed it to the pudgy little girl. She was still wearing her pink hat on her fat little head.

"What happened to the child?" Lillie was asking.

"She fell out of a grocery cart."

"You see it?"

"I think I'm gonna be sick."

"Did your momma hit that child?"

"No."

"Did she hit you?"

"That baby's in rough shape," Quinn said.

"Where is she?"

"St. Jude," Quinn said. "Her skull was cracked. Ribs snapped like matchsticks."

"She gonna make it?" Mara said. Her voice sounded small. Head dropped into her chubby hands.

Nobody said anything. The silence in the station was electric. The bottle of Coke just sat there, fizzing, with Mara frozen and staring into nothing. Quinn couldn't note any emotion at all until the tears started to come. But the face was passive and dull, almost bovine. She didn't even seem to notice the tears.

"Where are the other children?" Lillie asked.

Mara was silent.

"What about Ramón?" Quinn asked. "What's he do?"

"Nothin'."

"Are the children all Mexican?" Lillie asked.

Mara nodded.

"How many?" Lillie asked.

Quinn listened.

"Eleven."

"There were thirteen cribs."

"She only got eleven now."

"What's she do with them?" Lillie asked, taking a seat across from the girl.

"Helps them find homes."

"For a price?" Lillie asked, leaning forward.

Mara nodded.

"So she sells babies," Lillie said. "That's pretty illegal, Mara. I sure would appreciate you working with us. We're worried about those children."

Mara shook her head, took off her pink hat, and wiped her face and big eyes clean.

"Is she still in the state?" Quinn asked.

Mara shook her head some more. Lillie looked up to Quinn, Quinn leaning his butt on the desk with arms folded across his chest. He shrugged.

"Are you worried about the baby?" Lillie asked.

Mara was sobbing now, leaning down between her knees and making retching sounds. Lillie stood over her and rubbed her back.

"Sheriff, can you call about that child?" Lillie asked.

Lillie nodded to Quinn, and Quinn walked back to his office. He had the hospital number written on a yellow legal pad on his desk. He was transferred around a bit before he was able to talk to an administrator on duty. He'd spoken to the woman before, the woman obviously half asleep, but she promised to call him back with an update.

She called back a few minutes later, and Quinn walked back to the conference room.

Quinn said: "That baby is dead."

The heaving and sobbing and retching all came pretty fast and hard now. Mara fell from the chair and curled into a fetal ball, screaming and yelling. Quinn leaned against the desk. Lillie dropped down on a knee and soothed her back some more, telling her she was very worried about the other children and that Mara wasn't to blame.

The shuddering and cries broke down after a while, and the sobbing turned to a smattering of coughs. Lillie reached out her hand and helped the fat little girl to her feet. Her sweatshirt had a picture of Tinker Bell on it.

"Where's your momma?" Lillie said. "Is she still in the state?"

Mara's face was a reddened, puffy mess. She shook her head and wiped her bug eyes. "No, ma'am."

"Where?" Quinn asked.

Mara turned her eyes to him and coughed. "Memphis."

10

THE FASTEST WAY OUT OF TIBBEHAH COUNTY WAS TAKING THE NATCHEZ
Trace up to Tupelo. It was 0500 by the time Lillie drove the old winding trapper and Indian route by moonlight, passing through the thick
humps of Indian mounds and long stretches of virgin oak and pine,
Quinn riding shotgun and studying the scenery. They refueled just
after they got onto Highway 78, heading through the north Mississippi
towns of New Albany, Potts Camp, Holly Springs, Red Banks, and
Olive Branch. By the time the Jeep hit the state line, the sun had just
started rising over the Mississippi River. Lillie pulled off again, this
time for coffee and biscuits at a Shell station, and for Quinn to check in
with the shift commander at the Airways Precinct to see if they could
get a couple uniform officers to help them serve a warrant.

Lillie had explained, Quinn not knowing this, that the local law
had to be present not only in case some shit went down but because
they were the ones who had to make the actual arrest. They'd have to
extradite the Torres family—if they were able to catch them—back to

Tibbehah County. Lillie rolled down the window, lighting up a cigarette, and surmised they might need a horse trailer to truck Janet's big ass back to Jericho.

"Being inside that house makes me think these folks aren't even human," Quinn said.

"We aren't paid to be psychologists," Lillie said. "Just get them to court."

"You think those kids are still with them?"

"Don't know," Lillie said, flicking her cigarette out onto the road. "But let's not take any chances. We'll get the Memphis cops to go in first. I know you want to be the first to point that gun at Ramón and Janet, but, trust me, it'll make it go better with the D.A."

"I wonder how these two shitbirds met," Quinn said.

"Maybe found each other on eHarmony," Lillie said. "Both of them being good Christians that like going to the beach, puppy dogs, and sunsets."

"What's in it for him?"

"Maybe she pays him," Lillie said. "Maybe it's not a marriage at all but a business deal. Them being married gets his ass a green card."

"He earned it."

"We treat either one of them with some contempt and it'll fuck up the case," Lillie said. "I want them both in our jail, and I want you and me to file every bit of paper we can on these people. I want those children in a safe place, and I want the Torreses to be locked up in a cage a good long while."

"You know Kenny kept one of those dogs," Quinn said. "Spent five hundred on getting her cleaned up and dewormed and all."

"Yep," Lillie said. "That's something Kenny would do."

Lillie and Quinn followed 78 until it turned into Lamar Avenue in south Memphis, running through all those warehouses and big-rig garages, cheap motels for truckers to sleep, and barbecue joints to grab a sandwich, or western-wear shops for some new cowboy boots. The road soon turned into a clustered section of beauty parlors and pawn-shops, used-car dealerships, and storefront churches. The Stonewall Jackson Motel was a half mile off the I-240 loop, tired and haggard and having seen its best days when Ike had been president. There had been a pool at one point, but it had been filled in, with thick weeds growing in the center. The motel was one story and a deep U shape. Lots of transient cars with out-of-state license plates littered the parking lot, probably laborers cutting through town. The sign outside the small registration lobby boasted FREE HBO.

You could hear the trucks and cars zipping past the old highway on the bypass. The sound of it made the motel seem lost and insignificant.

"Sometimes the chickenshits are the worst arrests," Lillie said, parking and turning off the engine. "Domestics. Drunks. I had a crackhead bite me on the tit once."

"I'll be careful."

"Like you were with Boom?"

"I got him home."

"He gonna go back to the VA? See that therapist?"

"I don't know," Quinn said. "I thought about offering him a job."

"A one-armed deputy?" Lillie said. "Boom's strong, but he couldn't pass the academy physical."

"I got somethin' else in mind," Quinn said. "Something that would set his mind in the right direction."

Lillie and Quinn climbed out of the Jeep and joined up with a couple street officers with the Memphis PD. Both of them black men in their thirties in stiff blues. They made introductions, and the men pointed out Unit 22, where the night clerk said the Torreses had registered. The men were both drinking coffee. Lillie showed them the warrant signed that morning by a judge in Tibbehah County.

"Where the fuck is that?" one of the cops asked.

"South of Tupelo, north of Starkville," Lillie said.

"Never heard of it," the cop said.

"Neither have most people."

"Y'all in the hill country," the other cop said. "My people from Marshall County."

The night manager was a dark-skinned doughy man with badly thinning hair and the bulging eyes of a bulldog. He didn't bother to speak to any of the cops, only reached into an old pair of black dress pants and pulled out a passkey, muttering to himself about the couple being the only guests who'd paid for the week. Lillie showed him the warrant, but it didn't seem to make a difference, he didn't question anything they asked. He looked to be Pakistani, and Quinn asked him something in Pashto.

The man just stared at him with a blank look and walked to the door. He knocked a couple times. The man had sweated a great deal through a very threadbare Grizzlies T-shirt, the perspiration forming a V at the nape of his neck. He knocked some more, and Quinn exchanged looks with the cops. The man turned and shrugged, crossing his arms over a fat little potbelly.

"You hear something?" Lillie asked.

"I think I hear a kid crying," one of the men said. He gave Lillie a wry smile.

"Open it up," Lillie said.

The manager turned the key and walked back, the two Memphis patrol cops stepping up and pushing on inside with guns at the ready but below their waists. Quinn and Lillie followed, the lights cutting on, showing two unmade beds and piles of fast-food wrappers and pizza boxes, dirty linen and used diapers. The manager started into a roll of a language that Quinn didn't know as he threw open the old curtains and tried to raise a window that looked as if it had been painted shut years ago.

Lillie walked into the bathroom and quickly came out, holding her breath. "Toilet's backed up."

The manager had kept the door open, and the sound of passing cars filled the little room. He was already on his cell phone, dog-cussing somebody about the shithole he'd found.

"How'd they pay?" Lillie asked the man. The manager looked annoyed that she'd spoken to him and kept on muttering into his cell phone. Lillie took the phone from the much shorter man and repeated, "How did they pay?"

"Credit card," he said.

"Probably one of these," Quinn said, walking to a small writing desk that faced the window. A neat arrangement had been made of three credit cards and driver's licenses for both Ramón and Janet Torres. Besides the garbage, that's all they had left in the room. No luggage or clothes or even a toothbrush.

"They coming back?" one of the cops asked.

"Nope," Lillie said. "They wanted to offer a little F.U. to us. I guess they knew their daughter had given them up."

Quinn nodded to her, already walking to the door. She joined him outside on a weedy hill filled with busted bottles and candy wrappers and rusted hubcaps and shit off the streets. "They got some friends," Quinn said. "Got them some new IDs. New cards. They could be any-where."

"Yep," Lillie said. They watched the cars circle Memphis on I-240, spoking out to Nashville to the east, Little Rock to the west, or New Orleans south. Lillie smoked another cigarette as they stood there, kicked at a stray bottle, and walked back to the Jeep.

———

JOHNNY STAGG FOUND DONNIE working the register that morning at Varner's Quick Mart. Even though it was Friday, Stagg was dressed for Sunday with his shiny pin-striped suit, shined alligator boots, and a tie painted up with the head of a big buck. Donnie nodded to him as soon as he walked in the door and asked his cook, an old black woman named Peaches, to take the register for a few minutes. Donnie got his half-finished Mountain Dew and sat down at a back table, where old men were known to linger in the morning instead of tilling or feeding or whatever old country men do. He fired up a smoke and leaned back in a folding chair.

"You want some coffee?" Donnie asked.

Stagg shook his head. He'd just shaved, and there were nicks on his thin, papery skin. He grinned a big tombstone smile and leaned forward across from him. "Need to know more about your people."

"They ain't my people."

"I need to know who we're dealing with here," Stagg said. "You ain't exactly ordering up a load of discount Sheetrock."

"I don't think they want to be known, Mr. Stagg. If my money ain't good, I'll try somewhere else."

"You're making folks a little nervous," Stagg said. "They said Memphis has been crawling with federal folks in the last few months."

Donnie blew some smoke out of his nose. One thing he hated so much about his daddy's store was the smell of old grease and dead crickets he sold for bait. The smoke at least helped some with that, and to pass the time. Running a place like this, smoking's about all there was besides playing with his pecker. And you couldn't really do that in public.

"Your buddy from Memphis?" Donnie asked.

"One of 'em."

"Well, I ain't no FBI."

"We're talking smart business folks. They don't want to see these guns end up in some kind of Waco situation. You know what I mean? We got them crazy Nazi folks arrested or killed and finally out of Tibbehah County. But people read about it all over and it still makes 'em nervous."

"I know how much you hated to see Gowrie and his people go," Donnie said.

Stagg grinned. He leaned back and smoothed down his big buck tie. He nodded. Donnie squashed out the cigarette in the silver ashtray, noticing they'd run out of cracklins on the sale rack and he hadn't even called the goddamn Golden Flake rep to stock.

"Don't believe the bullshit," Stagg said, still grinning, still preaching. "Your buddy Quinn Colson spread around a lot of lies in that election. He hates that I'm trying to take this county out of the eighteen hundreds."

Donnie drank a little of the Mountain Dew and shrugged. He leaned back in the chair and looked over his shoulder at Peaches ringing up a couple teenage boys. Maybe she could order up the cracklins all his customers wanted to buy for lunch. A sack of cracklins and hot sauce was a cheaper meal than buying a burger or a chicken on a stick. These days, you spent most of your goddamn wage on the gas to drive to the work site.

"Believe it," Stagg said after a few seconds.

"These people ain't even American, Mr. Stagg," Donnie said. "Just some Mexicans who want some military-grade hardware. Don't know why and didn't ask, but I think they're part of some of them cartel folks who settled in after Katrina. I don't give a shit about what goes down in Ole Mexico. How 'bout you?"

"My people want to meet 'em."

"Nope."

"Why not?"

"Well, that kind of cornholes me, Mr. Stagg. I bet you're familiar with the phrase 'cut out the middleman.'"

Stagg grinned. He slowly nodded. He scratched the inside of his ear with his pinkie like he was trying to clear out the wax to hear Donnie a bit better. Like Donnie could surely not be questioning a great mind like Johnny T. Stagg. But hell, Donnie knew more about Stagg than Stagg knew himself. He knew the *T* in his name didn't stand for shit. He was born just Johnny Stagg. Not John. Not Jonathan. Johnny Stagg, the son of a manure salesman from Carthage, who took on a middle initial because he thought it made him seem respectable.

"They'll need reassurance," Stagg said.

"You want Dara to pat down my bulldog again?"

"I think that girl's taken a shine to you."

"Only thing your girls take a shine to is cash."

Stagg shrugged. That goddamn toothy smile on his face wouldn't leave, like he was a television preacher who'd been infected by the spirit of God and that happiness coursed through his veins like a drug. Donnie wondered if he should offer up a few amens for Brother Stagg's gospel of tits, grits, and cash.

Donnie just nodded.

"OK, I'll meet 'em," Donnie said. "But it don't matter two shits who I sell 'em to. All they got to figure is if the money is good. Money's good, and that should put their mind at rest."

Stagg stood up. He buttoned his shiny suit jacket and offered his long, skinny hand. His grin sliced even wider, his breath smelling like Listerine. "All I can ask."

"When?"

"You busy tomorrow night?"

"We got church the next morning."

"I know." Stagg's eyes wandered over him. "Who the hell you think is teaching Sunday school?"

11

QUINN HAD GOTTEN HIS OFFICE IN SOME KIND OF ORDER. THE RECKLESS-
ness of his uncle's paperwork, unfiled reports, and dirty guns sickened
him. He never saw that side of him growing up and wondered if the
sloppiness had spread in him like a cancer. Or maybe he'd never noticed
it. Hamp had been the lead Quinn had followed when his father left
town. A big, lumbering man who wore a tobacco brown ranch coat
and beaten Stetson, Hamp got him out of trouble more than once and
pushed him toward the Army. He took Quinn hunting from the time
he could hold a gun and taught him how to track animals and to fish.
He'd walk him around the muddy edges of the old pond and point out
the prints of raccoon and deer and bellies of cottonmouths. He'd given
him guns, taught him to shoot. He'd introduced him to the joys of a
good cigar on his thirteenth birthday. His funeral had brought Quinn
back again to a town that Hamp had always told him to escape.

When Quinn took the job, Hamp's longtime secretary, Mary Alice,
asked if she could burn all the files. Instead, Quinn had them sorted
and placed in a row of a half-dozen locking cabinets. He kept them all

in his office against a far wall as a visible legacy he'd inherited. A weak light shone in from the east window across his desk.

The old rancher coat hung on a hook by the office door, the leather worn smooth and soft by the elbows. Quinn's new ball cap hung next to it.

After he and Lillie got back from Memphis, Quinn sat at his desk, drinking coffee and going through the night's reports filed by Kenny and his six other deputies. A total of nine for the entire county. He learned Kenny couldn't spell worth a crap.

Someone knocked on the door, Quinn looking up to see Mary Alice peering inside. Mary Alice, who was gray-headed and plump, said a woman was out front who wanted to see him.

"She say the trouble?"

"She showed me a badge," Mary Alice said. "She's with ATF over in Oxford. She ain't that nice. Talks like a Yankee."

Quinn widened his eyes and nodded.

He stood when the woman entered. He would have stood even if she hadn't been a federal agent or had been coming to see him. She was average height, but lean and hard, with red hair and light gray eyes. Her skin was the color of milk, with light freckles across her nose and cheeks. She was carefully made up with lined eyes and a deep red mouth. Without makeup, she might've looked washed-out and pale.

She wore a crisp, fitted blue suit and two strands of pearls on her neck. She took his hand and held his smile with the intense, serious look of a woman who was used to men grinning at her and didn't have time for their shit. This woman was all business, reports and record keeping and making sure that her scores at the shooting range didn't just match the boys but embarrassed them. Quinn had known a lot of women just like her in the service. He admired them.

Quinn dropped the smile and offered her coffee.

"No thanks," she said. "You know, I expected someone a lot older."

"Sorry to disappoint."

She looked to be about his age, maybe a little older. She smiled, slightly. It was a professional smile but one that held little interest.

"Dinah Brand."

Quinn let go of her hand. She sat down.

"Don't be afraid of the coffee," Quinn said. "An Army buddy at Fort Lewis gets it in Seattle."

She cocked her head. "Hard to find good coffee in Mississippi," she said.

Quinn called out to Mary Alice. She placed a mug in front of Agent Brand and closed the door behind her. She took a sip and then set the mug at the edge of his desk.

"Not bad."

"I'm guessin' you didn't drive over from Oxford for a cup of coffee."

"I'd like to talk to Mara Black."

"Thought Mary Alice said you were ATF?"

Brand nodded, opened her purse, and placed on his desk a card with her name and *Special Agent* embossed in neat type. "We're interested in her stepfather."

"Ramón?"

"You know him?"

"To be honest, never met either him or Janet," Quinn said. "Thought we had them in Memphis this morning, but something spooked them. Most people recall Janet 'cause of her size. No one seems to recall the husband or daughter."

"Didn't her daughter go to school?"

"Dropped out two years ago to help with all those kids."

"I read there are thirteen children missing?"

"Eleven that we know about," Quinn said. "What's that have to do with ATF? The Torreses doing some moonshining, too?"

Brand took a cautious breath, one that let her think for a moment, decide what to say. She wasn't really sure about Quinn, not too sure if some hick sheriff could keep up with someone who trained in Washington. Always an enlisted man.

"Mr. Torres has some friends we're investigating," she said. "He may know where we can find them. We've been looking at Mr. Torres for a while now."

"What kind of friends?"

Brand's gray eyes roamed over Quinn's face, and she nodded after a few moments as if she'd just decided to take him into her confidence. She crossed her legs, and Quinn tried his best not to stare. It had been a long while between women. A sweet-hearted hairdresser in Columbus, Georgia, who needed someone to raise her two kids. And then a real estate agent in Phenix City who was twenty-four but acted like she was eighteen. And then there was the brief thought of Anna Lee when he'd come home, although she'd married Luke. But that whole idea seemed to make much less sense now that she was pregnant.

"We have a paid informant who thinks Mr. Torres works with the Los Zetas."

Quinn looked away from her legs. He smiled.

"Miss Brand, I've been away for about ten years," Quinn said. "You're going to have to get me up to speed. The only Mexican folks I know in this area are some people in the restaurant and construction business. A couple of them I played high school football with."

"There've been some changes in law regarding buying weapons," Brand said. "States that border Mexico have to report anyone who purchases a large amount of weapons."

"You're talking straw buys?"

"Yep," Brand said. "Cartels will pay a lot for good weapons. They used to back their trucks up to gun dealers on the border and get forklift loads of 39-millimeter cartridges. Nobody said anything to them. As long as they presented a clean driver's license, no questions asked."

"And now these cartel folks are sending people into the Deep South?"

"Mississippi doesn't have much bite in its gun laws."

"But we are last in education and health," Quinn said. "Where are you from?"

"Atlanta."

"How long have you been working with the Feds?"

"Since college."

"You married?"

Her face colored. Her eyes roamed over Quinn's smiling face. She looked up at the brick wall of a framed photo of his squad at the Haditha Dam. A photo of him and Uncle Hamp with a prize buck. A small school picture of Jason on his desk. There was always that beat of surprise when people saw Jason, because they saw the resemblance but also noted his color. Sometimes it was racism, often just surprise, not sure of how to ask if they were kin.

"Are you?" she asked, widening her eyes.

"Nope."

"Ever?"

"Never."

"Who's the child, if you don't mind me asking?"

"My nephew."

She tilted her head to the side and nodded.

"I came to see Mara Black," Brand said. "Can you set that up?"

"I can."

"Will you."

Quinn nodded and stood.

Brand stood and smoothed down her skirt. She reached for her purse as Quinn walked to the door and opened it wide. They shook hands. She smelled very nice close up, just a little perfume to draw you in and then cut your ass to pieces.

"You think you might stick around Jericho after you're done?" he said.

"I suppose you'll have questions."

"Yes, ma'am," Quinn said. "Lots. Maybe I could buy you lunch."

"I'd like that."

"SO YOU BUY HER LUNCH?" Boom asked.

"Bought her a hot dog at the Sonic."

"Bullshit," Boom said. "You took her to the Sonic?"

"Fillin' Station."

"That place just as bad."

"They do a mean blue plate," Quinn said. "Special was meat loaf with mashed potatoes and gravy and green beans for five bucks. Sweet tea and corn bread."

"You been in the Army too long," Boom said. "Eatin' MREs and shit on a shingle. Anything tastes good to you. She say she like it, she just bein' nice."

"Maybe so."

"She really look that good?"

"She did."

"Red hair and freckles. Nice body?"

"Yep."

"You think she really a redhead?" Boom said, grinning a little.

"Didn't get that far," Quinn said. "We were talking about Mexican drug gangs."

"You gonna try?"

"Kept her card."

Quinn had picked up Boom at his shotgun shack out toward Drivers Flat. The house wasn't much, just a ramshackle tin-roofed job built by

71

his great-grandfather, one of the original black landowners in the county, but it was surrounded by five hundred acres of cotton. The cotton would be ready for the gin in a few weeks, and Boom would work the tractor till every plant was harvested, splitting his cut with his father and eight brothers and sisters. By the time it was all divided, he barely had enough to live.

"Come out to my church Sunday and I'll get you fed," Boom said.

"Or you could come to my mom's house and get some, too. Without the three-hour service."

"White churches got an eye on the clock the whole time," Boom said. "Your mom can cook, though."

"How about tonight?"

"What's for dinner?"

"Does it matter?"

Boom shook his head. "Where you taking me now?"

"Got a proposition for you."

"I ain't into that kinda shit, Quinn."

"Business proposition."

"OK."

They cut up off Highway 9 through more acres of cotton in the little bit of flat land that there was in Tibbehah County and up over the Black River bridge, afternoon light gold and thick on the sandbars and dying leaves. The sluggish water moved under extended limbs of fat oaks and on past a rusting collection of junked cars piled ten high in Mr. Hill's pull-a-part junkyard. Quinn drove a mile or so east past the VFW Hall and turned south into some land that the county still owned. A sign reading COUNTY BARN, with arrows hand-painted on scrap wood, showed the way a good half mile down a twisting dirt path. The truck bucked up and down off the potholes, Quinn straddling over a dead raccoon surrounded by vultures. The carrion eaters kicked up onto a cedar tree until they passed.

"You ain't takin' me to no goddamn intervention," Boom said, "are you? Bring my family out and my preacher and my tenth-grade teacher cryin' and all that. I like to get fucked up. OK? I ain't no crackhead. Me and you just got a little lit last week, you don't see me callin' up Miss Jean and your uncles to come out and lay hands on you and all that mess."

Quinn didn't answer him, just slowed on the dirt path and turned up toward a big sheet-metal barn with two old gas pumps out front. A school bus with flat tires and three old sheriff's cruisers up on blocks sat in a weedy parking lot. A light fall wind brushed over the tops of the weeds, the whole space still and quiet. Someone had built a fire pit in front of the school bus, the ground littered with liquor bottles and ciga-rette butts.

"How much you payin' to clean this shit up?" Boom said.

"I'll get some folks to help," Quinn said. "But I need someone to run this place."

"Run what? This place is fucked up."

"Used to be the maintenance shed for all the county vehicles," Quinn said. "I'm going to the Board of Supervisors next week to get them to open it back up. We'd save a ton of money buying our own fuel and servicing our own vehicles. I got three years of receipts to prove it."

"What's this got to do with me?"

Quinn kept walking into the open bay door of the old barn. Inside, the barn was deep-shadowed and colder. The wind kicked up the grit and dirt at the mouth's edge, and you had to adjust your eyes to see in the deep corners. Chains hung from engine hoists, and large old metal barrels stood filled to the rim with filthy oil. Over an old workbench, someone had left a *Playboy* calendar from 1987, and the pages fluttered over sun-faded images of naked women. Boom walked to the bench and picked up a few tools with his good hand.

"Need me a mechanic."

Boom laughed.

"I'm serious," Quinn said. "I met a guy at Camp Phoenix who had a prosthetic hand with fitted spaces for ratchets and screwdrivers. He said once he got used to it, he could work the same as before. You know, the VA has to pay for that."

"I don't want no goddamn Edward Scissorhands. This won't work."

"So you just want to keep pissin' away your Guard check on shit whiskey and busting heads at the juke?"

"Maybe I like bustin' heads."

"What's that pay?"

"Jack shit."

"You want to keep bullshittin' or do you want to get to work?"

"I don't need no fucking charity."

"Ain't charity, Boom," Quinn said. "It's good ole-fashioned cronyism."

Boom nodded. He picked up a wrench in his good hand. The wind jangled the loose chains hanging from the ceiling. The oil stains splattered on the concrete floor were thick with fine gray dirt and leaves. Boom stayed in thought, standing there, chains turning.

"You scared it just might work out?" Quinn said.

Boom stayed silent for a moment, and then said, "Your truck does need work. You shoulda kept that Dodge Big Ram Stagg tried to give you."

"I keep hearin' that," Quinn said. "Can you do anything with that old Ford?"

"Nope. But I know where you can get a better one cheap. F-250. Put on a roll bar and a winch. Paint it myself. How's Army green sound?"

Quinn walked up to his friend and offered his left hand.

Boom took it.

12

JOHNNY STAGG DROVE NORTH TO OXFORD SATURDAY AFTERNOON AND
then west into the Delta, not talking much, only playing his easy-
listening music, humming along to Pat Boone and Don Ho, as they
crossed into the flat land of the Delta to a hunt club where they'd meet
his people. Stagg never said names, not that Donnie had asked. He just
talked about these people with a lot of respect and admiration. Stagg
was like that, thinking that men who were whoremongers, gun dealers,
and drug pushers could be admirable because it brought them nice
clothes and big houses and hunt clubs in the Delta. Stagg didn't have a
conscience, believing a man's wallet is all that separated him from others. A preacher might disagree, Stagg said, but in the end, money is
what gets respect.

"What's in this for you, Johnny?" Donnie asked.

"All I want is a finder's fee," Stagg said. "How's forty percent sound?"

"Twenty sounds better."

"Let's say thirty, 'cause if not, it's just chickenshit and not worth the
time."

"Thirty," Donnie said. "But Johnny, just give me your word that you won't cornhole me. You do, and I swear I'll come for you in the middle of the night."

Stagg smiled and kept on steering his big Cadillac as if he was steering a ship, cutting north on Highway 316 through Jonestown. The ragged old place looked like something out of a western movie except it was all black; the whole town made of clapboard and brick, broken windows, and ragged trailers. Rangy old black men in dirty T-shirts wandered out onto the stoop of a pool hall as they passed, holding cues and cheap whiskey bottles, eyeing Johnny Stagg's El Dorado sailing through to Highway 61. Don Ho sang "My Little Grass Shack," Johnny reaching down every few moments to grab a plastic cup full of ice and bourbon. His brand-new car reeked of cigarettes and cheap perfume.

"This land looks like somethin' outta the Old Testament," Stagg said, more to himself than anyone.

Cotton fields stretched in endless acres on each side of the highway. The sun was half gone over the river, coloring the billboards sending them on to the casinos on Tunica where BIG REWARDS TAKE BIG RISKS. Fat women and old blacks held big checks and grinned stupidly.

Stagg went up off the highway on Dog Bog Road like they were headed up toward the Mississippi River and Friars Point but slowed when they hit a big stretch of fenced land. He turned at an open cattle gate, driving maybe a mile up through the property, through acres flooded for duck hunting and a big forest perfect for getting all likkered up and shooting some deer and turkey.

"Don't get smart," Stagg said.

"Why start now? Got me this far, hadn't it?"

"Answer the man's questions," Stagg said. "But don't put on no show. He just wants to make sure you ain't a Fed. They'll probably pat you down and ask you about your service. I think it's the service part that spooks 'em. You gettin' one check from Uncle Sam already."

"Maybe I need to ask them some questions, too," Donnie said. "I ain't handin' over a hunnard thousand dollars in good faith. Unless you're gonna tell me we're meeting Jesus Christ himself."

Stagg ignored him, slamming the car door and slipping into a pressed suit coat he'd kept on a wire hanger. He popped a piece of Juicy Fruit in his mouth and ran a pocket comb through that dyed black hair. They walked together, strolling down the pebble footpath to the biggest log cabin Donnie had ever seen, with thick stone chimneys and a shiny green metal roof. Smoke pouring from one of the chimneys smelled pleasantly of red oak.

"Let me talk," Scagg said.

"What if they ask me the damn questions?"

"You can answer," Stagg said. "But do it with respect."

Stagg knocked on the front door, and when nobody came to it, he opened her up anyway and stepped into a wide flagstone hall decorated with all kinds of dead animals who'd never set foot in the Delta. There was a zebra and a yak, a polar bear, and even a goddamn elephant. The thick planked walls looked to Donnie like the inside of a barn, with everything set up in the wide open. There was a kitchen, and a space in the back with a pool table and a bar and a couple leather couches facing a flat-screen television turned to some kind of nature show with crazy-ass people in cages poking sticks at sharks.

A man was asleep on one of the couches but stirred when they came up on him. He wore khaki pants and a red golf shirt. He'd kicked his tasseled loafers off, and he had old-man half-glasses on a string around his neck. When he saw Johnny, he got to his feet and nodded, pulling out an old-school Zippo and firing one up. He was an average-sized guy, not fat but not in shape either, with small brown eyes and a large forehead from a receding hairline. He was real tan, like rich men always were, and wore a thick gold bracelet on his hairy wrist that jangled in the light when he lit the smoke. Donnie figured he was somewhere in his fifties. His golf shirt said OLE MISS ALUMNI ASSOCIATION, but, damn if he didn't need to shave his face and neck.

Stagg shook his hand and smiled and smiled.

Donnie stepped beside him and said, "You're Bobby Campo."

"This him?"

Stagg nodded.

His small eyes roamed all over Donnie's face.

"You want a drink?"

"I'll take a little toddy," Stagg said.

"Cold beer," Donnie said.

"I like that suit, Johnny," Campo said. "You get a deal at the funeral home?"

"My wife bought this for me last Christmas," Stagg said. "It's made in America."

"I'm just having a good time, Johnny," Campo said. "Don't get your dick in a twist."

Stagg swallowed and looked out a large bay window while Campo walked back behind the bar and set a glass of ice and a bottle of Jack on the counter. He cracked open some kind of fancy beer brewed in small batches and handed it to Donnie. Donnie took it and lit a cigarette, figuring if Campo smoked, there wasn't any harm. He drank some beer and studied all the animals looking down at him with those glass eyes. "You kill all these?"

"What's that?"

"You kill all these animals?"

"Shit no."

"Ain't this a hunt club?" Donnie asked.

"It's a fucking clubhouse," Campo said. "I shoot some deer and ducks and all that. I bought all that other shit."

"That seems kinda fuckin' stupid," Donnie said. "That's like me putting up some all-state trophies in my gun shop that I never won."

Campo looked to Stagg. Stagg's face was coloring a good bit. Donnie smiled as he watched the older man suck down a good half of the bourbon. Campo started to laugh and clasped his hand on Stagg's shoulder. He laughed until his eyes got a little teary. "If this kid is a federal agent, I'll cut off my own dick."

"Appreciate that," Donnie said.

"Guns," Campo said.

"Mr. Stagg said you could help us out some."

"I don't want no religious nuts or no Arabs," Campo said. "Couldn't live with myself."

"Just some Mexes who want to shoot up each other."

"I can live with that," Campo said. "Long as they don't fuck up my time-share in Cancún."

"I think what we got to do—" Stagg said, starting to talk.

"Hold up, preacher," Campo said. "Let me and this boy talk."

Stagg sucked down more bourbon, his jaw working on a piece of ice. Donnie studied the cold beer in his hand, wondering just what all that German writing said. He drank down another sip, still wishing it was a Coors, and took a deep breath. "I need U.S. Army Colts," Donnie said. "M4s. Military-grade. None of that Chinese-made shit, neither."

"I understand," Campo said. "We can truck it in? OK, preacher?"

"I ain't no preacher," Stagg said. "Get that straight, Mr. Campo."

"No?" Campo said. "That's what my boys always call you. They say you're the spitting image of Pat Robertson, with a little Jerry Lee Lewis thrown in for good measure."

Campo laughed a lot at that, looking over at Donnie to join in a bit. Donnie couldn't help but laugh a little.

"I'll excuse your manners because I can tell you're intoxicated," Stagg said.

"I've been sleeping down here in mosquitoville for five days now," Campo said. "My wife has hired two lawyers to keep me away. My oldest son said I was a selfish prick while he's driving a brand-new Mustang bought with pussy cash. And I have a restraining order on me, and federal agents trying to sweet-talk my bitch of a wife into letting them get a peek into my personal files. So don't deny me some fun, Johnny T. Stagg."

Stagg finished the bourbon and put down the glass.

"Truckin' sounds good to me," Donnie said. "Do the deal at the Rebel. Money will go through Mr. Stagg. We good?"

He passed over the gun list he'd made with Luz.

Campo blew some smoke out a big fat nose as he read. His big, wide forehead was peppered in sweat from the booze. He wiped it away with a cocktail napkin and walked back over to the bar and refilled his glass. He poured some more into Johnny's glass, and Johnny looked at the whiskey with some disgust. "Y'all want to have a drink on it?" Campo asked.

Donnie joined them and helped himself to another beer in the refrigerator. He cracked open the top on the side of the counter, drinking off the foam. He stepped a foot in front of Johnny Stagg, feeling his breath on his neck, and raised his bottle. "I say fuck your wife," Donnie said. "You seem like a hell of a guy, Mr. Campo."

He looked over at Stagg and winked.

"Maybe ole Johnny can make enough to buy a new suit."

Donnie and Campo laughed a little bit more. Campo reached around his shoulder and patted his back like a football coach.

Man, it was gonna be a bitch of a ride back to Tibbehah.

QUINN GOT BACK TO THE FARM at sundown. Hondo was on the front porch but stirred when he heard Quinn's truck and ran out to greet him, shaking the dust from his coat and offering his head for Quinn to pet. The cattle dog followed him up inside the old house, which was stark, bare, and airless as a church, Quinn leaving the front door open and letting the screen door thwack behind them. He'd spent most of the summer gutting the place and whitewashing the walls and sanding the heart pine floors. By the time he went through all his Uncle Hamp's junk, there wasn't much to keep besides a big kitchen table and chairs, a couple iron beds, and an old dresser that had belonged to his great-grandmother. He gave away about everything else or burned it. Now the house seemed empty and hollow but at least clean. Quinn set up an iron bed for himself and a little pillow for Hondo. He'd affixed a metal pipe against the bedroom wall for his pressed blue jeans, work shirts, and such. His cowboy and hunting boots were polished with saddle soap and waiting on the floor below.

He kept most of his guns in a hiding hole he'd bored into the center of the living room floor that he covered with a rug he'd shipped home from Afghanistan. He kept his service revolver on the nightstand after work. A Browning "Sweet 16" rested between a set of deer antlers above the fireplace.

Quinn took off his shirt and tossed it in a laundry bag. Now dressed in an undershirt and jeans, he removed his Sam Brown and cowboy boots and retired to the front porch. He lit up a La Gloria Cubana and brought out a rawhide for Hondo.

They sat on the porch for a long time, watching the sun drop over a small orchard of new and old pear and apple trees. The light grew gold and pleasant as it slid across the skeletal frame of a new barn Quinn was building. Hondo made a lot of noise as he chewed.

His mother never understood why he'd kept the old place. Johnny Stagg tried to buy it from him for a more than decent price. But he couldn't sell a piece of land that had been in his family since 1895, especially to a shitbag like Stagg. Besides, he liked it out here, a good ten miles out of Jericho, and on a good piece of acreage populated with

turkey and deer. He expected to have a full freezer by the end of hunting season and had already been able to put up a nice bit of beans, corn,
and peppers from his small garden. The idea of home such a strange
concept after living life in Conex containers, airplane hangars, and tents
for the last decade. One of the first things he'd learned as a Ranger was
make the most of your downtime. Quiet your mind and rest. You never
know what's around the corner.

A young doe wandered into his orchard and began to eat some rotten apples that had fallen long ago. He watched with interest as she
scoured for the remaining apples, ears pricked for the slightest sound.
Bats filled the sky as it turned to night, picking off mosquitoes in the
quiet hum of the country. There were frogs chirping in the creek. He'd
roll onto duty at four a.m. and would enjoy the last little bit of night left.

Hondo lifted his head from the porch.

Quinn put his hand on him and stood, looking down the long gravel
road to the main highway. A red SUV turned onto his road and
bumped up his circular drive. Hondo trotted out and barked at his
visitor.

Anna Lee stepped out, Hondo sniffing at her hand as she turned up
the path to the old white house. Quinn met her at the screen door, letting her onto the porch and inviting her to join him.

He hadn't seen her since Johnny Stagg's Good Ole Boy, but the same
feeling hit him in the pit of the stomach, something that he wished he
could control but couldn't. It had been that way since they were fifteen,
taking it all slow and easy as good buddies till it all became rocky and
wild and heated, kid promises made. She said she'd wait till he returned
and they could marry, but that didn't last long. A few years later, she
found a better situation when Luke Stevens came back from Tulane.
And how could he blame her? He'd only been five years into a war that
would take him another five to come home.

"Is this OK?" she asked.

"Just watching the bats."

"Is that what you do all the way out here?"

"Sometimes," Quinn said. "I don't have a TV. A few beers makes things more entertaining."

"Good to see you the other night."

"Always good seeing you, Anna Lee."

He offered to get her some sweet tea or water, but she declined. It was cool on the porch, but she fanned her face with her hand, the trip from the car to the porch a little too much. Hondo stood between them, panting and staring up at Quinn.

Anna Lee rested her tall boots on the ledge. She was fair and blond, with delicate features and a long, elegant neck. Besides the bulge of stomach under her long-sleeved brown dress, you wouldn't know she was nearly due.

"Haven't seen much of you since I've been back," Quinn said.

"Haven't been out much," she said.

"How much longer?"

"Eight weeks."

"Luke must be thrilled."

"He is."

"Sorry we haven't talked," Quinn said. "I guess there wasn't much to say after you got pregnant."

"I said all I wanted to say after you got shot," Anna Lee said. "You figure that wasn't enough?"

"You didn't say anything."

A silence cut between them for a moment, the only sound Hondo's panting and then the violent scratching of his back leg on his ear. The chain on his neck jingled as he worked. He went back to his bone.

"I put out a steak for supper," Quinn said. "I can make another."

"I can't stay, Quinn," she said. "How the hell would that look?"

"You came to see me."

"I came to talk to you about Caddy."

"I'm done with Caddy."

"How can you be done with your own sister?"

"After a while, you quit trying."

"Can you try for Jason?"

Quinn nodded. He watched two young calves playing in the pasture, head-butting each other and tossing their rear ends up in the air. The big cows grazed around them, chewing and eating, the big bull standing on the far hill, looking tired and old. He'd been the bull for as long as Quinn could remember, but his ribs were starting to show, and his eyes had taken on a yellow cast.

"She's been lying to Jason," Quinn said. "She'll promise to come see him and never make it. How's that look to a kid?"

"She's back now."

Quinn didn't say anything.

"Just got back from your momma's," Anna Lee said. "I watched Jason while your mom shopped. Caddy came in after I fed Jason."

Quinn nodded. "Twenty-four-hour hero," he said.

"She unpacked," Anna Lee said. "I think Caddy's home for good."

CADDY WAS THE CIGARETTES-AND-COFFEE CADDY THAT QUINN HAD SEEN a thousand times before. She'd sit in their father's old recliner and read the Bible or books of inspiration or some Christian romance novel with women and horses on the cover and begin reciting back things she'd read as if they were her own ideas. She was pale and skinny, with dark-rimmed eyes and bad hair. She'd stripped off all the makeup she took to wearing when she was all full of herself and toned down the sexy dress with a pair of jeans and a large T-shirt that hit her at the knees. She lit up and reached for a Diet Coke, finding her place in a book called *The Shack*, a novel Quinn had heard about that told the story of a man who meets up with Jesus in Oregon and talks it out.

When Quinn walked into their mother's house, she jumped up and hugged him as if they'd last left things in great order. Quinn recalled a shouting match in a Memphis parking lot where he told her to get her shit together. Caddy had been working for dollar bills at a gentlemen's club by the airport.

"Big brother," Caddy said, and kissed him on the cheek.

Quinn nodded and hung up his hat by the door. Anna Lee had followed in her car and closed the door behind them. She smiled at Caddy, both of them obviously catching up earlier, and she walked outside to join Jean, who was playing with Jason on a tire swing hanging from an old pecan tree.

"You still got the eyes for Anna Lee, knocked-up and all."

"She said you wanted to see me."

"You could've come tomorrow."

She sat back down in Jason Colson's recliner, the one they should have taken out and burned the day he packed up his shit and moved to California for good. She pulled on her cigarette and grinned at him in a knowing way, as if it were Quinn with the goddamn problems. Not Caddy, who'd moved home because she'd hit rock bottom with nowhere else to go.

"Anna Lee says you're sticking around awhile," Quinn said.

"Momma needs help."

"Oh, yeah."

"And I'd been missing Jason, with work and all," Caddy said. "It's ninety miles to Memphis."

About a hundred and fifty replies popped into Quinn's mind with that one. But he stayed silent, knowing a man never got himself in trouble by keeping his mouth shut.

"Sheriff Colson."

"I was sheriff last time you were home, too."

"Don't recall much of that trip."

"No fooling."

"It's not the same," Caddy said. "Not now."

Quinn nodded and walked back to the kitchen to snatch a beer that his momma kept in the refrigerator just for him. He popped the top on a Budweiser and returned to the TV room, knowing Caddy was a hell of a lot easier to take with a beer in hand.

"You know, you can let your hair grow out," she said. "You don't have to go with the high and tight."

Quinn shrugged and drank the beer. Caddy turned to the sliding glass door and watched Anna Lee and Jean pushing Jason between both of them. Jason laughing and kicking his legs, both women making sure that he didn't veer off path or go too high. Jason screamed with laughter.

"It's good to be home."

"You make it hard on him," Quinn said. "You just make it that much goddamn harder every time."

"You won't spoil this for me," Caddy said. "You hadn't walked in the door five minutes."

"You want to tell me how now is different?" Quinn asked. "Because Momma and I are going to have to clean up the mess when you get gone again. You ever try reading books to a child while he's crying?"

She nodded. "I've been meeting with a counselor," she said. "Three times a week. He wanted me to come home, address my issues with my family."

"You blaming us now?"

"We grew up in a shitstorm."

"I figure you wouldn't want that for Jason."

"I don't want to fight," Caddy said. "Momma's picked up dinner, and I thought we could all sit down together. I'm trying, Quinn. I am. I'm clean."

"How long?"

"Three weeks."

Quinn nodded. He'd heard it before.

"What happened to the new boyfriend?"

"He's a piece of shit."

"I think I told you that," Quinn said, the words out of his mouth before he could stop them. But Caddy still smiled at him, feeling something in the room that Quinn didn't. She was looking at all of Jean's stuff, and the sight of that ugly green couch and slick dining room table that they didn't use except for Christmas and Thanksgiving and even those old Elvis movie posters brought her some kind of happiness.

"You ever think that Momma might have done it with Elvis?" Caddy asked.

"Nope."

"You know she was a groupie, driving up to Graceland with her girlfriends in her short shorts and waiting for him by the gate. Daddy knew him. He knew Elvis through karate and all that. I don't know. I just think there's something strange about pining for a dead man."

"Maybe she likes his music."

"And the movies?" Caddy said, whispering. "Who likes the movies?"

Quinn shrugged. He'd yet to sit down. Anna Lee, Jean, and Jason were making their way down the hill, Jason between them, the women with one of his hands each, swinging him up high into the air.

"I just don't want him hurt," Quinn said. "He's doing good. He's in school. He's doing good."

"I'm his mother."

"And you remind us of that all the time," Quinn said. "He needs something stable."

"I am stable," she said. "That's why I'm here. I'm here this time. It's over."

Jason, Jean, and Anna Lee were on the back deck and making their way to the glass door. Quinn looked to Caddy and massaged the back of his neck, knowing how the next few weeks would play out and knowing how it would affect his nephew.

"We got to talk, Quinn," Caddy said.

"Isn't that what we're doing?"

"You know exactly what I mean."

——————

DONNIE HAD RETIRED for the night at his trailer at the gun range. Stagg dropped him off after they got back to Jericho, Stagg not saying a word on the ride back, still pissed about Donnie and Mr. Campo getting along so good. Stagg just turned up that Don Ho hula shit, cracked the window, and smiled at all the scenery passing. When Donnie would ask him a question, he'd just nod deep in thought and answer him with a nod or shake of his head. Guess the comment about the suit had really chapped old Johnny's ass.

Donnie lay on a pullout sofa mattress, smoking cigarettes and watching *The Magnificent Seven* with a bottle of tequila and a bag of chips for dinner. He'd promised his daddy that he'd be back at the Quick Mart at five a.m. to start cooking up sausage and biscuits for the farmers and truck drivers before church. Donnie was so goddamn tired of the smell of that place. Even good shampoo and Lava soap couldn't wash it out. He kicked back more of the tequila, Yul Brynner telling that dumb kid to clap his hands, "Fast. Fast as you can." And the kid not having the speed or the smarts to see how Yul was playing with him. So what does the kid do? He just gets piss-drunk and tries to shoot Yul. But it all works out in the end; he meets a nice señorita and lives it up in high tail. Donnie smiled with the thought and punched up a phone number he'd written on the back of a napkin.

"Yes?" Luz asked.

"You sleeping?"

"Yes."

"We need to talk."

Luz was silent.

"In person," Donnie said. His tongue feeling a little fuzzy, but, damn, if he didn't sound straight in his head. "Can you come on?"

"Is there a problem?"

"We got to talk, and phones make me a mite nervous."

"Where?"

Donnie told her to come on back to the gun range and clicked off the phone with a big shit-eating smile on his face. He walked on outside the old Airstream and plugged in a string of Christmas lights that he'd hung up through the pines and oaks surrounding a little fire pit he'd made from old bricks and river stones. He tossed some brush and logs into the fire and soaked it good with some diesel, lighting the son of a bitch up.

He'd found some fallen logs and arranged them around the fire pit. A hell of a good place to sit and drink and look at the stars. But, god damn, he was getting tired of Shane's jokes and Tiny's farts. That's about all those boys offered in way of company, corn and gas. But the boys had been with him every day after he'd gone up and nearly turned into a crispy critter. It was Shane who'd had the sense to reach for the morphine needle in his pack and stab Donnie with it after the explosion, when Donnie couldn't see worth shit with blood in his eyes and his damn hearing was nothing but a high-pitched electric sound.

After an hour, or maybe two, he saw a big truck roll down the dirt road and park down at the range. Luz was just a shadow in the moonlight, but he could tell it was her and her alone, no crazy-ass Alejandro or the kid shooter or those three crazy *muchachos*. She sure had a confident strut about her. Donnie wondered just where the carnival had ended up tonight.

He warmed his hands over the fire, facing the trail that she'd followed after seeing the Christmas lights and fire up on the hill by the old Airstream.

Donnie sure had to grin when he saw her. She wore a fitted red snap-button shirt and tight dark jeans with a straw Stetson set over her long black Indian hair. She looked clean and fresh-scrubbed, and he noticed the big turquoise bracelet on her wrist before he noted the Colt slid into her belt loop.

"Where were y'all tonight?" he asked.

"Place called Water Valley."

"Ain't shit in Water Valley."

"Tonight, we brought the carnival."

"So how does that work?" he asked. "Y'all do that full time and the guns on the side? Or is it some kind of cover for y'all while you buy guns?"

"We work for the carnival, and we have other business."

"I like your hat."

She nodded at him.

"You ride?"

She nodded again. "I grew up in Saragosa, Texas."

"No shit," he said. "That makes you a citizen."

"What do you want, Donnie?"

"I got the deal," Donnie said. He smiled. "It's all set up. And we got those extra fifty M4s just like y'all wanted. Be here next week."

"We will bring the money," she said. "Good night."

"Can't you stay for a bit?" Donnie said, grinning. "Please."

"You live here?"

"It ain't a mansion, but—" Donnie said, laughing. "But it ain't a mansion. Pull up a stump and have a cold beer or some tequila, and you can go on. All right?"

She looked at him like he was crazy but joined him by the fire pit and accepted a drink from his open bottle of tequila. God damn, he loved a girl who could take a swig off an open bottle.

"Down in Saragosa, that where you meet up with your boyfriend, the bad motherfucker?"

"Let's not talk."

"You kind of hold a lot of interest for me, Luz," Donnie said. "I mean, we're kind of in this together now, long down the road, me and you. I figure we could at least get to know a bit about each other. Ain't no harm in that."

She nodded and took another hit from the bottle.

"Where'd you get those scars?" she asked. "The ones I saw on your back."

"Some little shithole outside Baghdad that don't have no name."

"Were you in battle?"

"I was patrolling a goddamn bazaar."

"Is that why you came home?"

"No," Donnie said. "I went back, next time to Afghanistan, after I healed up. I guess my head is hard that way."

"Did you love it? The war?"

"I loved that paycheck."

They watched the fire, the crackling of the dry brush and logs, sparks flicking up into the Christmas lights and treetops. Donnie thought it didn't look too bad at his place, kinda like a Kenny Chesney video if they were at the beach and not in Tibbehah.

"You got to go back to Mexico when you get the guns?"

"I don't know."

"Up to your boyfriend?"

"Why do you ask so much?" Luz asked.

"I just don't understand why you're with those people," Donnie said. "Your buddy Alejandro looks like he should be living in a cage. No offense."

She nodded. She drank some more.

"You will do what you say?"

"I promised," Donnie said. "Say, how do you like the ole trailer? Belonged to my granddad. He bought the fucking thing in the fifties so he could go to the Grand Canyon. Son of a bitch had a heart attack right before he pulled out onto the highway. Whole time I was growing up, it sat under a tarp in our garage."

"That's very sad."

"But kinda funny."

"How?"

"The way God can bite you right in the ass."

"Sometimes you bite back," Luz said. She stared very hard into the fire. The night had grown cold, and Donnie just noticed their shoulders were touching as they leaned into the warmth. He turned and smiled at her, catching her eye. She didn't smile, looking downright sad to him, but not breaking away, either. Son of a bitch if he didn't have to do it, but he reached around her with his arm and pulled her close. The front of that western snap-button shirt looked like it was about to go and bust, and he caught a peek of a little lace on a black bra.

"Just how bad of a motherfucker is your boyfriend?"

Luz turned to him and kissed him long and hard on the mouth. When Donnie kissed her back, there wasn't nothing but air, and he opened his eyes with her standing above him. "Don't show affection in front of Alejandro," she said.

He held up his hand in a solemn promise.

"And you won't talk of me to your friends."

"You Catholic girls are damn superstitious."

He reached for her hand. She looked at him with a lot burning in those eyes, but he pulled her in close and hooked his fingers into her leather belt, pressing her hard against him and knocking her hat up so he could give her a decent kiss.

He felt her Colt digging into his forearm as he hugged her, but it didn't bother him a damn bit.

FOUR DAYS PASSED, AND QUINN FOUND HIMSELF AT THE FILLIN' STATION
diner, drinking black coffee and working on a plate of fried eggs and
grits. The rains had blown in from Texas the day before, and with dark
skies came a chill. It wouldn't be long until the heaters would cut on,
and he'd smell burning dust and propane that reminded Quinn of long,
bare winters. Mary, a tired old waitress who used to shack up with his
Uncle Hamp, refilled his cup. Quinn wondered if his wearing Hamp's
old rancher coat bothered her. She'd been with Hamp until the last,
spending his last years taking trips to Tunica and down to the coast.
When they buried him, the honor guard folded the flag and handed it
to her.

A few folks wandered in the front door of the old gas station and
nodded to Quinn, rain dripping from their coats. Some shook his hand
or passed on a few problems.

One man had lost a good dog. An old woman wanted to know about
any progress in the break-in at the Baptist church. Someone had stolen
six peach pies from the deep freeze. Quinn was patient and listened to

it all. After all, coming to the Fillin' Station for breakfast in downtown Jericho was better than keeping office hours. He learned more there in ten minutes than he'd probably learn all day behind his desk.

Quinn was about ready to leave when Lillie sat across from him and snatched a half-eaten biscuit—already buttered—from his hand. She wore a baseball cap with a ponytail threaded through the back and a satiny sheriff's office jacket that read CHIEF DEPUTY.

"Go ahead and help yourself," Quinn said.

"Didn't think you'd mind."

"How'd it go overnight?"

"Helped Joe Burney's dumbass daughter out of a ditch. Kenny issued some traffic tickets and looked for a stolen vehicle."

"What got stolen?"

"Nothin'," Lillie said. "Some kid didn't know his buddies took it and hid it out behind the car wash."

"Busy night."

"What's going on?" Lillie asked. Mary wandered over and rested her hand on Lillie's shoulder while sliding coffee in front of her. Lillie patted the old woman's liver-spotted hand. Mary smiled back as if in a daydream.

"Thought I'd try and talk to Mara Torres again," Quinn said.

"She prefers Mara Black."

"Well, I'll talk to Mara Black again."

"There's somethin' off about that girl," Lillie said.

"No kidding."

"No, *really* off," Lillie said. "She ain't right. I'd say she's operating on a different radio signal than most."

"Been through a lot."

"That's not what I mean," Lillie said. "I've spent a lot of time with her. She talks about people on *Days of Our Lives* like they're real people. She about shit her pants when she found out Sami might be pregnant, like Sami was a real person and it was a real baby. She talked for two days about whether it would be a boy or a girl. I let her come in my office every day at noon to watch her stories so she'll shut her mouth and cooperate."

"She made any calls?"

"She's got a public defender."

"Any friends?"

"Some women from her church came to see her," Lillie said. "They brought her some lemon cake and some bologna sandwiches. I got the feeling they didn't know Mara real well."

"I still can't believe what they were doing was legal," Quinn said. "They were bringing in babies with all the right papers."

"When the children come from developing countries, the only type of qualifications you need is some cash," Lillie said. "When you adopt that child, it's legally your baby. That has nothing to do with American laws. You think any of those Mexican officials gave two shits about where those kids ended up?"

"But how in the hell does a woman adopt dozens of kids and sell them off?"

"Foreign kids aren't looked after like wards of the state."

"That's dumber than shit."

"That's the law."

"Any news on the child's autopsy?"

"No," Lillie said. "But I spoke to the coroner's assistant up in Memphis. They got fingerprints, and signs of a severe beating. They're just making sure everything all makes sense for a jury."

Quinn nodded. "You want some more coffee?"

"Afraid I'll drink yours?'

Quinn smiled. Lillie smiled back. She was pretty when she lightened up a little bit, her freckled face brightening up like a kid's. He and Lillie had been decent friends in high school but better friends since he'd come back to Jericho and Tibbehah County. During the summer, Lillie had been his running partner, trailing down fire roads and country highways to keep his training in check. They'd shoot guns out on the range and sometimes drink beer after. They'd grown close, with things progressing over the summer. But they understood that'd be a bad mistake, knowing how crossing lines might be a recipe to fucking up a hell of a good thing.

"Listen, you got a second?" Quinn said, lowering his voice. He looked to make sure that Mary was out of earshot, Mary being the kind who'd wipe down a table for five minutes to hear some gossip. "I need to talk about something personal."

"You wetting the bed again?"

"If you can't handle it," Quinn said, "forget I mentioned it."

"Go on. Go on."

"I'm not really good about talking about stuff like this."

"That's kind of like EJ."

"Who the hell's EJ?"

"Fella on *Days*. He's gone back to being evil, and that's why Taylor has to leave him."

"Caddy's back."

"I know."

"She says she's clean."

"How many times is she gonna do this to her poor son?"

Quinn nodded. "My momma says it's our job to accept her back with no questions asked. She said she won't judge her or ask her where she's been. She tells Caddy that the light is always on at our house, and her bedroom will always be the same."

"She hasn't changed Caddy's bedroom?" Lillie asked. "How old is she?"

"Too old," Quinn said. "She's sleeping with a stuffed bear and staying up to watch Elvis movies with Jean. And she's getting real pious, asking me questions about my relationship with God."

"You doin' well with that?"

"It's nobody's damn business."

"You are a charmer, Quinn Colson."

Quinn leaned in and Lillie joined him. Their heads almost touched.

"She wants me to help her talk out some shit that happened to us when we were kids," Quinn said, whispering, watching the front door. "It's some unpleasant stuff, and things are best left unsaid."

"But it's troubling her?" Lillie asked.

Quinn nodded.

"Maybe she needs to pour some light in."

"Or maybe this is just some more of Caddy's bullshit."

"How bad?" Lillie asked.

Quinn let out a deep breath and twirled a coffee mug in his hands. He just looked to Lillie, and Lillie, seeing the horrible thing there, just nodded with him, knowing whatever it was just wasn't ready to come out.

Quinn's cell rang, and he picked up. Mary Alice let him know that he had someone waiting for him at the sheriff's office. He said he was coming on in now.

"Who's there?" Lillie asked.

"An ATF agent interested in Ramón Torres."

"Heard about her," Lillie said, staying seated as Quinn grabbed his coat. She wrapped her arm over the back of the booth in a cocky manner. "Also heard Ramón wasn't the only thing she was interested in."

"She believes Ramón was into guns like Janet was into selling babies."

"Watch out for those redheads, Sheriff," Lillie said. Mary slid a plate of eggs and sausage before Lillie without her even ordering. Lillie grabbed her fork and dug in. "Never knew a one that wasn't crazy as hell."

"THANKS FOR LUNCH THE OTHER DAY," Dinah Brand said. Her red hair had been combed straight back from her face and tied in a simple, tight knot.

They were sitting in Quinn's office again, and it was raining in sheets outside the lone window facing the back of the jail on the river. Again, Dinah was dressed for court, black pleated dress, black blazer, with real nice shoes. Quinn didn't know shit about women's shoes, but they looked nice, being suede and all. Her lipstick was very red, and it set off something nice and pleasant with her hair.

"Anyone ever tell you that you look just like Claudia Jennings?"

"Who's that?" Dinah asked. She smiled, mouth parted a bit, eyeing Quinn to see just where he was going with this.

"The queen of the B movie," Quinn said. "She was a friend of my dad's. She was in all these pictures like 'Gator Bait, Truck Stop Women, The Great Texas Dynamite Chase before I was born. She was a pistol."

"How'd your dad know her?"

"He worked in the picture business before I was born, and some after."

"What's he do now?"

"Don't know," Quinn said. "Haven't heard from him since I was in high school."

"Is that tough?"

"If you knew my dad, you'd know it made things much easier."

"Anything new with the Torres family?" Dinah asked.

"Nope," Quinn said. "You?"

"Zip."

"We're expecting back the autopsy any day now," Quinn said. "Plan on making a solid case once we can find these people."

"I think they're in Mexico."

"Probably."

"And you won't ever be able to touch them there."

"Can y'all?"

"Extradition from Mexico is complex."

"Didn't mean anything by saying you looked like that actress," Quinn said. "I meant it as a compliment. Hope that doesn't cross any professional boundaries."

"You work with many women in the Army?"

"We didn't have women Rangers, but yes, I did."

"Did you mind that?"

"Not at all," Quinn said. "I remember this one soldier, tough gal from Texas, who used to sit in the catbird seat of a Hummer, keeping watch at Camp Phoenix. One day some little Afghan kids started talking to her in some pidgin English. One of them asked her what was that she was holding, and she looked down at them and smiled and said, 'It's a big motherfucking gun, kid.'"

"And your chief deputy is a woman."

"So we're good?"

"How many people in this community have you interviewed about the Torres family?"

"You're welcome to the reports," Quinn said. "Talked to folks at the Dollar General, where she used to work, and at their church. They weren't regulars there. And they didn't have any neighbors to speak of. One of those 'keep to themselves' deals."

"Nothing more from Mara?"

"You spoke to her," Quinn said. "What were your impressions?"

"She's psychologically stunted," Dinah said. "It was like speaking to a twelve-year-old."

"Lillie, my chief deputy, says she's mainly interested in watching soap operas and eating cake."

"I hear you have a small Hispanic community here," Dinah said. "Have you reached out?"

"Some," Quinn said. "We're not exactly well staffed with Spanish speakers, but I have an old friend who runs the El Dorado restaurant here. We went out and talked to some folks. No one knew Torres. Nobody ever knew him to hold a job."

"Not to imply you didn't do a good job," Dinah said. "But do you mind if we drive back?"

"You want to tell me more about his connection to these bad men on the Coast?"

"They are known associates."

"That sounds a lot nicer than it is."

"We've scattered a big network out of Dallas."

"Bad people."

"We think Ramón Torres is part of a cell connected to a group that beheaded seventeen farmers over the summer."

Quinn leaned forward in his chair, his boots touching the floor. He widened his eyes and shook his head. "All drugs?"

"Drugs, guns, human trafficking," Dinah said. "Bad people."

"You speak Spanish?"

"And carry a big motherfucking gun."

15

THERE WASN'T MUCH IN THE WAY OF WHAT QUINN WOULD CALL A HIS-
panic community in Tibbehah County. There was a collection of about
twenty old trailers huddled together on a one-acre slice of land right
outside the Jericho city limits. Most of the folks who lived there were
day laborers taking on construction jobs or cleaning houses or offices.
Everyone knew they were mostly illegal, but no one made a thing of it,
because the folks had done so much to help rebuild a lot of the town.
Two Latino soldiers in his company had joined up to gain citizenship.
Quinn had a ton of respect for the immigrant work ethic. And there
was no more loyal, tough, and resourceful soldier than one who had a
clear sense and love for his new country.

The rain fell in a steady downpour and had turned the muddy clear-
cut land into a soup.

"I got some rubber boots in back of my truck," Quinn said.
"Might fit."

Dinah nodded, and Quinn got out and checked in his truck box for
the pair Lillie had left with him when they'd gone out and searched for

old Miss Magnolia, who'd wandered away from her house for the hundredth time.

"They're a little big," Dinah said.

"Deputy Virgil has big feet," Quinn said.

Most of the trailers looked as if they'd been picked up and put down in a lot of different places; sagging, tired, and worn on concrete blocks. Some of the folks who lived there had planted small gardens with peppers and tomatoes. Most of the tomato plants had died, the vines hanging lifeless and brown, but the peppers would last until the first freeze in a few weeks, growing bells and jalapeños as Quinn did on his farm.

When they went door-to-door, knocking, Dinah was good at the entrance, explaining in Spanish that they weren't with ICE or immigration, only wanting to find out if they'd seen this man. She'd carried a mug of Ramón Torres, a picture taken in Houston for a DUI arrest in '03. His face looked slick with sweat, eyes bloodshot, and he wore a yellow T-shirt. Most all who came to the door were women, many of the men already out on jobs. Some of the trailers didn't have electricity, and their residents used propane tanks to cook, many of the places smelling of tortillas and spicy burning fat. The women were smiling and polite but made nervous by the star Quinn had pinned on his shirt. He and Dinah stood there, rain sluicing down the brim of his cap, she huddled in a slicker, waiting outside maybe fifteen trailers. Some of them were abandoned or no one answered.

"You see any recognition?" Dinah asked. "When we were speaking?"

"Nope."

"Goes with your theory that he wasn't connected to anyone local."

"I'd like to know a little more about this cartel if they're planning on setting up shop in this county."

"I wouldn't worry," Dinah said as they walked back to Quinn's truck. "We just got the alert when the news came out about Ramón Torres. We'd been looking for him for the last two years."

"And you say these people are with Los Zetas?"

"Yep."

"And you believe they've got cells down on the coast."

"They control most of the Texas border," Dinah said, pulling off her slicker, folding it, and placing it in the back of the cab. "They got a pipeline of drugs and cash that heads up through Memphis and Chicago and over to Atlanta."

"But we could have a cell here," Quinn said. "Working with Ramón?"

"I guess it's possible," Dinah said as Quinn cranked the truck and headed back to town. The county road stretched long and slick before them, broken pavement with no shoulder, only long drops down into wooded land. "I bought some photo packs maybe you and your deputies could study."

"Sure."

Quinn stopped off at a roadside produce stand right outside Drivers Flat. The stand was a lean-to of barn wood and tin. It was late in the season, but they still had some peppers, pole beans, and tomatoes. The woman who worked the stand looked like someone you'd see out of a WPA photograph, rawboned and weathered, with a gaunt smile and long thin fingers. She exchanged a couple bucks for some beans. It had stopped raining, and soft mist rose off the rows and rows of pumpkins ripening for the fall.

"I promised my mother I'd pick some up if I was out this way," Quinn said.

"Most of your family here?"

"Unfortunately."

"Your mother must be glad you're home."

"You're welcome to ask her," Quinn said. "She does a nice spread every Wednesday after church."

"I better get back."

"Invitation stands," Quinn said, following the road back to Jericho, passing the Dollar General where Janet Torres had worked, Hollywood Video, and on past the Piggly Wiggly. The rain had left puddles in the potholes, and water sat stagnant along the drainage ditches.

"I'd like that," Dinah said.

Lillie was at the front counter at the sheriff's office when they walked back inside. And she did her best to not seem interested in Dinah Brand in the least. Quinn introduced them anyway, and Lillie looked up from some reports she was writing to give a friendly nod. Quinn grabbed a couple coffees, and they went back to the office. Dinah swung her purse on the back of the chair and sat down, opening up a thick black leather satchel she'd brought in from her trunk.

"How many deputies do you have?"

"Nine."

"For the whole county?"

"All we can afford," he said. "Trying to get a maintenance barn going. I've got to go in front of the county supervisors to beg."

"And you don't like to beg."

"You'd have to know our supervisors," Quinn said. "A bit like selling your soul."

"OK," Dinah said, opening up a three-ring binder and showing Quinn photos, three to a page, of Mexican nationals in the United States believed to be working within cartels in the Mid-South. Quinn walked behind his desk, turning the binder back toward him, and flipped through each page while sipping some coffee.

Dinah walked around his office, studying the photos on the wall and looking out the single window to the bridge over the Big Black River. There were thick bars over the window, and little wires within the glass.

He'd probably need to show the book to Lillie and then to Kenny and the others. Maybe he'd make another trip after working hours back to the migrant camp and see if he spotted anyone familiar.

"Can I keep this for a day?" Quinn asked.

"See anything?"

"Nope."

Most of the photos were of men, but a few women, too. Many of them were identified by gang tattoos or scars. Some pretty hardened hombres and even harder-looking women. They came from faraway places like Juárez, Monterrey, Zacatecas, and Tampico. They were all associated with the Zetas and with a man noted as El Tigre.

"Who's this El Tigre?"

"He goes by the name Tony the Tiger."

"Guess you're gonna tell me he's not a very nice man."

"I could tell you a lot of stories about him," Dinah said. "After a while they all sound the same. These people try to outdo each other in horrific violence. They kidnap and kill anyone suspected of going against them. The Zetas were always having a turf war with the Gulf Cartel, though they've mostly won now. Rivals, politicians, and their families will show up dead, hanging from trees, or their body parts scattered on roadsides. This stuff is like something out of the Middle Ages."

Quinn absently flipped through more pages, ready to call Lillie in and have her take the book for a while. If one of these guys had set foot in Jericho, he was pretty sure Lillie would know it. As he got into the final pages in the book, a picture of a woman made him return two pages back. The photo showed a slender, sad-faced girl with thick black hair pulled into a ponytail, wide eyes, and a full mouth. She stood against a board that showed she was *1.8 meters* and she held a sheet of paper showing her arrest was on *24-Diciembre—10. Zuniga Huizar.* Her first name was Laura. Quinn stared at the photo and pictured her with a shy hand across her face and downcast eyes as he leaned into Donnie's truck to welcome him back from the front.

What did Donnie call her? Luz?

"You see something?" Dinah asked.

Quinn shook his head and closed the book. "I'll pass it around."

BEFORE HE GOT A LOOK at the new guns, Johnny Stagg offered Donnie a piece of pecan pie. They sat in the main dining area of the Rebel Truck Stop in the back booth that was always roped off for Stagg himself. The booth sat up into the back corner, seats padded with seafoam green vinyl, the white walls behind them covered in even more photos than Stagg's office of more politicians, weathermen, and country music stars. He'd apparently spent a lot of time with the Tiffin family, a daddy, momma, and daughter, who'd cut a record called *Ain't But One Man.*

"What ever happened to the Tiffins?" Donnie said, digging into some pie. "They used to come every year and sing at church. I wonder if they're still out singing at tent revivals and street fairs."

"I hadn't talked to them for some time," Stagg said. "They implied falsely that I'd made advances toward their daughter."

"That's some hair they all got. Take a lot of hair spray make it that tall."

"Singers need to have some show about them," Stagg said. "If not, nobody will pay attention."

"Good pie, Johnny."

"You finished?"

Donnie nodded, and Stagg got up, walking into all the noise of the kitchen. Three large black women worked the grill, sizzling with bacon and burgers. An older black man worked the big brick barbecue pit built into a back wall. Some Mexican women washed the dishes, and a couple Mexican men were stocking the walk-in refrigerator with thin dinner T-bones and whole chickens. Donnie lit up an American Spirit before he even hit the back door and the rain that was soaking the wide lot where about fifty or so truckers had stopped off. Stagg had his lot lizards carrying umbrellas and wearing knee-high rubber boots. They wandered through the aisles. Within a couple hours, the big neon sign of the mud-flap girl would be shining down on Highway 45.

"How many?"

"Fifty, like you ordered," Stagg said. "These folks don't fool around."

"Well, shit," Donnie said. "I got the money. Who's drivin'?"

"You?"

"And as soon as I'm off this here lot, it's my ass."

"You want to bring in someone else?" Stagg asked, stopping dead still in the rain to run his hand over his red neck. "Figure it's smart we just keep this deal kind of local. I don't want to kick loose any of my cut, and nobody wants an extra mouth shootin' off. Can't you drive a semi?"

"I can drive anything with wheels."

"How long'd you drive with that outfit in Tupelo?"

"Two years," Donnie said. "Only lost my job 'cause the Guard kept sending me back. The Guard fucked me."

Stagg took him into the big maze of trucks, most of them Macks and Peterbilts, humming along, keeping that electricity going so the truckers could sleep in some AC, kick back and watch some movies in the cab, or make some friendly time with one of Stagg's girls. They turned another corner, and another, Donnie feeling his mouth getting dry, because if Stagg wanted to cut his ass out of this business arrangement, this would be the time and the place. Stagg could drop him right here and pack him in the back of a Tyson chicken truck headed for Tucamcari.

Stagg stopped at a tractor trailer marked BATESVILLE CASKET COMPANY. *Drive Safe. We're in No Hurry to Do Business.*

"Kind of a cute sign, ain't it?" Donnie asked. He stepped back and let Stagg be the one to open those doors. No way in hell would he let his ass be snatched and pulled inside. Stagg grinned at him, knowing he was making him nervous, and the thought of it pleased Johnny Stagg. He pulled out a set of keys from his hip and opened the big doors.

"Go on. Here, take this."

Stagg handed him a flashlight and hammer, and Donnie lifted himself up into the trailer, shining the light at floor-to-ceiling wooden boxes in lengths that would befit caskets. He let out a long breath, Stagg joining him inside, following the light. Stagg motioned him over to the row on the far right.

"Man, this is like Christmas morning," Donnie said, using the claw end of the hammer and pulling open the top. He found gun boxes packed inside instead of caskets, all in a mess of Styrofoam peanuts. He pulled out the first box and sliced through the plastic bands with a box cutter. He had the last bit of cigarette clamped into his jaw as he extracted the gun, the magazine and muzzle not yet attached. He turned to Stagg and then back to the gun, checking out the manufacturer details, noting that unless this was a hell of a fake, it was indeed made by the fine people at Colt in West Hartford, Connecticut.

He ghost-fired the gun without the magazine, feeling the quality of the mechanisms and the familiar feel of the weapon. During his time in Iraq and Afghanistan, he and his M4 ate, slept, and shit together. For a long while, it felt like a damn extension of his hand.

He looked over at Stagg.

"You want to check all the boxes?"

"Would I be a fool to trust you?" Donnie said.

"You gonna have to unload 'em," Stagg said. "You'll see what you got. All the same. All come from the same place."

"How'd Campo get 'em?"

"Does it matter?"

"Nope."

"Then I wouldn't ask, son."

16

THE TIBBEHAH COUNTY SUPERVISORS MET ON WEDNESDAYS, TWICE A
month, at the County Courthouse just south of town. It was an old
building, as most buildings were in Jericho, constructed sometime in
the early 1900s, with all the aesthetics of a hay barn. It had two func-
tional floors with a single courtroom, several musty offices, and a big
hall where the supervisors gathered on a high dais. Their seats were
backed by dark wood paneling embossed with the official seal of Tibbehah County, the head of Issatibbehah, the Choctaw chief who'd sold
his land in exchange for a one-way ticket for his people on the Trail of
Tears. Quinn and Lillie sat in the second row, waiting for the third
agenda item to get cleared up, a proposed tax on logging trucks using
county roads. The five supervisors spun the idea around and around,
debating just to show they possessed the skill.

About twenty minutes in, Johnny Stagg, the board president, finally
held up his hand and asked if they'd like to take a vote. District Four
supervisor DuPuy, a black slumlord who ran Sugar Ditch, was too busy
having a personal conversation on his cell phone. The supervisor from

the northwest part of the county where Quinn lived, a short, obese man named MacDougal, agreed with Stagg to never tax a money generator, but he seemed to agree with Stagg on most things. MacDougal was so intent on the consideration that he even took the time to remove his foot from the dais where he'd been clipping his toenails since the Pledge of Allegiance.

"Bet you wish you were back in combat," Lillie said.

Quinn didn't answer. They had two more agenda items to go until they got to the issue of opening up the old County Barn to fuel and service county vehicles.

"Whew," Lillie said. "This could've been for nothing."

They both watched as Betty Jo Mize, the editor, reporter, and owner of the *Tibbehah Monitor*, wandered in and took a seat in the front row, opening her steno pad. She was thin, small, white-haired, and enjoyed Jack Daniel's and dirty jokes as much as a Sunday sermon.

The supervisors didn't take but a minute to agree three members should attend a rural county planning conference in Panama City, Florida. The only dissenting vote came from Sam Bishop, the only voice on the board that Quinn respected. Sam's father still held the office as county clerk and had been Quinn's scoutmaster years ago. Sam Jr., the supervisor, was in his forties and ran the county co-op.

After a short discussion of a water association running line on a county right-of-way, Stagg coughed and shuffled his paper. "Next item is on the old County Barn."

Stagg looked to MacDougal, whose beard couldn't hide his lack of a chin or his fat neck. He peered over a pair of half-glasses as if this item was giving him gas pains.

DuPuy shut off his cell phone and began to shuffle papers, too, that being the thing you did when you did nothing. He smacked gum and listened to Stagg outline the proposal: "The refurbishment of the old facility, upkeep, and new employees would prove more than the county

can afford. But I believe Sheriff Colson wishes to speak on the matter.
That right?"

Quinn stood, dressed in his blue jeans, a stiff pressed khaki shirt,
and polished boots. He'd showered and shaved before driving over to
the meeting. His Beretta 9mm rested on his hip.

"Go ahead, Sheriff," Stagg said.

Stagg sat in the middle of the dais, scratching his neck, waiting.
DuPuy and MacDougal flanked his right. Sam Bishop and a spark
plug of a little redneck named Bobby Pickens flanked his left. Pickens
was the wild card, a self-proclaimed independent who'd been elected to
office because the previous supervisor had left his wife of thirty years
for a nineteen-year-old Piggly Wiggly checkout girl.

"I believe y'all have the rundown of expenses on county vehicles for
the last four years," Quinn said. "A pretty conservative rundown still
shows us cutting our expenses in half by using the barn."

Stagg smiled and shook his head, looking again at his buddy Mac-
Dougal for support and then over to DuPuy. Quinn could tell the matter had been decided as soon as it had turned up on the agenda. Stagg
sucked on a tooth, and gave a long, dramatic pause, before he began to
lecture down to Quinn. In the front row, Miss Mize sighed, knowing
she'd have to hear the same old argument.

"Sheriff, we all appreciate you bringing ideas to us," Stagg said.
"That's kind of the nature of what we do as county elders. But before
you bring up something, you might want to run some numbers on how
much this here thing's gonna cost." Stagg grinned some more, showing
off his big veneers. He shifted in his seat. MacDougal looked down at
the agenda but couldn't stop snickering like a third grader. "This thing
could cost us a couple hunnard thousand."

"Did you read my report?" Quinn said.

"I read it."

"It doesn't ask for new equipment or tools," Quinn said. "I've asked for three employees to be added to the payroll. A manager and two more mechanics. They will take care of the building. We're only one of two counties in Mississippi who don't purchase our own fuel."

Quinn saw Betty Jo Mize lean forward from her seat, scribbling notes.

"You know about hazards of gas pumps and safety concerns," Stagg said. "It ain't like fillin' up a couple canisters for your bass boat."

Quinn let him get it all out, let him hang himself as he threw out the facts. "I'm the one who had that old rickety barn closed when I took office," Stagg said. "It was a dangerous place. We had graft. County officials were fillin' up their momma and daddy's cars or their girl-friend's. I'm not backing any plan that opens up that can of worms."

Quinn looked over at Betty Jo, who had bit down on her lower lip, scribbling word for word.

"So almost all gas and maintenance should continue through your truck stop, Mr. Stagg?" Quinn said. "Maybe you might consider selling the county gas at cost."

You could hear the supervisors' chairs creak and a couple stray coughs from the crowd of four more folks. Someone behind Quinn laughed.

"It's no secret that I operate one of the largest truck stops in north Mississippi," Stagg said. "If you hadn't noticed, I do advertise the fact on big billboards out on Highway 45."

Sam Bishop nodded while he made some notes, waiting for Quinn's reply. Bobby Pickens stared at Quinn. Bobby was caught off guard, red-faced and sweating in his ill-fitting Sunday best, not sure which way to side. DuPuy gave a sly grin, watching Quinn work, savoring the moment. He tilted his head in a little bit of appreciation and put his feet up before him, hands behind his head.

"Give me one reason why the servicing and care of our own vehicles and buying gas at cost won't save thousands," Quinn said.

Stagg, rubbing the back of his red neck, let it all hang in the wind for a few moments. He cleaned his teeth with his tongue, checked out Mac-Dougal's glance that seemed to ask what to do, and then said, "We'll take it under advisement, Sheriff. We do appreciate your time. We got a vote?"

MacDougal shuffled his fat ass in his chair and made a motion to table the issue until the next meeting. He looked to DuPuy and Stagg to second.

Sam Bishop raised a single finger. He raised his eyebrows. "Hold up. You got someone to run this thing?"

"Boom Kimbrough," Quinn said.

Stagg cackled. MacDougal and DuPuy joined in. Pickens looked mildly confused by their laughter, smoothing down the front of his wide flowered tie. He took a long sip of water, spilling some on his crotch.

"You know a more qualified mechanic?" Quinn asked. "He's been working on tractors and cars his whole life."

MacDougal nodded, looking stuffed and self-satisfied on the dais. He had a little gleam in his eye as he leaned back into his leather chair, looked over his glasses, and said, "If you hadn't noticed, that boy got only one arm."

"He'll be my hire," Quinn said. "I'll put in our budget."

"This is the craziest notion ever put before this board," Stagg said.

"You ever heard of the Americans with Disabilities Act?" Quinn asked.

Stagg leaned back in his chair. He looked to his right and then to his left for full support, but not getting much. He again said the board would take it under advisement.

"He would be my hire," Quinn said.

"Where we gonna get that money?" MacDougal asked, still smirking.

"From the money the county saves by not buying gas from Stagg," Quinn said. "You need me to spell this out for you?"

Quinn felt Lillie's fingers slip into his belt and pull him back a bit. The motion was slight and sneaky, and no one noticed it. Quinn could feel her, tugging at him. No one said a word for several moments, and Quinn finished off the conversation by thanking them all for their time and saying he looked forward to a reply at the next meeting.

Quinn steadied himself and nodded to the men at the dais and walked to the back door, Lillie and Miss Mize trailing behind him. He drank a bit from the water fountain and turned to see both the women waiting.

"That was fun," Miss Mize said. "I do believe Johnny Stagg just shit himself."

"Maybe too far," Lillie said.

"Oh, no," Miss Mize said. "This is just getting fun."

"You didn't know about the gas?" Quinn said. "Thought everybody did."

"Can't write something from sealed information and secret meetings," Miss Mize said. "Might be done, but until someone airs it out in public, it's not game."

He nodded at the old woman. She winked and walked back into the supervisors' meeting.

"Thought you were gonna pull me down on top of you," Quinn said. "Tugging my belt like that."

"Slow down, Sheriff," Lillie said. "Give 'em some more rope."

DINNER AT THE COLSON HOUSE was served at seven. Jean was frying chicken, Quinn could smell as soon as he hit the front door. Caddy and Anna Lee were in the kitchen helping, Quinn a little surprised to see

Anna Lee since his sister was back, and Jean didn't need the help. Potato salad and some kind of carrot salad were already fixed. Soft white rolls sat ready to go in the oven, and the chicken popped and hissed in the deep fryer. Quinn's mother was very good at frying chicken. He walked past the women and reached into the refrigerator for a beer. Hondo trailed at his heels.

"What are you doing?" his mother asked. "Don't you dare bring that old nasty dog in my house."

"You invited us for dinner," Quinn said, popping the top on a tall can of Budweiser. "And he just had a bath."

"I invited you but didn't invite that dog."

"Hush, or he might hear you."

Hondo had already made his way into the living room to lick Jason's face. Jason was playing with a couple Hot Wheels monster trucks— Grave Digger and Swamp Thing—that Quinn had bought him at the Dollar General, and laughed and rolled on the carpet while holding on to Hondo's tail.

"She doesn't really hate the dog," Anna Lee said. They stood side by side, watching boy and dog roll around together. She smelled like honey-suckle.

"I know," Quinn said. "She let him sit in Daddy's chair the other night, and they watched the '68 Comeback Special."

"Thought Boom was gonna join y'all?"

"On his way."

"He driving again?" she asked.

Quinn nodded. Anna Lee wore a dress that looked like a man's faded plaid shirt over her bulging stomach. She had that healthy, flushed look that pregnant women get, her blond hair pulled back into a ponytail. No makeup, but not needing any, either. The ring on her finger shined big and bold in the light.

"Glad you came," Quinn said. He took a sip of beer.

"I dropped by to see Jason and then started helping out in the kitchen. I promised Luke I'd be home an hour ago."

"He did a smart thing calling me the other night," Quinn said. "If he hadn't, we might not have caught the Torres daughter and seen the situation at that house."

Anna Lee shuddered and put her arms around herself and over her stomach. She smiled at Quinn, both of them listening to all the commotion going on in the kitchen. Caddy had already gone back to familiar territory with Jean, not really arguing but more of a kind of snapping back and forth. *Watch out, Momma. That's too hot. Come on, move, I need to put the rolls in the dang oven.* Anna Lee had heard it for years, and they both laughed at the familiarity.

Hondo followed Jason, running past their legs. Anna Lee snatched Jason up and kissed him on the forehead and set him back, the little boy's legs staying in motion, hitting the ground running.

"Good-bye," Anna Lee said.

"Good night," Quinn said.

He stood at the front window and watched as Anna Lee's SUV pulled out and drove off. Not two minutes later, Boom's old truck rumbled into the drive to replace her.

Boom let himself in, like he had since he and Quinn had been kids, and removed his jacket with the pinned sleeve, muddy work boots, and cap at the door. He found his place beside Caddy at the table, and she turned and kissed him on the cheek as he sat down.

"Want a beer?" Quinn asked Boom.

"Sure."

"Get me one, too," Quinn said.

Boom smiled and walked back to the kitchen and grabbed a couple, one in his hand and one in the crook of his arm, and sat back down. Quinn forked a couple pieces of chicken and put them on his plate. Boom seemed pretty damn good at eating with one hand, setting down the chicken and using a fork on the potato salad and coleslaw Jean had loaded onto his plate.

"How you doin', Caddy?" Boom asked.

"You know, we forgot to say the prayer," Caddy said.

Quinn looked up from his chicken at Boom. Boom grinned but lowered his head anyway. Caddy launched into a prayer about the grace of God and blessedness of family and the sanctity of children before she finally wrapped it up. It sounded like something she had heard someone else say on television.

"Must be good to be God," Boom said, scraping up some coleslaw. "All these people just telling you how great you are."

"I heard some people dog-cuss him, too," Quinn said.

"You shouldn't do that," Jean said.

"Didn't say I did," Quinn said. "Just said I'd heard it."

"That's blasphemy," Caddy said.

"I know what it's called," Quinn said.

"When's the last time you've been to church?" Caddy said.

Jason looked from his mother to uncle to grandmother. He reached for a piece of chicken that had been cut into small bites.

"I go to church when I can," Quinn said.

"You didn't go Sunday," Caddy said.

"Nope," Quinn said. "We had a man go off his meds and threaten to kill his wife."

"You can take a break for church."

Quinn nodded. "Well, next time you're praying, please tell God to slow down the shitstorm during the Sunday service."

Boom took a sip of beer. He coughed. "How'd it go with the supervisors?"

"Not bad," Quinn said.

"What's goin' on?" Jean Colson asked.

"Trying to get Boom hired to run the County Barn."

Jean nodded and ate. She looked over at Jason and smiled at him. He smiled back. He'd yet to touch the carrot or potato salad. Jean would have to bribe him to eat anything beyond the chicken. She'd done the same when Quinn was a boy.

"Heard supervisors shot you down," Boom said.

"They tried," Quinn said. "But I put things in perspective for Stagg."

"So you got a county job?" Jean asked.

"Depends on how this town reacts to tomorrow's paper."

"Hope it works out," Jean said, winking at Boom. "Would y'all like some more to drink? We got plenty of chicken, too."

"Quinn, let me ask you a question," Caddy said, looking up from her sullen place at the end of the dinner table. She'd tied her hair in a red bandanna and wore an old gray sweatshirt and jeans. "If you died tonight, are you sure you'd be walking tomorrow with our Savior on the streets of heaven?"

Jean stopped by the door to the kitchen and waited.

Quinn put down a drumstick and wiped his mouth. "If you're asking if I've ever considered my mortality, you might want to consider where I've been for the last ten years. I thought about it every waking hour."

Caddy looked back down at her plate and ate a little potato salad. Boom looked to Quinn and raised his eyebrows. Jean went back to the kitchen for more food.

"How'd you do it?" Caddy asked.

"Do what?"

"Stop the man from killing his wife."

"I arrested him."

Caddy nodded. "You coming to church Sunday?"

"If I can."

"What's the most important thing to you?" Caddy asked. "If you made a list."

"Right now?" Quinn said. "Probably eating some fried chicken in peace."

"Do not curse the deaf or put a stumbling block in front of the blind, but fear your God."

"Appreciate that, Caddy," Quinn said. "Now, would you please pass the goddamn chicken?"

Caddy picked up and threw down her plate and ran for her bedroom. Quinn kept eating. Jason bowed his head at his plate. Boom kept eating, too, and drinking beer. Quinn didn't even bother to look at his mother, who'd come back to the table, knowing the scorn that would be there.

"Caddy said you hadn't talked to her since she'd come home," Jean said. "That's what she's mad about."

"I talked to her enough."

"She doesn't feel welcome here," Jean said.

"Because I'm not going to church regular?" Quinn asked. "I'm sorry, Momma. But this new Caddy is going to take some adjusting to."

Quinn put his arm around his nephew and kidded with him a bit while they ate. Caddy didn't return to finish or to help with the dishes. Quinn and Boom tried to get Jean to sit and relax while they cleaned up, but she said they'd probably put everything in the wrong place and insisted on helping. Nearly an hour passed before Quinn and Boom walked outside so Quinn could smoke a cigar.

"When did Caddy get right with the Lord?" Boom asked.

"Pretty sure it was last week." Quinn looked up at the sky, a cool, clear, crisp night. "Boom, let me ask you a question. Have you seen Donnie since the other night?"

Boom shook his head.

"What about that girl he was with?"

Boom shook his head again.

"I know he hangs out with Shane and that fat kid, what's his name?"

"Tiny."

"Ever see him with any other Mexicans?"

"Only at the El Dorado."

"Donnie's into some shit," Quinn said. "Lillie and I are working on it. Maybe you can ask around a bit without people knowin' you asking."

Boom nodded. "How deep?"

Quinn pointed to right under his chin.

17

THE SOUTHERN STAR BAR HAD BEEN OPEN FOR AS LONG AS YOU COULD buy beer in Tibbehah County, which was nearly two years. The Baptists fought hard to keep Jericho dry, but in the end, the loyal voice of the redneck spoke up and passed the resolution by six votes. Quinn wasn't back home then but had heard that signs outside the various churches protested the change by saying the road to hell was littered with beer cans and drunkenness. Every town needed a bar. One of the first buildings in Jericho had been a saloon, as pointed out during these hearings. The Southern Star was packed most nights, except for Sundays, of course, when Tibbehah went back to being dry for the Baptists' sake. Saturdays were the most crowded, when dispatch would have to call deputies to break up a fight or find the poor drunk bastard who'd walked out on his tab. Almost always it was a regular, a friend of the bartender, who swore he'd get good with it next week.

The building had been a hardware store when Quinn was a kid, and some of the old nail bins still hung on the far wall. It was a narrow shot of space, with the bar running down the long left side. There were a lot of neon beer signs and mirrors, a few deer heads, and even a stuffed wildcat displayed by the bathrooms.

Donnie Varner wasn't hard to find, perched at the corner of the bar, drinking a draft beer and talking to a curvy girl in tight-fitting blue jeans, black halter top, and boots. Lillie walked with Quinn as they approached them, and the curvy girl turned to study Lillie head to toe.

"Lillie Virgil, what the hell you doin' here? I paid that goddamn ticket."

Lillie nodded without emotion. "Go make yourself scarce, Dwana. We're here to see Donnie."

The only thing worse than impugning the honor of the redneck male was to impugn the honor of the redneck female. Dwana put her hands on her hips, stuck out her large breasts, and lifted her chin. "Just 'cause you wear that badge doesn't mean you have to be such a dyke bitch."

Donnie winced and drank his beer. Lillie took a step forward, smiling sweetly.

"Dwana, why don't you give your pussy a rest tonight," Lillie said. "Or you out to break some kinda record?"

Dwana stepped forward to meet her toe-to-toe. Lillie stood her ground and looked down at Dwana, who was quite a bit shorter. Donnie pulled her in and whispered something soothing in her ear, something that made sense to Dwana's honor, and she turned away with a flash of her highlighted hair.

"And here I thought you mighta mellowed since high school, Lillie," Donnie said.

"Girl deserves it," Lillie said. "That's what she gets for being born the preacher's daughter."

Quinn looked up and showed the bartender two fingers, letting Donnie know this was social. He was drinking beer and didn't come wearing his star or gun. "Heard you opened the gun range back up."

"Got to make money somehow," Donnie said. "Lost my job driving when the Guard called me back. Don't care to sell Cheetos and Marlboros the rest of my life."

"How's that going for you?" Lillie asked.

"All right, I guess," Donnie said. "Sellin' pistols, deer rifles, and all. You know I got permits. It's legal."

The bartender set down a couple Budweisers. The jukebox in the corner started up, playing that old David Allan Coe song, "You Never Even Called Me by My Name."

"I heard this song maybe a million times and still love it," Donnie said, drinking, reminiscing about good times. "Y'all remember how tore up we used to get out on the Trace at those field parties? Alma Jane would put those kegs down in the creek, and me and Colson here would be there till they'd emptied out."

Quinn smiled.

"Probably should be careful drinking a beer in public now that you're a servant of the people and all," Donnie said. "Won't sit right with some."

"I'm not changing who I am."

"How long you known Quinn, Donnie?" Lillie asked.

"My whole life."

"And what the hell did you expect?" she asked.

Donnie smiled and turned back into the bar, obviously a few beers and shots ahead. He was a little glassy-eyed and smirky and pretty much the way Quinn had hoped to find him. Quinn drank his beer, and David Allan Coe sang, most of the bar joining in to sing the part about "the perfect country-western song" at an ear-pounding volume. Nobody could talk till the jukebox settled into a downer from Dolly Parton about growing up poor and shoeless.

"All that groundwork for nothin'," Donnie said, looking at Dwana, who'd settled in with her pink drink at a table with two guys not too far out of high school. "Dang it, Lillie. I'd already bought her two god-damn drinks. Those beach drinks ain't cheap, either."

"Well, think of how much I saved you on penicillin."

"God damn, you rough, girl," Donnie said, lighting up a smoke. "You are rough."

Lillie shrugged.

"What happened to that good-looking girl I saw you with the other night?" Quinn asked.

Donnie narrowed his eyes, doing his best to look confused, tilting his head in thought a bit. "That little brown-eyed honey?"

"You got that many girls, Donnie?" Lillie asked, saddling up to a spot that opened up next to him. Quinn took the other side, the three of them facing their reflection in the bar mirror. The bar growing smoky as hell and thick with perspiration and bullshit.

"Oh, hell," Donnie said. "That wadn't nothing. Just making some time."

"She from around here?" Quinn asked.

"Nah, just some little Mex," Donnie said. "Hey, y'all want another beer? I'm buying."

"She speak English?" Lillie said.

"'Course."

"Thought that might be some kind of advantage not to understand you," Lillie said.

"What you driving at?" Donnie said, grinning and stubbing out his smoke. "That I can't pull some tail unless they don't know what I'm saying?"

"That's about the size of it."

"Rough," Donnie said. "Just rough."

"So she's not your girlfriend or anything?" Quinn asked.

"Nah, man," Donnie said.

"Reason I'm asking," Quinn said, "is that she looks like someone connected to a fella I'm looking for. You heard about Ramón Torres?"

Donnie shook his head.

"Ramón and Janet and all those kids," Lillie said, turning on her barstool. "Don't you read the goddamn paper, Varner?"

Donnie nodded. "Fat Janet? I didn't know that Mex she was married to. What they'd do, kill that child?"

"They skipped town," Quinn said.

"Your girl live here?" Lillie asked.

Donnie shook his head. He asked the bartender for another shot. "How about some tequila for my old high school buds? They got this thing they made up here the other night called a Bloody Maria. It's like a Bloody Mary, but it's with tequila, and a raw egg. So much hot sauce, it'll set your asshole on fire."

Lillie winced. "I'm good with beer."

"Beer," Quinn said.

The bartender cracked open a couple Buds and started into Donnie's Bloody Maria.

"What else you know about the girl?" Quinn asked.

"Just met her the other night."

"Where?" Quinn asked.

"I don't want her to get in trouble or nothing," Donnie said. "You guys ain't with border patrol last time I checked."

"Just trying to find the Torres couple," Quinn said. "Where'd y'all meet?"

"She come into the VFW Hall with a couple gals from the nail salon," Donnie said. "I bought her a corn dog. That ain't a crime."

Donnie laughed, leaned forward, and took a sip of his drink. Lillie looked over to Quinn and nodded for him to keep driving at him, push him a little. There was nothing like a drunk at the bar to open up all his problems to his world. When Quinn had needed to investigate a fight, a theft, or some bullshit with his Joes, he'd usually catch them at the bar, after hours and off base, and they'd get to the heart of it.

"You get that girl's number the other night?"

Donnie shook his head.

"She work at the nail salon, Donnie?" Lillie asked.

"Y'all seem to know more about her than I do," Donnie said. "Shit. I was just trying to get sweet with her. But she wadn't having none of it."

"Where'd you drop her off?"

"Nowheres," Donnie said. "She got mad after I touched her dang knee. Walked home from the Sonic. Thought I was trying to get into her pants."

"Were you?" Lillie asked.

"Sure," Donnie said.

"You are a real romantic," Lillie said.

"But you'll ask around," Quinn said.

"Sure, sure. Y'all gonna drink some tequila with me or not?" Donnie said.

Quinn shook his head. Lillie didn't bother to answer.

Donnie wandered off, right to the dance floor where Dwana was slow-dancing with another woman. He wrapped his arms around both of them, one hand full with the Bloody Maria and the other with a lit cigarette. Quinn figured he was having quite a time.

"You gonna check the nail salon?" Quinn asked as they walked out.

"Why? Son of a bitch is lying his ass off."

18

SUNDAY MORNING CAME EARLIER THAN DONNIE WOULD'VE LIKED, HARD
sunlight through the window of his Airstream and a loud knock on the
door by ole Luther himself. His daddy only knocked, figuring Donnie
mighta had a girl, but once he knew it was clear, he turned on the television and made a pot of coffee in the percolator. Donnie showered and
shaved while Luther watched the news out of Tupelo, the old man
suited and carrying a rebound leather Bible that he'd owned as long as
Donnie had known him. Donnie didn't feel much like religion today.
He downed a couple Motrin and a cup of coffee, following the old man
out to his old Chevy pickup, kicking the son of a bitch in gear and
heading into Jericho and the Calvary Methodist.

The church was built out of pine and cypress right before the turn
of the century—the last one—looking a bit like a one-room school-
house where they'd fitted in twenty pews, ten to each side, instead of
little desks. Once inside, there was some handshaking and waves, hellos
from distant cousins and friends. A smile from the friendly preacher,

Reverend Rebecca White, who once told an ornery elder that some-times you couldn't set a man's mind right with a brand-new gun.

Donnie and Luther sat side by side, Donnie's morning sweats com-ing on along with a strong hatred for tequila and most things Mexican as Reverend White led them through "A Mighty Fortress Is Our God" and "Blessed Assurance" and then right into the Call to Worship and the Lord's Prayer. The service was straightforward and old-fashioned, with hymns from the 1800s and a sermon that landed right on time and didn't require shouting to drive its points home. His grandfather and his great-grandfather had both been members here. His mother's folks, too.

Up front, Donnie took notice of Quinn Colson, and Quinn had his arm around that half-black kid of Caddy's. The sister and his crazy mother sitting right by Quinn in the pew. A few times, Quinn would turn that high-and-tight buzzed head around and study the church, eyes wandering over Donnie. Donnie thought for a minute that old Quinn may have conspired with Reverend White for her sermon about "Being Your Brother's Keeper" and how Cain didn't think his actions were anyone's business till God scattered his ass to the wind.

"Everything you do affects another human being," Reverend White said. "Let me say it again. Everything you do affects another person. Your actions can't be hidden from God. He knows your every thought. Good and bad. Cain said he wasn't his brother's keeper. But the Lord saw the blood spill from the soil."

Quinn Colson cocked his head and scratched his ear. *Son of a bitch.*

"Are you your brother's keeper?" Reverend White asked. "How do your life and your actions serve Christ? Every one of your actions sends a ripple through hundreds or maybe thousands of people. Do you pres-ent yourself with honesty and integrity, thinking of others? Or do you walk a selfish road, looking out for your own business, locked up tight in your own thoughts and deeds?"

Donnie studied the church bulletin, learning from the prayer concerns who was sick, down on their luck, or dead. He looked up again and found Quinn was back watching the preacher and taking care of his own business instead of messing with Donnie. The little boy had fallen asleep over Quinn's shoulder, his momma, Caddy, leaning back and watching her brother holding the child with a soft smile on her face. Donnie felt embarrassed every time he saw her, searching for words to say, because when you'd been with a woman, it was damn hard to smile and shake hands. Hell, she probably didn't even remember it, after five years.

Donnie'd been home before he left for Iraq, and Caddy was home for the holidays, and they'd met up at that shit beer joint off 45, near Stagg's place. She'd been with a pretty rough fella, a roofer from Calhoun County, and there had been a drunken exchange over a dart game. The roofer left her. Caddy had been on pills and drunk, and things kind of picked up momentum quick. Donnie had stayed, and they'd talked. First time they'd talked since school. And it didn't take long till they got sloppy over cold Coors and started kissing at the bar and then ended up at the trailer, where she sure as hell made him hurt. Donnie had been with a lot of women, but no one with that kind of rage in them. She bit and clawed and screamed till she passed out.

He seemed to recall she had a small tattoo on her right shoulder of a sunflower.

"Do you offer the Lord your bounty or the scraps of what you have left?" Reverend White asked.

Donnie had found Caddy sitting on the hood of his truck the next morning, smoking a cigarette and watching the sun rise. As he walked up to the truck, she didn't even hear him, too intent on crying and praying. He wasn't dumb enough to think it was on account of him; there was only so much self-hatred a Varner man could inflict. Her knees were cradled to her chest, cigarette loose in a hand from crossed arms. She turned to him and wiped her face. "What?" she said.

Donnie shook his head.

"Want to talk about it?" he asked.

Caddy tossed the cigarette and slid from the truck. She shook her head and met him toe-to-toe. "You got somewhere to be?" she asked. She stayed two days before she slipped out, and he hadn't seen her since.

Why did Donnie always end up with the head cases and women with problems? Surely there was just one girl he could meet who could cook him supper and knock boots with him and not make him crazy or get him killed.

Reverend White told everyone to please stand for the final hymn, and Donnie found the page for "Onward, Christian Soldiers." He didn't give a damn where the carnival had set down today, knowing he'd find Luz, not wanting to wait till they exchanged the guns for cash. He was tired of sitting on them, waiting for a phone call, while he kept that tractor trailer at Stagg's.

Quinn Colson turned back and eyed Donnie. He gave a nod, the kid asleep on his shoulder.

Donnie pretended like he hadn't seen him and kept on singing.

DONNIE FOUND her that afternoon in Tupelo, running the Ferris wheel and drinking a Mountain Dew. She was none too glad to see him and stood with her hand on her left hip and eyes lowered.

"We shouldn't be seen together," Luz said.

"But we look real good."

Her shirt was snap-button gingham and she wore tight dark jeans with a pair of cockroach-killer boots. The hard angle of her naked hip was visible when the wind kicked up the hem of the shirt.

"Can't hurt nothing," Donnie said. "Can you take a break?"

She shook her head. The teenage kid he'd seen unload the magazine on the M4 was loading folks from the wheel while Luz took the tickets. Sign said it took a whole five dollars just to ride. He handed her a ten, but she wouldn't take it. The little Mex kid smiled to himself, his teeth so white they looked bleached against his dark skin.

"How about me and you just take a couple spins around?" Donnie said. "When it sets back down, I'll head back to Jericho."

"Are you drunk?"

"I just got back from church, doll," he said. "I don't drink on Sunday. I'm too damn hungover."

She agreed, because she knew he wouldn't leave, and soon they were up and away, with a good view of the fair, this one being about five times as big as the one over in Byhalia, looking across downtown Tupelo and over at Highway 45. There was a little corral down next to the Scrambler, where they set monkeys on the backs of dogs and let them race. The sign read BANANA DERBY.

"Elvis grew up over on the east side of town," Donnie said. "You want, I'll take you over to where he was born."

"We shut down tonight," she said. "We work all night and leave in the morning."

"Where?"

"Bruce."

"God help y'all."

The Ferris wheel stopped, and they hung there at the high point, rocking in that passenger car for a moment. Donnie leaned in and placed his arm around her, studying her mouth and dark hair. Luz put a hand to his chest. He could tell she wanted to speak but didn't know what to say. She just studied the horizon and little buildings, the car finally steadied.

"You tell Alejandro we need to deal soon or else the price goes up."

"Are the guns safe?"

"Sure," Donnie said. "But I don't know for how long. Sheriff's been asking about you. He says y'all connected to this fella Torres and his fat wife. They were selling kids on the Internet or some crazy shit. You know something about that?"

Luz shook her head.

"As soon as we're settled at the next town," Luz said, "we'll come for the guns."

"I want to see you."

"I'm here."

"Away from this shit."

"Why?"

"You kind of left me in a precarious state, darlin'."

The Ferris wheel kicked back on and rolled back down to the ground, passing that crazy-ass teenage shooter who was at the controls now. He looked like he should be packing groceries at the Piggly Wiggly or pumping gas. He barely had a bit of fuzz over his lip.

"I'll cook you dinner," he said. "I'll grill T-bones. We'll drink some beer. Listen to some music and build a fire."

Luz didn't say anything, watching the brick downtown and a gathering of campers and trailers of all the carnival folks in a distant lot. The neon light clicked off and on, the sounds of the midway loud as hell even up in the air. The bells and whistles and crazy barkers screaming at the folks that filled the fairground. Everything smelled like burnt popcorn and cigarettes. Families with five dollars to their name and not a damn job on the horizon dished out two hundred bucks for screaming kids to win a fucking stuffed SpongeBob Square-Pants.

"You got a trailer?" he asked. Donnie rested his hand on her knee.

She removed it.

"God damn."

"You shouldn't have come here," she said.

"Alejandro needs to mind his fucking business."

"This is so much more than you think," Luz said. She tucked her hair behind her ear, the blackness of it shining like a crow's wing.

"I don't care what y'all are doing with them guns," Donnie said. "But we can't do it in Tibbehah no more. You understand?"

They went up and over one more time, the car slowing to a stop on the platform. The boy still stood at the controls, but this time it was Alejandro's bad self who unlocked the little gate. He didn't say anything to Donnie, most of the weird horns and scrawls and numbers on his face saying it for him. Donnie just winked at him as he passed, waiting on the steps for Luz to join him.

"If you leave now," she said, "I will call. We can talk."

"About the guns?" Donnie asked and frowned.

"Whatever you wish," she said.

"What about Alejandro?"

"This is none of his business."

19

QUINN AND JASON WENT FISHING AFTER CHURCH. CADDY CAME OUT TO pick him up a little while later, Jason passed out on the couch, tired from the sermon and lunch and catching bluegill and running wild at his uncle's farm. Caddy still wore her Sunday dress, but Quinn was back into his jeans and khaki sheriff's shirt. He'd been ready for her and had already fitted the gun on his belt as she drove up and met him on the path. The gravel road was rutted and muddy with the rains.

"Sacked out."

"You carry him?" she asked.

Quinn nodded and went back into the house, returning with Jason over his shoulder. He helped Caddy fit him into the safety seat, and she closed the door, smiling at Quinn and squinting to watch him. He nodded back to her.

"We're gonna have to talk sooner or later."

Quinn nodded.

"My therapist wants you to join us," she said. "She says that was a lot on a little boy."

"I got to go to work, Caddy."

"You want to pretend it never happened?"

"Nope," Quinn said. "I want us to remember it happened when we were kids and it's over."

"Not over for me."

Quinn leaned against her car, a beaten-up blue Honda that had taken her back to Jericho. He studied the two big pecans in his back acreage, a tire swing knotted over a big fat branch. Hondo was in the far field on his back, taking a nap, yellow grasses bending around him.

"Listen," he said. "I'll do whatever you want me to. If you want me to talk to your doctor and all, that's fine. But there's some places I don't care to go back to. You need to respect that. Why don't we make sure you're churning this shit up for a reason and not just to make me uncomfortable?"

"I love you for what you did, Quinn," she said. "You got to understand that. I want you to know it."

"I didn't do anything."

"You did everything."

Caddy reached over and took his hand. She smiled at him. "Can we quit fighting?" she asked. "I'm not like you. I wish there wasn't evil in this world. You've made friends with the idea. You think there's something you can actually do about it."

"Nope," he said.

"You do," Caddy said. "I just wish I hadn't been eight years old when I learned that lesson."

"I didn't do nothing."

"You saved me."

Quinn turned his head. He spit on the ground. His cell phone went off in his pocket, and he was glad for the call, Lillie telling him some crazy-ass hermit on County Road 32 was telling his neighbors he was an instrument of God.

"Hold on," Quinn told Lillie. "Is he armed?"

"Wouldn't be interesting if he wasn't," Lillie said.

Caddy kissed his cheek before getting behind the wheel and driving off.

THE MAN WITH THE GUN was a Vietnam vet named Nehemiah Davis, a white male, aged sixty. According to Lillie, he was new to the county, moved to Tibbehah about ten years ago and had parked his trailer on some logged-out land right off the road. Earlier in the day, he'd taken some shots at a woman who lived down the road. He said he'd been charged with protecting the land by God Almighty Himself.

"Who are we to interfere?" Quinn asked.

"He's toting a .45 pistol."

"God give him that?"

"I think the fella must be Catholic," Lillie said. "Keeps on talking about the Holy Mother."

"Thanks for calling."

"Figured you'd need to be in on this one," Lillie said. "Kenny thought we should just shoot him."

"Who are his people?"

"I think he used to go with the Jessup woman, before she died. Like I said, I don't think he's from around here."

Quinn placed his hands on the hood of Lillie's Jeep and stared down the short dirt road to the trailer on blocks. A dog trotted out from below, and a white curtain moved in the far left window. "The reason I appreciated you calling is that Caddy wants me to meet with her therapist. She wants us to talk about when we were kids."

"Couldn't have been easy growing up Quinn Colson's sister."

Quinn shrugged as Lillie reached into the back of her Jeep for a shotgun. She thumbed in four shells as Quinn said, "What's wrong with that?"

They walked side by side down the path. The windows to the trailer were closed. The dog ran up to greet them, a dirty red hound missing an ear and eaten up with fleas. A couple junk trucks, weight-lifting equipment, and various tools turned to shit littered the front path.

"Maybe Caddy's trying to help you," Lillie said.

"Come again?"

"I know, I know. She's a real pain in the ass. But she's your sister."

"Caddy does for Caddy."

The curtain in the window moved again. The brief lighting of a wild-eyed face and then nothing. Lillie saw him, too, and lifted the shotgun in both hands. The front door was closed, with a screen door in front of it.

"How was church?"

"Good sermon," Quinn said. "Cain and Abel."

"Never could figure out why Cain killed his brother."

"Jealousy."

"Over what?" Lillie asked.

"God didn't appreciate Cain giving Him the dregs of his grain. Abel was a shepherd and sacrificed the best of his flock."

"Pissed off his brother."

"Yep."

The dog circled away and trotted to the back of the property. A door or window creaked, and there was a thump. Quinn removed the 9mm on his hip and waited for Nehemiah Davis to round the corner and come tell them all about it.

"Also never did figure out how Cain met a wife," Lillie said. "If he and Abel were born to the first man and woman, where'd they meet women?"

"Must've been a bar," Quinn said. "Maybe over in Canaan."

"See him?"

"Yep," Quinn said.

Nehemiah Davis was little and skinny and wearing nothing but a pair of white undershorts. He hadn't shaved in a while, and the top of his head was balding and sunburned. He waved a .45 pistol up in the air and told them to disperse from this Holy Place.

"What's so holy about it, Mr. Davis?" Lillie asked.

"I'm the Angel Gabriel," Mr. Davis said. "I am charged to protect this land."

"You would've thought Holy Land would've called for a double-wide," Lillie said under her breath. "Mr. Gabriel, would you mind putting down the weapon, seeing as how you're an angel and all?"

"The Holy Mother is here."

"In your trailer?" Quinn asked.

Davis nodded, frail and bony, with a chest and shoulders covered in fine white hair.

"Y'all got cable?" Lillie asked.

"Don't push him," Quinn said.

Behind the half-naked man sat an Oldsmobile Toronado. Maybe a '69, silver with whitewalls, the top ragged and covered with a blue tarp. The back tires were flat, but the paint looked good.

"You get that car when you left the service?" Quinn asked.

Davis turned back, the memory of such a sweet vehicle a little too much for an archangel. Mr. Davis's eyes grew smaller, and he nodded a bit, the .45 lowered in his hand. He used his free hand to scratch his butt. The dog came up and sat down on his haunches, yawning.

"You got a 425 under there?" Quinn asked.

Nehemiah scratched his butt some more. He turned back to the car. And then back to Quinn, and then looked down at the dog. He mumbled something.

"What's that, sir?" Lillie asked.

"455," he said.

Quinn grinned a bit. He whistled for the dog. The dog trotted over, met him halfway, and Quinn moved on up to Mr. Davis. He kept on smiling. His gun was drawn but hanging loose by his leg. Davis had the saber tattoos on his bicep of a man who'd served in Airborne.

"You miss jumping out of planes?" Quinn asked.

Davis cocked his head, confused.

"82nd?"

"I am Gabriel," Davis said. "I am charged with protecting the Holy Mother."

"Sure like that car, Mr. Davis," Quinn said. "You kept it nice for a good long while."

Davis dropped the gun loose again. Quinn stepped forward a bit and cut his eyes at Lillie. She nodded slow. Quinn stepped forward and snatched the gun from the man's hand in a single breath. Davis looked at him, saddened, and dropped to the ground, where he buried his face in his hands and started to cry. The one-eared hound licked his face while Lillie called in the situation on the radio. She said they'd need some transport and a mental eval.

"You take the Holy Mother for a drive in that Olds?" Lillie asked.

Davis looked up. He nodded at her.

"I guess she would dig that ride," Lillie said.

Quinn spun open the old man's .45. The cylinder was empty.

20

QUINN DREAMED OF CADDY THAT NIGHT, AND THE BIG WOODS.

It was fall, as it was now, and the cotton had burst out in bolls as thick as his fists, the earth still warm and giving off heat on a chilled morning as he'd packed. He'd known the woods his whole life and hungered to get far into them, deep into the national forest, as Caddy trailed behind him. He could see the gentle roll of the green hills just beyond a forgotten tin-roofed barn, rusted and worn. The fields were choked with fog.

"Can we stop and eat?" Caddy asked.

"When we get to the forest."

"I brought peanut butter cookies."

"I got some dried peaches and jerky," Quinn said. "Salt and pepper and shortening. Cornmeal for fish. I'll catch us some brim for dinner."

"You think he'll follow?" she asked.

"You can bet on it."

Caddy was little, with light hair and dark skin from the summer. She wore overalls and cowboy boots, kicking at the clumps of earth between cotton rows. Her hair had been tied in a ponytail with pink string.

"I don't like that man, the warden," Caddy said. "He's got eyes like a pig. He looks at me strange."

"How do you think I feel?"

"He told Momma he was gonna arrest you for those deer."

"If he can catch me."

"He won't catch us," Caddy said. "We can live in the forest forever. We'll take care of each other. We don't need nobody."

"You shouldn't have come."

"You need me," she said.

"You're just a kid."

"What are you?"

"I'm not a little girl," Quinn said. "I wish you hadn't followed."

"I ain't leaving you."

Quinn didn't say anything. He kept walking through the fog, knowing the way up into the hill more by feel than sight. He couldn't see much beyond that old barn but knew the big woods stretched out for miles and miles beyond it, leaving Tibbehah County far behind.

"I can keep house," Caddy said.

"I brought a hatchet," Quinn said. "I know how to make a shelter like the Choctaw. We got a lot of work to do before it grows cold."

"What if the warden finds you?"

Quinn carried his Captain Planet backpack and his dad's .22 rifle.

"We run," he said. "He keeps coming, and I'll have to shoot him."

"I don't know why Uncle Hamp can't make him go away," Caddy said. "He's the sheriff. Why can't the sheriff tell him what to do?"

Quinn stopped and turned to his sister. She stood on a turnrow, making her seem taller.

"Those deer were killed on state land," Quinn said. "He's the law there."

Caddy kept following as the farmland ended and the trees bucked up far over the hills and into the west. A white fall sun tried to break through the clouds above.

"I heard Uncle Hamp tell Momma last night for you to just take your licks," Caddy said. "He said the warden was coming for you on account of what you did to his truck."

"He deserved it."

"You really have to cut his tires?"

"He was following me."

"And you dug that hole," Caddy said. "Covered it with branches. Is that how he got hurt?"

"I guess."

"He sure is mad," Caddy said. "Said you need to go into a state home for boys."

"Over two bucks."

"Warden said it was six."

"He's a liar."

"Momma said he'd been youth pastor since she was a kid."

"Doesn't make him any more honest."

"He sat on our porch waiting for you to come home from school," Caddy said. "He's probably still there."

"What's he doing?"

"I think he found Daddy's whiskey."

"Is he talking to Momma?"

"She's real scared, Quinn."

"Well, we won't be trouble no more."

They followed a fire road high up into the second-growth timber of red oak and birch and pine, big thick pines, not the skinny scrub stuff that grew on cleared land, Quinn remembered from when he'd found the hidden lake that first time. That was when his daddy had left, Quinn knowing he'd gone to Hollywood for good. Finding the lake had been some kind of gift.

"How much money did you bring?" Quinn asked.

"I got seventeen dollars."

"Aunt Halley will give us some money."

"What about Uncle Hamp?" Caddy asked.

"She won't tell him," Quinn said. "She's mad at him for not getting that warden off my ass."

"You're not as bad as people say. Why do you want people to think you're so bad?"

"I'm not bad," Quinn said. "I just don't have much luck. Seems like every stupid thing I do, I get caught. I'd like a break every once in a while."

"If something happened to you, I'd die, too. I can't sit at home and just pray."

Caddy stumbled on the slope of the hill and Quinn reached for her hand. He held her hand up and over the hill and around the twisting fire road until he found that deer path. The deer had led him to the secret lake, and that's where they'd live until there was no more trouble.

He'd wait there till forever.

21

FOUR DAYS LATER, LILLIE CALLED QUINN INTO HER OFFICE AND PLAYED the tape.

"When'd she make the call?" Quinn asked.

"Last night in the jail common," Lillie said. "Mary Alice logged it, and I played it right before you got in. By the way, did you know you were late?"

"A whole fifteen minutes."

"You're not gonna get fat and lazy on me, are you?"

"What do we do?"

"This will add pressure to Mara," Lillie said. "I say we play it for her, and let's see what shakes out. Momma sure was hard on her."

"Who's the girl's attorney?"

"Public defender out of Oxford," Lillie said. "I think he's a whole six months out of law school."

Quinn nodded.

"You look tired."

"Had a hard time sleeping last night," Quinn said. "Weird dreams. I think it's that old house does it to me."

"What happened to you bragging about falling asleep at will?" Lillie said. "You said in the Shitbox, you could close your eyes and sleep but still kind of be awake."

"Wasn't like that," Quinn said. "I finally got up, took out Hondo, and made a pot of coffee at three a.m."

"And still late," Lillie said.

"Do we have to call the lawyer?" Quinn asked.

"Mara will ask," Lillie said. "She's dumb, but she ain't stupid."

"Can you imagine growing up with that woman as your mother?" Quinn asked. "She called her own daughter a fat, lazy piece of shit. And then expects her to keep her mouth shut."

"She said if she talked, that she'd have her killed."

"Sweet woman."

"You know that's witness intimidation," Lillie said. "We got her now on more charges. Janet can just keep on talking."

"What about the phone number Mara called?"

"Came back to a disposable cell bought at a Walmart."

"We know which Walmart?"

"Working on it," Lillie said. "Don't expect much. If Janet and Ramón pitched their IDs and credit cards, they're not going to mind throwing away a twenty-dollar phone. Man, she was pissed."

"Well, at least we know Mara's been holding out if she knew where to call."

Lillie nodded.

"And playing that tape for her, whether she's got her attorney or not, may jog loose some details."

Lillie nodded again. "You want some coffee? Mary Alice also brought some homemade biscuits in. I sure like that woman. Nice hire, Quinn."

"After thirty years with my uncle, you know she came with the place."

Lillie's office faced the front parking lot. Quinn's old truck sat next to Lillie's Jeep and a couple aging patrol cars.

"Last time I interviewed Mara, I brought along the ATF agent from Oxford."

"You mean Dinah?"

"I know her name."

"I bet you do."

Quinn smiled.

"See it," Lillie said, pointing. "I see it right there."

"What's that?"

"That shit-eating Quinn Colson grin," Lillie said. "Since when are you into redheads?"

"I'll call her and tell her what's going on," Quinn said. "I worry your professionalism might be on the decline."

"You think I'm going to ask if the carpet matches the drapes?"

"You know, if I said that, you could have me fired."

"It's a bitch, ain't it?"

Lillie grinned at him and walked out to Mary Alice's desk, where she lifted a couple sausage biscuits wrapped in foil. She tossed him one and sat back down at her desk, lifting her boots off the floor and placing her hands behind her head. She spun her office chair back and forth on the swivel.

"You gonna ask her out?"

"Lillie, just set up the interview. I don't need for you to pass notes for me in class."

"She likes you," Lillie said. "I can see it."

"Set it up," Quinn said. "I want to know everything Mara knows. She can't hold out on us anymore."

"You mind just us talking to the girl?" Lillie asked. "You bring in a Fed and it's gonna spook her. This isn't about the guns to me. It's about those kids."

THE PUBLIC DEFENDER HAD a fraternity boy haircut and wore an awkward-fitting pin-striped suit. Quinn noticed his hands were sweating before they started the questioning. He kept on referring to Quinn as "sir," although he was only a couple years younger. Mara was "Miss Black."

Quinn and Lillie sat them all down in the interview room, a windowless cinder-block space that still smelled of sweat and cigarettes after countless pressure washings. Quinn had found a long table in county storage, and it comfortably sat about eight in folding chairs. Mary Alice served coffee. Mara and her attorney had Coca-Cola.

Quinn sprung for both bottles.

A lot of pleasantries were exchanged. Quinn learned that Mara's attorney had been a Sigma Chi at Ole Miss when Lillie was there. They didn't know each other. His father owned two McDonald's in Jackson.

Lillie pressed PLAY, and they all sat around and listened. Just as the attorney looked like he might protest, Mara starting to sniffle and cry, the tape was over. The whole exchange between mother and daughter lasted about ninety seconds.

"You don't owe her a thing, Mara," Lillie said.

"Your client had some pretty good information that she withheld," Quinn said.

"What's that?" the attorney asked.

"Momma Janet's phone number."

The attorney's face reddened. He asked, "Can we have a second?"

Lillie lifted her eyebrows. Quinn walked with her outside, where Lillie lit up a cigarette and blew some smoke into the wind. "Give him two minutes, he'll want to cut some kind of deal. You know the D.A.?"

"Met him at Johnny Stagg's party."

"What'd you think?"

"I think he had his teeth capped and gets fifty-dollar haircuts."

"This kid doesn't have to be Matlock to be working the Mara-as-victim defense," Lillie said. "Just let him roll with it. See if she'll tell us more about what was going on in that shithole."

Quinn nodded.

"She gets to the point of getting tired, emotional," Lillie said, "maybe we find out where they stashed those kids. Janet didn't say shit on that tape, but that doesn't mean Mara doesn't know. That woman has her scared shitless."

The attorney opened the side door. He asked for directions to the bathroom. His suit jacket looked two sizes too large.

After a couple minutes, they were back at the old school table. Quinn sat at the head and Lillie sat across from Mara and her public defender. "Miss Black wants to help out in every way with the investigation," he said. "You know she was taken out of high school to help her mother? She saw a lot of things."

Quinn nodded.

"But for her to implicate her own mother, she can't be charged as an accessory in the death of the child. Miss Black was as much a victim as those missing kids."

Lillie cut her eyes at Quinn. She nodded.

"Let's hear what she has to say," Quinn said. "If it gives us more on Janet and Ramón, I give you my word I'll put in a good word with the D.A."

"She doesn't know where they are," the attorney said. "But she wants to help."

"You mind me doing the asking?" Lillie asked. "Mara? I don't have any doubts about how rough you had it. We just need to hear it from you. What happened in that house? You shut down when we were talking last week. But we need to know."

Mara leaned back in her chair. She was crying pretty freely and used the back of her hand to keep her face dry. She shook her head and did some more face wiping. "She said she'd kill me then, too. This wasn't no different."

"What did she say?" Quinn asked.

"If I didn't change the diapers, keep them from crying. She hated the crying. She said it made her blood pressure go sky-high. Sometimes I'd try to calm the babies so she wouldn't come in screaming."

Mara dropped her head into her hands. She closed her eyes.

"What would she do if she was mad?" Quinn asked.

The attorney took some notes. He looked up from his notepad and listened, waiting for Mara to continue. He loosened his tie as if the real work was about to start and leaned back in the folding chair.

"She hit them," Mara said.

"For crying?"

"For crying, for being dirty. For it all. Sometimes there would be handprints on the crib. It was their own mess. You know, shit. Kids trying to clean the shit off themselves, and she got mad about that. If they wouldn't stop crying, she made me pour Tabasco in their mouths."

"She made you," the attorney said. "Right?"

"We heard her, Counselor," Lillie said.

"What else?"

"When they got older," Mara said. "You know, the ones we sold?"

"How many?" Lillie asked.

Mara thought about it for a few seconds. "I guess ten?"

"Same routine?" Quinn asked.

"Momma would strap them to their bed with a belt, so they couldn't move. They try to fight it. These were the kids who were two and three, and Momma would hold their heads under water in a tub out back. I tried to stop her. Jesus, I tried to stop her. She about killed two of 'em. I thought one was dead till he started choking out water."

Quinn didn't move or speak. Lillie rubbed her forehead as she listened. Mara's attorney's face dropped all color. He took a deep breath and sat up straight in the metal chair, cheek twitching.

"Where are they, Mara?" Lillie asked.

"I don't know."

"You knew a phone number," Quinn said.

"I don't know."

"I can't have anything happen to those kids," Lillie said.

"I had forgotten her number," Mara said. "It came to me last night. That's all."

"You can set this thing straight," Lillie said. "You never have to deal with your momma ever again."

The attorney stood up. He looked to Mara and motioned for her to do the same. He buttoned the top button of the big coat. "That's it," he said. "That's all. That's all."

"You have to go through law school to learn that?" Lillie asked. "We don't think Mara hurt those kids. Mara, what would happen if you disobeyed Momma?"

"She'd come at me," Mara said. "She'd hit me in the face. Take a belt to me. Said I was a worthless piece of shit. A fat nothing. She said she'd kill me. Just like she said last night."

"Where are those kids, Mara?" Lillie asked.

"I swear to Jesus, I don't know."

Quinn looked to her attorney and held up the flat of his hand. The attorney looked at Quinn with an open mouth but stayed silent. "If you were going to take a guess, where would you guess they are?"

Mara shook her head and watched Quinn with flat eyes. "They're in Mexico. Things got rough, that's where Momma said she'd head. Don't ask me where in Mexico, 'cause I don't know. But Ramón's people were there. Momma said they controlled the law."

22

JOHNNY STAGG HAD LOANED DONNIE A '99 KENWORTH WITH A 455-HORSE engine and a big condo sleeper in back. The rig was powder blue with a lot of chrome and an airbrushed Mississippi flag on the door that read *Heritage Not Hate*. The cab had a comfortable seat, still slick from a rubdown with Armor All, and a knicked and worn gear shifter that felt solid and smooth in his palm. Donnie wound the gears down, brakes hissing with a step on the pedal, as he took the exit off Highway 78 and onto Bratton Road, looking for the road Luz had told him about. He hadn't been out of Tibbehah County long enough for his coffee to grow cold in his Rebel Truck Stop travel mug. He wished maybe the trip was longer.

"How much farther?" Shane asked. He and Tiny were seated in the back condo cab, watching a movie where Nicolas Cage rides a motorcycle and turns into a demon.

"About a quarter mile," Donnie said. "Why don't y'all drop your dicks and come on and pay attention."

Donnie missed driving a truck, liking the freedom of it. Before the

Guard had called him back, he'd worked for a company out of Tupelo that took him all across America. He could stay up for days, jacked up on pills and bad coffee, living off truck stop T-bones and fried chicken, with a soundtrack playing Waylon, Merle, and Johnny Cash. A man didn't have to answer to no one besides the dispatcher. You could do it alone without a couple numbnuts taking up your air.

Tiny's fat shaved head leaned through the seats as he stared down the country road. "You should see this movie, man. His goddamn head turns into a burning skull."

"Turn that shit off," Donnie said. "Here we go."

Donnie crushed out a cigarette and squinted at the roadside, seeing the sign for the FREEWILL BAPTIST CHURCH and a livestock arena, the county road coming up fast on the left. He'd hoped Luz's people had enough sense to know he couldn't take the trailer up onto mud or gravel or under a bunch of low branches. He was glad to see it was nothing but pavement up to the cattle gate, where that little Mex boy from the carnival sat perched, talking on a cell phone. As Donnie tapped the brakes again and waited for him, the boy jumped off the gate and swung it open wide.

"That the same kid?" Shane asked.

"He could shoot your asshole out at a hunnard yards."

"Bullshit," Tiny said. "He wadn't that good."

"Turn your backside and fart," Donnie said.

The boy motioned the big truck forward with his straw cowboy hat in his hand. Donnie took a deep breath, jacking her into gear and forward down a long dirt road cutting through bare grassy hills dotted with Black Angus. The trailer bumped a bit in his rearview, and he felt the shudder in the cab.

The big red barn was maybe a quarter mile from the road, a good place to unload far away from state troopers. Donnie also figured it was also a good place to get shot in the back of the head and buried maybe ten feet down with a backhoe. Wasn't much, but Shane and Tiny were something.

"I don't like this," Tiny said. "None at all."

"Just step out and look mean," Donnie said. "Let 'em see your guns. And don't play with yourself."

"You worried?" Shane asked.

"If I was worried," Donnie said, "would my ass be here?"

Donnie couldn't see Shane, only hear his lazy ass lounging in the bed back there, the sounds of breaking glass and bullets coming from the television. He spotted Luz at the mouth of the barn, looking better every time. She didn't have to do much, wearing a man's flannel shirt tied up at the waist of her jeans and those Mexican cowboy boots. Her brown eyes looked as big as silver dollars. And, man, those lips.

She motioned him up and into the barn, another large door to exit on the other side, the place some kind of livestock arena, reminding him of that place where they had rodeos just outside Jericho. Sunlight cut in from the open slats on the side of the barn to let the animals breathe; the ground hard-packed, smooth dirt, smoother than the road cutting off the highway.

Alejandro and the three boys he'd met stood by him. He couldn't tell one from the other, all three stout with Indian faces and drooping mustaches. They wore boots and belt buckles the size of dinner plates. Alejandro didn't wear a shirt or shoes, the tattoos from his face and neck stretching down on his chest and veiny arms.

"Descarguen las armas de la camioneta ahora," Luz said. *"Tiene hombres con él Tengan cuidado."*

She watched him as he crawled out from the cab and stretched. Tiny and Shane got out on the other side, both of them holding M4s like when they were in the AFG. They didn't seem to like this situation one damn bit.

"Who are they?" Luz asked.

"Just my boys," Donnie said. "You got your boys, I got mine. Don't let 'em spook you. They're uglier than they are mean."

"Alejandro has your money," she said.

"And I got his guns."

"They're not his."

"Who runs this show, then?"

"We all do."

Donnie nodded and wandered to the back of the trailer, finding a key on his ring and fitting it into a Master Lock, opening up the two doors. Light spilled in on all the crates and boxes made for coffins. Alejandro bumped right on by him, bigger than shit, without even saying excuse me. He had a box cutter in hand and tore into the first plastic band and box. Didn't take him long before he found the first M4s and began piecing one together from the smaller box.

Alejandro walked out to the edge of the trailer, looking for some better light, and studied the fine American craftsmanship. He nodded to Luz and wandered back into the truck. He had the face of Jesus wearing a crown of thorns inked between his shoulder blades.

She handed Donnie a fat rucksack.

Donnie opened it up and found hundred-dollar bills bound in rolls by rubber bands, a hundred bills in each roll. There were a lot of rolls, more money than he'd ever seen, and he counted out every one. Tiny and Shane were hanging out by the tailgate, walking up and around the truck as he'd asked. They'd study the front and rear entrance to the barn, that big open mouth of light.

The boys exchanged glances with the mustached men, dog looks, nobody giving an inch.

"I don't like these guys," Shane said, whispering as much as Shane could whisper. "They smell like tacos."

"Shut up," Donnie said, placing the money back in the bag and watching Luz's boys take the smaller boxes out from the coffin boxes and stack them.

Luz had walked away and helped them arrange the boxes in neat rows. He tossed the rucksack over his shoulder and found her sweating, counting the guns. "Want some help?"

She shook her head.

"I'm gonna take a leak and stretch my legs," he said, hand on her shoulder. "Will I see you again?"

"This shipment goes without me."

"This one," Donnie said. "Y'all want another?"

Luz shrugged. "Perhaps."

"I'd like to see you soon," Donnie said. "I sure miss you, darlin'."

Luz didn't answer, only continued to pack.

Donnie smiled and walked away, catching Tiny's and Shane's eyes and winking at them before walking out the back entrance, a two-acre bass pond stretching out in the distance. The ground was dusty and uneven, big clumps of earth picked up and chewed up by the cows. He had to step around piles of shit as he walked to the edge of the pond by an old oak, the lone tree left on the land, where he took a leak.

Three trailers had been situated up on the far hill. Rusted and busted-up and on blocks. Someone had gotten a grill going, and he could smell the meat cooking from where he stood. A long line of laundry was strung from a couple metal crosses, blowing in the wind. Not much but some kids' clothes, and some drawers that looked bigger than flags.

Donnie lit up and twisted his head back to the barn. He looked back over the pond and up on the hill.

A woman was pulling pins from the laundry and stuffing them into a sack. Two small kids in diapers wandered after her. Donnie couldn't see much about the kids, other than them toddling around. But the woman, she was hard to miss.

She ripped down the big drawers off the line and snatched up the children toward the house. One tried to squirm from her arms, but she grabbed the child by the neck until it settled down. Donnie could hear her screaming voice all across the way.

Janet Torres wandered back into the trailer and slammed the door shut.

"God damn it all to hell," Donnie Varner said.

23

"IF THEY'RE IN MEXICO," DINAH BRAND SAID, "WE'RE ALL SCREWED. WE won't ever get them. Ramón Torres's brother is high up in the cartel, right under *el jefe*. He can do whatever the hell he wants. They could be anywhere."

"That's terrific news," Quinn said. "What about the Mexican police or *Federales*?"

"Don't you read the papers?" Dinah said. "The cartels own the police. They own the Army. Most of Los Zetas is made up of guys like you. Special Forces guys who decided to ditch the Army and run drugs."

"I wasn't Special Forces," Quinn said. "Just a Ranger."

"These guys have military training, and then they train the younger guys," Dinah said. "You have military-style operations in major cities, guys in black fatigues kicking in doors and executing top cartel members. Right now, Los Zetas is making a play against the boys in Sinaloa. Whoever wins will run the whole damn country."

"And that's why they need a shitload of guns."

"It's beyond drugs," Dinah said. "It's a war. Last summer, they took out the leaders of another cartel and had their heads dumped on the floor of a disco. Isn't much of a stretch to see this thing headed out of the borderlands."

Quinn sat on the edge of his desk. Dinah Brand stood, wearing a navy V-neck sweater and gray pencil skirt that hit her just at the knee. She wore brown riding boots that didn't look like they would fare too well in a pasture. Her red hair had been brushed straight back and tucked behind her ears. She looked freshly scrubbed.

"You want to talk to Mara again?" Quinn asked.

"You think it would do any good?"

Quinn shook his head. "The girl is tapped out. Can y'all help us with the phone trace?"

"If it's a throwaway, it won't tell us much."

"What about location?"

"Cheap ones don't have GPS."

"I'm sorry you drove all this way for nothing," Quinn said. He took a deep breath, sheriff's office ball cap in hand, crushing the brim into a tight curve. "I guess we could have talked about all this shit on the phone."

"You had promised me dinner," Dinah said, smiling.

Quinn looked up from the floor. "I know a good place."

"The Sonic?"

"I can do a little better than that," Quinn said, grinning. He walked to the coatrack and snatched up his uncle's old leather rancher. "How do you feel about catfish?"

PAP'S PLACE OCCUPIED a brick building in downtown Jericho that had once been a five-and-dime. The interior was a long, straight shot filled with tables covered in red-and-white-checked oilcloth, a tin stamped ceiling, and replicas of stuffed catfish hanging from wires. Icons of Elvis Presley—the owner a great pal and kindred spirit of Quinn's mom—and Jesus Christ hung on the walls. A framed advertisement for MISSISSIPPI FARM-RAISED CATFISH stood side by side with a cardboard tablet of the Ten Commandments. Everything was buffet style, steam and good smells rising from trays of fried catfish, French fries, hush puppies, macaroni and cheese, and collard greens. Sweet tea came in quart-sized plastic cups, with a pitcher left on your table. No alcohol of any kind was served or allowed, according to the sign by the door.

"You ever wonder why Mississippi is the fattest state in the nation?" Quinn asked.

"Not anymore," Dinah said, cutting into the catfish with a knife and fork instead of picking it up and eating it like a regular person.

"My family has always eaten like this," Quinn said and reached for a bottle of Tabasco. "This is the same stuff they ate fifty years ago, but back then, you'd spend all day tending to your crop and cattle. Now most people only walk from their couch to their cars or maybe their mailbox. One of my friends from high school weighs more than four hundred pounds."

"Maybe I should have gotten a salad."

"You see one on the menu?"

Dinah smiled and helped herself to another bite. The catfish was crispy, spicy, and very hot.

"I eat like this maybe once a week," Quinn said. "But I run. I try and run every day. I have hills up around my place. One of my deputies runs with me sometimes, too."

"Lillie?"

"Yep."

"I don't think she cares for me."

"Lillie doesn't care for most people," Quinn said. "Don't take offense."

"I don't think she's said two words to me."

"She knows you're looking for leads to the guns," Quinn said. "She only cares about those kids. She thinks your investigation is going to get in our way."

"Isn't it the same thing?" Dinah asked, taking another bite of catfish. "I get the guns, you guys get the kids. I have resources you don't have.",

"That's the way I see it."

Dinah ate for a while and looked around the room at all the framed pictures of Jesus and Elvis. A heavyset couple waddled toward the door, both with toothpicks hanging out the corner of their mouths. They wore matching Mississippi State sweatshirts.

A waitress wandered over and refilled their cups from a fresh pitcher of sweet tea. An elderly woman worked an old-fashioned cash register up front, where they sold candy to support Boy Scouts and packs of gum.

Dinah smiled at him. Quinn smiled back.

"You have a problem with this?" she asked.

"What's that?" Quinn asked.

"Sharing a catfish plate?" Dinah said. "Might start rumors."

"What's wrong with me having dinner with a federal agent? I'd call that cooperation among law enforcement. I'd do the same if you were a fat old man."

"Really."

"Well, that may be stretching it."

"You know, I did some checking up on you," Dinah said. She pushed her plate away and took a sip of tea. Her eyes were a light gray that went nice with the red hair and freckles. There was something kid-like about Dinah Brand that he liked, the hard shell from their first meeting dropped.

"Why's that?'

"You've been a busy man," she said. "How many tours?"

"Enough."

"And you were wounded? What do you have? Four Purple Hearts?"

"They give those things away when you twist your damn ankle."

"That's not true."

Quinn shrugged and kept eating the catfish. He watched the cook come back from the kitchen and dump out dozens more fresh from the fryer. He doused another fish with Tabasco.

"And then you come home last year and run into some really fine people."

"There were some issues needed to be addressed," Quinn said, stripping away meat from bone. "That's all done."

"About your uncle? He was into this?"

"I'm not one to judge," Quinn said. "There was a bad situation in this town, and I wanted to help. That's pretty much it. I don't think my uncle knew how deep of a shit pile he'd stepped in."

"But some people got killed?"

"Did you know they have a dessert bar?" Quinn asked. "Do you like banana pudding?"

"A lot of those meth peddlers are in business now with the cartels," Dinah said. "I worked a case over in Shelby County, Alabama, last year. Five Mexicans were executed on a farm there. I think you all are about to have the same problem."

Quinn watched her and stopped eating for a moment.

"That's how it starts," Dinah said. "These organizations will have cells in small towns and counties. Your county is ideal, because it's got access to the highway, and it's far enough from a major city to escape attention."

"I pay attention."

"You're not the typical backwoods lawman."

"Appreciate that."

"And much younger than expected," she said. "How old are you anyway?"

Quinn told her.

"You've been kicking in doors since you were eighteen?"

"I hit the ground running when I joined up," Quinn said. "This is my retirement."

"So why'd you come back? You could have left being a Ranger and gotten an Army desk job and drawn a hell of a retirement before you were forty. You wouldn't have to work for the rest of your life."

"I grew up here," Quinn said. "My uncle left me a nice bit of land. My mom, sister, and her boy live in town. He's three."

"Is your dad living?"

"I guess," Quinn said. "Like I said, I haven't heard from him in years."

"What was it like growing up the son of a stuntman? Guess it was hard for him to tell you to be careful."

"This isn't fair," Quinn said. He motioned for the waitress and ordered some coffee.

"What's that?" Dinah Brand asked, smiling, having some fun with him. He felt her foot kicking at his boot.

"You got a file on me, and I don't know much about you," he said.

Dinah leaned in over the table. Quinn met her halfway and grinned.

"What do you want to know?" she asked.

"You got to head back to Oxford tonight?"

"I'm an adult."

"You want to come back to my place for coffee?" Quinn said. "Let me interrogate you?"

"You good at it?"

"Talking?"

"Interrogating."

Dinah eyes moved over him, and her mouth pursed into a wicked smile. The waitress came back and started to fill his glass. Quinn lifted his hand and said he'd changed his mind.

"I got a great dog, too," Quinn said. "His name is Hondo. I want y'all to meet."

"Like John Wayne."

"He walks just like him."

"Coffee?" she said.

"Brew it myself," Quinn said.

He felt her foot rest against his as he reached for the check.

24

IT GOT PRETTY HEATED ON THE COUCH BEFORE DINAH BRAND USED THE flat of her hand to push Quinn away and pull down her sweater. They'd been on the couch a good long while, and the nice, slow kisses had turned into something a lot more rushed, with some heavy breathing and wandering hands. He'd put a Tammy Wynette record on his uncle's old stereo, and he figured that "I Don't Wanna Play House" had been the one that had pushed her over the edge, lying long and prone on the couch, taking Quinn's face in her hands and letting out a long sigh as she reclined. Quinn had tried to hold her hand and pull her back to his bedroom, but that's when Dinah Brand, Special Agent, returned, and she shook her head with that palm on his heart as she said, "Easy. Easy. This is way too fast, Sheriff."

Tammy Wynette sounded so sweet, singing from the salon with the lights off and a nice fire going in the old stone fireplace. Hondo didn't even lift his head as the drama had been going on. The fire kicked up sparks, popping and hissing.

"I got a spare room," Quinn said. "You could stay over. It's too late to drive back."

"I'm a big girl."

"I get that," Quinn said.

"How about a drink?" Quinn asked.

"I said I need to drive home."

"Coffee?"

"OK. Coffee would be nice."

Quinn used an old speckled percolator on his gas stove, spooning in some of the grounds his buddy at Fort Lewis had sent. Good dark-roast stuff from Seattle. Quinn took good whiskey, bacon, and coffee as required items.

"I meant to tell you we connected a few folks in Memphis to a cell in Houston."

"Yeah?"

"They work the carnival circuit," Dinah said. "How about that? We think that's probably how they're running drugs and guns."

"No kidding."

"Same group set up a Ferris wheel for your harvest festival."

"I was there," Quinn said. "I brought my nephew."

"That's probably where they did some business with Ramón."

Quinn nodded.

"We know they'd put the word out to some gun dealers," Dinah said. "We got them making some straw purchases in Grenada and some more in Southaven. But I don't think they got all they were after. I showed you a picture of a couple of them. You remember a woman named Laura? Zuniga?"

Quinn shook his head. He leaned against the edge of his kitchen counter.

When the kissing and hands had started, they'd both laid their guns on the kitchen table, and Dinah Brand reached for hers before taking a seat. Quinn moved his gun to the kitchen counter with a smile, the water starting to boil. Hondo padded into the kitchen and looked up at him before Quinn let him out the back door and he rushed out barking at some deer. The screen door closed behind him with a thwack.

"You don't keep much but the basics here," Dinah said.

"I got what I need."

"What do you need?"

"Coffee, whiskey, and books."

"And guns?"

"I got that safe after I got this farm," Quinn said. "My uncle had a lot of collectibles. He had them lying all around the house. I found some under his bed and in boxes. This place was a real mess when he died."

"And the town, too."

"Some people turned him," Quinn said. "They preyed on his weakness. He wasn't right in the head."

"Johnny Stagg?"

"You've read up."

"He seems as slippery as they get."

"I'm working on it," Quinn said. "Milk and sugar?"

Dinah nodded, and he poured her coffee into a thick ceramic mug. He placed a sugar bowl and glass bottle of Brown Family Dairy milk, along with a spoon, before her. Hondo was scratching at the back door, and Quinn let him back inside. It had grown chilly outside, and a gust of wind kicked into the kitchen. There was no moon tonight, and the farmland was still and quiet.

"I really do have a spare room."

"You could get me in a lot of trouble," Dinah said. "You do know that?"

"You can sleep in my room," Quinn said. "Bed is better. I'll take the couch. I got a nice fire going. It's no trouble."

"What time is it?"

"One."

Dinah nodded. She poured a little milk into the coffee and stirred in some sugar. Hondo rested at her feet and looked up with his mismatched eyes at Quinn. Her face had been chafed from all the kissing. He hadn't meant to, but her sensitive skin was marked up pretty good.

"How long have you been in Mississippi?" Quinn asked.

"This is my first year."

"And before that, you were in Alabama?"

"I've pretty much been in the Southeast from the start."

"You always like this line of work?"

"Sure," she said. "My father was in the FBI. I admired what he did. Hey, is that your family?"

Quinn looked up at the wall at a shot of the Beckett family. Quinn's grandfather was one of five barefoot kids standing with his great-grandfather and great-grandmother in front of the farmhouse. The photo was sort of a *Southern Gothic* without the pitchfork, more a family milling about for a traveling WPA photographer in the 1930s.

"This is the same house?"

"Our family built this place in 1895."

"And you must love that history."

"We've been in this county since right before the Civil War."

Dinah nodded and drank her coffee. She dropped one hand and rubbed the scruff of Hondo's neck. He liked it so much, his back leg twitched and scratched involuntarily.

"I do the same thing if you scratch me," Quinn said.

Dinah smiled. She took another sip of coffee.

"You have an extra toothbrush?"

"Yep."

"And some pajamas?"

"I can round something up."

Quinn walked ahead and showed her the simple room where he

kept the iron bed, a footlocker, dresser, and nightstand. The only thing hanging on the walls was a flag flown at Camp Spann in Afghanistan. Colonel George Reynolds had presented him with it on what would be his last tour with the 3rd Batt. All of his other mementos—beret, weapons, medals—were locked up tight in the trunk. He hadn't opened it since he'd been home.

Quinn cut on a small lamp on the nightstand and pulled back the cover.

Dinah was there as he turned, and she grabbed his hand, and kissed him on the cheek. She used the flat of her hand, this time to push him down on the edge of the bed, and she walked to the door and closed it with a light click.

"Don't talk about this."

"No, ma'am."

"To anyone."

"Yes, ma'am."

"Especially to the deputy who doesn't like me."

"Lillie."

"Especially Lillie."

"You bet."

Dinah laid her weapon on the nightstand, stripped out of her clothes, and clicked off the table lamp.

25

ANNA LEE STOPPED BY THE SHERIFF'S OFFICE THE NEXT MORNING TO TELL Quinn that his sister had gone batshit crazy.

"Tell me something I don't know."

"She's at Jason's daycare right now and won't leave."

"Least she's spending time with her son."

"She called the woman who runs the place a Nazi Bitch."

"Mrs. Shelton?"

"What it all boils down to is that Caddy thinks Jason is being treated differently."

Quinn nodded, put down the morning reports, and stood up. Anna Lee looked as if she wanted to say more, Quinn knowing what she wanted to say, thinking: *What the hell is the big deal?*

"Treated differently because he's a Methodist?"

"Son of a bitch, Quinn," Anna Lee said. "You know what I'm saying. 'Cause he's half black."

"Holy shit," Quinn said. "Which half?"

Anna Lee shook her head and frowned. "You can make fun of this all you want, but your sister is making quite a scene down there. She's blocked the other parents from leaving the parking lot till she gets an apology."

"Just what did Mrs. Shelton do again?"

"Quinn?" Anna Lee said.

"Yep."

"It's Caddy."

"Ten-four."

Quinn had brought Hondo to work with him that morning, and the cattle dog rode shotgun high up in the old truck, the doors creaking and shocks squeaking. The passenger window had stopped working, and a tractor had thrown up a rock last week, spiderwebbing part of his windshield.

Quinn put in a call to Boom, checking on that new truck. Boom didn't answer. He tried his mother and got voice mail. He really didn't want to handle this but figured putting a deputy on it would be cowardly.

True to what Anna Lee had said, Caddy's Honda had blocked the entrance to the ABC Learning Center. Caddy was standing toe-to-toe with Mrs. Shelton, finger waving in her face, a lot of yelling. A dozen cars were backed up behind her. Mrs. Shelton nodded with Caddy, looking nervous and apologetic.

Quinn thought about hitting the flashers and trying out the siren.

Instead, he told Hondo to stay and approached the women, Quinn just catching the end of Caddy's speech about Mrs. Shelton never wanting Jason in her school and the way she was always looking at him like he had some kind of disease.

"Morning," Quinn said. "You think we might move this inside and let these people head on?'

"Do you know what this woman did?" Caddy asked.

"Hello, Mrs. Shelton," Quinn said.

Mrs. Shelton took a long breath and closed her eyes. Caddy launched into a story about how Mrs. Shelton had divided the kids into different groups yesterday and made a big deal about how Jason was an African. She even had him point out parts of Africa on the map. "Can you believe that shit?" Caddy asked.

Mrs. Shelton shook her head and closed her eyes. She kept shaking her head.

"This is a traffic issue right now," Quinn said. "Let's work on that family issue somewhere else."

"I'm not moving my car," Caddy said. She crossed her arms across her chest and clenched her jaw. Old Mrs. Shelton had walked away, talking to the parents who were waiting in line, trying to get out.

"This ain't the best way to handle it."

"What the hell do you know?" Caddy asked.

The keys to the Honda flashed in Caddy's hand, and Quinn plucked them from her fingers, crawled inside, and moved the car off the road, parking along the shoulder of Main Street. Hondo watched him from the driver's side of the truck, panting up a nice fog on the window.

"Don't you care?" Caddy asked. "Don't you give a shit what she called your nephew?"

Quinn kept walking. The cars moved on out of the way. Most of the parents knew him, and they knew Caddy, and passed with an apologetic wave. Caddy followed him inside the school, where Mrs. Shelton waited. The hall was cinder block and lined with finger paintings with a Halloween theme. Pumpkins, skeletons, a few bats.

"Your son offered the information," Mrs. Shelton said. "He pointed out on the map that his family was from Africa."

Quinn rubbed the back of his neck. His cell phone rang. Quinn saw it was his mother and turned it off.

"I can settle this," Quinn said.

"I want an apology," Caddy said. "He's three years old, and if the children start seeing him as something scary and different it will change his whole life. He'll be an outcast in this shitty little town."

Quinn held up his hand.

"I told him his people were from Africa, Caddy," Quinn said.

"What?"

"Hell, he asked. I have that big *National Geographic* map at the farm and I was showing him all the places I'd been. I showed him different spots in Iraq and Afghanistan, and over in Scotland where our people come from. He asked about his daddy's people, and I showed him Africa. I didn't see any harm in that."

"You didn't?" Caddy said. Her face had turned red. "What the hell were you doing?"

"I think they call it geography."

"I don't like this," Caddy said. "I think he was made an example. It's sick to do that with a child."

Caddy turned, ripped the keys back out of Quinn's hand, and hustled back to her Honda. She left the parking lot with a big screeching noise.

Quinn turned away. He smiled at the older woman.

"I'm sorry, Mrs. Shelton," Quinn said. "My family is sorry. Did Jason see any of this?"

Mrs. Shelton shook her head, walking Quinn into the daycare and letting him watch Jason sitting cross-legged in front of a teacher reading a story.

Jason looked very content with the tale, his eyes flashing up at the illustrations with a big grin.

"God love her," Quinn said and left.

QUINN AND CADDY MADE CAMP *by the hidden pond at twilight. He'd fished for the last thirty minutes, not needing long to catch a mess of sunfish.*

*He strung them through their gills and carried them back to the small
lean-to where Caddy worked. She'd pulled branches off pine and oak to
fashion walls.*

"You don't need to sweep a dirt floor."

*Caddy didn't listen and continued to sweep using the end of a pine
branch. She hummed along as if it were the most natural thing in the
world.*

"You've gone crazy," *Quinn said.*

"So?"

"I'm gonna build a fire."

"What about the warden?"

"He's too fat and lazy to track at night," *Quinn said.* "By morning we'll
be gone."

"What about the camp?"

"We'll build another."

"But I like this one," *Caddy said.* "It's pretty, and by the lake."

"We walk at a good pace and we can get out of the forest tomorrow,
maybe make our way toward the interstate. We can hitch down to New
Orleans. I can get a job there."

"Can we call Daddy?"

"Hell no," *Quinn said.* "You think he gives a shit about us?"

"That sounds like Momma talking."

"He's the big shot in Hollywood who thinks all that shit he sends at
Christmas means something," *Quinn said.* "I ain't calling him for nothing. He can go ahead and live it up with that big-titty whore he's seeing."

"That's a lie."

"Nope."

"Can I keep sweeping?"

"Sure."

Quinn found some rocks and fashioned a little ring by the edge of the pine. He had a matchbook he'd taken from the Rebel Truck Stop and set fire to some pine bark and shavings from a birch tree. After the fire grew nice and hot, he collected some branches and cedar logs. The cedar would give the fish a nice taste.

He used a folding knife with a serrated edge to cut off the fish heads, gut and scale them. He washed the fish at the edge of the pond and threw the heads and guts way out into the water. The sun was almost done now, lights fading through the thick pine trees and oaks with yellow and red leaves.

Caddy sat next to him as the little skillet he'd packed heated in the fire. She leaned into his coat, and he stretched his arm around her. They watched the final light crossing the land, bleeding out until they were all in shadow.

A wind whipped fast and cold up across them, knocking down part of the lean-to. Caddy ran and picked up the branches and again made her wall. The wind was cold and brisk and made the woods seem even larger and more hollow than they were.

Everything was so quiet way up here, almost like some kind of holy place.

Quinn loved it. But Caddy was scared.

He opened up the dried peaches and let her eat first while he turned the fish in the hot oil. The fire brought a nice comfort to them, smelling of sweet cedar and spiced cornmeal and fish.

The pines swayed in the night breeze as the fire popped and hissed.

The fish was crisp and delicious, and after he scrubbed the skillet clean in the pond, Quinn reached into his coat for some tobacco and he chewed a bit, spitting into the fire.

Caddy stayed and leaned against him.

"Can I read to you?"

"What did you bring?" Quinn asked.

"*What was on your shelf.* Last of the Mohicans *and* The Tales of King Arthur."

"*You'll like King Arthur.*"

"*I would have brought my own books but had to hurry.*"

"Caddy, if there is trouble, I want you to run," Quinn said. "Can you find your way home?"

"*I think so.*"

Quinn reached into his mackinaw and handed her a compass. She clutched it in her little hand and smiled, pulling her knees up to her nose and kicking her feet with excitement.

"There won't be trouble," Caddy said.

"Walk west and you'll hit the interstate," Quinn said. "Call Uncle Hamp, and he'll get you. But if something happens, you run. Don't stay on account of me. I got to settle this myself."

"Why won't you call Daddy?"

"He quit on us," Quinn said. "Somebody quits on me, and I don't have no use for him."

"He still loves us."

"Can you read to me?" Quinn said, spitting into the fire. "I like that story about Gawain and the Green Knight."

Caddy thumbed through the pages, reading to the sounds of owls and wandering deer, night birds and bats. She smiled as she read, and kept smiling in her sleep.

Quinn pulled his mackinaw over her and watched the fire. He filled his rifle with .22 longs and waited.

26

THE BEAUTY OF OWNING YOUR OWN BUSINESS WAS ROLLING YOUR ASS out of bed and walking straight down the hill to work. Donnie had three trailers he kept on his old family hunting land: the old Airstream, a single-wide he rented out to Tiny, and a double-wide he used as the gun store. In the gun store, he kept six old candy cases he'd taken from the movie theater downtown—before it had become that crazy church—where he displayed his pistols and automatics, handcuffs and mace. Behind the counter, he kept the rifles and assault weapons in a locked gun rack. Most folks just came by the range to buy some ammo and rent those assault weapons. Businessmen from Tupelo would bring a cooler of beer and shoot AK-47s into targets of Osama bin Laden or President Obama. Not that Donnie was political, that's just what seemed to be selling that year.

He opened up at nine, unlocking the cattle gate at the end of his road. Tiny's fat ass wasn't even up yet as Donnie bounded up the wooden steps to the shop and turned on the lights and turned off the alarm. A lot of what he did at the shop was answering phone calls and taking orders off the Internet. He'd get maybe two people stop by on weekdays. Saturdays were his busiest time when it wasn't hunting season or football season.

He ate a bowl of Frosted Flakes as he checked his e-mail and leaned back into his seat to fire up his first cigarette of the day. Someone was looking for a Smith & Wesson .38 with a six-inch barrel. Another fella wanted to know if he could get him a good deal on a Henry rifle. There was the daily devotional his aunt had forwarded, and a couple messages from a girl he used to date in Eupora. She wanted him to know she was getting married in the spring, saying it in kind of an ugly way. Tiny had sent him a pornographic picture of a woman having sex with a pickle.

Donnie shook his head and shut down the computer. He had a week to come up with another order of guns for Luz and her banditos. She said this would be their final order for a while, maybe their final order ever, because they all had to boogie on down the road to Louisiana and then back south of the border.

He'd asked her how they got the guns back in.

She just smiled at him.

He figured they did it with those carnival trucks. You could hide a mess of guns in those contraptions. And he imagined it wasn't too hard to grease the wheels of the Mexican border folks. They weren't looking for drugs coming into Mexico.

Donnie hadn't asked her about Janet Torres and those kids.

He didn't even mention them to Shane and Tiny. That wasn't his concern or his business. He didn't even think Luz knew about them. And if she did, that was something she'd have to make right with Jesus, Mary, and Joseph in the confessional. Donnie ran guns. Luz had ordered them. If he started trying to make judgments and getting involved in things that didn't involve him, everything he'd worked hard for in Trashcanistan would come tumbling down. Shit, it took a five-grand investment to grease those wheels in the AFG.

Donnie didn't have shit to come home to, and bringing them M4s with him was about the smartest thing he ever did. All those guns were supposed to be given to the goddamn local police. And what would happen to those guns? As soon as Uncle Sam's ass pulled out of the armpit of this earth, those guns would wind up with the Taliban, al-Qaeda, or some other assholes with barrels aimed back at Americans. If he wanted to sell them to a bunch of Mexicans so they could kill one another, he figured he was doing this country a goddamn service.

Donnie walked outside, flicked his cigarette into the kudzu, and heard a truck approach from down the road. He thought it was probably Shane, wanting his cut from the truck run up to New Albany. He knew it wasn't Luz, the girl just shining him on till she got what she wanted and could hit up the next dumbass with a nice arsenal for sale. He'd called her ten times since yesterday, not getting a voice mail or nothing.

Quinn Colson drove up and stopped not two feet from him. He waved and smiled at Donnie.

"You want to do some shooting?" Quinn asked.

Donnie smiled. "Shit, why not?"

Donnie rounded up a couple targets, basic bull's-eye patterns he set out at fifty yards. Both he and Quinn were wearing guns. Quinn had a 9mm Beretta and Donnie had a Glock he'd brought down from the shop. It wasn't his favorite weapon, but it was there and handy and loaded.

"I just nearly had to arrest my sister."

"What did Caddy do now?" Donnie asked before squeezing off all seventeen rounds into a tight center pattern.

"She stopped traffic at her boy's daycare," Quinn said. "She wouldn't move her car till she got an apology from Mrs. Shelton. Can you believe that shit?"

"What'd Mrs. Shelton do?"

"Nothing," Quinn said. He stretched out his arm and unloaded his Beretta. "She was scared."

Donnie watched Quinn unholster his gun. "You like that Beretta?"

Quinn nodded and squeezed off those rounds. The shots cracked through the wilderness. He was good. Better than anyone Donnie had ever seen. Quinn could always shoot like that, like he'd been born to it.

"It's served me well," Quinn said. "I guess I got used to it."

"You might think about getting some new guns for the department," Donnie said. "Your uncle used to carry that lever-action Winchester with him like it was the damn eighteen hundreds. I don't think he ever updated even a pistol."

Quinn nodded.

"I can get y'all a good deal," Donnie said. "You can bid it out, but I'll make it worth your time."

"Might be a while before the county supervisors give me another nickel," Quinn said. "I just got Boom hired to run a maintenance shed, and they acted like I was trying to rob them. You know we're pretty much the only county in the state that doesn't service our own vehicles?"

"Yeah, I heard you and Stagg got into it."

"I made it known Stagg didn't want a shed so he could keep selling fuel out of the truck stop. At a nice profit, of course."

"Stagg never heard of a conflict of interest," Donnie said. "Don't come natural to him."

Quinn reloaded his Beretta from a box of bullets Donnie had brought from the shop. Donnie dropped out his magazine and did the same. A soft gold light fell across the rolling acres of kudzu and skinny pine trees and shone hard off the top of his silver Airstream. Up the hill, he saw Tiny walking out to his front stoop to take a leak. He waved with his free hand.

"Reason I came by is I wanted to talk to you more about your friend, the Mexican girl."

Donnie nodded.

"We need to talk to her, bud."

Donnie shook his head and snicked the clip back into the Glock. "I don't know what to tell you. I met the girl, took her to the Sonic, and tried too soon for the sugar patch. I hadn't seen her since. You know, this morning I got a goddamn e-mail from a woman I seen maybe three times. She lives over in Eupora and wrote me some crazy-ass letter about her getting married. Saying it real ugly, telling me that her fiancé had a good job at the Kroger meat department. What does that mean to me? Discount T-bones?"

"Lillie went looking for your girl at the beauty shop," Quinn said. "The women there didn't know anything about her."

Donnie shrugged.

Quinn fingered in more bullets, doing it quick and easy, not even paying attention to the loading, as natural as a man could breathe. "You said that's how you met her. You'd think a looker like that would be pretty known in Jericho."

"I said I thought she was friends with those women. Hell, I don't know. You come over here just to bust my nuts?"

"I came down to shoot," Quinn said. "If I don't shoot a target, I may just have to shoot my sister."

"You hadn't gotten used to Caddy yet?"

"She's come home to make trouble," Quinn said. "And she'll leave like she always does."

Donnie walked out to the targets and replaced them with new ones, tacking them up with long pins into Styrofoam. He handed Quinn the one he'd shot up. The pattern was as neat as if he'd sketched it with a paintbrush. Donnie was just as accurate, killing the target just the same, but it was loose and wild-looking up close.

"You know me and Caddy got together while you wasn't here," Donnie said. "I couldn't handle her, either."

"She doesn't want to be handled," Quinn said. "I think that's most of her trouble. She doesn't know what the hell she wants."

"She's just wild," Donnie said. "That may piss you off, saying that, man. I'm sorry. But you know you can do nothing about a person when they gone wild."

"You forget how I used to be?"

"Army straightened your ass out."

Quinn nodded.

"Didn't do that for me," Donnie said. "I hate people telling me what to do. When to eat, when to sleep, when to shit. You know, I had to study a diagram on how to properly put in a latrine? A fucking ditch where we would piss and shit. We had this lieutenant right out of West Point who handed a blueprint to me as if it had come down from Mount Sinai. We lit us a little fire under there while he was on the commode."

Quinn smiled.

"I need you to find that girl," Quinn said. "I don't care what you're into with her. Doesn't matter to me. But I got to find those kids."

"You ever figure out how that woman ever got all those children?"

"Bought 'em," Quinn said. "Her daughter said some of the older girls were sold on the Internet, taken to Atlanta, and pimped out. They were what? Twelve? Thirteen?"

Donnie felt his face color, a nauseous feeling down deep. He turned and spit. He pulled out a pack of cigarettes and started to thump them, shaking his head to let Quinn know the whole thing made him sick.

"What she's got now is six little girls and five little boys," Quinn said. "They're all under five years old. Two of them have special needs. Her daughter Mara told us they came cheaper that way. Like dented-up goods at a grocery."

"Bad stuff."

"I can't imagine a person who'd beat a child like that. She poured hot sauce into their mouths if they cried. If that didn't work, she'd dunk them in water till they passed out. She'd fly into rages, and ole Ramón and Mara had to restrain her."

Donnie nodded, the smoke clouding Quinn's face as he spoke. "Bad stuff."

"You help us out?" Quinn asked.

"What do you think she'll do with the kids?"

"We're not talking about stable people here," Quinn said. "We think she may already be in Mexico. But if not, she'll probably try to get rid of the kids before she travels."

"Well, that's good."

"I don't think she wants to leave any evidence," Quinn said. "Understand?"

Donnie started a new cigarette before the other one had even gone out. His hands shook as he lit up, and Quinn noticed the shaking.

Quinn holstered the Beretta and tipped the brim of his baseball hat.

"You know where to find me," he said.

27

"WELL, YOU AIN'T GONNA GET JACK SHIT FROM DONNIE VARNER," BOOM said. "You know you can't trust his ass. Remember that time we did all that work planting those trees, and Donnie took a cut of what we made? What did he say when we confronted him?"

"He said he deserved it," Quinn said, "because he was the one who got us the job. He called it a finder's fee."

"It's always been chickenshit like that. He'd sell you out for a Coca-Cola, man. You know that's the truth."

"You think he's the one who gave us up when we borrowed that fire truck?" Quinn asked.

"I know it was him," Boom said. "He got caught, and your uncle leaned on him. He figured he'd get it easier if the sheriff's nephew was in on it."

"I never found out."

"Who else knew we took that thing?"

"Wesley Ruth. Your girlfriend."

Boom looked up from under the hood of a Ford truck up on blocks. He grinned and turned back to his work. "You had Anna Lee on your lap the whole time. You think ole Luke Stevens know that?"

"Doubt it."

"Why we do that crazy shit back then?" Boom said.

"'Cause there wasn't much else to do around here."

"What will you do if you catch some kid doing the same?"

"Put him in jail."

"Ain't that hypocritical?"

"I guess," Quinn said. "How's that truck coming along?"

"Be better if I had more help," Boom said. "I got a fella comes and helps in the morning. But all the supervisors did was OK me for the job and the delivery of two hundred gallons of fuel out here. You know how much they payin' me?"

"Nope."

"Me neither," Boom said, standing up, reaching for a grease rag and rubbing his fingers along it. "Guess it don't matter. I appreciate the job. We'll see about all that crazy bionic shit at the VA. I hear it's a crapshoot and a lot of paperwork to get that kind of device. Right now I can do it, but I drop a lot of shit."

Boom had brought in his own set of tools on a big rolling chest. In the week since the meeting, without an official vote, the county had kicked on the electricity, and small lamps shined down the length of the barn on piles of junk and ragged scrap metal. Quinn made a mental note to bring out a work detail of prisoners to dig into the mess.

"What do you think?" Boom asked.

The big Ford F-250 was up on blocks and stripped of its tires, the windows covered in brown paper, but large and bold in the center of the barn. Boom stood back from the engine and admired the truck. Quinn couldn't see what he was admiring but trusted him.

"You think you'll get her running by Christmas?" Quinn said. "I don't know if the one I have now will make it through the week. Engine sounds like it's about to throw a rod."

"Damn, I just started to work two days ago," Boom said. "First week on the job, and you already giving me shit."

"Let me ask you something," Quinn said. "Did you know Donnie Varner had been seeing Caddy?"

"Man, everybody knew about that," Boom said. "They weren't too private about it."

"She's been giving me a lot of shit since she's been back," Quinn said. "I'm waiting for her to make her dramatic exit and let us all get on with our lives."

"What's Jason think?"

"I think it's confused him."

"But does he like her being around?"

"I don't think the up and down is good for anybody," Quinn said. "This latest act won't last, and then what?"

"Why don't you just try for custody, then?" Boom asked. "You got a history of her ditching town, and with all the drugs and mess."

Quinn shrugged. The wind was bright and cold coming from the mouth of the shed, and the room smelled of gasoline and fresh grease. Boom had swept the dirty concrete to a polished shine. Quinn looked back to Boom and shook his head.

"Caddy had it rough growing up."

"'Cause your daddy?"

"Some," Quinn said. "But other fathers have left. When we were kids, some bad stuff happened to her. Sometimes I forget what that must have been like."

Boom nodded. The right arm of his flannel shirt was neatly pinned at the elbow. His only arm was as thick and hard as the branch of an old oak.

"What happened?" Boom asked.

"You remember when we were kids and I got lost?"

"Yeah, man," Boom said. "Everybody remember that. I thought you was dead. Whole town looking for your ass. It made the papers in Jackson and Memphis. What did the headline read?"

"COUNTRY BOY CAN SURVIVE."

"If it'd been me been lost, wouldn't been no headline. Maybe a little story about a dumb black kid can't find his way home."

"Caddy was with me."

"That's not right," he said. "You were alone."

"She was part of the time," Quinn said. "I got caught poaching some deer, and we ran away. Caddy wouldn't leave and tagged along. We camped out in the National Forest, trying to make our way to New Orleans."

Boom placed a cigarette in his mouth and then reached down on the edge of the truck for his lighter. "What happened to y'all out there?"

"You drinking these days?" Quinn asked.

"I hadn't stopped."

"This is a drinking conversation," Quinn said. "Between us. I don't want you telling Lillie about it. Only man who knew about it is dead."

"Your uncle."

Quinn nodded.

Boom walked over to the wall where he'd hung his coat. Quinn made his way out to his old truck and opened the door, the radio squawking inside. He picked it up, cigar smoldering in the ashtray.

"Where are you?" Lillie asked.

"County Barn."

"You need to make it out to the Traveler's Rest Motel," Lillie said.

"Someone not pay their bill?"

"I don't think this son of a bitch is ever gonna pay his bill."

"Bad?"

"I'm guessing this fella looked better before he got shot in the head," Lillie said.

QUINN WASN'T A STRANGER to seeing dead bodies. In fact, every time he'd get back stateside, he'd think it was strange to go a day without seeing bodies lying in the street. But this was the first time as sheriff he'd been called to a scene of a killing. There had been some near killings, most domestics, a woman trying to cut off a man's pecker, and there had been many natural deaths and two suicides. But there wasn't any mistaking what had happened inside the room of the Traveler's Rest sometime in the last twenty-four hours. Whoever killed the man had stuffed his body up under the bed. The maid had seen the blood spilling out on the carpet.

The body was still there, but the bed had been moved slightly so the body could be photographed. Lillie did the photographing with a digital camera. She wouldn't let anyone else inside the room, making Quinn put on some plastic hospital booties and gloves she kept in the back of her Jeep.

Kenny stood guard outside, waiting for Luke Stevens to arrive.

"Can we move the body?" Quinn asked.

"What do you think?"

"This a quiz?"

"You're in charge," Lillie said. "You tell me."

"And I rely on you to tell me the proper thing to do," Quinn said, catching just the shoulder and stray leg of the dead man. He wore dark jeans and boots. "Don't we have to dust for prints and collect DNA and all?"

"I called the crime lab over in Batesville," Lillie said. "They're sending some techs over."

"What can we do?"

"You're looking at it."

The foot of the bed had been raised a foot by a couple concrete blocks. Lillie handed Quinn a Maglite, and he dropped to one knee to shine the light on the man. He had black hair and a mustache, with a pockmarked complexion that looked like he hadn't shaved for a few days. His black eyes were wide open, and a purplish tongue hung loose in his mouth. He was a big man with a thick body. The blood spilled out in a halo from the back of his head, the wound was small and neat, easily seen after the hair had been parted with a bullet.

"OK if we turn him over and check for an ID?" Quinn asked.

"Already did," Lillie said. "Guess you figured he's not from around here. He has a Mexican driver's license. Francisco Quevedo Sanchez from the state of Chihuahua. Thirty-five years old. Of course he's not in our system. He has what looks like a real visa in there, too. Runs out in two weeks. Place of employment is an outfit out of Houston called Lone Star Amusements."

"That's something."

"You better call your girlfriend," Lillie said. "She might be of more help to us than just entertaining the troops."

"Can we put the bullshit on hold today?" Quinn asked. "Y'all check for his vehicle?"

"He doesn't have any keys on him," Lillie said. "All the cars in this shithole are accounted for."

"Finest motel in Tibbehah."

"It's where you stayed when you first came back," Lillie said. "Good enough for you."

"That's a close-range gunshot," Quinn said. "I'd bet on a .22."

"See, you aren't as bad at this as you think," Lillie said. "What else do you see?"

"Can I check out the drawers and space or will that mess shit up?"

Lillie shook her head, stepped back, snapped some more photos, a flash going off in the small room. The blood had dried in a thick pool around the man's head, but when he walked a few meters toward the bathroom, Quinn saw more blood misted on the wall of the shower and on the rear of the shower curtain. The drawers were empty of any personal items. It looked like he'd just taken a shower, with wet towels on the floor and some dirty clothes kicked in the corner.

"How long till the state people get here?"

"Maybe an hour," Lillie said. "They'll process all this sometime next year."

"You're kidding me."

"State lab is backed up till Easter, they say," Lillie said. "Even then, it's going to take some political pull and a swift kick in the ass. This state doesn't have the money or resources. What we see here is what we get. Besides, looks like someone was real careful on this whole thing. Moved the poor son of a bitch into the tub, might've worked him over there. You see the marks over his eyes? Probably see the same thing on his body. Guess Francisco didn't give it up, and they took his ass out."

"Or he gave them an answer they didn't like."

"There's always that," Lillie said, replacing the memory card in the camera. "Can't help but wonder if this isn't tied in with Ramón Torres. I know, just 'cause this victim is Mexican doesn't mean shit. But, hell. We got two major crimes this month, and it's folks from south of the border. What do you think?"

"I think I'll call Dinah."

"Good excuse as any," Lillie said. "After she meets Francisco, you could take her down to the Fillin' Station for dinner. I hear it's chicken-fried steak night. Give her enough time and she can put on a fresh pair of panties."

Quinn just stared at Lillie. Lillie grinned.

"You know that Mexican woman Donnie was with the other night at the Sonic?" Quinn said. "I saw her picture in a photo pack that Dinah showed me the other day. She was tied in with some cartel along the Gulf."

"Terrific."

A framed picture on the wall of the motel celebrated the sweet potato harvest in 1978. Big blooms surrounded an orange spud. Kenny leaned in the door and looked from Lillie to Quinn and then ducked out the door. Quinn could smell Kenny's cigarette smoke as he stood guard.

"What's the ATF think is going on?"

"I didn't tell her yet," Quinn said. "I wanted to talk to Donnie first."

"That's a mistake, Sheriff."

Quinn reached for his cell phone in his coat and stepped outside. Kenny leaned back into the room, and Lillie told him she'd punch him in the throat if he took one step in her crime scene. Kenny ducked his small goateed chin and said, "Yes, ma'am."

Quinn dialed Dinah's number. He'd have to tell her everything.

28

QUINN LEARNED ALL OF THIS FROM HIS UNCLE, MUCH LATER AFTER IT ALL *happened. His uncle said he never had much patience or time for fools, the man being the most foolish man he'd known. Hamp told Quinn that the warden Porter had waited overnight at the Colson home, worrying the hell out of Jean, asking for some cold fried chicken and downing a six-pack, using her phone and cussing to high heaven. Jean didn't need any more trouble, as those had been the days when she'd drown herself in boxes of wine and stories about Elvis rather than facing what Jason Colson had done to her.*

Porter had been so drunk on some Jack Daniel's that Quinn's daddy had left behind that Hamp Beckett had to kick his legs out from under him to wake him up. Porter's eyes narrowed on the sheriff, fired up with frustration and plain meanness.

"You got 'im?"

"Nope," Beckett said. "Not my job."

"Well, it should be your job, since that boy is your nephew," Porter said, pulling himself to a few inches below Hamp's chin, trying to look like

a lawman in charge. They'd stood on the back deck of the Colson house, loaded down with dead potted plants and Jean's flowers that had burned up in the first frost.

"How far can a kid get?" Porter said. "Holy Christ. Where the fuck would he have gone?"

"You know if I knew, I sure as shit wouldn't tell you," Hamp said. "Why are you here? You're drunk as hell and worrying the crap out of my sister. I'll call you when I find them."

"Them? Who's them?"

"If he killed those bucks like you say, he'll have to answer for it. But why you think you can run roughshod over this whole family is a riddle to me."

"He broke the law," Porter said. "He slashed my tires. Rurned my property. And you said 'them,' god damn it."

"OK," Hamp said. "He killed some deer. But he's also a ten-year-old boy without a daddy."

"I don't get involved in no family drama," Porter said, taking a pack of Red Man out of his shirt pocket. "His sister with him? I knew it. I think she come back here for some supplies. His momma said they're missing some food items. Sounds like someone taking to the woods."

"Then what are you doing dead drunk on this porch?"

Porter made a show out of taking a generous spit and headed back to his state truck, the back window obscured with a loaded gun rack. A hand-painted sign on the door, bragging on the title the state had awarded him. He hung off the door and watched Hamp Beckett follow.

"I don't care if they're kids or not," Porter said.

"You better care, you cocksucker."

"What did you say?"

"I said you are a lazy, stupid, splayfooted cocksucker," Hamp said. "Don't you know who I am?"

"I know who you are."

"Know who I am from some time back?" Hamp said. "You remember me from when those black students from up north went missing? When they found them all buried twenty feet down on Ronnie Hankins's land. They burned Ronnie's ass up like a candle, but he didn't do it alone."

"You're crazy as hell."

"And you ran the backhoe, you cocksucker," Hamp said. "People like you have nothing in your soul, still passing the collection plate on Sunday with a smile on your face."

"That mess don't have shit to do with that boy," Porter said. "And I'll sue your ass out of office, I hear that talk again."

"Sue me, cocksucker."

"I'll fix you."

"Go ahead."

"They got supplies," Porter said. "They took to the woods. I'm the best damn tracker in this county. You better pray you find them first."

Porter slammed the door and pulled away.

Hamp walked back into the house and held his sister's hand. She had already finished off half a box of wine.

"Quinn had a special place, Jean," Hamp said. "He said there was a lake or a pond in the National Forest. What's he told you about it?"

"I don't like that man," Jean said. "He smells rotten."

"That's 'cause he is rotten," Hamp said. "Where's that special place? Can you draw it for me?"

29

QUINN'S MOTHER SAT IN THE DARK WITH JASON ASLEEP ON HER LAP, watching a late-night movie starring Robert Mitchum as a hell-raising moonshiner. He couldn't remember the name of the film but recalled it being one of his daddy's favorites. Jean put a finger to her lips and began to carry Jason back to his bedroom, but Quinn met her halfway and tucked him in himself. Jean had recently converted Quinn's old bedroom, since it was larger than the guest room, into Jason's. And Quinn was proud to see that Jason wanted to keep some of his old things: a picture of a samurai warrior and a hand drawing of the Knights of the Round Table. The bookshelf had changed some, with *Treasure Island*, Greek mythology, and Nick Adams hunting stories side by side with *The Very Busy Spider* and *Duck Goes Potty*.

Quinn softly laid the boy in bed and closed the door. Jean had the sound off on the television and had lit up a cigarette.

"You want some dinner?" she said. "I put some up for you. I kept the oven warm. Some chicken spaghetti, and I left you a little salad in the refrigerator."

Quinn made a plate and brought it out to the dining room, where you could still see Mitchum on television running shine and ducking cops.

"At least you don't have to chase down moonshiners," Jean said.

"Want to bet?" Quinn said. "We still got the old-timers up in the hills around Carthage who love it. I can see how a man would make shine when the real stuff is illegal. But can you imagine liking the taste?"

Jean shuddered and blew out a trail of smoke by lamplight. "Your granddaddy sure loved that stuff."

"I'll stick to beer."

"Heard you had quite a day," she said.

"Yep."

"Poor Caddy," his mother said. "I know in her mind she was trying to do the right thing. She was supposed to just drop off Jason. I thought it would give her some responsibility, make her feel good about being a mother. Jason must've said something to her on the way to school about all that Africa mess."

"You know I was the one who told him his people came from Africa?"

"Oh, Lord, yes," Jean said. "Caddy told me."

"So now she's pissed at me?"

"She's just mad in general," Jean said. "She's keyed up. I think she's coming down from whatever kind of high life she's been living. Makes her edgy."

"You know what she was on?"

Jean shook her head and walked to the kitchen. She poured a little coffee and sat across from Quinn. The chicken spaghetti was very good. He added a little ranch dressing to his salad that wasn't much more than some lettuce and a slice of tomato. A piece of garlic bread sat at the edge of his plate.

"What I'm worried most about is probably the same thing that worries you," Quinn said. "Stop me if I'm wrong. I'd love to be wrong. But Caddy has come to town with some kind of agenda. She may believe she's going to get her life straight and take Jason back to Memphis."

As soon as he'd said the word he wished he hadn't, as his mother's face changed hue. Jason was her entire world.

"But then it will fall apart, and Jason is going to be the one switching schools and being around God knows what. She pulls that crap again, and I want us to get an attorney."

"I believe she's changed."

"Since when?" Quinn asked.

"We've talked at length."

"About everything?"

"Some of it."

Quinn walked back to the darkened kitchen and fetched a beer. He sat back down. "Just what did she tell you?" Quinn asked.

"She wouldn't tell me some specifics, but talked about some rough stuff that happened when y'all were kids. I was hoping you could shed a little light."

Quinn took a deep breath and dug into the chicken spaghetti some more. Probably the one thing he missed more than anything being away from home for ten years was honest-to-God real food. If he could only eat in peace without the world coming to head over a set table, he'd like it even more. He stopped eating for a moment and studied the wall. He didn't know quite what to say.

"Quinn, honey?" Jean said. "I asked you a question."

Quinn nodded. He drank some beer. Black-and-white images flicked across the living room. "I think that's something that's up to Caddy, Mom," he said. "It's not for me to speak for her."

"But you know," Jean said. "You know what she's talking about? Did it happen to you, too?"

"Shit, what does it matter now?" Quinn asked. "It's all over. It's been taken care of a long time ago."

"Did someone hurt you two? Was this something that happened when I was drinking? Lord God. Please tell me it wasn't while I was such a mess. Please, Quinn."

"Momma, you didn't do anything," Quinn said. "What happened, happened. I don't want to talk about it. OK? In fact, I never want to talk about it. But if Caddy does, that's her own deal."

Jean stared at him for a long moment. She drank some coffee. When Jean wanted to show you her disapproval, she grew very quiet. His mother was the master of the long silence.

"Caddy is getting too old to make a scene like she did today," Quinn said. "And I don't think you need to coddle her, either. She blocks traffic again, and I'm going to have to arrest her. You know that?"

"I know, I know," Jean said, adjusting the narrow old watch on her wrist. "What she did today wasn't smart. It was a step back to her old ways even though she thought she was looking out for Jason. But this thing, whatever it is in her, has been bottled up so damn long. If she could make sense of it, it would be like cleaning house, throwing open the windows. I want to help her with that. I think you should, too."

"You can't make sense of it," Quinn said. "And it's not my place. But I'll talk with her. If that's what she wants."

"You know, Quinn," Jean said, "this may be that one step she has to take before she gets her life in order. I had to make myself understand that your dad was gone and wasn't coming back before I straightened up. We all got things that we have to set right in our heads."

"All that was twenty years ago," Quinn said. "You make decisions, act on them. If the outcome doesn't work, you study it a bit. But you don't let it sink you. You start to backtrack, and it can kill you."

"Army talk?"

"It's the truth."

"I think a preacher might put it another way."

"I'd rather listen to a warrior than a holy man."

"Just like your father."

"He wasn't a warrior," Quinn said. "He was a pretender. He's the one where you should place the blame. Not you. You were trying to hold us together. OK? This thing didn't have anything to do with you."

Most everything in the house was untouched, the same as he always remembered it. The framed pictures of Elvis and Graceland and cheap oils of rolling farmland and simple white houses. Jason had changed some of that and had added a lot of life to the house and to his mother. Everything felt so still here and safe.

"Mitchum was one handsome man," Jean said, trying to compose herself. She snuffled and smiled a bit, trying. "Did you know he was sentenced to time on a Georgia chain gang? I think he wasn't but fourteen or fifteen. He escaped and went to Hollywood."

Quinn reached for his mother's hand and squeezed. Jean Colson started to cry and wiped away the tears with the back of her hand. She gave a weak smile and turned back to the television.

"He was good as the drunk sheriff in *El Dorado*."

"You want some more supper?" Jean asked, picking up the empty plates. "Or another beer?"

"I'm good."

"So how's the rest of your day?" Jean asked. "Anything else interesting happen?"

30

DONNIE WENT TO THE TIBBEHAH HIGH SCHOOL BALL GAME ON FRIDAY night to deliver the gun money to Johnny Stagg. Stagg had told him through Leonard not to even think about dropping by the truck stop unless he wanted a mess of federal agents crawling up his ass. Donnie told Leonard that he preferred not getting his ass crawled and for Stagg to let him know where he wanted to meet. When Leonard called back, Donnie broke out a new pair of Levi's, his best pair of boots, a white T-shirt, and his old Wildcats letter jacket. He'd been a wide receiver for the Wildcats back in the day, playing ball with Boom and Quinn Colson and a fella named Wesley Ruth. In truth, they weren't worth a shit, losing as many games as they won. But like they say, you only get better with age, and to hear the class of '99 tell it, they all could have played D-1 ball if they'd had the grades.

The home bleachers were old and concrete, with narrow steps stretching up to the high seats. The lights shined bright across the crisp green field where Tibbehah and Water Valley were tied up at the half. 7 to 7.

Donnie walked up the far corner of the packed stadium and took a seat by Johnny Stagg. Stagg ate salted peanuts from a paper sack and threw the busted shells at his feet. He wore a bright red sweater and an Ole Miss ball cap, not even acknowledging Donnie as he reached into the sack and grabbed a handful.

"I knew a boy one time who put his pecker in a peanut sack," Donnie said. "Waited till his little lady got hungry."

"You got the money?"

"Hell yes, Johnny," Donnie said. "Jesus Christ. You mind if I stay and watch the third quarter?"

"Water Valley has a colored quarterback who ain't afraid to run, take some hits," Stagg said. "He's one to watch. Heard he already committed to Arkansas. I don't know why we can't keep the good blacks in this state."

Donnie dropped a heavy backpack between him and Stagg. He reached into the sack for a few more peanuts, waiting for the band to clear the field, all of the music an off-tune medley of new country by Keith Urban, Lady Antebellum, Miranda Lambert, and all that assorted bullshit. One of the flag girls wasn't too bad, her cheeks painted up all rosy, and a tight little ass set off in gold sequins.

"This is the first time I've ever known Tibbehah to be undefeated," Donnie said.

"Won state in '63," Stagg said. "Had two players go to Ole Miss. Another fella went to Auburn. We got a senior playing defensive tackle who's a top prospect. I got his momma a job washing dishes at the truck stop."

"You goin' to the game in Oxford?" Donnie asked, not 'cause he gave a shit, but because it was a way of passing the time with Stagg before they talked business. "I know you love the Rebels."

"I own season tickets," Stagg said. "We got a hell of a tent in the Grove."

"Think you might invite me sometime?" Donnie said, cracking a whole peanut shell in his back teeth and spitting out the shells. "Or would I embarrass your high-dollar friends in Oxford?"

"You're welcome anytime, Donnie," Stagg said. "Bring your daddy out, too."

"You know Luther, he don't take off Saturdays," Donnie said. "Besides, lots going on right here. You hear about that dead Mex at the Traveler's Rest?"

Stagg said nothing. The players took the field, stretching out before the kickoff.

"He was of those carnival folks," Donnie said. "They got some kind of fighting go on with each other. Doesn't concern us. They got it straight now. I don't want this spooking you."

The crowd yelled and clapped as the ball sailed into the air, the players for both teams crashing together, knocking the hell out of each other. A little black kid for the Wildcats ran the ball about two yards before being swarmed by the Water Valley Blue Devils. The folks who'd driven over from Yalobusha County all yelled and screamed from the pissant stands across the way, ringing cowbells and sounding air horns.

"I heard a man on television say there was nothing like football in the South," Stagg said. "He said it was because Southerners were defeated people and appreciated the idea of going to war every week."

"Football ain't war."

"It's like war," Stagg said. "You don't think those folks from Yalobusha wouldn't love to come down here to give us a good ass-whipping? This is their clan they sent to show us up. Look at them girls across the way with war paint on their faces."

"Ain't the same, Mr. Stagg," Donnie said.

Stagg chewed on some peanuts, and they watched the game for a while. Donnie thought the Wildcats looked like they had lead in their ass tonight, loafing from play to play. If he'd walked across the field like that, his coach would have chewed him out good.

"We can't be seen together no more," Stagg said. "You hear me? Don't come 'round the truck stop."

"Leonard told me," Donnie said. "That's why I wanted to give this to you personal."

The Water Valley quarterback tossed the ball to a halfback who put on the afterburner and rammed it down the throats of Tibbehah, getting a first down and then some. Donnie clapped as the back bounced up and started talking some shit to a couple Tibbehah players. The sidelines bulging, both teams ready to bolt onto the field and break out some whoop-ass.

"Feds have been giving Mr. Campo hell these last few weeks," Stagg said. "A couple 'em come by the Rebel yesterday, asking me about business I have up in Memphis. I don't think it's anything for us to worry about. But you can't be too careful, son."

"I got an order for one more load," Donnie said. "Same as before."

Stagg laughed. He cracked some peanuts and watched the game. Water Valley drove it down the field in three plays, scoring on a twenty-yard pass to the end zone. Those Yalobusha bastards really raising hell now with their cowbells and horns. They finally got quiet after the extra point was kicked, and Stagg leaned over to Donnie's ear and said, "You got to be shitting me."

"Promised twenty grand on top of what was paid this time."

Stagg sucked a tooth, clearing out a lodged peanut.

"Twenty grand?" Stagg asked.

Donnie nodded.

"No." Stagg shook his head. "Can't do it."

"OK."

"What about the dead Mex?" Stagg asked.

"He ain't my problem."

"Anything bother you about this here deal?" Stagg said. "You gonna do business, you need to know who you're dealing with. What the hell do you know about these damn Mexicans? They're shooting up their own people. You don't think they'd shoot us up when they got what they needed? I read on the computer that these people hang their rivals off highway overpasses, messages spray-painted across their dead bodies. I don't want any more of this."

"What about Mr. Campo?" Donnie asked. "You speak for him, too?"

"He's out, too," Stagg said. "You can ask him if you like."

"I just might do that," Donnie said. "Ain't but ninety miles to Memphis."

Donnie stood up to leave.

"Appreciate the business," Stagg said, watching the game but offering his hand. "Come see me when the shitstorm passes."

Donnie shook it just as Leonard's fat ass lumbered on up the stairs, sitting on the opposite side of Stagg. He'd brought a couple hot dogs and Cokes.

The Wildcats had the ball now. Donnie had lost track of the game but turned back now as the quarterback scrambled with those Blue Devils over him like flies. He threw a damn turkey up high into the lights, ball dropping right into the hands of a Water Valley defensive back. God damn if he didn't have some running room, sprinting by everyone and scoring a touchdown.

Donnie shook his head. "Guess this ain't Tibbehah's year."

LUZ CAME TO SEE HIM a little past midnight, letting herself into Donnie's Airstream and finding him half asleep, half drunk on the bed, watching a show about rednecks who hunted alligators. He passed her the bottle of Jack, but she put it down on the coffee table, crawling onto the bed and straddling him, kissing him full on the mouth in a real famil-iar way. Donnie looked up at her from flat on his back and said, "Well, hello there."

Luz hadn't said a word since she'd walked inside, a cold wind shift-ing the old Airstream a bit. The only light in the place came from a strand of chili pepper lights he'd strung above the bed. Luz smiled down at him and pulled off her jeans jacket and kissed him again, this time longer and slower. She lay down next to him, pulling herself in close, where Donnie could hear her breathing.

"I tried to call you," Donnie said. "You ditch that phone? I thought y'all had left."

"Everything is a mess."

"You gonna tell me more about why y'all are shootin' each other?" Donnie said. "Ain't nobody gonna do business with folks who kill each other. What the hell?"

"That wasn't supposed to happen."

"Son of a bitch didn't kill himself," Donnie said. "What was his name?"

"Vincente."

"Vincente trip and shoot himself in the head?"

"He was a good man."

"Apparently not for y'all."

"Alejandro believed that he was stealing from us, taking guns and money to use against us," she said. "I don't know what happened. But Alejandro killed him. He's a violent man. A *sicario* who's worked for the narcos since he was a boy. He enjoys the killing and thinks nothing of it."

"Well, then. I sure am glad you brought him my way." Donnie shook his head. "So, was he?"

"What?" Luz asked, rolling over on her side, propping up her head with an elbow.

"Did Vincente try and double-cross y'all?"

Luz shook her head. She lay back down, pillow under her head, hand on Donnie's chest. "They are impatient. These people want the guns and money we have. They want us to return now. But we're not ready. Not yet."

Donnie nodded. "So that's why you're here," he said. "You want to know how we're doing with those guns?"

"It's not the reason," she said. "I wanted to see you. You know that."

Donnie rolled off his back, snatched the bottle back, and planted his feet on the floor. He took another hit of the Jack and turned off the show about the rednecks hunting gators. He hadn't had dinner and thought about heading back into town for a Sonic burger or maybe seeing if the Fillin' Station was still open. You could get bacon and eggs damn near anytime.

"How can I call you?" Donnie said. "Your number ain't good no more."

"I have another."

She leaned in and wrapped her arms around Donnie. She snuggled in close, making it seem as if she really felt something, and nuzzled her nose against his ear. She smelled sweet and good.

"Ain't necessary," Donnie said. "I'll get your guns just the same. Don't sugarcoat it."

She pulled away and sat down next to him. Her eyes looked very sad and dead as she watched his face. She just shook her head as if she'd grown disappointed in him. Donnie knew that look. A lot of people had tried it out on him his whole damn life.

"You, too?" he asked.

"What do you mean?"

"You need to tell Alejandro he needs to take some anger management or some shit, because if he keeps killing folks here in Tibbehah, he's gone get arrested," Donnie said. "Our gun supplier don't want to work with me no more 'cause of all this shit. I don't know how you do it in Mexico, but you can't just start killing folks you don't like in the USA. Our police will investigate. Did you know you got federal agents looking for you all? *Federales?* You know?"

"You can't get the guns?"

"What it all boils down to," Donnie said. "Don't it, sister?"

She reached out and grabbed his hand and looked long and hard at his face. Her eyes were so damn big and brown, and Donnie wanted to believe her if she said the world was flat and gumdrops fell from the sky. He looked away and drank some more. He got up and hunted up a T-shirt to cover his scars.

"Is that what you think?" she asked. "That I am with you only for the guns? You were paid. I am not part of that."

"All right. All right. You want some more whiskey?"

She tilted her head, making some kind of decision. She stood and touched his face and ran her hand long against his naked back, feeling for the contours of the scars. She held his hand and ran it up under her shirt and across her rib cage, where she had her own thick scars. She moved his fingers back and forth across them.

"How'd you get that?" he asked.

"I lied to someone once."

"Your boyfriend cut you?"

She let Donnie's hand drop and held it in hers, snatching his other with her opposite. The cold wind buffeted around the trailer, Donnie having had enough Jack Daniel's to remember being on the flip side of this earth and having to clean out the sand from his boots and ears every time the wind blew. Sand getting goddamn everywhere again as soon as you finished.

"You want to stay the night or something?" he asked.

Luz nodded. Damn, Donnie had never realized how lonely this trailer could be. She pulled his hand and made him find the flat of her back. Donnie wanted to pull her so damn close but stopped himself and asked the question that had made him drink half that bottle in half an hour: "What are y'all doing with those kids?"

Luz's face turned sad. She shook her head as if she didn't know.

"That fat woman, the American? What in the hell is she doing with y'all?"

"I saw her and I saw the children," Luz said. "The man, her husband, has friends in Mexico. He is trying to leave the country."

"And y'all going to give him a ride?"

"I don't know," Luz said. "Who is she?"

"She killed a child. She's beaten and tortured the others," Donnie said. "Y'all need to let those kids go."

Luz shook her head. "I'm sorry. This is why you're angry?"

"I don't know what y'all do, and I really don't give a shit. But when you start hurting kids, that makes my stomach turn."

"I can find out," Luz said. "There is so much you don't know."

"I know enough."

"Vincente was my friend."

"I'm sorry."

She pulled the Jack Daniel's from his hand and drank down a generous portion. She sat at the edge of the pullout bed and held her head in her hands, black hair spilled over her face.

She began to cry a bit.

"Just what the hell is going on?" Donnie asked. "I feel like I walked into this picture show kind of late."

QUINN HAD FALLEN ASLEEP AT THE FIRE, BUT THE HARD KICK OF A BOOT *knocked him awake and down on his side. He turned and looked up into the double barrel of Warden Porter's shotgun, the flat of his boot across Quinn's chest. The man was red-eyed and unshaven and breathing hard. "Get up," Porter said.*

He stepped off Quinn's chest and let the boy get to his elbows and then knees.

Porter knocked him across the mouth with the butt of the shotgun, sending him sprawling down by the edge of the pond. Quinn's mouth began to bleed.

Caddy screamed and ran to him, trying to block the way between the old man and her brother. Quinn regained his vision and wiped the blood from his lip, feeling like his jaw might be broken. He pulled Caddy back as Porter approached, the old warden wearing a dark rain slicker and slouch hat.

"You kids give me trouble and I'll sink y'all both in that there pond," Porter said. "Don't matter to me."

"My uncle said you were a cocksucker," Quinn said.

Porter moved on him, Caddy trying to push him away and getting the back hand from the older man, sending her onto her butt in the mud. Quinn rushed the man, a flurry of little fists and elbows, not really knowing how to fight yet, and the man gripped his small fist and pulled it hard behind his back, hard enough that Quinn heard the pop in his shoulder. Porter held him facedown in the mud before he jerked him up and bound his wrists with thin rope, telling his sister to quit her bawling.

"We got a good eight miles to go through this forest," Porter said, picking up his hat from the ground. "I'll pull the boy, but don't make me rope you, too. You hear me?"

Caddy didn't say anything.

Porter screamed it again, veins bursting in his neck.

Quinn spit blood at the man.

"You 'bout broke my neck when you set that trap for me over that ravine, you little shit," Porter said. "Don't try and be a man."

Quinn spit out some more blood and watched as Porter kicked dirt over the fire, sending smoldering smoke up into the gray sky. He pulled some Red Man from a pouch in his coat and set a fat chaw in his cheek. He looked to Quinn and his crying sister and shook his head with disgust. Porter yanked at the rope tying his hands.

"Don't worry, Caddy," Quinn said. "Don't you worry about nothing."

Porter lumbered over at the lean-to and kicked over the carefully placed pine and oak limbs. He studied the way Caddy had arranged all the food she'd taken from the house on a rock shelf and laughed as if it were the funniest thing he'd ever seen. He marched back to the smoking fire ring and reached down for the .22 Browning that had once belonged to Quinn's grandfather. He roughly pulled out the loading pin and shook loose the long bullets inside. He threw the gun over his shoulder, spitting in the dirt fire, and grinned at Quinn. The man had dared him to say a word.

He'd left about four feet of rope hanging from Quinn's wrists and used the loose end to yank him to his feet. Porter kicked him hard in the backside, setting him forward and stumbling and right to his knees. Quinn called him a fat old bastard. The old man kicked him again.

"You can be as tough as you want, boy," Porter said. "But the next kick is for your sister. You want that?"

Quinn shook his head, and the man marched them forward up the fire trail and over the first great hill and the next, taking them out the opposite way from the way they'd entered the woods, the long way.

"Why are you headed west?" Quinn asked. "It's shorter back toward Tibbehah County."

"Sometimes I figure out things on a walk," Porter said, taking a moment to study the darkening sky. "Hadn't figured out what to do with you all yet."

Caddy's face was a mess, but she had quit crying. She walked alongside Quinn, step for step, until Porter reached for her shirt and yanked her back with him. When Quinn turned back and stopped walking, Porter slapped him against the back of the head.

"You lay a hand on her, you bastard, and I'll kill you."

"Sure like to see you pull that off, kid."

It started to rain a few miles in, the trail wandering and wild, overgrown with thorny brush and blocked with fallen, rotting trees. But Porter knew the way, as Quinn did, and they pushed ahead. The rain coming down hard in Quinn's eyes as he felt his jaw swell to the size of a baseball. Caddy was quiet, and every so often, Quinn would look over his shoulder to make sure she was OK. She walked right in front of Porter, and Porter lowered his eyes on the wetness of her shirt and small figure, spitting now and then into the brush.

He called her "girlie" and tried to make small talk. He said he was sorry for the rain. He said he was sorry her no-account brother caused all this trouble. Caddy didn't answer him. The trail spread out into four or five fingers, dipping up and down the rolling hills of north Mississippi, until they connected with a well-traveled path through a patch of new-growth trees that thinned down and long into an open clearing of cotton land. An old rusted barn stood alone in the new growth of the forest, the farmland being reclaimed by nature.

Porter moved fast ahead and yanked rough on Quinn's wrist, pulling him forward like he was a dog, taking him under the sloping roof, rain pinging hard above them. Quinn and Caddy were soaked to the bone, both shivering. Porter shook the rain off his slicker and hat. He put his hat back on and looked around the barn, finding an old metal bucket to sit on and stare outside.

There was thunder and stillness.

"No, sir," Porter said. "I hadn't quite figured out what to do."

Quinn gave him a hard glance. Porter kept staring at his sister. Quinn readjusted himself between his legs.

"You need to peepee, little boy?" he asked. "Come on. I ain't holding it for you."

He loosened the ropes with one hand, Quinn's wrists red and chafed. His fingers had turned a purplish blue. Porter pointed the end of the shotgun all loose and wild at Quinn, waiting for him to take a leak in the rain, water coming down cold off the cedar and down his neck and back.

When he finished, Porter spit again and bound a single wrist and yanked him toward the cedar, tossing the end of the rope around the trunk and binding Quinn there in the rain. Quinn muttered to himself, calling Porter a fat piece of shit.

Porter didn't even smack him. He sauntered on up the hill and back into the ramshackle, forgotten barn. The rain tap-tap-tapped on the metal roof and stopped for a long, slow moment, thunder growling far out to the west. A deep electric silence far up into the waiting barn.

Caddy screamed.

Porter yelled. "Just lay down. Lay down, damn you."

Quinn had lost feeling in his wrists and fingers and tugged hard as he tried to loosen himself. The minutes stretched out. He dropped to the ground and placed his feet against the trunk and pushed and wriggled and felt the rope burning and tearing into his skin until he bled. The rope was wet and slick, and with a final kick and tug, one hand broke free, and the other, both dead and asleep and clumsy as he made his way to the yawning mouth of the barn and stepped into the darkness. There was more thunder out in the gentle gray light, and the metal humming with it all.

Porter had hung his rain slicker all neat and civilized on a nail by the door. His hat and 12-gauge rested on a ledge with an old Coleman lantern.

"Lay down, damn you," Porter said from high up in the loft. A home-made ladder built of two-by-fours lifted on up into the crooked ceiling. Quinn rubbed the blood back into his clumsy hands as he reached for the shotgun. Caddy screamed at a higher pitch like bubbles popping at the surface of a pond.

"YOU AWAKE?" Dinah Brand asked from beside Quinn in the old iron bed. It was late night, a soft storm passing outside, only an old quilt his Aunt Halley had made across their naked bodies. As Dinah turned in shadow, hand propping her head, the curve of her hips and smallish breasts were clear in a sliver of light from the hall.

"It's raining," he said, on his back, staring at the ceiling.

"You need to let your dog in?" she asked, whispering.

"He's got a door in the back."

"Were you dreaming?"

"I haven't slept."

"Sounded like you were dreaming."

"No," Quinn said. "I'm fine."

"You worried about what we're doing?" Dinah asked, staring down at him. Her voice had a husky edge to it. "Because I'm not. This is my personal business on my personal time."

"I'm not worried. Couldn't sleep is all."

Dinah backed in closer to Quinn's body. Quinn's arm wrapped around her. The rain and storm pinged off the edge of the roof as it had in his memory. Her skin was warm to the touch, and her hair smelled of sweet shampoo. His feet stuck out the bottom of the quilt. "You want some water?"

"Please."

Quinn scooted out as Dinah righted herself, reaching for one of Quinn's old flannel work shirts, slipping inside and buttoning. In bare feet, she followed him to the kitchen, a single light on over the stove as he filled a canning jar from the tap.

"What's the matter?" she asked.

Quinn handed her some water. Lightning flashed from far off, the thunder low and grumbling out across the pastures. He shook his head.

"Just some family drama," Quinn said. "You really want to meet my family?"

"I really do."

"You might think less of me."

"I doubt that."

"My mother is a good woman," Quinn said. "And my sister. Well, she walks a pretty rough road. It's not her fault."

Dinah Brand looked natural in Quinn's old shirt, red hair loose and a bit wild, bare feet twitching on the floor by the kitchen table. Her eyes almost translucent in the light, long white shapely legs with really nice knees.

"You got great legs," Quinn said.

Dinah stretched on her right leg and turned it this way and that. She smiled. "I do. Don't I?"

Quinn nodded. Hondo padded on in from outside and shook his wet coat. He'd been asleep in the mudroom, and he stretched out long and yawned. Quinn tossed him a biscuit from a tin on the counter.

"Hungry?"

Dinah shook her head.

"Thirsty?"

She shook her head.

"Want to go back to bed?"

Dinah nodded.

She clutched the edge of his shirt in her hands and tiptoed across the room to him, hands across his neck and a warm, welcoming slow kiss. He reached around her waist and pulled her up into him, letting his hand drop down below her narrow waist.

He had begun to back her down the hall, working on the old shirt's buttons, when the phone rang.

Quinn said, "Son of a bitch."

It had to be way past midnight. But late-night calls were common. Lillie and the other deputies checked in at all hours. Quinn told them he'd be mad if they didn't let him know about something important.

"Sheriff?"

Quinn did not recognize the man's voice.

"Who's this?"

Dinah tucked her head on Quinn's shoulder. He felt the soft curve of her back under the flannel shirt with his free hand. She stared up at him.

"I know where those kids are at," the man said.

Quinn waited. His hand stopped.

"Don't worry about tracing this call," the man said. "I'm at a pay phone, and don't have nothing to do with this mess. But that fat woman and the Mex are about to boogie on down the road. If you're quick, you can still catch them up in New Albany."

"Where?" Quinn asked.

"You need a pen or can you listen to me straight?"

32

"I AM IMPRESSED, AGENT BRAND," LILLIE SAID, WINDOW CRACKED, CIGA-
rette in hand, as the night highway flew past. "You sure made good
time from Oxford. I mean, it was what? Maybe thirty minutes from
the time the sheriff got the call? Damn, you federal people are sharp.
The best. I'm telling you what."

Dinah didn't answer, only glanced back at Quinn as they headed up
45 North in Lillie's Jeep and then cut west on 78 into Union County.
Lillie drove with Dinah in the passenger seat; Quinn sat in back,
exchanging phone calls with the sheriff in Union County, making plans
to get on the farm where he'd been told the children were stashed. He
said he'd meet Quinn with a couple deputies but couldn't guarantee a
warrant. They could try for a welfare check only and then see how to
proceed. By the time they hit the county road where they were supposed to find Janet and Ramón, it was 0500 and dark as hell.

Quinn liked it that way, always preferring night.

"What else did the man say?" Lillie asked.

"Told me about this property, said to hurry, and then hung up."

"You recognize the voice?" she asked.

"If I did, wouldn't I have told you?"

"A little testy this morning, Sheriff," Lillie said. "You hit the wrong side of the bed?"

Lillie had been quiet most of the ride up, trying a few remarks out in the quiet car, knowing full well that Dinah had just rolled out of bed with Quinn. She hadn't wiped the smirk off her face since they'd arrived at the sheriff's office about three a.m., Lillie smiling at both of them, lighting up a smoke, taking them both in, studying them with much interest.

"What's your move, Sheriff?" Dinah asked between making phone calls to Memphis and Oxford, touching base with the folks she worked with in the ATF.

"The way I'd plan this is different than the way we have to do it," Quinn said.

"Quinn would like to call in an air strike," Lillie said. "Flatten the shit out of everything and comb through the wreckage."

"Nope," Quinn said. "I found some high ground on the map I downloaded. I'd find a nice spot to set up my rifle and start picking off anyone over three feet tall."

"See what I mean?" Lillie said.

"Didn't say I would do it," Quinn said. "I'm just saying that's the most efficient. You pick off a couple, and more will come out to see what's going on. That's how you clear an area."

Lillie turned off the exit. "I've been working on Quinn about certain laws we have in Mississippi. We've just gotten beyond shoot-to-kill being frowned upon."

Quinn ignored her, getting better and better at that, and asked Dinah what she thought.

"If these are the folks I'm looking for, I wouldn't knock on the door and say hello. Maybe get as close as we can and try and force a reaction. How far from the road are the barn and trailers?"

"About a mile," Quinn said.

"Too far for an air strike?" Lillie asked.

"Hell, I wouldn't call in an air strike," Quinn said. "Those kids might be there."

"What if you knew it was only Janet and Ramón and some of their compadres?"

Quinn was silent.

"See what I mean?" Lillie asked.

THEY GOT A HALF MILE down the farm road before the first bullet spider-webbed the passenger window, maybe three inches from Dinah Brand's head. All three of them ducked, Quinn yelling for Lillie to cut off the lights. The Union County sheriff and deputy, braking behind them, did the same. Quinn was out of the Jeep and taking cover behind the vehicle almost at the same time. He fired five times with his Beretta auto and slipped the Remington pump over his shoulder with a home-made sling. There were no lights on the road, only the faintest of illumination well beyond a bend in the open, rolling field. A single white light shone near the mouth of a red barn.

Two more shots sounded, and Quinn spotted the quick flashes from a ravine at forty meters. He returned fire six times before he met Lillie and Dinah on the driver's side of the Jeep. He kept a fresh magazine in his pocket and reloaded.

"Two guns," Quinn said. "There's a ditch to the north."

He looked to the south of the road, gentle hills without trees, only cows, a bright white frost coating the brown grass, terrible cover for all. The Union County Sheriff's car, a maroon Dodge Charger, pulled up within a couple meters of where they stood. The sheriff, a portly man in his seventies named Drake, and a young deputy, a muscle-bound black man in his thirties, joined them behind the cars. Drake removed his ball cap and looked to Quinn. "That warrant shit was a waste of time. Wadn't it? Holy Christ. These crazy sonsabitches mean business. I got eight units headed this way."

Four more shots came from the ravine, shattering glass in the Jeep and thudding against the doors of the Charger. "God damn," Drake said. "Just had this car painted."

All five of them squatted down behind the cars. Quinn introduced the sheriff to Dinah, the agent he'd told him about who was tracking guns out of Memphis. Dinah had her red hair tied up in a bun and wore a thick black ski coat.

"You really think they'd keep those kids in there?" Drake said. "I mean, shit. We gonna have to wait it out now."

"I got tipped there are three trailers down that road," Quinn said. "Up and over that hill."

"That makes it a bitch to see," Drake said. "We got shooters out on this road saying hello, and God knows what's waiting for us."

"All part of the fun," Lillie said with a grin.

"Sheriff, this is my chief deputy, Lillie Virgil," Quinn said.

Lillie nodded.

"I used to ride horses out here when I was a kid," the sheriff said. "I don't even know who owns it anymore. Tax record says it's in bankruptcy. Don't recall the trailers."

"When we get some more folks out here," Quinn said, "I'd like to head back to the main road and backtrack. I'd prefer to introduce myself from a different direction."

"What do you think we got in there?" Drake asked Dinah.

"Maybe a shitload of automatic weapons headed back to Mexico," she said. "They could be armed to the teeth with assault rifles. Grenade launchers."

"Real cute," Sheriff Drake said. "I was supposed to speak to the Ruritans this morning at eight. I was gonna give the opening prayer, and brag on our low crime rate."

"You want us to pray now?" Lillie asked.

"Might help," Drake said, turning to Quinn. "You really want to double back on them?"

Quinn nodded. Drake smiled at him as if recognizing an old pal.

"I knew your uncle real well," Drake said. "Me and him had been sheriff about long as anyone in this state. He sure was a good ole fella. You favor him."

Sirens sounded off down in the distance, and the flashers came up hard and fast from the main road, bounding over the gravel. The shooters were silent down in the ravine. Quinn watched for their shadows to return, heading back to the barn or out into the woods, where he planned to follow into the cleared land.

"Don't matter to me if you go on," Drake said. "You want a couple deputies go with you?"

Quinn nodded, Drake saying they'd meet him on the main road. Dinah and Lillie followed. Dinah carried a Sig Sauer P226 with a laser sight. A gun was usually the second thing he noticed about a woman. Lillie walked confident with a Mossberg pump and standard-issue Glock. Lillie was tall and lithe, good body, but with a tough walk. Dinah walked more girlish in her tall boots, and with more caution on the loose rocks and dirt.

Back at the county road, Quinn used his Leatherman tool to cut into the barbed wire and track alongside the ravine in some low-growing pines that had been planted in the last ten years or so. The pine needles were soft and quiet, muffling their steps as the group followed him.

Quinn saw the sheriff's cruisers and Lillie's shot-up Jeep from the edge of the clearing. The ravine sat about twenty meters from the edge of the pine. Quinn spotted two shadows, holding hunting rifles at their sides. The men were speaking Spanish and watching as two more patrol cars joined the mess in the center of the dirt road.

Quinn could take both men out from where he stood and clear the path to the barn and the next objective.

"Don't think about it," Lillie said behind him.

"These boys are fucked and they know it," Quinn said. "Folks are scariest when they got nothing to lose."

Quinn quietly radioed to Sheriff Drake to spotlight the ravine. Two patrol cars hit the lights on the wide-open space, and the two men fired again at the deputies in the clearing. Quinn and Lillie fired at the same time into the ravine, dropping both men where they stood. A stillness fell over the early morning. Lillie let out a lot of air and dropped her weapon, refusing to look at Quinn. She walked across the open ground to the ravine, staring down at the dead men.

Quinn grabbed her arm and pulled her from the light, taking her back into the pines with him. "What the hell's the matter with you?" he asked.

"You know what else is up that road?" Lillie asked.

"Don't ever walk out into the open like that," Quinn said.

His voice had some edge about it, and although he knew Lillie didn't like it, she said, "OK." Dinah caught his eye, Sig Sauer loose in her hand, and followed Lillie without a word back toward the main road and the gathering of deputies. Union County had more than half of their department out on the farm road, spinning red-and-blue lights, radios squawking. The early morning had a bright chill to it, a frost spreading up on the rolling hills where the cows stood and made grumbling sounds.

Quinn didn't ask but followed the path along the pines to the east and the lone barn, where he expected to find more trailers and more guns and maybe the kids. You always wanted to get a feel for the enemy before they saw you, know their size, their weaponry, their immediate location. You also never wanted to take a chance you didn't have to. If the local sheriff agreed to march on in and start kicking in doors, fine by Quinn, but he wanted to know every damn detail.

Quinn was joking when he said it, but he wouldn't mind having his old M24 sniper rifle in hand with a nice night vision scope. For most of his life, he worked on a simple premise: eradicate the enemy with as much speed as possible. He could pick off any opposition, man-for-man, within inches of those children, making sure no harm came to him or the kids. But there were laws and courts for even the most evil bastards in this nation, and he knew not to fire unless fired upon.

Those two men in the ditch back toward the road had made their choice. Quinn tried not to dwell on that stuff.

The thick pine plantings ended abruptly a half mile down, running next to the large barn. As promised by the tipster, three trailers sat up on blocks with four 4×4 trucks parked outside. A light shone down from a utility pole, and strobed light from a television flashed from inside the middle trailer. Two of the trucks were older-model Chevys with a lot of aftermarket supplies, KC lights, and glasspack mufflers. The third was a brown-and-tan GMC with a heavy chrome roll bar on top.

He called in his position to Lillie and the Union County folks.

The ground was beaten and uneven, with a thin layer of gravel spread out around the trailer encampment. The barn stood dark and quiet, only cows softly wailing by the feed troughs and buckets of molasses. Quinn kept watching the barn until a tall Hispanic man, maybe in his early twenties, wearing a black cowboy hat with a Concho band, walked out into the open holding an M4. Quinn was quite intimate with the model and made a call on his cell. Four more men joined him from the trailers, heading to the group of trucks, speaking Spanish, Quinn unable to hear what they were saying even if he had had great command of the language, which he didn't.

The sun would be up soon, and the deputies would be bottlenecked on that road.

Quinn called into the sheriff to see if there was a back road or a fire trail the gunmen might use to try to escape arrest.

No one seemed to know.

All of the men carried assault rifles. The hills obscured the sheriff's cars down the road. The men held the ground as Quinn watched the light of the television flashing inside one of the trailers, thinking back to another nameless village where his platoon dragged two American soldiers out from a Taliban safe house, the soldiers' faces beaten to shit. The Rangers left no one standing within a hundred meters of the landing zone. Everything was done with quickness and speed, getting in and getting out, taking care of the enemy without discussion. Quinn tried to slow his breathing, clear his mind, not think so much.

If he moved a little bit out of the pine concealment, Quinn could take out all four men before they could squeeze off a round. He raised his Beretta 9 and aimed at a man in the black cowboy hat. The man wore a big denim coat with a Sherpa collar and continued to speak on a cell phone. A cigarette hung from his mouth.

Quinn took a breath.

He heard the cry of a baby from one of the trailers. The men turned, and a young Hispanic woman walked out, a baby against her shoulder, patting its back and yelling to the men. A toddler in pink pajamas waddled to the open door and looked out into the crisp night.

33

"I WENT AHEAD AND CUT THE POWER TO THE SONSABITCHES," SHERIFF Drake said. "I got six deputies in the woods surrounding the trailers, and the only road is blocked. If they try and shoot their way out, we'll cut 'em down. I guess it's their move now."

The sheriff spread a large topographical map on the hood of a patrol car parked on the side of the county road, a few cars slowing to view the commotion. Quinn and Lillie stood on either side of him, Lillie smoking a Marlboro Light, and Quinn drinking coffee someone had brought in a Styrofoam cup. The sheriff tapped a pen to the location, circled it, and looked to both of them for a reply. The wind brought a razor chill to the back of Quinn's neck, nearly taking his ball cap with it. Dead leaves tumbled out in the street and spun in a little vortex.

"If I wasn't worried about those kids," Quinn said, "I'd say let's go ahead and hit them right now. But a five-mil round from one of those M4s will eat up those trailers. We don't want to risk it."

"You get an ID on the fellas in the ditch?" Lillie asked and blew out a long trail of smoke in the cold.

Drake shook his head. "Working on it," he said. "But I'm betting they ain't from Tishomingo."

Lillie's face had grown tight and stern. She was never pleased with herself when she fired her weapon. She'd want to know every detail of the dead men until she could set in her head that she'd done right. It didn't matter to Quinn. He had learned long ago to leave the dead where they fall. Most of the men he'd killed were nameless and faceless, and he preferred to keep it that way. He did his job and moved on. Keeping score only weighted you down.

"Can I borrow one of your .308s?" Quinn asked. "And for Deputy Virgil, too. I'd like to scout those boys out one more time before sunrise."

Drake nodded. Quinn sipped his coffee.

"If only this was easy as talking to an archangel," Lillie said.

Drake looked to her, confused, and folded up the map.

"The other day Sheriff Colson talked down this old coot who said he was protecting his land for the Virgin Mary," Lillie said, smoking down her cigarette and crushing it under her boot. "He's pretty good at the negotiation. Too bad these fellas don't speak English or whatever the hell they speak in Afghanistan."

"I got a couple deputies who took Spanish in high school," Drake said. "Damn menu at Taco Bell confuses 'em."

Lillie leaned close to Quinn and whispered, "I meant you spoke crazy."

Drake walked over to the muscular black deputy Quinn had met first thing that morning and asked him to bring in a couple rifles.

Quinn looked past the open gate and along the long dirt road. Frost coated the hills in a brittle white, cows huddled next to one another for warmth, taking hay from a round steel feeder. Quinn finished the coffee and stared down the row of cedar posts to the place he'd cut into the barbed wire a few hours ago. Once he had those men in the crosshairs, it'd be hard not to take the shot. With Lillie watching his six, he could take out all four of them and work with the locals on clearing those trailers.

"Let me talk to them."

Quinn turned to see Dinah standing behind him. Strands of red hair crossed her pale and freckled face, making her seem almost kid-like.

"They won't shoot a woman," she said. "Machismo culture and all that."

"I don't like that plan," Quinn said.

"OK." Dinah shrugged. "You got a better one?"

"Sheriff says to wait 'em out," Quinn said.

"What do you say?" Dinah asked.

"Not my county. Not my call."

Lillie stood between them, hands on her hips and fresh cigarette in her lips, maybe enjoying being a spectator.

"And if the kids are in there with armed men, and that Torres family's feeling the heat?" Dinah asked, leaving the question hanging out there. She looked up at the long dirt road cresting the hill and disappearing on the other side. She shook her head at the prospect.

"You just walk right in and say hello?" Quinn asked. "That it?"

"I think she'd actually say 'Hola,'" Lillie said. "'¿Cómo estás?'"

"I don't like it."

"You said that already," Dinah said. "You know, I am trained in this type of situation. Say what you will about Mexican drug runners, they won't shoot a woman."

"Got to love machismo," Lillie said. "Makes you stupid."

Dinah smiled at her. Lillie nodded with appreciation.

Drake walked up and handed a lever-action Browning with a tactical scope to Lillie. "Ladies first," he said. Lillie studied the rifle, cigarette clamped in her lips, and opened the breech with the lever. Drake passed along a pack of .308 bullets. She nodded and loaded the weapon and snapped it shut with a hard clack.

Drake handed Quinn the same setup.

"Guess you're pretty good with this," he said.

"Lillie might be better," he said. "What were you on the Ole Miss rifle team?"

"Team MVP," Lillie said.

"Hot damn," Drake said. "Ever think about leaving Jericho?"

"Yep," Lillie said. "Pretty much every day."

Lillie smiled as she passed Quinn and followed the cedar posts to the opening in the fence and disappeared into the pines. Dinah Brand stood sure-footed at the edge of the patrol car, two 18-wheelers blowing by, and removed the Sig Sauer from her holster and worked her way into a Kevlar vest. She fitted a jacket reading ATF over the bulk.

"What are you thinking?" Sheriff Drake asked.

"I want to talk to them," Dinah said. "Let them know their options look like shit."

"Can you say that in a nice way?" Drake asked.

"I'll smile at them when I lay it out."

Dinah looked to Quinn and raised her eyebrows. She started down the dirt road.

"I sure as shit hope she knows what she's doing," Drake said. "It's on my ass. Yours, too. Those Feds never get their names in the papers."

Quinn nodded and followed Lillie's lead, keeping a fast pace to catch up.

"WHAT DO YOU HAVE?" Quinn asked on radio.

"I got the Pancho Villa bastard playing pocket pool, and Antonio Banderas talking on his cell phone," Lillie said.

"You targeting the man with the mustache and the curly-headed fella at his flank? Denim coat?"

"Like I said, Pancho Villa and Antonio Banderas," Lillie said, answering back. "Holy crap, Quinn. Get a goddamn sense of humor."

Quinn set down the radio, finding a good spot to lie prone, elbows and body against the earth, finger on the trigger, and two targets in his crosshairs. He focused on a gaunt man with an unnaturally long face, a neatly etched mustache, and hair under his lip. The other gunman stood a few inches shorter and broader, mustached and scruffy-faced. Both wore crisp dark jeans and large gold belt buckles, trucker jackets with Sherpa collars. They both looked as if they'd stepped out of a hundred-year-old photograph. A few minutes later—maybe ten—he heard Dinah calling out a warning in Spanish from the other side of the hill.

The long-faced man turned to the others to discuss, shouldering the M4, taking aim on where she'd walk, saying, *"Venga solo. Vamos. Vamos."*

Quinn let out his breath, breathing slow and easy, falling into a comfortable place. He felt his whole body grow loose, still not seeing Dinah but knowing from the reaction of the men that she'd crested the hill. The long-faced man was speaking in a conversational tone with her now, gun still in the crook of his elbow, but he seemed to relax. After a few moments, he lowered his weapon, his attention on Dinah. Quinn pulled away from the scope and reached for a pair of binoculars. Three other men stepped away from Dinah and the long-faced man to watch the hills and long road past the barn. One looked up directly where Quinn waited but kept scanning right along the length of the pine woods.

The long-faced man reached for Dinah's arm and pulled her toward him. Quinn reached for his rifle but then put it back down as the man's hand roughly searched her, running hands under her coat and down her legs, coming up hard to her crotch and smiling as he searched. He pushed her away, speaking louder now, harsh words in Spanish that Quinn could barely hear and didn't understand.

Dinah kept her cool. Quinn appreciated the loose way she stood and talked with the gunman, shrugging and nodding.

She waited a beat and then yelled back to the man. The man approached her with dead eyes, and Quinn wanted very badly to end the entire discussion. He reached for the rifle. The other three men had wandered, their backs to him. Quinn stared through the scope and let out a breath.

It started to rain a little.

Dinah turned and walked back on the dirt road toward the barn and over the hill. Just as she reached the top, a limb cracked and broke behind the trailers.

The gunmen turned and opened up with their assault rifles. A stream of bullets erupted, bringing Quinn back into a familiar place and zone, the .308 back in his hands, firing two shots at two figures, dropping both as the others fell to the ground, the others falling from someone else's gun.

The battle took less than ten seconds.

The bodies lay in the dirt road, rain dimpling the puddles and blood coloring the water, as deputies came out from the woods. A sheepish skinny deputy with a red face covered in dirt followed. It wasn't hard to tell, he'd been the one who'd broken the branch. The deputy looked up at the dark clouds and thanked Jesus he hadn't been shot.

Lillie was up to the first trailer as patrol cars raced down the road with a lot of lights and useless sirens. She tried the door handle as Quinn reached her at the steps, dropping his .308 and carrying his sidearm. He motioned for her to step back and kicked in the door, moving fast and hard into the space, finding the long shot of the trailer open and empty. A television played from a far corner, Lillie checking the rooms, Quinn covering her, both moving out and away, rain pinging across the dirt road puddles and the trailers. The Union County deputies stormed the second trailer, and Quinn and Lillie found their way into the third, hearing the children even before the door was open. A teenage Mexican girl in a pink bathrobe fell to the ground and covered her head with her hands, praying to the Holy Mother and various saints that she wouldn't be shot, Dinah pulling her to her feet and pushing her into the trailer, where there were more cries and children all around. Quinn stood in the center of the trailer, the inside now crowded with law enforcement, harder and harder to hear what was going on with the crying children, the crying teenager, the shouting deputies, and the rain against the trailer roof.

Lillie held up a wailing baby, naked and cold, and clutched it to her chest. There were two more children in portable cribs, and another in a back room that reeked of soiled diapers and spoiled milk. Sheriff Drake entered the trailer, removed his hat with sorrow and remorse as he listened to all the children, reaching down for a baby not more than four months old who had fallen into the cushions of a ratty and torn sofa. He placed the child inside his satin sheriff's jacket to give it some warmth and met Quinn's eyes with tears running down his weathered face.

"What's the count?" Quinn asked.

"Five in the other trailer," Sheriff Drake said.

"Six here," Quinn said.

"Janet and Ramón?" Lillie asked.

The old sheriff shook his head.

"They're gone."

Dinah Brand walked in out of the rain. "But we got a shit ton of cocaine, meth, and a hundred or so assault rifles in the barn," she said. "This is gonna hurt them real bad."

Quinn gave her a solid nod. She nodded back and smiled.

He looked over to Lillie. She softly sang to the small naked child, holding the baby tight, the rain and the wind kicking up harder outside.

34

LUZ FOUND DONNIE WORKING THE COUNTER AT VARNER'S QUICK MART just as the five o'clock rush was coming on. The rush meant more than two people in the store at one time, and right now there was maybe eight, Luz motioning for him to come outside to talk. He looked back at her, trying to let her know "You got to be kidding." But she didn't pay him any mind and wandered up and down the short aisles, grabbing a couple packs of bubble gum and waiting in line like a good customer until it was her turn. "We need to talk."

"That'll be ninety-five cent."

Luz put down a dollar. "Now."

"My daddy won't be back till seven," Donnie said. "Come on out to the gun range. We can talk there."

He looked to the front doors of the mart, a steady cold rain coming down, night falling early. He nodded to a couple fellas he knew from Ackerman who'd come out to do some tree planting up around Providence. They were covered head to toe in mud, looking like they'd slid back down those hills and into their truck.

Luz took the gum without a word.

"'Preciate it," Donnie said to her back.

SHE WAS THERE when he drove up in his truck and killed the engine. She sat on the stoop of his Airstream underneath the green canopy that spread out over a table and some chairs. The girl was chewing the damn gum, contemplative. Donnie made a run for it up past the gun shop and along the path to where she stood. His damn jacket and hair were drenched.

Luz didn't say a word or look happy to see him. She just studied his face and blew a bubble, shaking her head like she was pissed off at something.

"What'd I do now?" he asked.

"You talked to your friend, the sheriff, about those children."

"What the hell are you talking about?"

"He's your friend," Luz said. "You wanted him to know where they were hidden."

"Bullshit."

"I see it," she said. "I see in your face. You are lying."

"So what if I am?" he said. "Those kids were being treated like animals. And that woman Janet ain't even Mexican. Why should you give two shits?"

"The police raided the farm," she said. "It was owned by some of my people."

"Hey," Donnie said, smiling. "Come on in, and we'll have some whiskey. Let's get out of these wet things."

He put a hand to her shoulder, but she shook him off hard, staring into his eyes, full of all that crazy-ass Latin rage. "You know what this means to us? You shouldn't have done this. There is so much loss. It's all such a mess."

"I didn't do jack shit," Donnie said. "You want to come in or not? 'Cause if you don't want to come in, it don't matter to me. Freeze your ass off out here. See if I care."

Donnie opened the door and stepped up into the trailer, his flannel shirts and *Guns & Ammo* magazines tossed on the floor where he'd left them. He reached into the cupboards for a half bottle of Jack Daniel's and stripped out of his jacket and T-shirt. He sat down on the bed and wiped his face with a towel. Luz walked into the doorway, hanging right there in the open space, her arms on each side of the threshold. Through the little round windows, Donnie saw mud and water sluicing off the logged-out hills, cutting little rivulets down into the ravines and creek beds that would run into the Big Black River and out to better places.

"They took the guns," she said.

"Shit. How many?"

"All of them."

"Oh, hell. I'm real sorry."

She shook her head, walked inside the trailer, and removed her jeans jacket. Donnie hadn't turned on the lights, and they stayed there in the darkness of the tin room for a long while, rain drumming above them as they studied the floor. "Shit. Shit. Shit."

"Did you tell the sheriff?" she asked.

"Shit, woman. I said I didn't."

"Alejandro had been there," she said. "He left only a few minutes before they came in with guns."

"Well, that's some luck right there. Right?"

"Six of our people were killed."

Donnie upturned the Jack and reached for the cigarettes in his coat.

He offered the bottle to Luz, and she refused. He looked over at her, black hair and purple T-shirt wet, and he wanted to reach for her, peel her out of those clothes, and forget about damn-near everything.

"Alejandro wanted to come for you," she said. "I came instead."

"He can take his crazy ass somewheres else," Donnie said. "Ain't me. Hey, come here. Sit down."

He patted his seat. She shook her head.

"And don't want a drink, neither."

She said no.

"Say, what makes you so damn special?" Donnie said, taking another hit of Jack. "You come in here accusing me, talking down to me like I'm trash."

"You're a thief," she said. "You stole guns from your own Army. How can I trust you?"

"And what makes selling drugs better than damn guns? Hell. That's some fucked-up logic right there."

Donnie drank some more and watched the water run down the side of the small hill and the rain beating against the glass. A hard wind shook the little Airstream. He looked to Luz and her soft brown skin and eyes.

"I'm sorry," Luz said, her eyes downcast.

"Have I ever asked you anything about your business, just what the hell y'all are up to? I mean, shit. Y'all are a bunch of dope peddlers who want to cut the competition off at the knees. I don't judge you. I figure you got a reason to be in the life. Just like I do. I like money. But that doesn't make me dirty."

"Everything is dirty and tainted," Luz said.

"Pretty harsh, sister." Donnie walked over to a basket of clean clothes and fished out a plain white tee to cover up his scars. He sat back down across from her and said, "I seen me a break in the system. OK? Every day that Uncle Sam forced my ass to be over in that shithole, I got more and more pissed off. I hated everything about the place. It made my dad's stories about Vietnam seem like paradise. Least there were girls there. Who gave a shit about taking over a craphole in the desert? Some stupid-ass politicians gonna get me shot up, fucked up. When I saw the chance to get even, I did."

Luz nodded. "I shouldn't have said what I said. I'm sorry."

"I got about fifty M4s supposed to be for the National Police," Donnie said, pointing the end of his cigarette at her. "You figure those guns ain't gonna end up pointing at some other stupid-ass American like me someday? Hell, I'd rather give it to you narcos and let y'all shoot it out over your cocaine runs. OK? So what the hell is your story? Why are you peddling dope? You have a problem with cleaning houses, washing dishes?"

Luz took a deep breath. She shook her head and stood.

"Be careful," she said. "If you were lying, Alejandro will find out and will kill you."

"Tell that marked-up, bald-headed fuck to bring it on," Donnie said, pointing to himself. He singed his chest with the cigarette butt. "Son of a bitch."

Luz made it to the door.

"Don't go out in that, baby," he said. "We're both kind of fucked up and dirty. Why don't we just be fucked up together?"

She shook her head.

"Will I see you again?" he asked.

Luz didn't say anything. Everything was getting dark outside, and Donnie could no longer see the water eroding the dirt hill. He walked to her and pulled her in close. Her body stiffened, not fighting, but unmoving and soulless. She smelled very sweet.

"You ever want to get out of this mess?" Donnie asked. "I got some money. You say the word, and I'll leave this craphole right now."

"I can't."

"Because of your boyfriend?" Donnie said.

"No."

"You afraid of him?'

"That's not it."

He held her hand as Luz stepped back. Donnie held on to her hand even though she wouldn't meet his eyes. She took back her hand and sighed.

"You better get on, then," Donnie said, feeling his face redden. "Git. Because you don't make a bit of sense."

Luz walked to him, stood on her toes, and kissed him hard on the mouth. Then he watched her big red truck disappear down the road, rain soaking his face and clean shirt. He shrugged as he slammed the door, said "Fuck it," and fell asleep dreaming of folks screaming in a bazaar and nurses who watched him like angels.

35

"YOU WANT SOMETHING TO EAT?" LILLIE ASKED.

"I'm good," Quinn said.

"You just gonna sit there in the dark and smoke that big cigar? Be contemplative and sort out this screwed-up world?"

"Yep."

"You mind me sitting with you?"

"Pull up a chair."

Lillie sat across from Quinn's desk, lights off and a slow cold rain falling outside. They sat there for a long while in silence, welcoming it after hours spent in Union County recounting every step they took and every move they made until they found the kids. The locals photographed the dead until the rain got too bad and they took them away. They had long Spanish names coming from places in Mexico that Quinn had never heard of, some with criminal records in the States. Others would take a while to identify.

"I wish I could say I feel bad," Lillie said, pulling the cigar from Quinn's fingers and taking a few puffs before handing it back to him.

"But I don't feel anything for those folks I shot. I only care about those kids, glad this mess ended for them. Or maybe started. You think they'll try and send them back to Mexico?"

"I don't know how that all works."

"I feel sick about that one child," Lillie said. "You know, the one I carried for a while?"

Quinn nodded. Lillie had carried the baby in her coat until the sheriff said the little girl had to go to the hospital and get checked out. Quinn had seen her cry a bit when the child left her arms, but he'd never mention it. The kid was maybe six months old, with dark skin and downy black hair. Lillie asked the Mexican woman who'd been in the trailer the child's name. The woman had said she didn't know. Lillie had started to call her Rose, the name of Lillie's mother who had died of cancer two years ago.

"That cigar isn't too bad," Lillie said. "It smells worse than it tastes."

"Don't worry about that baby," he said. "They'll take care of her."

"Yeah, fuckups never happen in the foster system. They always do a bang-up job finding houses with picket fences."

Quinn nodded.

"You think it went down the right way?"

"Sure," he said. "Those men made their play. What choice did we have?"

"Does it bring back some bad memories for you?" Lillie asked. "Fuck your head up?"

"Kenny is always asking me shit like that," Quinn said. "This was nothing like what I did in the Army."

"How's that?"

"What if I told you it felt a lot safer doing this on American soil?"

"I'd say you have a hell of a point," Lillie said, again reaching for the cigar and taking a puff. She returned it back to his fingers. "Have to say your gal is pretty stand-up, walking into that nest of narcos. You probably know different, but it seems she sure has a big pair of brass balls."

"She did good," Quinn said. "You did real good. Doesn't have shit to do with balls."

Lillie stood up. "'Preciate that, Sheriff."

"Good night, Lillie."

Lillie saluted him with two fingers and headed to the door, nearly bumping into Mary Alice, who sidestepped her. Mary Alice looked to Quinn and said, "Boom Kimbrough's been calling you."

"You got the number for the County Barn?" he asked, leaning back, feet on the desk.

"Last time, he called from that black juke down in the Ditch," she said. "He told me not to bother you. But I figured you'd want to know."

"Any trouble?" Quinn asked. "Was he drunk?"

"Nope," said Mary Alice. "Not as far as I could tell. Just the calls."

IT WAS NIGHT BY THE TIME he made it down to Club Disco 9000. Spam had clicked on the colored Christmas lights he kept up all year; a single lamp burned from a utility pole in the gravel lot. There was music inside and a few cars outside, Quinn seeing Boom's dad's truck parked at an odd angle. *Here we go again,* he thought. Of course he felt good that the place wasn't burned to the ground yet. That was a start.

Spam nodded to Quinn as he walked inside. He offered him a beer and pointed him to a back table, far from the jukebox, where Boom sat alone and still. His face was a large mass of odd angles, colored by the bar neon.

Quinn was off duty and took a quart bottle of Budweiser, declining the illegal moonshine offered. He had to leave the three dollars on the bar, Spam saying he refused to take his money.

"I told Mary Alice I was fine," Boom said. "You didn't need to drive out here. I heard about y'all's trouble in Union County. Holy shit."

"Wasn't pretty."

"But you got those kids?"

"We did."

"You find Janet and her man?"

"Nope."

"Sorry to hear that," Boom said. "People should burn for doing shit like that to children. You'll turn 'em up quick."

"I think they've gone back to Mexico," Quinn said. "May never find them."

"Woman like Janet would stick out in Mexico," Boom said. "Poor country can't afford to feed her."

"Why'd you call, Boom?"

Boom shrugged, a couple empty glasses in front of him. Quinn drank his beer.

"Well, went like this," he said. "'Cause I know you gonna ride my ass until you hear something that makes sense. I came down here after a pretty good day. I guess to celebrate. Did I mention I got your truck ready? Fine job, if I do say myself."

"I want to see the truck," Quinn said. "But tell me why you called."

"I don't care for some of the folks at the VA center," Boom said. "I ain't made of glass. I drink 'cause I like it. It don't hurt nobody."

"Maybe not the drink, but your fist works pretty good."

"The other night? Yeah, I guess I got a little loose. I guess tonight I didn't feel like getting like that. Figured I'd call. Shit, I don't know. I didn't want you coming down here and holding hands and saying prayers and shit. I can do that with my daddy."

"There's no weakness in calling a friend," Quinn said.

"You shoot those men today?"

"Some of them."

"Why didn't you bring me?"

"'Cause you were fixing my truck," Quinn said. "How many have you had?"

"Just a couple. Moonshine ain't bad. They make it with strawberries. Mellow out that gasoline taste."

"How do you know? You ever drank gasoline?"

"Not on purpose," Boom said. "Man, I guess I called because I don't like getting owned by this shit. I'm getting sick and tired of being pissed off about a situation that I didn't make happen. I can't go back to Iraq and find the motherfucker who did this to me. I get mad. I get so fucking mad, so mad that this was taken from me. I don't know shit. I curse myself, blame myself. I blame God. My father said that's some blasphemin'."

"Probably."

"I think the reason I like to drink is that it cools me out some," Boom said. "VA folks call it self-medicating. I think I get fucked up because I don't feel in control."

"You get out of control to be in control?"

"I told you it don't make no sense," Boom said. "All I know is, I could maybe use a ride. That OK?"

"It's always OK."

"You think it makes me weak?"

"Nope."

"I say that because I know how you feel about your sister, about how she goes carrying on and with the drugs and all. You told me she needed to get her shit together. I guess you cut me some slack 'cause you know where I live. You been to the same place."

"I have."

"I guess some people get to that place in their heads," Boom said. "You don't have to go to war and get your shit blown apart for that to happen."

Quinn nodded. He sipped his beer. They didn't talk for a long, steady while.

"The other day at the barn, you were telling me something about Caddy," Boom said. "About something that happen to her. You said your Uncle Hamp was the only other person who knew about it."

"I guess I was talking too much."

"You said it was a drinking conversation."

Quinn nodded.

"Well, we're drinking, or at least you're drinking," Boom said. "If I have one more, you turn me in to the VA?"

"As I've said, it's not my place to judge."

Boom walked to the bar, ordered another from Spam. Spam looked to Quinn and Quinn nodded. Spam looked worried as he served Boom. Boom sat back in front of Quinn.

"So what happened when y'all were kids?"

"Let's see that truck."

"Now who's the one who's got a problem?"

Quinn took a deep breath and told him.

36

THE LADDER REACHED UP INTO THE HAYLOFT, WHERE QUINN FOLLOWED HIS
*sister's cries over slatted boards that creaked and broke under his boots. He
could not see into the darkness, only hear animal things that made his heart
race and hands quiver on the stock of the shotgun. "Lay down, god damn
you," the man repeated. Quinn reached the end of the loft, a wide space that
opened up into a ratted-out corncrib, cobs cleaned long ago by yellowed
teeth and left in rotting heaps. The man was a dark shadow in the recesses,
guttural rhythmic sound from him and awful whimpering noises from
Caddy. Porter had torn off Caddy's overalls and his pants, and what Quinn
saw took his breath away, leaving a long, cutting stillness, everything seeming to stop. The rain drummed the roof as Quinn stepped forward, searching
for a way to get to her, get Porter off, when the old board gave way under
his feet, and he fell down from the loft into the rotting corncribs, tumbling
onto his back, letting go of the shotgun stock, the last time a gun would ever
fall lose from his hands. But, damn, if Porter didn't quit what had brought
a sheen of sweat to his balding head and unshaved neck. He crawled off*

Caddy and moved on Quinn, teeth clenched, a mind carried somewhere back to an animal place, walking with a purpose that left little doubt in Quinn's mind that he would die.

The shotgun lay half covered in rotting cobs, but the blued edge of the double barrel shone bright and clear. Quinn stumbled and reached for it, Porter gripping his arm. But Quinn reached back and bit into the man's furry hand, pulling away gristle and flesh. Porter yowled and fumbled back. Quinn turned the shotgun and saw Caddy in the corner of his eye. Time stayed like that, him knowing there was no going back for any of them. She was torn and broken and uncovered, openmouthed and vacant.

As Quinn raised the gun, he knew his sister had been taken from him.

He pulled on both triggers at once, sending fattened Porter back with a mule kick to the barn wall. His head landed with a thud against a hard floor beam.

Even in the horror, Quinn marveled at the way a shotgun could open up a human body.

Caddy stood there. Everything was silent and crisp. The blood smelled like old pennies.

Quinn pulled off his coat and covered her. He reached for her torn overalls and underthings. He gathered Porter's clothes to cover the man's face, frozen in a final confusion.

He pushed Caddy ahead, finding two-by-fours hammered into the wall, to get back to the loft. In the high corner of the barn, two pack rats, white and gray and as large as opossums, looked down with their red eyes and hissed at the disruption. Caddy's teeth chattered, and her entire body shook. Quinn carried her back down the ladder and into the yawning mouth of the barn, where they could see the gray daylight and the steady fall of rain.

Quinn found several pieces of scrap wood and old corncobs and kicked up a fire, smoke billowing up and out of the open barn.

"Caddy?"

She sat on the ground, knees reaching her chin. She was crying, although not hysterically, and rocking back and forth.

"Caddy?"

She did not answer. Quinn kissed her on the forehead.

"Are you sick?" he asked. "Did he hurt you?"

She nodded.

"Hurt you bad?"

She nodded.

Quinn found his .22 and those things that Porter had stolen from them. He discovered a half-empty bottle of whiskey among some Log Cabin pancake mix and pure maple syrup. He mixed the pancakes in a coffee mug, using rainwater to make batter, and set an iron skillet on a rock he placed dead center in the fire. The fire hissed and popped, embers glowing as night fell. Caddy had yet to speak.

Quinn cooked some cured bacon and added the batter to the grease. He set the pancakes and bacon on a tin plate and set it in front of Caddy. "We got to walk out of here tomorrow. You'll need your strength. Come on, eat."

She took the plate. She took a few bites.

Quinn ate three pancakes and bacon.

He watched the fire and the rain. The embers glowed hot and steady.

"You still have the compass I gave you?" he asked.

Caddy nodded.

"You follow that thing due west till you hit the interstate," Quinn said. "You hear me? You flag down a ride or call Momma from a fillin' station."

Her eyes turned on Quinn.

"I can't go back," he said. "Not after what I done."

"But." Her mouth was parched and clumsy as she spoke.

"Don't worry," Quinn said. "Don't cry. You hear me? I'm a bad kid, and *he was a bad man, and something happened out here. But ain't no one gonna catch me now. I'll head out west. Maybe I'll find Dad out in Los Angeles. Hell, I don't know. I just know I can't go back."*

Caddy started to cry again. She pulled her knees up even with her nose and started the rocking again.

"Aw, hell. Don't do that. All you got to do is get safe. You promise me that? You get safe."

She nodded.

"Finish those pancakes, it's a long walk."

"Quinn?" Caddy asked.

"It's all going to be fine."

Quinn reached his arm around Caddy. He was very cold now without his jacket and he took some warmth from her as they watched the fire for a long time. She left her plate unfinished. He added more wood to the fire until there was a slow, even heat in the barn, woodsmoke catching the wind and scattering out into the rain. Every time he would move, she would call to him, and he'd return quickly by her side.

"What if he comes back?" she asked.

Quinn said that wasn't going to happen.

Caddy fell asleep some hours later, and he held her until morning. The rain clouds scattered, leaving a crisp blue day. She cried—hadn't stopped crying, really—but she stood tough as he pointed west, that compass in her hand. He would walk south and catch the Natchez Trace, follow it as long as he could.

He didn't have plans much beyond that.

Quinn tried to give her his .22, but she wouldn't take it.

"I packed you some cookies and pancakes we didn't eat. OK?"

Her little blond head was bowed as she walked away, step for step, and Quinn hoisted his pack on his shoulder. Down the long, winding fire road they'd followed with Porter, he saw a darkened figure in a suede rancher coat and slanted Stetson. The man whistled out for them both.

Caddy turned. "It's Uncle Hamp. It's Uncle Hamp."

Quinn wanted to run away, but his legs felt lazy and wooden as his uncle came up on them out of breath. He looked to Caddy, set down on his knee, and studied the scratches and bruises on her little face. "What in the hell?"

Caddy turned her head away from him.

"Did he find you?" Uncle Hamp asked.

Neither one of the children spoke.

"Quinn?"

"The son of a bitch is dead," Quinn said. "He come after Caddy. I shot the bastard, and I'm glad I did it."

Uncle Hamp removed his hat and studied the cloudless sky. He picked up Caddy, still wearing Quinn's oversized mackinaw, and walked with her over his shoulder, heading around in circle after circle. Hamp's big hand on her back, soothing and comforting, wordless to Quinn but saying many words to his sister. When they looped back again, he set Caddy's feet back on the ground.

"He in there?" Uncle Hamp asked.

Quinn nodded.

"Can you find that old Indian mound?" Uncle Hamp said. "Down on the Trace?"

"Yes, sir."

"You walk that way," Hamp said. "Don't talk to nobody."

"Yes, sir."

"I'll come for you."

"Yes, sir."

Quinn headed out on a narrow path, trod by deer.

"And Quinn?"

Quinn turned.

"None of this ever happened," Uncle Hamp said. "You got that? We all got to get straight on that."

———

"WHAT DID THE SHERIFF DO?" Boom asked.

Quinn stopped his old truck outside the County Barn. He killed the engine, it continuing to knock a bit.

"He buried Porter somewhere out in the forest," Quinn said. "He never told me where. I tried to talk to him about it a few times, and he acted like nothing happened. He told Caddy the same thing. We were afraid if we did talk about it, something bad might happen. Might put me in jail or something."

"And you walked out of those big woods a hero," Boom said.

"I did get lost," Quinn said. "Caddy had my compass. My uncle didn't find me for another five days."

"Why didn't your uncle just bring it all out?" Boom said. "After what that man did, nobody would blame you."

"He thought it shamed Caddy," Quinn said. "He was a proud old man. He didn't want anything to stain her. He and Aunt Halley never had children. He loved her very much."

"Shit."

"Yep."

"I won't tell nobody," Boom said.

"We thought we were doing right by my uncle to leave it alone," Quinn said. "It's corroded her. How in the hell did we think it couldn't have?"

"Jean know?"

"Nope."

"Wish we could go find that son of a bitch out in the woods and shoot him again."

"I don't know what to do, man," Quinn said. "I've always blamed myself for getting her into my shit. She wouldn't have followed me out there if I hadn't shot those deer and started that mess. I was always in trouble, doing stupid shit to show off."

"This man got off on hurting kids," Boom said. "Hadn't been you and Caddy, been someone else. It's a sickness. You know? Man like that. Ain't but one way to deal with it and you did that."

"I was ten."

"And did the right thing."

"I've been hard on her."

"'Cause you carry your own water and think she need to do the same."

"We're not the same," Quinn said. "That man broke her."

Boom nodded. They sat in the truck for a long while, leaves blowing past headlights shining onto the County Barn. The barn's metal doors locked up tight with a chain. "I'm sorry, man," Boom said. "I'm real sorry. What are you going to do now?"

"It's been a rough twenty-four hours," Quinn said. "I don't know. Shit."

"Come on," Boom said. "Let's take out this new vehicle for a spin. Fine by you? We don't have to talk or nothing. Just ride around like we did when we was in high school."

Quinn nodded, and Boom opened up the barn with one hand and rolled back the doors.

37

DONNIE REACHED OUT TO BOBBY CAMPO IN MEMPHIS A LITTLE PAST midnight. He didn't have a number but knew Campo owned all those shake joints in south Memphis near the airport and kept on calling ones until he found someone at Southern Belles who said they'd relay a message. Campo called him back maybe five minutes later and asked if he wanted to meet up for breakfast at a CK's Coffee Shop right across the street from East High School. At five-thirty in the a.m., Campo was there as promised, sitting in a corner booth facing the window, adding some ketchup to a big mess of scrambled eggs. He didn't look up as Donnie took a seat, only scooped the mess up into his mouth and chewed for a long time before he said, "You Mississippi people are going to give me a fucking heart attack."

"Does that mean I can't get a cup of coffee?"

Campo shrugged. He wore a bright red Ole Miss sweatshirt—advertising the school as *The Harvard of the South*—with a big gold Rolex on his wrist. He didn't seem to take any notice of Donnie as Donnie made a little small talk with the waitress, trying to show all was cool and easy this morning, and ordered some biscuits and gravy with black coffee.

"You see the *Commercial Appeal*?" Campo said, pushing across the A section. "Christ. Just what happened down in Union County? Are those your Mexicans?"

"Ain't my problem," Donnie said just as the waitress returned. "Thank you, sweetheart."

"Where's Stagg?"

"He's out."

"Because of Union County?"

"He was out before that mess," Donnie said. "He made his money. He's more interested in making speeches for pancake suppers these days. I sometimes doubt his sincerity."

Campo nodded and ate some eggs. He drank some ice water, cubes rattling around in the glass, and studied Donnie's face to see if he was making a joke.

"I can't help you," Campo said. "Not now. Not after all this shit. Did I tell you my wife is speaking to the Feds now? I'm pretty sure she's screwing them, too, pillow talk about what an asshole I am. You know what an asshole I am? I paid for sixty-five thousand in plastic surgery to get her tits and ass lifted. Me? I can get the best grade-A snatch outside an Ole Miss sorority house. But you think I fooled around on her? Not once. And I'm the one who's living in a hotel by the airport with his dick in his hand. This is the best meal I've had in three days."

"I'm sorry."

The waitress slid Donnie's biscuits and gravy in front of him. He started to dig in as Campo craned his head to watch a big black sedan pulling off Poplar. When an old woman and an old man climbed out of the car, he turned back to Donnie. "I feel like I can't take a shit without being watched. I got high blood pressure and asthma. It's gonna kill me."

Donnie scanned the story on the front page of the paper, reading how six men had been shot and eleven children had been recovered. The story said that Janet and Ramón were still wanted and the dead men had criminal records from Texas, possibly associated with the Zetas Cartel. There was a big photo of Janet's and Ramón's ugly mugs and a faraway photo of a woman deputy carrying a child. Donnie couldn't tell from the angle but was pretty sure it was Lillie Virgil.

"They get all the guns?" Campo asked after he'd scraped the plate clean.

"Yes, sir."

"Didn't you say you had some of your own you were going to sell?" Campo asked. "Colts, just like the others?"

"They got those, too."

"So you're tapped out," Campo said, tapping his index finger on the table. "And want to see if I'll help out again."

"I can guarantee the same price."

"That was a fine price."

"You let me know where to find the rig, and I'll drive it over the state line."

"Yourself?"

"Yes, sir," Donnie said. "I can drive any damn thing with wheels."

"You know it's crazy to do business with me right now," Campo said. "I'm a fucking leper. Even a creep like Johnny Stagg doesn't want to be seen with me. That's why he's out. When someone like Stagg walks around you, that's when you know you got problems."

"Who knows how Stagg thinks."

"Just how much do you know about ole Johnny?"

"My daddy says he's trouble."

"Your daddy is a smart man," Campo said. He drank some more ice water. A neon sign down the street on Poplar clicked on, rotating clicks of light around a tire logo. "Stagg has owned that shithole county for nearly thirty years."

"He tell you about the new sheriff?"

"Had trouble with the old one," Campo said. "That didn't last long."

"Old man killed himself."

Campo raised his eyebrows and threw back the empty glass, finding some ice cubes and crunching them with his back teeth. He stared at Donnie for a moment. "Is that what you think?"

Donnie didn't say anything.

"Don't call me again at the shake joints," Campo said. "If I make this work, someone will call you. But you're in luck. I could use the fucking money."

"I knew we were gonna be buds, Mr. Campo."

"You like Ole Miss football?"

"Always been a State man myself," Donnie said.

"I invited Johnny Stagg to join me at my tent before the LSU game last year," Campo said. "My guests thought he owned a funeral home or was a roadside preacher. He wouldn't have been a bigger hit if he were a capuchin monkey. One woman handed him her empty plate with chicken bones and asked him to take care of it. Here the bastard drives all the way over from Tibbehah County, wearing his best sweater and loafers, and people still think he's the hired help."

"Johnny Stagg."

"I don't want you talking to him, either," Campo said. "This is between us. If it worked for Stagg, he'd be just like my fucking wife and sell me out to the Feds. You see, they were in on this raid, too. Christ Almighty, I must be fucking nuts."

Donnie put out his hand to shake.

Campo shook his head and reached for his wallet. "Never give the bastards anything like that to take a photo of. They'll blow it up bigger than shit and present it at trial like it was painted by Da Vinci."

"Yes, sir."

Campo set down his wet glass, dropped a twenty, and walked to the door. Donnie took his time with the biscuits and gravy. The neon light spun around and around that old tire sign as cars flew by on Poplar. Donnie drank his black coffee and thought of Luz. Damn if he couldn't wait to tell her what he'd found out. Only a man in love could be such a dumbass.

"THAT'S ONE GOOD-LOOKING TRUCK," Dinah Brand said. "When did you get it?"

"Last night."

"The old one was kind of growing on me," she said. "Dents and all. It had a lot of charm."

"And two hundred fifty thousand miles with a bad transmission."

They stood in the middle of the sheriff's office parking lot. Quinn opened the passenger door of the rebuilt Ford for Hondo, and he jumped inside. The dog moved over behind the wheel and looked out the window, panting.

"He acts like he owns it," Dinah said.

"Hondo's not a very good driver."

"Got some news," Dinah said.

"I thought maybe you just wanted lunch."

"Where have you been?" Dinah asked. "I've been waiting for an hour, talking to Lillie."

"She being any nicer?" Quinn asked.

"She is," Dinah said. "Kind of strange. I don't know what to think."

"I believe you now have her respect."

"And she mine," Dinah said, smiling. "You want to go inside? It's cold as hell."

"What's up?" Quinn asked. "Might get more privacy out here."

"Got IDs on all the folks from yesterday," Dinah said. "You should've been faxed those this morning."

"Got 'em."

"And some more stuff I didn't want to send." Dinah looked down at the pavement and raised her eyes back to Quinn. "Most of those guns got traced back to a big shop outside Oklahoma City. We're working on that."

"And the others?"

"Property of the U.S. Army."

"Come again?"

"That's all we know right now," Dinah said. "Showed up stolen from a base in Afghanistan."

"Which base?"

"I'm just learning all this," she said. "We'll know more today."

"I was afraid of something like this."

"How's that?" Dinah asked.

"This is how the personal gets messed up with the professional." Quinn leaned against his truck. He could hear Hondo jumping to the other side and panting against the glass. Quinn shook his head and looked to the ground.

"Go ahead," Dinah said. "OK?"

"I've been working on some things here," Quinn said. "I didn't want to say anything because I still don't know anything for sure. I just have some suspicions."

Dinah Brand was pretty good at setting her jaw. She stuck her hands inside a black raincoat and waited for Quinn to explain. She wore big tall galoshes with jeans tucked inside.

"There's a fella I know here in Jericho," Quinn said. "He runs a gun shop."

"He have access to military weapons?"

"Just got home from the Guard."

"OK," she said. "But we're talking about forty-six M4s."

"It could be done."

Hondo's breath had fogged up the glass in the car. Kenny walked out to say hello, big smile on his face, but saw the toe-to-toe talk and took a quick turn to his patrol car. He waved with two fingers as he drove off.

"OK," she said. "That's something. But I don't see the big deal. You got gun dealers all over the place in Mississippi. What's so bad about this guy?"

"He's not bad," Quinn said. "In fact, he's a friend."

"And."

"I just didn't want to screw him if this was nothing," Quinn said. "But after yesterday and all that happened, I had to tell you. Things have changed."

"What's his name?"

"Donnie Varner," Quinn said. "He was in the National Guard. Just got back from Afghanistan. He was in the 223rd, which is basically a lot of construction work and truck driving. But there are a lot of guns floating around those bases. A company up in Hernando got caught stealing some a few years ago. It happens."

"OK."

Quinn took a breath. "Can we go have some lunch?"

"You act like you want to tell me more."

"I'm sorry," Quinn said. "I was trying to find out more on my own. I should have been more honest."

Dinah waited. She was still setting her jaw and switching the weight from one foot to another. She didn't look very pleased and let the silences really play out.

"I recognized a woman's picture you showed me the other day,"

Quinn said. "Her name was Laura something or another. I've seen her. She's been here."

"With your pal?"

"That's not why I kept it from you," Quinn said. "I wanted to find out more."

"That's a big omission, Sheriff."

"I didn't know you that well."

"And now you got into my pants, you feel better about cooperating?"

"This is where the personal muddies things," Quinn said. "Hell, that doesn't have a damn bit to do with it."

"You had ample time to whisper into my ear while we were in bed," Dinah said. "Who's stupid now?"

Dinah looked around the empty lot. She leaned in closer to Quinn, jaw clenched and speaking in a lowered tone. "You're goddamn right you should have told me. Don't you realize who these people are? We all could have been killed yesterday, and you knew that you had a local here working with them, supplying the guns."

"We don't know that."

"Want to bet?" Dinah asked. "Damn it, Quinn. If she's the one I'm thinking about, she's in the company of one mean bastard, MS-13 gang-banger out of Texas named Alejandro Umana."

"And who's he?"

"The son of a bitch I've spent the last two years trying to catch," Dinah said. "He operated a cell out of Galveston a few years ago and left a group of rivals headless in a ditch behind a Popeyes Chicken. Jesus Christ, you don't know how bad these people are. Do you?"

"I'm starting to get the idea."

"Why didn't you tell me?'

"I wasn't sure," Quinn said. "And I didn't know if I could trust you."

"Well, you're in it now," Dinah said. "I think I know where to find this woman."

"OK."

"Want to come along?"

"How about Hondo?"

"Not unless he speaks Spanish, too."

38

THE CARNIVAL HAD SET DOWN IN SOUTHAVEN, MISSISSIPPI, JUST OVER
the Tennessee border and right outside a big Harley-Davidson dealership and civic center that mostly hosted monster truck and livestock
shows. The tractor trailers had unloaded the rides and games, and
workers in bright yellow ponchos scrambled to put the massive parts
together, fixing lights and unrolling canopies, shimmying up big metal
arms and crawling up and down ladders. The parking lot was filled end
to end with RVs and trailers, a small army setting up to bring the MID-
SOUTH FAIR to north Mississippi *Wednesday Night Through Saturday Only*.

Quinn sat beside Dinah in her car. The rain had stopped, and the
carnies seemed to be busting their asses to make sure they opened up as
planned. He noted a lot of tough wiry old rednecks working as carnies,
but a lot of Hispanics, too. One trailer featured the talents of the FEAR-
LESS FLORES FAMILY, a set of motocross bikes parked in front. "What'd
you say her real name was?" Quinn asked.

"Laura Zuniga," Dinah said. "If you saw her, you wouldn't forget it.

She was some kind of Miss Rodeo beauty queen in Texas before getting mixed up in this mess."

"And how will I know Alejandro?"

"Hard to miss a guy who has tattooed numbers and symbols all over his head."

"I'll try and be alert."

Quinn stretched his legs and checked the time on his watch. Dinah stared straight ahead as the midway took shape.

"Just how stupid is your pal Donnie?" Dinah said. "Why would anyone want to get involved with an outfit like this?"

"Donnie kind of has a knack for bad choices," he said. "I used to get myself in just as much shit, but was caught less frequently."

"Would you ever sell U.S. Army weapons to a Mexican drug cartel?"

"Maybe he's doing it for the girl," Quinn said. "Donnie one time broke into a rich man's hunting lodge and said it was his, all to impress some girl from Memphis."

"He should know, then, that this girl's boyfriend and Alejandro's boss goes by the name of Tony the Tiger. This guy operates one of the biggest cells down on the Gulf Coast."

"Donnie won't care."

"When the Tiger was down in Mexico, bands wrote *corridas* about him. You know, like folk songs about old bandits? One group wrote this song about his sexual prowess and how his enemies would die in a rain of bullets or something."

"Love to hear that."

"It sounds much better in Spanish."

"Donnie's mother died when he was young, and his daddy let Donnie do whatever in the hell he wanted. He couldn't cross Luther or anything, but it was like he was told to be a man from the time he was born. I think that kind of rearing can work or make a kid reckless."

"How about you?"

"Same."

"Reckless how?"

"Just stupid shit," Quinn said. "Adding liquor to the punch at a church picnic, stealing a couple goats and leaving them in a teacher's car. One time, Donnie and I stole a change machine from the coin Laundromat. Chickenshit stuff."

"And you didn't get caught?"

"Hell yes, I got caught. But Donnie got it tough from his daddy. Luther never had much of a sense of humor."

"I think I like this Quinn Colson," Dinah said, a big grin on her freckled face. "I thought you always had your boots spit-and-polished and jeans ironed with a crease."

"If my uncle hadn't led me into the Army and the Rangers, I might be running things right along with Donnie."

The door opened to the trailer of the Fearless Flores Family, and a young woman walked out dressed in a leather jacket and pants. She checked over one of the motocross bikes, straddled it, and gunned the motor, peeling out through the maze of trailers. A beaten old man wandered through the cars and trailers, carrying big clear plastic bags stuffed with pink-and-blue cotton candy. A younger man pushed a rolling cart filled with balloon toys of Dora the Explorer and SpongeBob.

"How'd you know Laura would be here?"

"We know her through Alejandro," Dinah said. "That's his trailer right there."

She pointed at a small camper hooked up to the back of a red dually Chevy. Even though it had quit raining, the windshield was flecked with water drops. They'd been watching the carnival for the last hour.

Quinn leaned up toward the windshield. The door to Alejandro's trailer opened, and a very beautiful black-haired woman walked out. She walked up to a large Mexican man and spoke to him for a long while and then moved away and answered a cell phone, looking out into the parking lot and passing right by the window where Dinah and Quinn sat.

"She know you?" Quinn asked.

Dinah shook her head.

"Well, that's her," Quinn said. "That's the woman Donnie called Luz."

"What exactly did he say when you asked him about her?"

"He said he'd just picked her up, tried to get into her pants, and she left."

"You country boys are such charmers."

Dinah got out from the driver's side and walked out into the sideshow. "Stick tight. I want to get a look up close."

DONNIE WATCHED LUZ walk all the way from the civic center lot to where he'd parked at the Harley dealership. He leaned against his Tundra and smoked, tired from the drive up to Memphis that morning and hoping all this would come together. He didn't care to drive all this way again for nothing. It was more than a hundred miles to Memphis and another hundred back home.

"Why are you here?" Luz asked.

"Well, hello, doll," Donnie said. "This your last stop, right? Ain't it?"

"After this, we leave for Texas."

"Without guns?"

"That's all finished," Luz said.

"Didn't you want to say good-bye?"

Luz shrugged and tried to walk away. Donnie grabbed her by the arm and pulled her toward him. "I don't need any more money. Go ahead and try to find you some M4s down at the El Paso Walmart."

"Be quiet," Luz said. "Let go of my arm."

She twisted away, Donnie's hand still on her but his grip loosening. A girl on a motorcycle rode right past his face and then zipped around a curve, doubling back, and came up behind Luz. Donnie felt for the .38 at his back, but she gunned her motor and took off into the civic center lot.

"Friend of yours?"

"She and her brother do high-wire stunts, ride motorcycles in circles in a big round cage. She will jump through a flame. I've never met anyone like her. I admire her."

Donnie smiled and said, "Maybe you're just attracted to crazy people."

Luz looked around the wet parking lot, her eyes settling back on Donnie, not so much as cracking a grin. "So, what do you want?"

"Y'all want the same deal? It's there."

"Still?"

"Yep."

"I will talk to Alejandro," Luz said. "It's not for me to decide."

"Let's go see him right now. I ain't driving all the way back to Tibbehah without knowing what y'all want."

"He's not here."

"OK," Donnie said. "I'll wait."

"You are crazy," Luz said. "He blames you for what happened at that farm. Six of his men are dead. Don't you understand what he does?"

"Condolences," Donnie said, cupping his hand to the wind and lighting up a smoke. "Call him. Tell him I'm ready to deal. Same deal one more time. If he doesn't want it, then *adios* to all y'all."

"It's not the same as before."

"If you don't call him, how 'bout I march right on into the carnival and ask around?" Donnie said, blowing smoke sideways out of his mouth.

"You'd make trouble because you are mad at me? You want to show me that this is all about the guns."

"Hell, it was fun. We both got what we wanted."

"So I'm like a carnival ride?"

"I didn't say I got gypped or nothing."

"Such a fool."

"Bible says never to call a man a fool," Donnie said. "Jesus said it was a one-way ticket to hell."

"Only if it is not justified," Luz said. "The self-righteous are always fools."

"Call that freak show and let me know the deal," Donnie said. "This is all business. Let's not take a detour over to Bullshit City."

Luz looked him over as things clicked around in her head. She finally nodded and said: "Where?"

"There's a Huddle House two exits south," Donnie said. "You know where I'm talking about? I'll keep my phone on."

Luz nodded.

DINAH CLIMBED BACK IN the car and wheeled out of the lot, windshield wipers clearing off drops of rain.

"What did you see?" Quinn asked.

"Your buddy and Laura Zuniga having a heart-to-heart."

"Did they leave together?"

"Nope," Dinah said, reaching for her cell phone, looking at the screen and setting it down. "He headed back to the interstate, and she walked back into the carnival. I don't know what they were talking about, but Laura didn't look happy."

"Now what?"

"Well, I guess I need to take you back to Jericho."

"Can you stay the night?" Quinn asked as she curved onto Interstate 55 South. "I'll send Hondo outside. I'll cook you breakfast. We can head out and pick up Donnie in the morning."

"Too late for that."

"How's that?"

"Expect to meet a few more agents in the coming days," Dinah said, taking the car to up toward ninety. "This was fun, Quinn. But we're going to have to cool it for a while."

"Y'all are going to set up some wiretap, surveillance, and the whole show on Donnie?" Quinn said.

"I'm sorry about your friend," Dinah said. "But gunrunning over several states and a national border isn't a local problem. You should've known that."

"Yeah," Quinn said, studying the passing countryside and occasional roadside exit. "But Donnie Varner definitely is."

Dinah turned to him, briefly.

"God help him," Quinn said.

39

DONNIE WAS ON HIS FOURTH CUP OF COFFEE WHEN HE SPOTTED Alejandro's big red dually pull into the Huddle House parking lot. For some reason he hadn't noticed the airbrush detail on the pickup gate: Jesus, Our Lady of Guadalupe, and a busty woman all stood by a golden-haloed pickup. *Dear Lord and Holy Mother, please pray for my transmission.* Donnie laid down some cash and walked around the side of the Huddle House, plenty of truckers cutting into their steak and eggs and peering out the window to keep Donnie safe. Another truck pulled in right beside Alejandro, and a couple more hombres piled out of the beaten Ford with its exhaust hanging by some baling wire. Donnie waited for everyone to get out and settled, the walkway on the side of the restaurant and over to where Alejandro stood with his elbow cocked on the gate, maybe fifteen feet. Alejandro saw him but didn't acknowledge it.

Donnie walked halfway and nodded to Alejandro.

Just about the time he thought this mess was a dang waste of time,

Alejandro motioned him forward with one hand. The kid shooter was with him, way the hell out in some dead-weed field, staring out at traffic.

Donnie looked back to the big wall of windows and the truckers jawing or picking gristle from their teeth. He took a breath and took the steps toward them, walking confident on shaky legs.

"Buenas noches," Donnie said. He grinned, all cool and easy, and nodded to the big thick men. "Can I interest y'all in some country-fried steak?"

Alejandro looked to his men. One of the beefy guys with the Wyatt Earp mustache relayed something in Spanish to Alejandro. Alejandro set on Donnie with those dead black eyes and nodded.

"So, we got a deal or not?" Donnie said. "Don't mean two shits to me."

Donnie took another long breath, scratched the back of his neck, and fired up a smoke.

The kid shooter walked back from the field and spoke to Alejandro. Alejandro jawed something back to him and studied Donnie some more. Donnie figured they were doing some serious thinking about how to make this work one more time. The traffic flowed steady way out on the overpass, red and white lights blurry far out in the distance. Donnie knew it'd be a good two hours home.

Donnie smiled at Alejandro and offered his hand to secure the deal.

Alejandro looked at it and then cut his eyes at the two men.

The kid whipped out a little .38 with a two-inch barrel and jabbed it into Donnie's stomach while the big men snatched his ass up off the pavement and tossed him into the backseat of that old Ford. The kid took Donnie's gun, and a heavy one sat on his legs and covered his mouth, a gun jabbed down hard into his ear.

They played that Mexican polka music for a long while, not

speaking once, till he felt the road go all bumpy under him. That's when Donnie decided maybe he should've thought this whole thing out before driving out of Tibbehah that morning.

DINAH WAITED FOR QUINN to check in at the sheriff's office and then drive back to the farm. She was sitting with Hondo when he walked into the kitchen. He'd brought a couple blue plate specials from the Fillin' Station diner for supper, fried chicken, greens, and black-eyed peas with corn bread. She'd made some coffee, and said she needed to drive back tonight. All were anxious to get going on Donnie Varner bright and early.

"So we cool it," Quinn said after they finished dinner and he walked her to the door.

"We don't have a choice."

"And you're going to drive back tonight?" he asked, leaning in.

Dinah nodded.

He tucked her hair behind her ear and ran his thumb down her jaw to her chin. She looked down, and he lifted her chin up to him. He wrapped one arm around her and moved his mouth to her ear. "You have to leave right yet?"

She nodded.

He began to unbutton her blouse, pushed her backward, and walked her into his bedroom. She didn't speak, only leaned back into the bed as he undressed her, holding on to the metal headboard, twisting out of her clothes, porch lights bleeding through curtains and across her pale skin. Lips parted and eyes closed, she wore only lace panties and a very thin silver necklace.

Quinn took off his shirt just as Dinah stretched her body with a long breath, tugging at the headboard, and said, "Damn you."

DONNIE NEVER FIGURED digging his own grave would be any church picnic. And he'd figured just about right. Alejandro's boys had driven him to the one section of Mississippi or Tennessee or Arkansas that he hadn't seen and kicked him out into a forest. Alejandro threw him a shovel as one of the big men went to the back of their truck and returned with a sack of lime. When Alejandro pointed his own gun at Donnie, Donnie didn't need a diagram. He started digging way out on some no-name road, out in the Booger Woods.

The boys watched him as he worked, leaning against their pickups and smoking cigarettes. The headlights on both trucks shined through Donnie and deep into the woods. At one point, Alejandro told a joke that really tickled them all, and that was about all Donnie could take. He stopped digging, placing the shovel handle under his chin in the now knee-deep mud, and said, "Alejandro, what's it like to be so damn ugly? You know, even a stray dog wouldn't want to fuck you."

Alejandro looked to one of the big men, who translated: *"Incluso un perro callejero no te jóde."*

Alejandro didn't think it was all that funny. He pointed his gun at Donnie and fired off a couple rounds into the hole. Donnie shrugged and asked for a cigarette. That didn't seem to need any translation in the dark, and Alejandro pulled a pack from his shirt pocket and bent down to light it for him. Donnie guessed this was one of those crazy Mexican respect things. You can shoot a man in a grave he dug, but you shouldn't deny him a damn smoke.

The night was cold, a lot colder than it had been all year, and when they'd stripped Donnie of his weapon, they'd also taken his coat. He felt like his shirt and jeans were made of paper, and the soft earth below his boots felt colder than hell. But the cigarette was some sort of gift to him, nice and warm, bringing him to the idea that at least he'd be dying in Mississippi. Coming back home hadn't always been a certain thing. If he'd been maybe two steps closer to that damn Haji, he would've been scrambled eggs across that bazaar. Coming back from all that, skin grafts and all, sure put things in a different color scheme. After it all, he'd enjoyed every smoke like it was going to be his last. And here it was, his last smoke, and a damn menthol.

"Only folks I know smoke menthols are blacks and women," Donnie said, flicking the butt of the smoke into the woods and continuing on with the grave. He figured there would be a point when they'd see fit he'd done his work, not having to make it regulation or nothing. Digging was taking his breath but not warming him up none, now hitting a mess of thick roots and stone, face filling with blood as he tore into those roots, cutting through them with the dull blade of that shit shovel. He looked up to the mustached banditos, not getting a glance back. But the kid, that damn kid shooter, did the strangest thing. He looked to Donnie and nodded. He smiled for a moment.

Alejandro spoke to his fellas and then walked to Donnie, pistol extended but loose in fingers, coming for him.

Donnie caught his breath, tossed the shovel far into the woods, and stood deep down in that hole and looked at the Mex bastard right in the eye.

"I took your guns and coke, man," Donnie said. "You were correcto. *Por teléfono policía.* Fuck you and fuck your *mamacita.*"

Donnie outstretched his arms and looked deep into the dark woods behind the trucks, saying a silent prayer for Jesus Christ to please forgive an unforgivable stupid bastard like him. *Ain't no sense to it, doesn't make it right, but Christ forgive me.*

He closed his eyes in that hole, body jumping a bit when he heard that pop-pop-pop.

Donnie opened his eyes just as Alejandro fell in beside him.

He stared up at the kid shooter. Each of the big Mexes flanked him.

One of the men outstretched his hand to Donnie and said, *"Vamos. Vamos. Estás vivo."*

The big fella lifted him out of the hole while the other hoisted that big sack of lime up in his arms and dug into it with a pocketknife, coating Alejandro's face and tattooed body. Alejandro's mouth was open, and the white powder filled it and streamed over his eyes and head. The man threw the empty sack in the grave, and the other walked into the woods, still lit up with truck light, and retrieved the shovel. He started to fill it in.

Donnie's body felt bright and raw, his mind shocked back to hell.

"¿Por qué? That means 'Why,' right? *¿Por qué?"*

That little skinny kid with the nothing mustache stared at him and pointed down the long stretch of dirt road. A red truck bumped over the ruts, dual lights shining into the nothingness of the woods, and then darkness again. The door opened and slammed shut, and a shadowed figure walked in front of the headlights.

"You are filthy."

Luz smiled at him as that shovel kept scooping earth and filled in that big ole hole.

40

JASON WAS OUT OF SCHOOL ON MONDAY, AND QUINN INVITED CADDY TO
bring him to the farm that morning to kick around since they'd missed
their weekend together. The day was cold and gray and harsh, speaking of the long winter to come. Quinn planned on building a fire down
in the fire pit and asked Caddy if she'd like to stay. He said he and Jason
liked to cook breakfast on a skillet and sit out and talk in his field.
Caddy smiled, seeming nervous and curious, and decided that would
work fine.

Jason helped him gather the wood from fallen limbs and branches
and tossed them into a pit surrounded by old stones from the house's
original chimney. Caddy had brought from the kitchen an old black
skillet that had been their Aunt Halley's and a loaf of bread, bacon, and
eggs. When the fire got going good, Quinn set the skillet on a flat stone
and waited for it to heat.

"You always liked to cook for me," Caddy said. "Always liked to
cook outdoors."

"I prefer being outside," Quinn said. "Jason is pretty much the same.

Did I tell you what a good fisherman he is? He can't help it. A natural."

Jason turned around with a smirking smile and turned back to the fire. He walked away from the ring searching for more branches.

"I also heard you let him shoot some," Caddy said.

"Just BB guns."

"He's not even four."

"He wanted to use the bow and arrow," Quinn said. "But I put my foot down. Next year, I'll teach him to drive my truck and pick up women."

Caddy cut her eyes at him but smiled, sitting in an Adirondack chair he'd set by the fire, legs tucked under an old horse blanket. Quinn stepped up to the firestone, feeling the heat rising from the skillet, warming his hands.

"You used to make pancakes," she said.

Quinn peered up and set some bacon in the skillet, the fat starting to slowly crackle and pop. Jason joined them at the stone ring again, tossing small limbs and fallen branches into the center. He smiled as they caught to flame and walked backward, stumbling into his mother's knees. She scooped him up and tucked him under the blanket, covering him up all warm to the neck.

Quinn turned the bacon with a long fork and sat down in an identical chair next to Caddy, stretching out his legs. Somehow the grayish day didn't seem to matter around the fire. He had his cell phone in case he was needed before his late shift. Or if Dinah called about Donnie or joining him for a Colson family meal.

"Might have some company at dinner Wednesday."

"The redhead?" Caddy asked.

"Her name is Dinah."

"Not a lot of kids named Dinah these days," Caddy said. "Old-fashioned. But pretty."

Quinn nodded, stood, and turned the bacon again.

"Of course, Anna Lee has the most old-fashioned name I've ever heard," Caddy said.

Quinn cracked some eggs in the skillet, bubbling and popping.

"She's due real soon," Caddy said.

"I saw."

"I'm sorry, Quinn."

"About what?"

"Guess it doesn't matter now."

Jason craned his neck to watch the bacon and eggs. He was enjoying the fire, not listening to his mother or uncle.

"I'm glad you're back, Caddy," Quinn said. "Hope you stay."

Caddy didn't look at him, but he could see her face light up. She tickled Jason under the blanket. "I was up till two last night," Caddy said. "Momma is already planning Christmas."

"So you'll be here?" Quinn asked.

"I don't have any plans other than find a job. Problem is that this county doesn't seem to have any other than waitress or secretary or homemaker."

Quinn squatted by the fire, flipping the bacon one last time, and pulled off a few pieces onto a plate. He dropped in a slice of butter and added a couple pieces of thick-cut bread to make some Texas toast.

"I'm glad you're staying," Quinn said as he slipped off a fried egg onto the plate and browned the toast. He handed the plate to Jason, and he and Caddy ate together. The coffee got going good, and Quinn strained the grounds for a cup, checking out the sky, wondering about rain and slick roads. There would be accidents today. More reports and work.

Quinn had settled into his chair with his coffee and plate when he saw Lillie's Jeep appear over the hill by the old farmhouse. She walked toward them and waved from far off. Jason turned over Caddy's shoulder, smiling at her, yelling, "Miss Lillie."

"You can't beat them off with a stick, can you?" Caddy said, whispering.

"Lillie and I do work together."

"You got lots to learn, brother."

Quinn put down his plate and walked out to meet Lillie with coffee in hand, well out of earshot of Caddy and Jason, still huddled by the fire.

"Something smells good," Lillie said.

"How about some eggs?"

She shook her head.

"What's up?" Quinn asked.

"Miss McCullough called me out to the house because she said someone stole her car keys."

"They on the hook?"

"You've done this before."

Quinn nodded.

"How'd yesterday shake out?" Lillie asked.

Quinn looked over his shoulder at Caddy and Jason. Caddy waved over to Lillie, and Lillie waved back.

"It's time for Donnie to come to Jesus," Quinn said.

"You told her?"

"Did I have a choice?" Quinn said. "I'm lucky she didn't charge me with obstruction."

"Shit," Lillie said. "She don't want to obstruct you for nothing."

Quinn opened his mouth and closed it. He eyed Lillie and shook his head.

"Coffee?"

She nodded and walked in step with him down the hill to the fire. Quinn tossed out the rest of his coffee and poured her a fresh cup in the same mug. He added a couple sugars, knowing how Lillie liked it. She took the coffee and thanked him, making herself comfortable in his chair.

"I saw her yesterday," Lillie said.

"Who?" Quinn said.

"The little girl," Lillie said. "Caddy, did Quinn tell you about the baby I found? There were eleven of them. All precious, but this one little girl came right to me. She was in a crib, hands reaching up, and just clung right to my neck, like she was waiting for us. She didn't cry or nothing. Just settled right into my body under my coat."

Quinn put his boot to the edge of the fire ring and looked from Lillie to Caddy.

"You must feel like that all the time," Lillie said, face flushing right after the words left her mouth.

Caddy saw her embarrassment and nodded, quickly saying, "Not enough."

"Where was the baby?" Quinn asked.

"DHS placed her with a family in Saltillo."

"For how long?"

"I don't know," Lillie said. "They seem like good people. They have three children of their own. Mother knows what she's doing. Child feels comfortable."

"And the others?"

"Same," Lillie said. "This family has one more. The others are in good places until DHS can find something permanent. It's not going to be easy. Some of those kids have special needs. But I guess you saw that."

Caddy looked up from where she held Jason in her lap. She smiled at Lillie and said, "Did she recognize you?"

Lillie's face lit up in a way Quinn had never seen before, soft, warm, completely content. "She did," Lillie said. "She knew me. She held on to my finger and wouldn't let it go. You should have seen her eyes, Caddy. So big and brown."

Quinn looked at the fire, listening, knowing this was a talk between his sister and Lillie. Lillie knew what Quinn would say, expecting him to tell her not to keep visiting the child. It would only make things rougher.

"I call her Rose," Lillie said. "Like my mom. And the family started calling her that, too. She is the most beautiful child I've ever seen. I don't know; this may not seem right to some. But I don't give a damn. I'm going to try and adopt her."

Quinn and Lillie's eyes met.

"I know what you're going to say, Quinn. You're going to tell me this isn't the same as Kenny taking that Lab from their property and setting her out in his backyard. This is a whole lifelong commitment, and me becoming a mother right away. But hell, I'm almost thirty now, and I don't see me changing my life for just anybody."

"Lillie, I think you should," Caddy said. "I think you should help that child. Miracles are rare. But I think things happen for a reason. God put that child in your path."

Lillie drank some coffee and nodded. "What says you, Sheriff?"

"I think you better take some time and think on it."

"I have," Lillie said. "How about you write me a nice recommendation for saving your ass so many times?"

Quinn reached down and took Lillie's coffee from her hands. He took a long sip, handed it back, and nodded. "Yes, ma'am."

41

"WHY?" DONNIE ASKED.

"Does it matter?" Luz said.

"Damn right, it matters," Donnie said. "I just got done digging my own damn grave and pissing down my leg before your boys decide to take out their boss. I think I have a right to inquire about why God's smiling on my sorry ass."

Luz had taken Donnie back to his truck at dawn before she'd followed him down to Highway 6 and drove ninety minutes east to Tupelo. She'd rented a room at an old motel called the Town House, where he'd showered and cleaned the dirt off his jeans and wiped down his boots. When he'd gotten halfway straight, they drove in his truck up Gloster Street to find a McDonald's or Burger King or anyplace half decent to eat. Donnie drove. Luz rested her head on her fist, seeming to sleep but suddenly saying: "Can you still get the guns?"

"The guns?" Donnie asked. "Are you shitting me? You just get finished telling me you can't do jack without Alejandro and then y'all kill the son of a bitch. Just who am I talking to? Did you kill him for me?

Or were you pissed at him anyway? I don't mean to be unappreciative, but what are y'all gonna do with me if I deliver?"

"He killed a friend," Luz said. "The man at the motel. He was growing paranoid, believing some were working against him."

"Ain't paranoia if you're right, darlin'," Donnie said. "Just what in the hell is going on?"

"Can you still get the guns?"

"No," Donnie said. "I mean, shit. I don't know. I guess."

"Now that Alejandro is dead, men will come for us," Luz said. "Do you understand? These are the people I told you about. This man Tony."

"Wait, wait, wait," Donnie said, holding up his hand. "Hold the goddamn phone. I thought you killed Alejandro for your damn boyfriend. Now you're crossing your boyfriend, too? I kind of feel like I walked into this movie a little late."

"If you can get the guns," Luz said, "we will need them tomorrow."

"Tomorrow?" Donnie said, laughing a little to himself, spotting a Burger King down the road and turning on his blinker. "Oh, sure. Christ Almighty. This thing is going to take some time and phone calls. People gotten real paranoid. My damn hands keep shaking."

"Listen," Luz said. "Be quiet. OK? Listen to me. There is too much to tell. Too much to explain. It won't make sense to you."

"You ever hear about Parchman prison? It's a place in the Delta where they skipped right over the damn twentieth century. They got men in there look like gorillas and take fellas like me as their damn tree mates. You are a real looker, and I care about you, Luz, but I don't want to spend the rest of my life being cornholed by the missing link."

"I can't explain everything. It won't make sense to you or any American."

"Darlin', do I look like I used to take the short bus to school? I made a B plus in Social Studies."

———

"DID YOU HEAR what's been happening on *Days of Our Lives?*" Lillie asked Mara in the interview room of the Tibbehah County Jail. "Abigail sure laid into Chad for kissing Melanie. And now Daniel wants that DNA test to prove he's Maggie's son. Lots going on in Salem."

"Was my momma there?" Mara asked. "At that farm with the children?"

Lillie sat down, and Quinn hung back again, lightly closing the door, standing and watching Lillie take the lead. She pushed a Coca-Cola across to Mara, dressed in that XL orange jumpsuit and picking at her cuticles, nervous, but a little wild-eyed, too. She seemed to Quinn like someone just waking up from a dream, everything still a little fuzzy and out of focus.

"We found some evidence that she and Ramón had been there," Lillie said. "A woman we arrested said they'd left a few hours before to go shopping."

"That's my momma," Mara said, nibbling on a cuticle. "Loves to shop."

"They hadn't left much in the house," Lillie said. "There wasn't formula for the babies, and none of the children had been changed in some time. They had sores."

"I'm sorry."

"Why are you sorry, Mara?" Quinn asked. He had his arms crossed, leaning against the wall in shadow. "Wasn't your fault."

"My momma isn't that bad," Mara said. "She was doing the best she can. She has a thyroid disorder that she got from my mee-maw. Reason she got so big. Everything she's done has been out of the love she has for the kids."

Quinn looked to Lillie, Lillie not taking her eyes off the girl.

"Mara, she threatened you," Lillie said. "You don't need to protect her. We need you to make things right."

"She's scared," Mara said. "Don't you bet? Don't you bet she's scared out there with y'all chasing her? How come no kids got shot at that farm? Y'all can't shoot guns around kids."

"We're chasing her because she killed a child," Quinn said. "What are you trying to do?"

"What will happen to them?" Mara said. "If you catch them?"

"You said you'd help," Quinn said. "I thought that was pretty stand-up."

Lillie looked up to Quinn, telling him to back off, and then back to Mara. "What about Gabriela?" she said. "Don't you care what happened to her?"

Mara was silent, slack-shouldered and chewing on a nail. She hadn't touched her bottle of Coke. She slumped in her chair, looking deflated.

"Mara?" Lillie asked.

The room stood still and very quiet, only the steady tapping of the keyboard, Mary Alice at work, from down the hall. Quinn rolled his shoulders, still standing back, spotting an old calendar for the Bank of Jericho on the wall. A quail hunt with pointers, men with guns walking through the grass. His uncle's shaky scrawl noting certain trial dates and events back from five years ago. The paper had curled yellow from sun and tobacco smoke.

"What happened that day, Mara?" Lillie asked. "I need you to explain."

Mara didn't speak for nearly a minute. Her large eyes finally lifted, looking at Quinn, not Lillie, and saying, "It's not like you think."

"What's that?" Quinn asked.

"Momma's not bad, you know. She was trying to help all those children. That's what she was trying to do."

"Go ahead," Lillie said. "Tell us."

DONNIE TOOK A RIGHT into the Burger King parking lot and killed the engine. He leaned back into the driver's seat and turned to Luz. He hadn't slept in a long while and he was sick of Luz speaking in code, toying with him. The ashtray in his truck was overloaded with spent butts, Mountain Dew cans at his feet. He felt like he'd been on full tilt for days now. Luz kept on staring out the passenger window, not facing Donnie, not speaking or making a move.

"Luz? You owe me a story."

"Really?" Luz said. "What about Alejandro?"

"What about him?"

"We saved you."

"OK," Donnie said, those burgers smelling pretty good. "I'll give you that. But that's where things get a little fuzzy."

Luz shook her head and stared at the window. Donnie could see the smoke coming from the top of the burger joint. "Holy hell, I'm hungry. Can I get you something?"

"We can talk later."

"Nope." Donnie shook his head. "Right now. If you want me to make that call, you and me gonna have to have a come-to-Jesus."

Luz turned to him and stared, unsure just what he was talking about. She studied his face, waiting.

"A come-to-Jesus?" Donnie asked. "If you're gonna get me killed or in prison, I'd like to know what team I'm playing for."

He leaned in and put his hand on her knee, smelling the sweetness of her soap and the shampoo in her black hair, and said as softly as he could, "I'm walking inside to get me a Whopper and fries with a chocolate milk shake. When I come out, tell me your deal in all this. You want something?"

Donnie kissed her cheek. She raised her eyes at him and nodded. He smiled back and snatched the keys from the ignition.

"Just in case you ain't in the talkin' mood," Donnie said. He grinned and walked inside.

When he came back, Luz's eyes were closed, using a jeans jacket for a pillow. She turned, waking, as she watched him unwrap that Whopper and squeeze out some ketchup for the fries. He hadn't said a word and started to eat as Luz said, "Have you ever heard of a place called Cherán?"

Donnie's mouth was full. He shook his head and listened.

"WHAT WAS SHE TRYING TO DO?" Lillie asked. "What happened to that child?"

"It's not like you think," Mara said.

Quinn moved from the wall and sat down at the table, not looking at Lillie, knowing he'd only find a dirty look. He bowed his head and looked down at his hands, not speaking, trying to let some silence work on the girl.

"I don't want him here," Mara said. "He hates me. I can see it on him."

"He's the sheriff," Lillie said. "He doesn't hate you."

"Well, I don't like him."

"I can leave," Quinn said.

"What you say to me goes to him," Lillie said. "You want to tell me what's going on with you? Did your momma send you another message? Is that what's wrong?"

Mara dropped her head into her hands. Quinn figured it was some act of contemplation.

"What will you do to my momma?"

"We won't do anything," Lillie said. "It's up to the courts."

"Will they kill her?"

"Nope," Lillie said. "She'll go to jail. The way she kept those children and those animals was a sickness. You don't take anger out on a toddler, Mara."

"I told you she had the thyroid. She couldn't go nowhere without people laughing at her."

"Doesn't excuse what she did," Quinn said. "She killed that little girl."

"That's a lie," Mara said as her face grew red, grinding her hands into her temples. "That's a damn lie."

"How do you figure?" Lillie asked in a calm, easy voice. "What happened?"

"Please don't kill her," Mara said. "I heard y'all shot six men. If she'd been there, you would have shot her, too."

"Does she carry a gun?" Quinn asked.

"Quinn," Lillie said.

Quinn stood up and turned for the door. He was tired of the cramped room, tired of Lillie getting on his ass, and of whatever Mara was planning. He said, "I'm tired of this shit."

"I killed that baby," Mara said. "Jesus, Lord help me. Jesus, Lord help me."

Quinn stopped and turned.

"I don't believe you," Lillie said. "Did your mother threaten you again? This won't help her. It just makes things harder for you."

"I killed Gabriela."

"No, you didn't," Lillie said. "Your mother has a sickness."

"We tried to sauce her," Mara said, wiping her face. "She was crying and crying. I poured Tabasco down her throat. Screaming. I never thought no kid could sound like that. I shook her real good. But she wouldn't be quiet. I couldn't stand it. Holy Lord. You don't know how it makes you crazy. Quit hunting my momma. Leave her alone. I killed that baby. I threw her. She hit a table. I didn't mean it. I didn't mean it."

Lillie dropped her head. Quinn watched Mara cry for a long moment.

"You sure this is what you want?" Lillie asked. "Is this your confession?"

Quinn tilted his head and scratched his neck. He looked to Lillie. Lillie let out a long breath and looked up at the ceiling. Mara stared at them both and nodded.

"Deputy Virgil, you want to call up her attorney and get the D.A. down here from Oxford?"

Quinn walked out of the room, and Lillie followed. He closed the door. Mara was crying as she did the first night they found her.

"Jesus Christ," Lillie said. "You believe it?"

"I hate to say it," Quinn said, "but I sure do."

DONNIE SWALLOWED. "Thought you said you were from Saragosa, Texas?"

"My mother and father were from Mexico," Luz said. "Nuevo Laredo. They moved to Texas before I was born, and as I've told you, my father was a narco in El Paso. My mother and I lived away from him so we'd be safe. When I would visit my father, there was a woman who cared for me. She was from Cherán. She became my second mother."

"OK," Donnie said. "Sure you don't at least want some fries?"

"I am not a narco," she said. "I am not like my father."

"Sure, baby."

"You speak more than you listen."

"You know, my daddy always says the same thing," Donnie said.

"They killed her and her husband," Luz said. "The narcos who work for Tony shot them and burned their bodies. They were found by the spring in Cherán to send a message to all the informers and people fighting them there. The entire town had been destroyed. All of it had been so beautiful, up in the mountains with thick forests. The narcos came and stole the land, logged everything."

"Was it their land got logged?" Donnie asked.

"My friends had tried to protect what was left," Luz said, shaking her head. "The townspeople stood guard in the woods, checking every truck that would try to enter or leave. The loggers worked for the narcos. Los Zetas. They killed my friends. You see? I have done things in the last two years that make me hate myself and grow sick of everything I touch."

"What the hell are you thinking?" Donnie said. "We're all gonna get killed. For what? Some fucking trees?"

"I do this out of respect for my friends, for everything they tried to accomplish. That boy with me is their son. Luis and Javier had family in Cherán. Vincente, too, which is why Alejandro killed him. If we can get these guns to the village . . . You see? This is something. This is something for us."

"And y'all had planned on double-crossing these bastards the whole time?" Donnie shook his head. He drank some milk shake. "Just how long till Tony the Tiger shits a golden turd and comes looking for Alejandro? And his guns?"

"Soon."

"Terrific." Donnie wadded up the burger wrapper and tossed it into the bag. "You know, this is some shit to spring on a man without something to drink. How about I find a liquor store, and we head back to that motel?"

"And then what?" Luz said. "They will know Alejandro is dead. They will come for us. They know who got him the guns and believe you told the police. They will blame all of us."

"Son of a bitch." Donnie grinned and pulled out into traffic. "Wait until I tell my daddy what I've gotten myself into. He'll never believe it."

42

BOTH MEN WORE NAVY SUITS, REDDISH TIES, AND SCUFFED-UP DRESS shoes. Dinah took a lot of care to address Quinn as Sheriff Colson and the men as Special Agents Willis and Caruthers. Willis was black and Caruthers was white. They both smiled in a good-natured way as Quinn shook their hands and asked them to take a seat. They didn't want coffee. Yes, it was their first time in Tibbehah County. No, they weren't from Mississippi but liked being assigned to the Oxford office. Dinah seemed pleased with the way things were going, waved to Lillie when she passed by the open door, and took a seat with the other agents. They'd all driven down from Oxford that morning.

"I guess y'all want to know all about Donnie Varner," Quinn said.

Willis was light-skinned and a little thick in the neck. He grinned at Quinn and nodded. "Yeah, I guess we would."

Caruthers nodded, too. He was short and bulky and wore a crew cut. He had asked for a paper cup to spit some Skoal while they talked. Quinn figured him for Army at one time, but probably long ago. Both men were in their late forties.

"I don't know how he got those guns," Quinn said. "He's always been pretty smart and resourceful. You make the right friends, and things like that can be done. I guess y'all know that."

"You know how he fell in with the Mexicans?" Caruthers asked.

"I was talking with Agent Brand about that the other day." Quinn smiled to Dinah, hoping she'd appreciate his professionalism. "We were buddies a long time back. I hadn't seen him for years until he got home this last time. That's when I saw him with this woman Laura Zuniga, the one who goes by Luz."

Dinah nodded, knees together, hands in her lap. She looked uneasy, restless. Quinn wished he could have told her to relax, that he had no intention of leaning over and kissing her in front of her people.

"Forty-six of those M4s we recovered were traced back to his Guard unit," Willis said. "Got any idea where he got the rest?"

"We didn't exactly have a heart-to-heart when I asked him about his girlfriend. He pretended like he didn't know her that well. Or know what she was hooked into."

"DEA arrested Ramón Torres in Houston a few years back," Caruthers said. A light blond beard was showing up on his jaw, his skin reddened and wind-chapped. He took a break to spit, feeling comfortable away from a federal office. "And he was connected to a case last year with teenage girls being turned out in a motel in south Memphis. Some of them were twelve, thirteen. Class-act stuff. We think he sold a lot of babies, kept some for himself and his wife or whatever she was. We figure he met her moving children and teenage girls up to Memphis. Made more money trafficking in people than crystal meth."

"I don't think anybody can make heads or tails of that relationship," Quinn said.

"Business partners," Dinah said. "She had a very active online life, trading dolls and collectibles. I heard from some people in town she was involved in beauty pageants."

"Only contest she could've won was for livestock," Quinn said.

"Lillie told me about Mara confessing," Dinah said. "You think she's taking a hit for her mother? I don't see her acting out on a child like that. She's pretty meek."

"Bets are off in that house," Quinn said. "I can't imagine what it would do to a girl that age, having a mother like that."

"And a stepfather like Ramón," Willis said. "You know he's hooked into some cartel folks. Men on the coast by way of Houston and El Paso, MS-13, Los Zetas. Some real nice people."

Quinn nodded, trying to see just where the Feds wanted to take it, making sure it was an easy transition muscling him out of the way. He just listened, waiting for them to get the hell on with it.

"These folks make those meth peddlers you ran up against last year look like church deacons," Willis said.

"Well, one of them was a pastor," Quinn said, smiling.

"That the one they hung from the cross?" Caruthers asked. "I read about it in the *Commercial Appeal*."

Quinn nodded.

"OK," Caruthers said, leaning back into his seat, smoothing down his tie as he spit. "We believe Donnie Varner entered the picture through Ramón Torres. Torres may have sought him out at the gun range, hoping to make a few straw buys with Janet and then moving on down the line. When they found out Mr. Varner had access to more military-grade weapons, they must've thought they hit the damn jackpot."

"And now what?" Quinn asked.

Dinah looked to Willis, and he noted a subtle nod.

"We have an informant that says Varner has one more shipment moving in the morning," Dinah said. "Looks like an eighteen-wheeler loaded down with a couple hundred assault weapons is headed for Tibbehah County in the next twenty-four hours."

Quinn leaned back and blew out a long breath. "Terrific."

NEARLY TWENTY MINUTES BEFORE, Ramón Torres had showed up at Donnie Varner's gun range and asked to speak to Alejandro. Donnie hadn't seen Ramón since before he'd sent him up Highway 78 to the carnival, and, truth be told, the little Mexican had looked much better. He was skinny and smaller now, with stick-thin arms and a teenager's mustache. Ramón sported a pair of rubber farm boots and one of those jackets you get from Marlboro after smoking a thousand packs of cigarettes.

"Alejandro ain't here," Donnie said. "Aren't you supposed to be on the run? I seen your picture at the post office."

"I have a message for him," Ramón said. He didn't have much of an accent, just a weird way of screwing up a couple words. Message sounding a lot fancier coming out of his mouth.

"You got a cell?"

"Yes."

"I'll have him give you a ring."

"I'll wait," Ramón said. "What about Luz?"

"She ain't here, neither."

"Go get her."

"I don't like the way you're saying that, partner," Donnie said. "Guess you didn't see my name out there on the property sign."

Ramón just looked at him, a black-eyed little banty rooster. Donnie wasn't sure, but he could bet on a semi-auto under that cheap-ass coat.

"I will wait."

"Go ahead," Donnie said, motioning to an empty strip of land. "Take a seat on that stump over there. I'll be back sometime tomorrow."

"You tell Alejandro to call Tony," Ramón said. "Do you understand?"

"How's the wife, Ramón?" Donnie said. "Those pictures I seen of her in the paper sure put on a few pounds. I know she's looked better."

"She's a fattened pig."

"No arguments there, brother."

"When I came to you," Ramón said, those dead eyes fixed on Donnie, "I was told you were a man I could trust. A man good to his word."

"And?"

"You brought those lawmen to where you traded the guns," Ramón said. "I could have been arrested. You've made some men I work with very unhappy."

"Sorry to piss down your leg, but I didn't do jack shit," Donnie said. "That's the cost of living, doing business up in here in north Mississippi. Sometimes the law gets wind of business. They ain't all on the take like the taco brigade down in Chihuahua."

Ramón stared at him. In the silence, Donnie fired up a smoke.

He blew out a long stream and said, "Well, it's been good seeing you, Ramón. Best to the little woman."

Ramón turned and walked back to a white Nissan pickup, kicking up loose gravel as he hit the road.

Donnie pulled out his cell and punched up Luz's number.

"Let's get this thing done," Donnie said. "Just saw Ramón Torres. Better put in a word with Mother Mary. Some bad motherfuckers are truckin' this way."

QUINN WALKED THE AGENTS out to the parking lot, Dinah hanging back, waiting while Caruthers and Willis made cell phone calls by their vehicle. She stopped a few feet outside the sheriff's office door and peered up at Quinn, smiling at him a whole lot more than she did in the thirty minutes she'd sat in his office.

"How'd I do?" Quinn said, giving a lazy salute to Willis.

"Just fine."

"You want to tell me about this source of y'all's?"

"Might be easier to introduce you," she said.

"OK," Quinn said. "That mean you're staying in town?"

"They're staying, too," Dinah said, motioning to the other agents and squinting in the harsh sun. "Got a recommendation for a good motel?"

"Sure," Quinn said. "I always stay at the Traveler's Rest. Just make sure they request the room without the blood on the floor."

"I'll let them know."

"You want to ride with me?" Quinn said, walking toward the new truck.

"I do like the new ride," Dinah said.

"We hit some back roads, and I'll even let you turn on the siren."

"I WANT TO GO WITH YOU," Donnie said.

"You're crazy."

"Yes, ma'am."

"Do you know what you're in for?" Luz asked. "Once we get to Cherán, we won't leave for a long while."

"I love Mexican food."

"Listen to me, this is a poor place," Luz said. "This isn't going down to the beach and drinking a six-pack of Tecate."

"Don't they sell beer?"

"It's dry," Luz said. "They made alcohol illegal so the loggers working for the narcos wouldn't stay."

"Well, shit," Donnie said. "Maybe I can bootleg some in."

"These men have killed nearly fifty villagers this year and promise only more violence and killing until the people stop fighting back."

Donnie slid up on the tailgate of Luz's truck and passed the cigarette into her waiting fingers. They looked down into the empty ravine, stripped of trees and littered with busted car parts and rusted refrigerators and the like. Donnie thought about things as they smoked, starting a new one, passing it on, thinking some more.

"When I thought I was dead," Donnie said. "I'll explain the whole thing to you sometime later. I wasn't quite awake and not quite out, but I had some crazy, crazy dreams about angels and Jesus and my dead momma, who still looked the same as she had when I was a kid. Somewhere mixed up in all of it, I remember standing in the middle of some land that looked like the other side of the fucking moon. I was alone and cold and guess it was night or outer space or whatever. But everyone was gone. The whole show was done. I felt like all the air had been sucked from me and I woke up gasping, goddamn promising myself that I would never die here in Jericho."

"But you would die in Mexico."

"I'm headed out with you, Luz," Donnie said. "I don't give a good goddamn what happens. I am pretty sorry at saying good-bye."

Luz nodded, passed the smoke back to Donnie.

"OK," she said. "When can we leave?"

Donnie looked at the old Airstream and ratty trailer where Tiny was sleeping one off. He shrugged. "Just waiting on the phone call."

"Can you drive?"

"Baby, I'm hell bound and down."

DINAH DROVE QUINN OUT to the Indian mounds on the Natchez Trace and parked right by the historic marker telling them about the race of hunter-gatherers and basket weavers who'd lived there. Dinah got out of the car and stretched, walking out to an empty welcome center with a few tables and chairs under a tin roof. There were four mounds out in a wide field, subtle bumps that hadn't made a lot of sense to the white settlers until they cut into them to plant crops. Inside, they found bones and arrows and hatchets and broken pottery. Some at least had the sense to understand these were holy places and leave them the hell alone, not like most of Tibbehah that had been stripped to the bone time and again by soulless men who grew fat from timber and on the backs of unskilled workers.

"Until this is over, let's calm this down a bit," Dinah said.

"You already told me that."

"In case you were trying to get me to stay with you tonight."

"Wouldn't think of it."

"I know you," Dinah said. "You would ask me over for coffee or a drink or to say hello to your dog."

"Hondo has taken a shine to you."

"But it won't work."

"Till this is over."

"I just hope we can end this thing as friends."

Quinn had his hands deep in the pockets of his rancher coat, sheriff's office ball cap low over his eyes. He studied her face and smiled, thinking she was being coy and funny but not seeing any of that, only a stern face looking down the Trace for whoever in the hell was going to tell them about Donnie Varner's gun deal.

"I thought this was a temporary cooling off," Quinn said. "What are you saying now?"

"You got to understand I don't make the decisions here," Dinah said. "I came here to look for Ramón Torres, work with the locals on what comes next."

"Sure."

"But I don't have anything to do with a lot of this."

"OK."

"But you'll blame me," Dinah said. "Hate me. I don't have any doubt about that. I know a lot about you, Quinn Colson. You are a man to hold a grudge."

Quinn reached out for her hand and pulled her in close. He brushed back strands of hair from her cheek and leaned in to kiss her on the forehead, make sure that she knew that he wasn't ready for any of this to end.

"Don't get crazy," was all Quinn said, before seeing a maroon Cadillac slow on the Trace and flick on its blinker, taking a lot of time to round into the lot and slow to a stop.

He let go of Dinah's hand. Dinah walked back a few paces and dropped her head.

Johnny Stagg crawled out from the driver's seat and waved to the federal agent like an old friend.

43

DONNIE GOT THE CALL AT ONE A.M., LUZ ASLEEP IN HIS ARMS, TELEVISION playing some infomercial about the history of classic country music, pictures of Hank Williams and Patsy Cline flashing across the screen. A grizzled old Mickey Gilley, wearing an open shirt and showing off a hunk of gold jewelry on his hairy chest, telling everyone they'd be a fool not to buy this collection of the best music that was ever made. Donnie pushed himself upright, not recognizing the caller's number, and just said, "Start talking."

The whole conversation was one-sided and took about three seconds.

"Go time," Donnie said, shaking Luz awake. She was wearing one of Donnie's old Tibbehah High baseball T-shirts, the one with the Wildcat head, and a pair of cotton panties speckled with blue flowers.

They were dressed and back in Donnie's truck in fifteen minutes, down to the Rebel Truck Stop in thirty. They sat there in the cold, heater cranked, waiting until they'd get a second call about a truck rolling in and where to leave the money.

"Riding around with all this cash makes me feel like I got a target on my forehead."

"Don't you trust these people?" Luz asked. "The man who you met in Memphis?"

"I trust him about as far as I can sling a piano."

"But you trust me?" Luz asked.

"You know it."

"Why?"

"I guess you got to trust somebody."

She nodded. That was good enough for her, the time coming up on one-thirty. The radio station out of Tupelo had called for a freeze that morning, the first of the season. All the truckers heading into the Rebel wore thick jackets and ball caps, coming out with hot coffee and biscuits. A sign outside the diner advertised a steak dinner special with pumpkin pie.

"You trust the boys with you?"

"Didn't they save your life?" Luz said. "You should trust them, too."

"I guess so."

"They can catch up with us in Texas before we cross."

"I'm not driving their rig south," Donnie said. "I'm not that goddamn stupid. You hear about that trucker in Houston that got ambushed by those cartel boys? You don't know who the hell is watching us."

Luz had pulled on jeans and boots, keeping on the Tibbehah High tee under her jeans jacket. Her hair was pulled back tight in a ponytail, big brown eyes watching the thick lot of parked trucks glowing red and green in the night. Donnie's .38 dug into his back as he turned in his seat.

His phone rang just about the time a purple Peterbilt, hauling a trailer for Little Debbie snack cakes, turned off the highway and drove up under the portico. A big man in a leather jacket and baseball cap hopped outside, hooked up the pump, spit, and walked into the truck stop.

"If I don't come out," Donnie said, "you go ahead and buy that collection of country music that Mickey Gilley was talking about. Play it at my funeral."

"What song?" Luz said, sliding behind the wheel of Donnie's pickup as Donnie climbed out.

"How about 'King of the Road'?" Donnie said.

"And if you do come back?" Luz said, smiling.

"Follow me back to the range," he said. "We'll switch the guns out there. Tiny can bring this one back tomorrow. We reload tonight, get out of here before dawn."

"Let's just go," Luz said. "Let's leave."

"If Stagg wanted out of this deal," Donnie said, "how come I got a handoff at his place? Nobody gets out of Jericho without paying tribute to that son of a bitch. This here deal isn't free. I want my own ride, free and clear, and headed out clean. OK?"

Luz nodded and handed him the thick Army duffel bag. He threw it over his shoulder, like a trucker out to change into some fresh clothes and get ready for the next leg.

He slammed the door behind him, breath clouding in front of his face, and marched right for the front doors of the Rebel Truck Stop.

"THERE HE GOES," Dinah said, sitting in the driver's seat, Quinn next to her. "Your pal is pretty stubborn. He gets into something and he sees it through."

"I guess that's one way to look at it."

Quinn had gone into the Rebel and gotten some coffee for them an hour back, the coffee cold and bitter and terrible. But he sipped it anyway. The worst cup of coffee he'd ever had in Afghanistan or the Cole Range at Fort Benning was still better than nothing at all.

"You recognize the rig's driver?" Dinah asked.

"Nope," Quinn said. "You?"

"Hard to get a good look with that hat," Dinah said. "One of Campo's flunkies. He'll have someone picking him up or have a car stashed. We'll follow him home."

"And we follow Donnie?" Quinn said.

"You mind being in the car with me that long?"

"Nope."

"You haven't said a lot since we met with Stagg."

"You met with Stagg," Quinn said. "I just listened."

"He did tip us," Dinah said. "And it wasn't me who got him involved. I knew you'd blame me. The more you stick around law enforcement, you'll do plenty of business with folks a lot worse than Stagg."

"I just don't like to be ambushed," Quinn said.

"I know you blame him for what happened to your uncle, and I know his reputation in this county," Dinah said. "To be honest, I didn't quite know how to tell you. And if I told you, I knew you wouldn't come with me to meet him. I wanted you there with me, let him know that you were in on this thing, too."

"In case he tried to screw the Feds."

"In case he thought he could work around you."

Quinn shrugged. He drank some of the Rebel's cold coffee.

"You got someone inside," Quinn said, "watching this exchange with Donnie?"

She nodded in the shadow of the parked car.

"I keep on waiting to see how Stagg is going to flip on us," Quinn said. "I don't know where or when, but it will happen. I just hope Donnie will make it out alive."

"We got six agents on this," Dinah said. "We're in control."

Quinn shook his head. "How do you figure that?"

THE BIG MAN HAD HUNG his leather coat over the wall of the shitter. Donnie saw his boots under the door along the row of stalls, a skinny old country man washing his hands with pink soap next to him. Donnie washed his hands, too, just for something to do, money at his feet, the old skinny man saying something about how it was colder outside than a Minnesota well digger's ass. Donnie didn't answer him, waiting for the old man to go ahead and get so he could get the hell out of here.

With one hand in his jacket, feeling the butt of the .38, he laid the duffel to the tile floor and kicked it under the stall. He heard the big faceless man spit, flush the commode, and unzip the bag. Thirty seconds later, a set of keys slid out on the floor, the man coughing, Donnie thinking that maybe he really was in there making a deposit with six hundred grand between his legs.

He didn't waste any time finding out, snatching up the keys and heading back into a long hallway of showers and phone banks, and a television room where two old truckers sat watching *Lord of the Rings* with open mouths and half-closed eyes.

One of those old boys had a cigarette hanging loose in his wrinkled fingers. Donnie came around the corner and took off through a side door, a long distance between him and that Peterbilt. The pavement seemed to grow and expand like it did in movies when people felt shaky, a whole long walk, lots of trucks all around him, a few hard fellas pumping gas. Donnie watched their hands and looked to open windows, wondering who in the hell might be in the back of that cab. He sure didn't want to knock that big engine into gear and head out onto the highway just as he felt a long thin wire cut into his neck.

Motherfucker. He sure needed to rethink his career.

"DID YOU KNOW tomorrow night is Halloween?" Dinah asked.

"Hadn't really thought about it."

"You don't like Halloween."

"No, I like it," Quinn said. "When Caddy and I were kids, my mom outlawed it for a while. She started going to some crazy church, not the one where we go now, with a pastor that said it was the night of the devil. My mom has mellowed out a lot since then. That preacher was involved in some kind of pyramid scheme that bankrupted the church."

"Will you take your nephew out?"

"Probably," Quinn said. "Caddy called me and asked if she could borrow my Army helmet. I guess I know what he's going to be."

"Where's his father?" Dinah asked.

"Never asked."

"You met him?"

"I don't know if Caddy knows who he is."

"That bad?" Dinah asked.

"Worse."

"Has Jason asked about his father yet?"

"We try and avoid that subject," Quinn said. "I think my mother told him that his daddy was out west with my daddy."

"That's where your father went when he left?"

"Last I heard."

"We don't need to talk about it."

"Better than talking about Stagg," Quinn said. "Jesus. I still can't believe a federal agent trusts someone like that bastard."

Dinah cranked the car, spotting Donnie walking cocky and cool out of the front of the Rebel, flipping keys in his hand. They watched as he opened the passenger door of the rig and leaned inside, both legs still on the steps. He closed the door, hung up the pump, and then walked around the cab, got behind the wheel, and snapped on the headlights.

"Sorry, bud," Quinn said.

"See?" Dinah said. "We got this."

DONNIE CALLED TINY AND SHANE and told them to go ahead and drive that cargo van onto his land. He said he was headed that way and they could start transferring the cargo in twenty minutes. Tiny said OK, but he still didn't know what the hell was going on.

"Don't ask me no questions, and I won't tell you no lies," Donnie said, clicking off and rolling up and down the hills into the Jericho city limits. He didn't have much he wanted to take with him. He already had packed a bag of T-shirts and jeans and shit. He snagged a dozen or so CDs for the trip, some Jason Isbell, Heartless Bastards, Chris Knight, and Lucero. The old Victorian and wide-porched single-story houses passed by his windows, some of them lit up in black and orange, witches and skeletons hung on the doors, cobwebs strung across windows. Somehow Halloween seemed to suit Jericho, Donnie thought, time running up toward three a.m.

Donnie slowed to a stop near the Sonic and Dollar Store. He thought about his daddy, knowing he'd be about to open up the Quick Mart, putting biscuits in the oven with Miss Peaches. He could call him, tell him to hang tough, and send him a postcard soon.

Or, he could let Shane and Tiny earn some money while he did the right thing. He figured it would be right to look the old man in the eye and say good-bye.

———

"I DIDN'T SEE THIS COMING," Dinah said, watching Donnie hang a right into the gun range road by the sign reading WE RESERVE THE RIGHT FOR YOU TO KISS OUR ASS. She slowed and U-turned on the county road, the car pointed back to Jericho. She made some calls to the other agents strewn around the county.

"Headed back to the roost," Quinn said. "Guess the deal's not ready yet. Donnie usually does business on his own time."

"That's not what Stagg said."

"You're a sharp woman," Quinn said. "I know you know a hell of a lot more than me about the way gun deals work. But you need to trust me as the expert on Johnny Stagg. Did you all pay him as an informant?"

"Nope."

"Did you contact him or did he call you?"

"I'm not supposed to say."

Dinah turned off her lights, pickup trucks and the occasional car blowing by the empty county road. They sat there in the dark, waiting for Donnie to head back out, neither one of them saying anything for a long while, a cold wind buffeting the car.

"The Varners' land backs up to the Byrd property," Quinn said. "Take me to my truck, and we can ride the fire road on in. Should give a pretty good vantage point to keep tabs on Donnie."

Dinah didn't say anything.

"There's a family cemetery up on a ridge," Quinn said. "When they start moving those guns, we can radio down to the road and stop them. Or we can work on getting a warrant, go ahead and stop them before they leave."

Dinah didn't speak, her pale face shadowed. She was listening to

Quinn, staring at the long county road winding up into the hills, head resting on her right hand.

"I can spare a few deputies," Quinn said. "But Donnie won't give you trouble. He'll know he's beat. That makes things easier on us all."

"Quinn?"

He nodded. Dinah's voice sounded thin and a bit shaky.

"What if I asked you just to walk away from this?"

"From us?"

"From Donnie and the guns."

Quinn smiled a bit. He rested a hand on her knee.

"Let 'em go," she said. "Those guns have to walk from Mississippi. We bust Donnie and we screw up the bigger picture."

"What if he gets away?"

"I'm asking you to step back," Dinah said. "OK? It has to be this way."

"Are you prepared to live with a hundred assault rifles turned loose?"

"I am."

"For the greater good?"

"We never had any intention of stopping things here," Dinah said, turning to look at Quinn. "I've made some promises to make sure that happens."

"Helps to have a hick sheriff in the sack, doesn't it?"

Dinah kept staring straight ahead, silent, before she turned the key and headed back into Jericho. Quinn stepped out into the jail parking lot near three a.m. without either of them speaking a word. Dinah wheeled out of the lot, twin taillights disappearing along Main and toward the Town Square.

Quinn waited a minute, settling his thoughts before he pulled out his cell and called Lillie at home.

"You up?" Quinn said. "We need to talk. And please don't say a word about being right."

44

THE BACK LIGHT WAS ON IN VARNER'S QUICK MART, AND LUTHER'S BEATEN GMC was parked around by the tanks, busted milk crates, and Dumpsters. Donnie walked around back and knocked a couple times, Miss Peaches letting him into the kitchen, her hands covered in flour, a big pile of biscuit dough waiting for her on a stainless steel table. Donnie winked at her, the old woman paying him no mind as he headed through a long hall filled with racks of white bread and overstocked candy bars, finding Luther stocking cigarettes behind the register in the thin light shining from the bank of refrigerators. He had fired one off already, the whole place smelling of thick smoke and grease.

"Daddy, you got a second?"

Luther turned around, face craggy and wind-chapped, and said, "Sure. Let me put on a pot."

He filled up the coffeemaker, taking care to restock the creamer and sugar in the dispensers and finding a seat before Donnie by the plate-glass window, pumps still off, big sign outside saying gas was going to take half your paycheck. Donnie slumped in his seat, the dripping sound of the coffee echoing through the mart.

"I'm gonna be gone for a while," Donnie said. "Just wanted you to know."

Luther raised his gray eyebrows, stubbed out his cigarette, and reached into his mackinaw coat pocket for his pack, shaking one loose. "You get a new job?"

"Something like that."

"What's the vocation?"

"Truck driver."

"Same outfit out of Tupelo?"

"International corporation," Donnie said, amusing himself. "Got offices in Texas."

"When do you leave?"

"This morning."

Luther nodded, cigarette burning down low and slow in his bony fingers. He wiped a speck of tobacco off his lip and leaned into the booth. His arm rested on the edge of the seat as he motioned lightly with the cigarette butt. "I guess I can get someone to fill in for you. Don't worry about that."

"Appreciate that, Daddy."

"When will you be back?" Luther asked.

"That's the hell of it," Donnie said. "I don't know. It might be real long. I don't know."

Luther nodded. He got up and stretched his long legs, tucked in crisp Wranglers, and wandered back to the coffeepot on arthritic knees, filling two large Styrofoam cups to the rim, stirring in the sugar and creamer he knew his son liked.

"What you gonna haul?" Luther asked, sliding the coffee before him.

"I don't know," Donnie said. "Different stuff."

"This have something to do with that Mex gal I keep hearing about?"

"You can't fart in this town without someone hearin' it," Donnie said. "But, yeah. It's something like that."

"You thinkin' of marryin' her?" Luther said, taking a sip of hot coffee. "Call me if you do. I'd like to see that."

"You're gettin' a little ahead of yourself," Donnie said.

"Figured."

"People will talk, Daddy," Donnie said. "But don't listen to them. You need to trust me that for the first time in a while, I got things figured out."

Luther opened his mouth and then closed it. He smoked a bit more of the Marlboro red and took a long sip of coffee. He looked at Donnie from those old hooded eyes that had seen a mess of Vietcong drop in rice paddies, and he smiled. He nodded with acceptance.

"You be careful," Luther said. "I don't like men knocking on my door in the middle of the night. Sheriff Beckett was the one who come out and told me that you'd been wounded. He was straight up about it, said he didn't know if you were dead or not. I walked around for five miles when I heard, thinking back on when we'd lost your mother. Man, I felt like a real failure all over again."

"I'm just driving a truck."

Luther nodded.

The smell of baking biscuits and frying bacon and sausage came from the open door of the kitchen. Peaches hobbled out into the room, peering over at Luther and Donnie sitting in the corner. "Y'all want something to eat 'fore we open up?"

"You set me up a dozen sausage biscuits?" Donnie said. "I'll take 'em to go."

"Mr. Luther?" Peaches asked.

He shook his head. Donnie stood up across the table.

"The woman's worth it?" Luther said.

Donnie nodded.

"OK, then." Luther stretched out his long fingers, offering his hand to his son.

"I TOLD YOU that she couldn't be trusted," Lillie said, not two minutes after meeting Quinn back at the sheriff's office.

"Don't you recall how I started this conversation?"

"Well, it was stupid," Lillie said. "I think that should be said. But I guess I won't say anything about what part was doing the thinking for you."

"That had nothing to do with it."

"Well," Lillie said, sliding out of her coat. Her hair was looped through the back of a ball cap. "Did you at least get laid out of the deal? I mean, if you're gonna be fucked one way, might as well be fucked in the other."

"You do realize I pay your salary?"

"Nope," Lillie said. "This county pays my salary, and Mary Alice writes the checks. You rather have someone sugarcoat the way the world works?"

"Have I ever?" Quinn asked.

"What do we do now?"

Quinn shook his head. He walked over to his office window, looking out on the jail, seeing the moon shining across the width of the Big Black River and a portion of the old metal bridge that spanned it. He heard the flick of a lighter and smelled smoke coming from Lillie's way. When she spoke, she had that tight-mouthed way of speaking that people get with a cigarette between their teeth. "You want to get Donnie Varner a going-away present? I'll chip in."

"Nope."

"Maybe a bottle of Jack," Lillie said as Quinn turned. "Isn't that what he always drank when smoking dope? I swear, it impaired that boy's brain. Do you remember when he painted that piece-of-shit Cutlass camouflage?"

"We could arrest him."

"What would the Feds say about that?"

"I'm trying to protect him."

"I know what you're trying to do," Lillie said, taking off her ball cap, working the brim into a tight circle, and then slipping it back on her head. "But the dumb bastard made his play. This is his own private shithole."

"And Ramón and Janet?"

"Yeah," Lillie said, smoking a bit. "I guess they kind of get lost in the shuffle. I didn't figure the ATF was that big on finding out what happened here. They only wanted Ramón's narrow little ass. Nobody gives a shit about what those kids went through."

"What do you think?"

"Do the Feds want our help?"

"Nope."

"Have you always liked redheads? I told you they were crazy as hell."

"Get Kenny up on the radio and have him watch the road out by the Varner land," Quinn said. "I want to know when that truck heads back out on the road and out of the county."

"You think she might've warned you about Stagg."

"I kept some things from her, too," Quinn said. "I didn't tell her that I'd seen Donnie with Luz. I'd like to say I was protecting Donnie, but that wasn't it."

"You wanted to handle this without the Feds holding your peter?"

"Lillie, you sure got a way with words."

"I'll call Kenny."

Quinn settled into his office chair, tired but not feeling like he needed sleep. He was used to spending days on end without rack time. Always the hardest thing about a mission was the damn waiting. You'd make camp, prep your gear, and wait for the word. He never dreaded it, more just wanted it to happen, capturing airfields, offering support for a rescue, or clearing houses. One of the most popular T-shirts you could buy at Fort Benning read *Jump out of airplanes and kill people. What do you do?*

Pretty much how Quinn's life worked for nearly a decade.

He cracked his window, feeling the first bit of winter blow into his office. He had half a La Gloria Cubana waiting cold on his desk. He fired it up with a Zippo and leaned back, thinking about trying to get to Donnie through his daddy before he made a play that would land him in federal prison for the rest of his life or get his name in the paper with the headline TOWN MOURNS DEAD SON.

Quinn could do without another soldier headline. He picked up the phone to call the Quick Mart when Lillie walked back into his office.

"You think Donnie might be throwing a keg party without inviting us?"

"How's that?"

"Kenny just saw four dually pickups with Louisiana and Texas plates turn down the road to Donnie's gun range," Lillie said.

Quinn reached for his ball cap, rancher coat, and gun.

"Put that out," Lillie said. "Don't even think of smoking in my vehicle."

"It's OK," Quinn said. "We're taking mine."

45

"THIS PICTURE JUST GETS PRETTIER AND PRETTIER," DONNIE SAID, STAR-ing out the window of his Airstream and rubbing a fist in his eye. "Holy Christ. It's four in the morning."

"How many?" Luz asked, getting up from the couch and coming up by Donnie's side. They'd just walked up the hill to grab a few things and go ahead and hit the road.

"Four trucks, I think," Donnie said. "Ain't nobody's gotten out yet. Engines still running. I can see the exhaust. You guess this your boy-friend come up a little early?"

"Can they see where you parked the truck?"

"Nope."

Luz punched up some numbers on her cell and talked in fast Span-ish to Javier, Luis, and the boy, Donnie not needing a translation. Luz probably saying something like "Move that shit right now, here comes Tony the Tiger and a few of his asshole buddies."

"You think he got the Lucky Charms fella with him, too?" Donnie asked. "Or ole Count Chocula? These cartel folks love those crazy-ass names."

Luz reached for a Glock she'd left on the table by Donnie's smokes and Wild Turkey and said, "The truck is ready. Is there a way around them? In the woods?"

Donnie poured a handful of bullets from a Dixie cup into his palm and filled his pockets. He reached for the .38 and also grabbed a Browning 9 and a couple spare clips and walked to the back door, opening up and motioning for Luz, turning to look right into the pockmarked face of a Mex with a busted nose and bristled mustache under a flat-crowned cowboy hat. The man had three of his buddies with him, pointing some AKs at him, taking the damn weapons from his hand and kicking his ass to the ground. The main dude in the cowboy hat reached for Luz's waist and pulled her back into the trailer.

She got off one clean shot, before they grabbed her, and one of the boys fell, and, damn, if it wasn't Ramón Torres, holding his leg and cussing up a storm of hellfire and shit from where he was bleeding in Donnie's kitchen. The big man knocked Luz across the face with the back of his hand. Ramón screamed some more, and yelled at Donnie as if he'd been the one who'd pulled the trigger.

What a mess.

"YOU GONNA CALL DINAH BRAND?" Lillie asked.

"Would you?"

"Hell no," Lillie said. "She'd probably just set up a conference call after the shooting was done."

"She said to ignore it," Quinn said. "That's not gonna happen."

"May put the damper on that romance."

"I think that's already in the shitter."

"If it's any consolation, I bet she had a good time doing it with you," Lillie said. "Probably wasn't all about her business with the cartel."

"Sure appreciate that, Lillie."

Quinn slowed the F-250 onto the shoulder of the county road, turned off his KC lights, and met up with every available deputy in Tibbehah County. Boom stood with Kenny by a loose group of patrol cars and pickup trucks. The ATVs Quinn had called for had been unloaded, time coming up on past 0400, headlights off on the vehicles, everyone grouped and waiting for Quinn's word. Besides Boom and Kenny, he found Dave Cullison, Chris Smith (who was Dave's stepson and had served with Donnie in the Guard), Art Watts, and Ike McCaslin. Quinn was pretty sure Art was a second cousin of Donnie's but wasn't exactly sure how that tree all worked out. McCaslin was Quinn's only black deputy, tall and bony, with the thickest redneck accent he'd ever heard.

Quinn laid out a legal pad on top of the nearest patrol car, probably Cullison's, and sketched out the loose topography of the Varner land, the gun range, and to the south, the Byrd property, where they'd meet up at a rally point halfway down the fire trail. The trail ran about a mile before they got to what was the Byrd house decades ago, now falling in on itself and rotting, the family cemetery all overgrown with weeds and kudzu, thick sweetgum trees breaking through the graves. Most of the men, and Lillie, had hunted the land and knew it well.

Quinn drew a sweeping arrow from the rally point to where he'd take Boom, Kenny, and Ike with him. He told Lillie to post the rest of the deputies and set them two to four yards apart on the ridge overlooking the gun range since they were all the best with rifles. They'd work off signals from their radio, cell phones not worth a shit this far out. Quinn got his cigar going again with his lighter and stood back as the deputies studied the points.

"I know y'all got hunting rifles in your county vehicles, right?"

Everyone went to their cars to grab their .308s, .30-06s, and .30-30s. None of them looked like they were hurting for ammunition. Quinn nodded at Boom, knowing Boom didn't have to be here. Boom smiled back, his .44 Anaconda tucked into his thick western belt.

"Once we get to the rally point, we go dead silent," Quinn said. "They won't hear the motors from the fire road, but once we move, night sounds will get you killed."

"And a full moon," Kenny said, shaking his head.

"Full moon is good," Quinn said. "We walk the woods and stay in the dark. The land is wide open down at Donnie's place. The moon will light 'em up."

They unloaded the ATVs, riding out onto the rough trail, what had been a cleared road now thick with young saplings and clogged with vines and broken branches. They rode single file, bouncing up and over the ruts and around the logs, limbs and loose branches clawing at the Carhartt coat Quinn had grabbed from his trunk along with his Remington pump, loaded with twelve rounds, and a pair of field glasses. He had his Beretta 9 and six spare magazines with fifteen rounds each. He led the way, lights turned off on the moonlit path, scattered and wild, up and around the old shack where the last Byrd had lived up into the 1970s, his body undisturbed for nearly two months before a relative came looking. There was still an old outhouse standing upright and a barn that had settled at an awkward angle.

Quinn stopped short of the family cemetery and a small clearing where a deer stand stood tall in a waist-high field of yellowed grass. The moon above was big and round, glowing blood red on the blowing grass. The ATVs fell silent behind him as everyone stopped and waited.

Quinn ground his cigar underfoot and made his way down the ridge to a decent vantage point and focused his field glasses on the trucks. He saw the four jacked-up pickups Kenny had described. One had Texas plates, another Louisiana. Four, five men stood by the trucks.

Lillie walked up to his side, and he passed her the glasses.

"That all of 'em?" Lillie asked.

"I hope."

And then they both heard the shot.

THE ONE THEY CALLED TONY tied Donnie to his own kitchen chair and started beating the ever-living shit out of him. It wasn't fair to say it was all Tony, some of his boys joined in, including Ramón Torres with his injured leg. He was hobbling on that damn thing, strips of bloody bed-sheets working as some kind of cheap-ass tourniquet. Guess the bullet had gone straight through. There were a lot of fists and pointed boots coming at Donnie, fast Spanish with a lot of threats that didn't make a lick of sense. He just tried to take it, laughing at them dumb shits, because he sure as hell wasn't gonna give them the satisfaction of seeing fear in him before they put a bullet between his eyes. Luz was holding on to his arm, screaming at the men as they worked out their social problems, screaming and crying. Donnie's eyes about swelling shut as he cracked out a whispered "What did you ever see in this guy? The damn cowboy hat?"

A couple fists knocked his lights out twice. He didn't mind the pain as much as the coming to with more fists flying. Luz screamed more, running for the door. Donnie wondered what had happened to Javier and Luis, thinking those boys weren't as stand-up as they promised. He'd even take that kid shooter right about now. Donnie's head lulled to his chest, looking at the world crazy and cocked and bloody as hell, his trailer more fucked up than he'd ever seen it. Four of them huddling around one another, talking, smoking, worn out from giving the goddamn beating, bless their hearts.

"They want to know where you've put the guns," Luz said, whispering, crying in his ear.

"Don't you tell 'em."

"They'll find them anyway."

"Give your boys a chance," Donnie said. "They can get out."

"Didn't you hear what they said?" Luz asked. "They want to cut off your head. Leave a message."

"I don't like the sound of that," Donnie said, spitting blood across his shoulder. "I bet that's gonna hurt like a bitch."

LILLIE LED THE THREE DEPUTIES down on the ridge, all spacing themselves among the trees, looking down into the little gulley, watching the men below walking around with AK-47s, smoking cigarettes, drinking beer, and laughing. Faraway music from a car stereo lilted through the air. Quinn walked ahead of Boom, Kenny, and Ike McCaslin, telling them to leave their ball caps with the ATVs and unzip the front of their jackets, leaving space for their undershirts to show a bit.

"Why?" Ike asked, not butting up against Quinn but more making talk as they wound through the headstones.

Quinn turned to him, crooking his head to the side, showing what the bill would look like in silhouette. "An open shirt gives another vertical line. From far off, you'll look like another tree."

"Kenny's been thinking like a tree for years," Ike said.

From back behind him, Quinn heard Kenny give a quiet "Fuck you."

The headstones lay crooked and lichen-coated, sculptures of wood stumps for loggers and small lambs for children. Lots of names Quinn knew from growing up in the county, the dead, long-gone relatives. He found the footing along the hill to his liking; all the recent rain had made the October leaves as soft and silent as wet cotton. Soon they were headed down the slope to the objective rally point where he'd give Lillie the order to start shooting at the men by the trucks, maybe flush out whoever had fired that pistol. Quinn didn't like the sound of that single shot and silence.

Boom walked up at his flank, Quinn walking with the Remington pump in hand, pockets loaded down with the extra magazines for the 9mm he wore on his belt.

"Donnie's dead," Boom said.

"Sounds like it."

"This gonna get you in trouble with those Feds?"

"They asked me to let them go," Quinn said. "I got to respond to shots fired."

"Part of your job."

"Thanks for coming."

"I'd been pissed if Lillie hadn't called."

"What were you doing?"

"Wide-ass awake," Boom said. "That's the bitch of not drinking yourself to sleep."

Quinn judged the distance before they'd stop. He radioed Lillie and within seconds heard her call down the ravine with a bullhorn for the men to put down their weapons and put up their hands. The reply came in assault weapons, zipping a continuous stream of bullets up onto the ridge.

Quick, loud, cracking rifle shots responded from the deputies. The men by the trucks ducked for cover and fired up to the ridge with their automatic weapons. Quinn was at a quick run now, Boom, Kenny, and Ike following, ready to sweep in behind the men and take control of the Varners' land.

"Now?" Boom asked, Ike at his side. Kenny huffing up behind them, stifling a cough in his jacket.

Quinn held up his hand. He shook his head.

He watched the men taking the fire from the ridge. He waited until the sound broke slow and ragged, some spacing out their shots, some changing out ammo. He ran hard and fast to the rally point where they'd regroup before heading toward the trucks. But at the edge of the clearing, standing on a path to the gun range, Quinn spotted two big men. He slowed and stopped, the men not hearing him, and walked forward with the shotgun jacked full of deer slugs.

46

THE BIG MEN HELD UP THEIR HANDS AND DROPPED TO THEIR KNEES, A damn teenage kid walking from the shadows, sweaty palms up, yelling in English in a thick Mexican accent for Quinn not to shoot. Quinn shifted the Remington pump to the men and the boy, Boom and Kenny kicking the men to the ground, searching them for weapons. The boy pleaded with Quinn, as shots echoed through the ravine, telling him he was not a part of this, he was a friend to the owner of the gun range. Up behind the men, an 18-wheeler sat parked with its lights off and the back trailer doors wide open.

"Who's with you?" Quinn asked.

"Two men inside the truck," the boy said. "I don't know their names."

"You know Donnie Varner?"

The boy shook his head, not hearing him with all the shooting going on. During a lull, Quinn asked again.

The boy motioned up to the Airstream on the hill, Christmas lights strung from a ragged canopy to four-by-fours poking out of the ground. Quinn told Kenny and Boom to zip-cuff the men and the boy while he moved toward the big open doors of the 18-wheeler, shining a Maglite held next to the barrel of the shotgun into the open mouth, seeing two Anglo men turn, both sweating, dirty, and out of breath, slowly looking to Quinn like their asses had just been busted. "God damn," Tiny said. "You made me shit my drawers, Colson."

"Y'all get the hell out of there," Quinn said. "Who's got Donnie?"

"Them crazy-ass Mexes," Shane said. "Shit, Quinn. Donnie said for us to go on in case this mess got started. You mind?"

"Who are these two men? That boy?"

"They work for Donnie's girlfriend," Shane said. "They're just good folks."

"I bet."

Shane dropped his head and walked out with Tiny's big ass, jumping to the ground first and then helping Tiny out. Both of them had big pistols on their waists, and Quinn took the weapons, stepping back and making his way back to the clearing. He heard the shooting every thirty seconds or so, volleying back and forth from inside the ravine.

"You stand with us, and the judge might make things easier on y'all," Quinn said.

"For what?" Tiny asked, trying his best to look confused.

"Tiny, outwitting a man has never been your strong suit."

The gunshots through the ravine went from the quick hard shots of the deer rifles to the rat-ta-tatting of assault rifles. Quinn moved around the wide berm of dirt littered with clay pigeons, beer cans, and tattered pieces of paper targets. The assault rifles flickered hot and orange in the night, the outline of the shooters standing behind their trucks clear and clean in the moonlight.

"You got ammo for those M4s?" Quinn asked Tiny.

Tiny shook his head.

"Well, that's no help," Quinn said.

He handed the pistols back to Tiny and said, "Your mother taught me in kindergarten. You shoot me in the back, Tiny, and she sure is going to be disappointed in you."

ONLY TONY THE TIGER AND RAMÓN were left with Donnie and Luz. Tony walked around with the AK dropped in his left hand while Ramón found a spot on the couch to change out his bandage and scream a little bit, face turning white, eyes rolling upward some. Luz held a wet towel to Donnie's face, crying, gripping his hand and saying everything was gonna be just fine. It reminded Donnie a bit of his mother as she was dying, telling him stories about tap dancing in heaven and ice-cream socials up in the clouds.

"How you like Tibbehah so far, Tony?" Donnie said.

Tony turned to him and pointed the gun at them. He was really an ugly son of a bitch, in his forties, with sandpaper skin and fat jowls, looking for all the world like damn Wayne Newton playing Roy Rogers.

Ramón kicked his foot up and down, yelling some more, biting down on torn strips of sheets, saying some kind of crazy-ass prayer.

"I think God's taken you off the short list," Donnie said, feeling Luz squeeze his fingers, closing her eyes tight, waiting for that final shot. A damn war cracking and popping all down the range, sounding tinny and compact in the old Airstream.

Ramón kicked and screamed again, pleading for Mother Mary and Jesus, and, damn, if Tony didn't open up that AK and finish the job that Luz had started. Ramón Torres dropped hard and fast, lights out, sliding down on the couch.

"*Déjale vivir y voy en paz.*"

Tony agreed with what Luz said and reached for that long black hair and yanked her off her feet, away from Donnie and toward the door. Donnie yelled at Tony's back as he found his feet and rammed the chair against the wall, breaking free of the rope. The thin Airstream door hung wide open, battering off the wall of that ole tin can. He looked down to Ramón Torres, dead and bloody, and felt sorry for him for a good two seconds before finding a .45 in his jacket pocket. Donnie ran to the mouth of the door, seeing Tony dragging Luz behind him, his neck thick and hairy under that cowboy hat.

Donnie's shaking hand lifted that .45 as they moved down the hill, spitting blood to the ground and squeezing the trigger.

QUINN GAVE THE RADIO SIGNAL for Lillie to change the field of fire, the shots coming on stronger now but Quinn knowing they'd swung north, clearing the southern land between the berm, an outbuilding, and those boys hiding behind their luxury trucks. Quinn moved up and over the berm, the men following him across twenty yards to a metal shed, not even catching their breath before they all spread out side by side and headed right for those trucks, opening up fast and hard. Quinn squeezed off slug after slug at the center of shadows, falling *one, two, three*. Shots came from his side, zipping from the muzzles of the rifles, sparks of firelight, more cracking shots off the hills. Man after man falling, time stopping, heart racing, mind heading back to a rocky crag of some outer edge of hell in Kandahar, a plan to drag back a couple dead pilots before the sandpeople torched their bodies and carried off plane parts and weapons to use against Joes trying to rebuild a nation that wasn't worth two shits in the first place.

In the periphery, Tiny jogged forward, yelling a war cry, two pistols in his hands, before being cut down to his knees. The shots now popping from a couple rifles. Two shadowed people, darting between bullet-riddled trucks, Quinn getting within *thirty, twenty, fifteen* meters. The shotgun was spent and empty of all twelve rounds, and he tossed it to the ground, pulling the Beretta, finding the lick of fire from the rifles and quieting both.

Two, three more cracks from up on the hills, and then that strange silence that follows battle. Boom and Kenny ran ahead, Kenny finding some kind of need to shoot a couple more times, probably from nerves. Ike McCaslin walked slower, falling in step with Quinn and asking, "You got any of them cigars left? They shore smelled good."

DONNIE MISSED TONY THE TIGER three times before shooting the ugly bastard three times in the back, Luz falling from the man's grip and tumbling down the hill. The guns went silent. A short pop-pop-pop, and damn nothing but cold Mississippi wind. His eyes were good and fucked up, and he knew he'd cracked at least two ribs, but Donnie made his way down to Luz, the girl trying to find her feet in the mud, a solid shiner below the left eye, black hair fallen wild from the ponytail and covering her face and busted lip.

She'd never looked prettier than when she brushed past Donnie, lit up good from the Christmas lights, and walked up to Tony's worthless body. She kicked him good and proper in the face, taking that flat-crowned cowboy hat from the ground and twirling it on her finger, a souvenir.

Luz tripped down the hill, hat in hand, and met Donnie down on the footpath to the gun range. She wiped the mess of his face and said, "Can you still drive?"

LILLIE AND HER THREE DEPUTIES emerged from the skinny pines and thick oaks at the base of the ravine. Quinn had hit the headlights on a couple trucks, lighting up the seven fallen bodies, one draped through the open window of a truck.

Two enemy men were alive. Kenny called dispatch.

Tiny was dead, lying facedown in a mud hole with his big flannel shirt riding up, showing off his wide, naked white skin and the spot where the bullet went clean through. His camo baseball hat floating in the dark water.

"Where are we, again?" Boom asked.

"You want to check on Donnie?" Quinn asked.

"Nope."

Lillie moved up to them, rifle in hand, confident, and lifted her eyes up to the trailer on the hill lit up in all those multicolored lights, a setting from a country music video but silent and still. "Nice trailer," she said.

"I'll call on Luther," Quinn said.

"Maybe he's still alive," Lillie said.

"I should have pressed him."

"Donnie sought out these folks," Lillie said. "He brought them here."

"He didn't bring Ramón Torres," Quinn said, moving up toward the hill, light silver and bright and strong. Moonlight shed across the hill and soft rolling mounds of man-made berms, sloping, giving space and height along the length of the gun range. Quinn reached into his pocket for a fresh cigar, listening to the strange sounds of the pumping accordion music coming from one of the shot-up cars.

"Can you do me a favor?" Lillie asked.

"Turn off the music?"

"I sure would love to be with you when those ATF folks find out what happened," Lillie said. "You know the word 'conniption'?"

Quinn fired up the cigar, sorry for what happened to Tiny. He'd known Tiny since they'd played Little League football together, but somehow couldn't recall Tiny's real name. Even as a kid, he'd always been looking for trouble, the bar fighter, the sore loser at pool, working as a landscaper, a roofer, a fella who'd never be worth more than a side-kick to Donnie Varner.

"Feel like home, Quinn Colson?" Lillie asked.

"Ain't we all gonna live forever?"

"Come on," Lillie said, nodding her head up the hill to Donnie's Air-stream. "Both of us will go."

Sounds in the night become magnified. A snapping branch is a gun-shot. Night birds can pierce the darkness. And the sound of a rum-bling, grumbling motor of a Peterbilt in a skinny ravine can sound like a crackling, booming summer storm. Quinn saw the headlights, the brightness slicing down that narrow gravel road that Luther Varner had laid twenty years ago, growing closer. Quinn squinted and then ran with Lillie in step back down the hill, watching that length of 18-wheeler roll, big and bold, bumping and running, heading straight for the mess of Mexican trucks. Its headlights crisscrossed over dead bodies and deputies scurrying out of the way, who pulled out their still-warm guns and aimed at the truck, barreling right toward them. The Peterbilt scattered and twisted those big pickups, twirling, dumping one truck on its side, and running for hell and Highway 45, a long toot-ing whistle of "Fuck you" as it jostled and rolled on out.

Quinn reached out on the radio, calling dispatch to get the highway patrol to stop that truck.

DONNIE GAVE A REBEL YELL as he rammed through the trucks and cleared the path, that old Dodge van shooting out from the fire road in his rearview as he hit the county road, Donnie turning south and the van turning north. Donnie took a cut up and around Jericho and found a service road out to Highway 45, smiling big as shit when he hit the highway south, wondering for a good long while if he hadn't pulled the son of a bitch off, planning to meet up with Luz and her boys down in Meridian at the truck stop they'd discussed. He drove from Jericho out of Tibbehah and then into Monroe and Lowndes County, finally seeing those flashing lights in his side mirror, laughing a bit, thinking of making a run for it, maybe hitting a country road and bailing out where there was a good mess of woods, calling Tiny to come pick him up, finding another way down to Mexico. But, damn, if there weren't more asshole troopers blocking the road up by a filling station, flares in the road, chains with spikes and all that shit, and what is a man to do but tap the brakes, slow a bit into the early light, and find his license and proof of insurance.

He finally stopped a good ten yards short of the roadblock, light coming on a pale purple about six a.m. Donnie was tired and ragged, worn out, hungry and thirsty and flat-ass busted. Donnie rolled down the window to a thick-necked trooper meeting him with a Glock pulled out straight in his hands.

"Was I speeding, Officer? I swear to Christ I was in the flow of traffic."

"Hands up," the thick-necked trooper said, opening the door. "Hands up."

"I get the idea," Donnie said, hopping down to the asphalt, a couple troopers being first-class assholes and wrestling him to the ground just 'cause they could. They dragged him to his feet and pushed him toward a cruiser, Donnie asking if they would mind if he smoked on the way. The troopers didn't answer.

"You boys sure love to work out," Donnie said as they nudged him along. "Y'all do that together?"

47

"YOU'D LET ME KNOW IF I GOT A POSTCARD, OR PHONE CALL OR SOME-thin'?" Donnie asked.

"You bet," Quinn said.

"It's the law. A prisoner got rights, too."

"I heard about that, Donnie."

"You know, this jail is a real shithole," Donnie said, touching the bruises turning yellow and blue on his face. "Don't you think it's about time to rebuild? Hell, this thing was built back in the fifties."

"Sixties," Quinn said. "Nineteen sixty-one. Maybe you can ask your pal, Johnny Stagg, about funding that project."

"He's not my pal."

"Don't you care how he rolls in shit and comes out smelling like a rose?"

Donnie shrugged.

"Or that he was the one who turned on the Memphis folks," Quinn said. "You ever met a man named Bobby Campo? Feds just raided two of his strip clubs."

"You know, jails don't have metal bars like this anymore," Donnie said, absently lighting a cigarette, staring up at the ceiling, while Quinn stood above him. "You get locked solid doors and stainless steel commodes. This looks like that jail in *El Dorado*. Maybe I could whistle for Hondo and have him bring me the keys to the lock."

"He's too smart to throw in with you."

"Guess you're right."

Quinn waited for Donnie to get up to escort him out into the yard to talk to Luther through the chain link. It was Saturday, visitors' day, and already the yard was filled with the drunks, drug abusers, and honky-tonk brawlers telling their families they were about to change, that tomorrow was going to be brighter.

"You know what I see in my mind?" Donnie asked, not turning once to Quinn, lying there in a dream state as he had for the last week.

"Love to hear it."

"I see Luz on a beach somewhere," he said. "Like in that movie *Shawshank*, and she'd be like that fella that escaped prison. The one working on his boat."

"Tim Robbins."

"Yeah, but good-looking. Like, she's in a bikini, drinking a Corona, feet in the sand, and waiting till I get that postcard and find her. Maybe a Kenny Chesney song playing at some bar made out of driftwood, looking over the ocean."

"From what you told me, I don't think she was the bikini type," Quinn said. "That little town where she was headed, the one up in the mountains, is pretty much dead center of a battle zone between those cartels. It's an ugly scene, partner."

"You mind letting me have my dreams?"

"Sure, Donnie."

"But you'd tell me about a postcard if it came?"

"I'd deliver it in person."

"Would those Feds tell you if they caught her and the boy?"

"I don't know," Quinn said. "I'm not exactly one of their favorite people."

"Where'd they find that old van of mine?"

"Queen City truck stop outside Meridian."

"That on Highway 20?"

"Yep."

"So they were cutting over to 55?"

"Looks like it."

"And they stole a truck?"

"They did."

"Where'd y'all find that?"

"New Orleans."

"And that truck?"

Quinn shifted his weight on his boot heels, watching Donnie stand up, slip into his laceless canvas shoes, walk to the toilet, and toss in the spent cigarette. Donnie scratched his bruised and scratched-up face and waited for Quinn to answer.

"They didn't find that truck," Quinn said. "I told you all this already."

"Yeah," Donnie said, pushing himself up and getting off the bunk, grinning. "But I love hearing it. I wonder where they crossed the border? Damn if they didn't pull that shit off."

"You do realize you're going to be formally charged in federal court with gunrunning on Wednesday," Quinn said. "I'll see if I can't take you to Oxford for your arraignment."

"Appreciate that, Quinn," Donnie said. "But I think I'd rather ride with that redhead who came to talk to me last week. She about set the room on fire. You know if she's got a boyfriend? Didn't see a wedding ring."

Quinn didn't say anything.

"Hell, do I need to draw you a map?"

"Come on, Donnie," Quinn said, opening up the jail door. "Luther's waiting for you. He brought you some biscuits from the Quick Mart."

"Miss Peaches sure can cook."

"You mind if I ask you a question?" Quinn said. "Between us?"

"Shoot."

"How'd you get all those guns out of Afghanistan?" Quinn asked. "Did you hide them in the heavy equipment y'all brought over? Or you catch some customs officer with a goat?"

"Nope," Donnie said, grinning.

"I'm not working for the Feds."

"OK," Donnie said, smiling wide. "We fitted those Conex containers with fake floors, raised 'em up about four inches, enough to fit in whatever we please. Customs folks would clear out the containers, walk around on those floors, and not suspect a thing. A buddy, who will remain nameless, helped me take 'em apart and refit them over in the Shitbox."

"You've got vision, Donnie," Quinn said. "I'll give you that."

"It's a gift," Donnie said, walking ahead out in the long dark hall. "Sometimes I wish I could turn the damn thing off."

LATER, IN THE SPRING, the children played outside after the church held Sunday service with doors and widows open, daffodils flowering, grass coming back to life, a soft, warm wind blowing across picnic tables set between the headstones in the nearby cemetery. Quinn stood inside with Caddy, hearing the kids squealing and laughing while they played tag, running wild up and around the graves, too young to know they were stepping on the dead. Caddy wore a new denim dress, face freshly scrubbed, and worked to take the cakes and pies out to the tables. The other church members finishing off their cold fried chicken and potato salad; open jars of homemade pickles and pimento cheese spread out on the table. Somewhere their mother was among them, gabbing, bragging about Jason.

They called days like this Dinner on the Grounds. Old church members and those who'd left Jericho long ago would often return, recall old times about people they'd buried long ago with a smile and a laugh. Since the fall, a soldier had come back home, another small American flag staked by the grave. Another just like him lay nearby, dead since '05. Quinn knew them both, had grown up with them.

Caddy took the pies outside and returned to fill pitchers of sweet tea. She looked confused as Quinn smiled at her. "What?" she said. "You drinking?"

"It's good to have you back, Caddy."

She nodded. "Can you still drive with me to Tupelo on Thursday?"

"Wouldn't miss it," Quinn said, standing alone with his sister. The wind shooting through the open doors smelled of warm sun and budding leaves and flowers.

"I know you hate going, all that talk."

"Nope," Quinn said. "No reason we can't talk about it. We're not kids. You were right."

"You mind me writing that down?" Caddy said. "Never heard my brother say that before. You sure you haven't been drinking? Maybe a little of that strawberry moonshine Boom likes?"

"Nope."

"I'm good," Caddy said. "I don't even know who that person used to be."

"Day by day, right?"

"It's over, Quinn. Everything is different."

Quinn was quiet, just smiled back at Caddy. He wished everything was as simple as she imagined it.

Quinn walked to the open doors and stared down the sloping hill at all the folks sitting at the tables among the headstones. Boom ambled up to the steps with an empty Styrofoam plate in his hand and joined him at the threshold, turning back to see what Quinn was watching. They stood side by side, and Boom nodded his head, seeing it, too. Lillie was showing off the child she'd adopted, the lost girl from the trailer park. Good to her word, she'd named her Rose after her mother, who was buried down that hill. Quinn had never seen Lillie smile so much. Boom wondered aloud if Lillie knew just what the hell she was doing, raising a child by herself, a child she didn't know a thing about, finding it like a wandering animal on the side of the road.

"You want to question Lillie's methods?" Quinn said.

"Nope."

"Lillie will figure it out."

"Kid's not right," Boom said. "Hadn't walked yet. Baby over a year old. God bless her for trying."

"Sometimes a hard head is an asset."

Boom walked back into the church for a second helping of lemon icebox pie or chocolate pie or coconut cake. Quinn drank a little more tea while Jason played war among the headstones with two boys and a tough little girl in a pink dress, time seeming to move in reverse. Quinn's eyes again falling on Anna Lee with her child, the little girl born in November. She was probably talking to Lillie about long sleepless nights, diapers and baby clothes, as she readjusted the child in her arms, Luke nowhere to be seen, probably sticking with the Episcopalians in town. She turned to Quinn at a distance, like she could feel him staring, and waved. He returned a loose wave back and smiled, Anna Lee still looking eighteen with her blond hair tied back in a black ribbon, long flowered skirt showing under a bright red jacket. A dozen years ago, there had been a summer afternoon on a secret creek, cutoffs and tank top tossed onto the hill, jumping out, wild and free, toward Quinn as he treaded cold water.

"Don't even think about it," Lillie said, meeting him on the steps and handing him her adopted daughter. Quinn hoisted the kid into his arms, all big brown eyes and long lashes. The child was attentive and beautiful, but as light as a bird, almost like holding air.

"I'm just watching the kids," Quinn said. "Making sure Jason doesn't bust his head on one of those stones."

"Bullshit," Lillie said. "You know she still looks at you the same. Same as when we were in high school, and you had her name written in your truck's back window. She shouldn't do that. It'll mess your head up, and I need you whole."

"I'm here."

"You think that redhead you were seeing knows anything about where to find Janet Torres?"

"If she did, she wouldn't tell me."

"You can do better than that tight-ass," Lillie said. "I do feel for Mara. If her lawyer can't put fat Janet on the stand, jury won't be able to make sense of the hell she lived through. She was a victim same as those other children."

Quinn nodded and passed the baby back to Lillie, admiring the natural way Lillie took the child, held her, made her smile and laugh. Lillie always had seemed a lot better with children than grown-ups. He wondered about the other kids they'd found, not knowing where they'd been placed or how things had turned out after all that the Torres people had done to them. Lillie handed Quinn a piece of coconut cake and a fork, and Quinn sat on the church steps, eyes coming back to Anna Lee, her arms empty now, standing there alone in her bright red jacket, blond hair, and red mouth.

Anna Lee met his gaze for a long moment and then turned away. She seemed almost angry, maybe a little confused. He'd seen that look plenty of times before they broke up. She collected her child from a white-headed woman and marched down the hill, out of sight and out of reach. Quinn finished the pie, helped clean up, and then drove back to the farm.

The old tin-roofed house stood stark, shadowed. Hondo waited, tall on the hill, barking at his return.